JOSEPH

ᐧTERRI L. FIVASHᐧ

Terri L Fivash

6/23/03

REVIEW AND HERALD® PUBLISHING ASSOCIATION
HAGERSTOWN, MD 21740

The author assumes full responsibility for the accuracy of all facts and quotations as cited in this book.

This book was
Edited by Gerald Wheeler
Designed by Saschane Stephenson
Electronic makeup by Shirley M. Bolivar
Cover illustration by Robert Hunt
Typeset: Bembo 12/14

PRINTED IN U.S.A.

06 05 04 03 02   5 4 3 2 1

R&H Cataloging Service
Fivash, Terri L.
    Joseph.

        1. Title.

ISBN 0-8280-1629-1

DEDICATION

This book is dedicated to my Aunt Mary Ann who, back in 1965, gave me my very first book about Joseph and started my lifelong love of this story.

ACKNOWLEDGMENTS

I wish to express my many thanks to all those who helped in this project. Special thanks to Dr. Leona Running, who so graciously gave of her time and expertise to review this manuscript. Thanks also to Dr. Alice Williams for her critique, and to Gerald Wheeler for his time and efforts in editing my writing.

Very special thanks go to my husband and boys for their patience the summer Mommy was "in Egypt" and to my own Mom and Dad for their encouragement, interest, and support.

Thank you also to Via Langteau and others who encouraged and cheered and listened and listened and listened . . .

A WORD ABOUT NAMES AND PRONUNCIATION

The Egyptians had, perhaps, some of the most confusing naming practices on earth. Each Pharaoh had five names in his royal name in addition to the name(s) given to him at birth. His mother most likely used a short nickname when speaking to him, unless he was in trouble, at which point I'm sure the entire name came out of her mouth, just like today.

Royalty did not have a corner on long names, however. Common people routinely gave children lengthy names to honor one or another of the gods. In addition, they might offer exactly the same name to three or four sons or daughters. No one was confused, however, because each child had a different nickname that he normally went by.

For instance, one might name a son Pediamennebnesttawy or Hekamaatreemperkhons. I'm certain that the Egyptians considered both of them quite nice names, but as an author I am lazy, and I refuse to type Pediamennebnesttawy all the time while I am writing. In addition to that, I seriously doubt any of my readers want to pronounce it!

I have, therefore, carved up such names and only used portions of them. Those of you who read further in this book will recognize Menneb and Hekamaat. If you look carefully, you will find Tawy as well.

As for pronunciation, no one today has any idea how ancient Egyptian was pronounced. Most ancient languages wrote down only the consonants. Vowels were unnecessary since anyone reading a text could speak the language already (right?), and would automatically supply the correct vowel sound as they read.

Because of that, we often find variant spellings for the same word/name from different historical texts. Amun versus Amon or Ra versus Re. Frankly, no one knows if either or any is correct. So, to make reading this book as easy as possible, I have taken the most common pronunciation of the vowels as follows:

a sounded as "ah"

e sounded as short "e" in "met" or as long "a" in "fate" if at the end of a word

i sounded as long "e" in "meet"

o sounded as long "o" in "mole"

u sounded as "oo" in "cool"

y sounded as long "e" if at the end of a word

kh sounded as "ch" in "loch"

Also note that every vowel is sounded. Ancient languages rarely, if ever, had silent vowels. Therefore, "Tate" is pronounced "Tah-tay" and "Maat" as "Mah-aht." Both have two syllables.

Now about Joseph's Egyptian name. Most readers will have seen it as "Zaphenath-Paaneah" or some variant spelling of the same. In any case, it's quite a mouthful. Remember that in Egyptian only the consonants would have been recorded, and the three consonants which make up "Zaphenath" are exactly the same as a common Hebrew word. However, if the last two consonants of "Zaphenath" are reversed, the Hebrew word becomes a very familiar Egyptian phrase—"he who is called"—which was used again and again when identifying Hebrews living in Egypt. The Hebrew name would be given, then the phrase "he who is called," then an Egyptian name.

It is possible that the Hebrew scribe recording Joseph's new name inadvertently reversed the last two consonants of the familiar Egyptian phrase to make an equally familiar Hebrew word. Thus, the "Zaphenath" would not actually be part of Joseph's new name. I have accepted this theory about Joseph's name in the interests of simplicity.

The "Paaneah" part of the name is simpler to deal with. "Aneah" with variant spellings means "life," or "is alive," and is often seen spelled "Ankh." Joseph would have been introduced to Pharaoh's court then, as "Joseph, who is called Paanekh, meaning 'He is alive.' " Very appropriate considering his past history.

Now, if I haven't spaced everyone out on linguistics, let us consider chronology.

For those readers who are historically inclined, or those who are just interested, I thought I would include a word about the time period I have chosen for this book. Egyptian history is divided into sections beginning with the Pre-Dynastic period before Egypt unified as a country. The Old Kingdom follows during which the pyramids were built. Then comes the First Intermediate Period; the Middle Kingdom; the Second Intermediate Period; the New Kingdom with Hatshepsut, Thutmosis, and Ramesses; the Third Intermediate Period; and the Late Period followed by the Ptolemaic Period and the Roman Period. Dating these periods is always fraught with error, and naturally the farther back in history one goes, the greater the chance for error.

Historians of all stripes, therefore, argue incessantly about dating. Very few dates are accepted by all, and in Egyptian history, the earliest date firmly in place is 664 B.C. when the Assyrians sacked Thebes, marking the end of the Third Intermediate Period. Every date prior to 664 B.C. rests on educated guesswork, and again the further back one goes, the more guess there is in the work.

The Patriarchal Period in Palestine is usually dated to the twelfth dynasty of Egypt in the 1600s B.C. during the Middle Kingdom. However, many historians argue that Joseph had to be in Egypt under the Hyksos Pharaohs of the Second Intermediate Period at the end of the Middle Kingdom some 150 to 200 years later.

I chose to place Joseph in the twelfth dynasty because during the reign of Senusert III and his co-regent/son Amenemhet III the nobility inexplicably disappeared from the Egyptian scene, never to play an important role again. The only extant explanation for this sudden and complete collapse of a thriving and powerful noble class appears in the biblical account of Joseph. Scripture states plainly that Joseph reduced the Egyptians to servitude, and bankrupted both Egypt and Canaan. By the end of the famine, Pharaoh owned all the land and all the people in Egypt, and all the wealth in both Egypt and Canaan. Only the priestly class retained wealth and land, and for the rest of Egyptian history, the only challenges to Pharaoh's absolute power came from the temples and the priests. (See Gen. 47:13-26.)

I have taken literary license on one point, however. Whether Senusert III was still alive when Joseph became governor of Egypt is debatable. But rather than confuse readers with a Pharaoh and a co-regent, I chose to simplify. At the same time, I could make Amenemhet close to Joseph in age, and create a political situation that favored Joseph's appointment.

Needless to say, I have had to conjecture on the exact political maneuvering. We do know that assassination attempts occurred during the twelfth dynasty. Also we have evidence that storing food for one or two years against possible famine was routine and expected of each noble house. Therefore, Joseph's plan to store grain was not unusual except for the length of time the famine would last. If the nobles ran out of grain before the famine ended the only explanation is that they didn't believe Joseph when he told them how long the famine would be, and that opens up a myriad of possibilities and provides much food for thought.

I hope you enjoy the possibility I followed with its attendant food for thought.

PRINCIPAL CHARACTERS

- Amenemhet III ~ Pharaoh who elevates Joseph to office of Tate.
- Amony ~ Noble from Thebes who covets the throne.
- Aneksi ~ Daughter to Minemhet. Dependent on Lord Potiphar.
- Asenath* ~ Joseph's Egyptian wife.
- Chaf ~ Joseph's body guard.
- Defatsen ~ Friend of Inti's. Dependent on Joseph.
- Chety ~ Father of Mahesa. Merchant in Thebes.
- Hazor ~ Syrian Royal Servant who first befriends Joseph in Egypt.
- Hekamaat ~ Syrian/Egyptian in charge of Lord Potiphar's herds.
- Hernofret ~ Lord Amony's son.
- Hesy ~ Orphan girl dependent on Lady Asenath.
- Hetepi ~ Female scribe and Inspector of Pharaoh's prison in Memphis.
- Hordef ~ Lord Treasurer to Pharaoh.
- Hutor ~ Superintendent of the Works for Lord Potiphar's tomb.
- Huy ~ A dependent of Lord Potiphar. Becomes a well-known entertainer in Memphis.
- Imenhet ~ A chief herdsman dependent on Lord Potiphar. Also a famous potter.
- Inti ~ Crippled soldier who becomes gatekeeper to Joseph.
- Irtisen ~ Jewelsmith who made a seal and signet.
- Isaac* ~ Joseph's grandfather.
- Iteti ~ Lady Tanefret's chief steward.
- Iutem ~ Dependent of Poti-Phera. Tries to poison Lady Asenath.
- Jacob* ~ Joseph's father.
- Jetur* ~ Son of Ishmael who purchases Joseph from his brothers.
- Kemi ~ Weaveress for Lord Potiphar.
- Khafra ~ Overseer of the Treasury Scribes to Pharaoh.
- Khay ~ Orphan dependent on Lord Potiphar who becomes Joseph's right-hand man.
- Kinen ~ Herder for Potiphar.
- Mahesa ~ Young scribe to Lord Potiphar. Becomes Joseph's chief of staff.
- Manakh* ~ Chief Baker imprisoned by Pharaoh.
- Menneb ~ Scribe on Lord Potiphar's estate.
- Meritifi ~ Nomarch of the twelfth nome who plots for the throne.

- Minemhet ~ Chief cook and baker for Lord Potiphar.
- Mishma* ~ Jetur's son. He doubts his father's assessment of Joseph.
- Mose ~ Nomarch of the first nome.
- Nekhty ~ Personal Scribe to Pharaoh.
- Neshi ~ River boat captain from whom Joseph buys purple dye.
- Nofret ~ Mahesa's mother. Wife to Chety.
- Onami ~ Joseph's chariot driver.
- Paanekh ~ Joseph's Egyptian name.
- Potiphar* ~ Captain of the Guard to Pharaoh who purchases Joseph.
- Ptahhotep ~ Chief of the guards in the Memphis prison.
- Renseneb ~ Joseph's chief opponent in the markets of Egypt.
- Reret ~ Chief steward to the former Tate.
- Sabestet ~ A barber.
- Saf ~ Illegitimate son of Lord Amony who becomes Joseph's steward at the Memphis residence.
- Sekhmet ~ Scribe under Imenhet, who becomes an assassin.
- Setne ~ Keeper of the Memphis prison.
- Sety ~ Nomarch of the twenty-fourth nome. He is a candidate for the office of Tate.
- Shenbu ~ Engineer who solves any problem Joseph gives him.
- Sheshon ~ Public scribe hired to assist Hutor with Lord Potiphar's tomb.
- Siamon ~ Herder for Lord Potiphar on the Delta. He designs a granary that keeps grain dry in the Delta.
- Snefru ~ Chief overseer of Lord Potiphar's Memphis estate.
- Sosamen ~ Chief steward for Ueb Poti-Phera.
- Tahsit* ~ Chief Wine Steward imprisoned by Pharaoh.
- Tais ~ Manankh's son.
- Takamenet ~ Saf's mother.
- Tanefret* ~ Lord Potiphar's wife.
- Teti ~ Inspector of the Works for Lord Potiphar's tomb.
- Ueb Poti-Phera* ~ High Priest of Ra at On. Lady Asenath's father.

* *indicates a biblical character.*

PROLOGUE

I am old now, having fulfilled the perfect Egyptian life span of 110 years, and I feel I am soon to die. Before I am gathered to my fathers, I wish to share the secret of all my glory. It is very simple: Serve the one true God, the Creator greater than Ra, with all your heart.

It is simple, but it is not easy. Yet the reward is unspeakably great. When God becomes your friend, the glory of it is more than mortal humanity can hold.

My great-grandfather Abraham knew this glory intimately, as did my grandfather Isaac. Jacob, my father, fought for it one night by a brook called Jabbok. And I? I have come to know it slowly, gradually, learning through the years the sacred and precious honor that God gives to human beings.

When one serves my God, one never knows where He will lead. Great-grandfather Abraham had to leave his estates in Haran and wander as a nomad the rest of his life. But how many have sat and eaten with God in human form?

My grandfather Isaac also roamed many of his days amid hostile peoples who drove him out many times. Yet who else can say the literal hand of God saved him from death?

And my father saw God face to face and lived, uniquely blessed.

As for me, following my God led me to the heavy responsibilities and cares of governing the greatest nation in the world. Only a miracle could have placed me, a foreign slave, into this office that I have held for so many years. So you see, all my glory comes from God. It has no basis in wealth or power, else Pharaoh never would have bowed so eagerly to receive the blessing of my father.

But, in the beginning, certainly there was no glory . . .

CHAPTER 1

"You can't! You can't do this to me! Come back! You can't leave me here—Abi loves me best!" The dark and damp stone curving above me threw my screams back into my face. Light from the small round opening directly above blurred as tears left wet streaks down my cheeks. "Abi loves me best," I repeated, choking on my sobs.

I lay on the cold floor of the abandoned cistern and gradually controlled myself, wiping the hated tears from my eyes several times. Father intended me to have the birthright and it was unseemly for a prince to cry. Brushing my face with the sleeve of my undergarment, I thought bitterly of all the times I had done exactly that during my 17 years. I didn't have time to cry now—I needed to think.

Slowly I pushed myself up, gasping at the sudden stab of pain in my side. Looking down, I saw blood oozing from one knee. I tried to stand anyway and collapsed immediately, both ankles screaming at me. They had taken the full impact from the drop into the cistern. Not that I could have gotten out, I told myself, looking again at the rough walls curving over me to the small opening above.

Settling back, I hugged my side and gingerly tested my ankles. They probably weren't broken, but they were going to hurt for a long time. A long time. Hastily, I stuffed my fist into my mouth to keep from screaming again and squeezed my eyes shut against the tears. Fear roiled in my stomach. They'd left me here to die. Better than killing me outright, Judah had said. Better for whom? Should I slowly die of thirst and starvation just so they wouldn't get my blood on their hands? As if that mattered! They already had blood enough on their hands, especially Simeon and Levi.

Hugging myself tighter, I rocked slightly to control my fear. When I remembered the look on Simeon's face, I started to sweat. Gulping down another sob, I forced myself to think. Father had taught me that I must remain calm and think at all times to be a good prince. Who might be persuaded to help me? Not Simeon—or Levi, for he followed wherever Simeon led. Judah usually had a cool head, but he was using it against me, that was plain. Dan—well, he had a definite sense of justice, but being Bilhah's first-born might make him think he had at least a remote chance at the birthright if death carried away some of the rest of us.

My thoughts stopped there. I could indeed die. Once again fear washed over me, and I shivered uncontrollably, making my side throb. Again I glanced around at the dark prison that held me. I couldn't die! What about my dreams? And my coat? Father had it woven especially for me, making sure the colors in the cloth and the rich embroidery matched my unusual blue eyes. He had even had it trimmed with the softest lamb's wool dyed with the expensive new color from Tyre. They called it purple, and it had a special glow. Only a prince would have need of such a garment. Father wore one like it when he met with the princes and kings of the cities around us. Blinking back the hated tears again, I told myself that I *would* be prince and get the birthright. Hadn't I had *two* dreams?

In the first one, my brothers and I stood in a strange, half-reaped, wheat field. The harvesters had cut the stalks close to the heads instead of near to the ground. Then they had laid two bundles end-to-end and tied them with a rope to form a double-headed sheaf that they left lying on the ground. Piles of these strange sheaves surrounded us, three or four sheaves to each pile. I thought, in my dream, that the grain would be ruined if left lying there on the ground, but the sheaf could not have stood up, since both ends had grain on them. Then, as I watched, the sheaves moved, rising upright despite the double heads of grain. The strange wheat had more than one ear per stalk. Suddenly my brothers' sheaves bowed their heads to mine.

Naturally I told the exciting dream to my brothers the next morning. But they laughed and made fun of me about it, jeering at cutting grain short and making a sheaf with a double head. Everyone knew how ridiculous that was. Judah waved his fingers at me, imitating the multiple ears I had seen on the stalks. Only Abi didn't laugh when I described it. He just looked at me strangely and got very thoughtful.

The next dream was even more important, for the sun and the moon and 11 stars all gathered around the place I stood and made obeisance to me. In my dream, I stood on a stone floor as I watched the heavens. Above me hung a strange square pattern that I looked through to see the sun. Its blazing fire was bright, but I could look at it unhindered. It dipped downward, passing two bars of the pattern, then climbed back up. The moon followed, a brilliant white disk brighter than any I had ever seen. And last came 11 stars, the center one brighter than the others and pulsating in a regular pattern. The stars were arranged in a ragged line, and they also moved downward past the pattern, back up, then faded from view.

Maybe I should have kept that dream to myself, especially since Father did get a little upset over it, clearly dubious about my ever being so great that he would bow to me. But he had watched me closely since then and taken me with him on more and more occasions. He even insisted that I be able to both read and write Canaanite.

Now I realized my brothers must have taken those dreams seriously after all, or else why was I down in this pit? Once more panic choked me. "Don't think about that," I told myself sternly, forcing my thoughts elsewhere. Now, once again, who could help me? Neither of Zilpah's sons had a chance at the birthright, although Gad seemed to think he might. Anyway, the maids' sons—Bilhah's Dan and Naphtali and Zilpah's Gad and Asher—deferred to Leah's four oldest. They were afraid of Simeon. So was I—now.

Thinking of Simeon brought the slaughter at Shechem forcibly to my mind. Judah had taken Dinah with him into town one day. When the servants returned without them, father began to worry. Then Prince Hamor himself came to our camp with Shechem and a proposal for Dinah's hand, letting us know where the girl was. Judah never did say where he'd been. I suspected he'd gone to a certain house he visited when he got restless, despite the fact that he had a wife and sons of his own.

I don't know why my brothers took such offense at Shechem. He loved Dinah and wanted to marry her so badly that he promised to pay any bride price they demanded to make up for any offense he might have caused. And Dinah was ready to be a princess someday.

Simeon must have had it all planned out when he insisted that all the men in town undergo circumcision in order for Shechem to marry Dinah. They were still helpless from the pain when Simeon and Levi slaughtered them and dragged Dinah back home. The rest of my brothers looted the town, driving off the flocks and grabbing women and children for slaves.

Father exploded when he learned what had happened. Simeon made some excuse that the only reason Hamor wanted Shechem to marry into our tribe was to steal our wealth, but that didn't make any impression on Father. Thundering at them that even the idol worshipers around us wouldn't do something so abhorrent, he said that only God's intervention prevented the people around us from killing us all. After cleansing the camp of idols, we moved to Bethel.

The hurried relocation and the stress and fear of the situation were not good for Mother, who was carrying Benjamin then. It all caught up to her at his birth. I know Father blamed Simeon and Levi for Rachel's death.

And soon after that Father caught Reuben in Bilhah's bed. Reuben! He was my best chance. Stifling the surge of excitement I felt, I thought back as best I could through my chaotic and bewildered fear to when my brothers had ripped off my coat and dragged me to the cistern. If I remembered correctly, Reuben kept urging them not to kill me. If he could take me back to Father alive, Abi would likely forgive him for his indiscretion with Bilhah, and he would be back in the running for the birthright.

He might have a chance at it too, for the others would accept Reuben as their prince much easier than they would me. Father might give it to him in the interest of family unity. But I didn't think so. I'll never forget the shock, betrayal, and fury on Abi's face with he found Reuben with Bilhah. During the scene that followed, Reuben hadn't dared to look at Father, being too busy abasing himself in hopes that Father wouldn't have him executed. Reuben never had been good at thinking through the consequences of something.

And now, he would do absolutely *anything* to get back in Father's good graces—even if it meant making peace with me. I hugged myself harder against the chill and waited, wishing I had my coat. I hoped it hadn't got too damaged in the struggle. I shuddered in shock. My brothers had clawed at me like wild animals, and the expression on their faces scared me. What would they want with my coat? Why didn't they at least toss it down to me? I wanted to feel the soft trim and see the wonderful new color again. It was Father's best gift ever to me. I needed its comfort now.

How soon before Reuben returned? Sure that he'd take this chance in spite of the others, I decided I'd say a good word or two to Father about him. Nothing overdone, of course, but Abi would listen. He had certainly listened when I reported to him how careless the maids' sons had been with the herds. They had allowed the donkeys to stampede, losing two foals, and then let the sheep graze the pasture down to dust. Also they lost *three* lambs to wolves in a week. Still, I hadn't planned on saying too much. There might really have been a lion stalking the donkeys and frightening them, and I've had trouble myself tracking down a wolf. But being careless with the nanny goats the women were milking was too much. We didn't have enough milk for more than a week, and I love goat milk. After that, I really did have to talk to Father.

Father had been very sharp in his reprimand. Dan should have known better, and Father let him understand that he expected better. Come to think of it, that must have been the first time Father had even looked at him or Naphtali since their mother had disgraced herself with Reuben. Maybe that's why Dan hadn't tried to stop the others from hurting me. Perhaps he still held a grudge, which was very wrong of him since he *had* been careless.

Glancing up at the small patch of light again, I wondered how long it would take Reuben to come. My stomach growled with hunger. I had brought a whole pack of foodstuffs on the donkey, and I'd purposely not eaten any of it because Father had asked me to be sure the others got some. Maybe I could maneuver Reuben into getting some for me before we left. I—

When the piece of sky above me suddenly shrank, I squinted upward. I'd been right! Exaltation swept through me. Reuben had returned, just as I knew he would. I'd definitely say a good word about him to Father. Now I wouldn't die! And my dreams would come true after all. When I grabbed hold of the rope he let down, he started to pull me up. Trying to make it easy for him, I remained as motionless as I could. Hands pulled me the last way up, and I rolled over on the ground, blinking in the brightness.

"Reuben!" I said, then stopped. Staring at me sullenly, Issachar and Zebulun jerked me to my feet and shoved me down the trail. I stumbled on my painful ankles. What was going on? Where was Reuben?

I fell from the shove Issachar gave me, landing on my hands and knees and gasping from the stab of pain in my side. Again, where was Reuben? And what were my brothers planning now? If Reuben wasn't here, why had they taken me out of the cistern? Hurriedly I glanced around. To one side was the food I'd brought, half eaten. My coat still lay discarded on the ground not far away. Then I saw the camels.

Traders. One of them at the head of the caravan talked to my brothers, Judah obviously their spokesperson. Still no sign of Reuben? Simeon left the group and strode over to me. The look of triumphant satisfaction on his face chilled me.

Without a word, he reached down and hauled me to my feet, his grip on my arm painfully tight. I wanted to say something to him, but my mouth was too dry. Then he half dragged me toward the others, my ankles making it difficult for me to walk. My knee landed on a sharp rock when he flung me to the ground, opening the cut wider. I bit my lip to keep silent and glanced upward.

Ishmaelites, or Midianites, I wasn't certain which. As I looked the caravan over I started to stand. A blow from Simeon between my shoulder blades sent me stumbling to the ground again. Anger flared in my stomach. He'd pay for that. When I told Father what had happened—

Someone jerked my face up.

"He's not much to look at," the trader commented. "What did you do? Break both ankles? Damage like that will affect the price. Ten pieces of silver is the highest I can go."

"He's strong," Judah answered. "The ankles aren't broken. Having worked with herds all his life, he knows much. He can manage the herders as well as animals. Egyptians pay well for that. They don't like to care for their own flocks. Thirty pieces sounds fair to me."

Puzzled, I looked up at Judah. Who was he talking about? He didn't have the right to sell any of the herders! Only Father could do that. Besides, none of the servants were here, just my brothers. What could Judah possibly be selling?

First my brothers had moved from Shechem to Dothan without notifying Father or getting his permission; and then someone had obviously bargained with the local authorities for grazing rights, something only Father could do; and now this! Judah would be—

The Ishmaelite yanked me roughly to my feet and looked me over. I tried to pull away, resentful of his familiarity, but he was much stronger, and his grip hurt. I noticed another trader standing off to one side, studying the encampment.

"No more than 12," the man holding me said. "He looks too young to be credible as more than a herd boy."

I noticed the cruel amusement in Simeon's eyes, and suddenly everything went cold. Unable to breathe, I could only stare, stunned, into those hard, triumphant eyes. I glanced at Levi, standing beside Simeon, then Gad a little beyond. They both looked right through me.

They were selling *me*. Choking, I searched around wildly.

Where was Reuben? Surely he would stop them! He needed me—he had to have me to make amends with Father.

Instinctively, I jerked, wanting to run, but Issachar and Zebulun stopped me.

"Let go," I said. "You can't do this."

They ignored me.

Suddenly, my heart pounding in my chest, I felt as if I had split in two. One part of me, the part that was really me, floated up above my head somewhere and watched this whole nightmare from the safety above. The other part of me stood very still, trying to understand what was happening, trying to speak, trying to find a way out of this horror.

Shaking my head, I managed to say, "You can't sell me." My stomach twisted painfully. I couldn't feel my knee or my ankles. I saw the Ishmaelite's mouth moving, but I couldn't hear anything over the roaring in my ears. Judah replied to the trader, gesturing toward me.

The other Ishmaelite came up and said something into the first man's ear. For an instant he glanced around, staring at something on the ground beyond my brothers. Then he looked back at me, his eyes suddenly sharp.

"Twenty pieces. That's my final offer," he said flatly.

Suddenly I could hear. I could breathe. And I could scream.

"*No!* Judah, no!" I cried. "You can't do this to me. What will Abi think?"

Judah just looked at me, his face hard and closed.

Breaking away from Issachar and Zebulun, I flung myself down in front of Judah, clutching his robe. "Judah, please, no." I gasped. "No. Don't sell me. You can't. It's not right." But all I saw in his face was flinty anger, and a bitter, bitter hatred.

"Levi, Dan, Gad," I said wildly, whirling around. "You can't do this. Stop him. Don't sell me. I'm not a slave. Please, please, don't."

The others edged away. Naphtali turned his back and left, looking uncomfortable. I screamed again. I couldn't be a slave. Slaves didn't have dreams. They didn't live long enough. And not in Egypt. Egypt was wicked, a place that did not respect El Shaddai, my father's God. Who knew what could happen to me there? I started to shake.

"What do you want?" I gasped, finding myself clinging to

Simeon's robe now. As I looked up in horror he yanked my hands behind me and started to tie them there. Although I fought him, he stopped me by twisting my arms cruelly.

"May you die, and your dreams with you," he said, the expression in his eyes freezing my insides.

"Then put me back," I pleaded. "Take me back to the cistern. Don't sell me." I didn't care that tears streamed down my face and that I choked on sobs. I couldn't be sold. I'd give anything—*anything*—to stay. I'd face death in that pit. I'd give up the birthright. I'd crawl to them the rest of my life.

"Don't sell me! Please, please!" I begged.

Simeon just pulled the rope tight.

"Eighteen, 19, 20." the Ishmaelite said, his voice tight. He nodded to the other trader, who started toward me. When I shrank away, Simeon shoved me toward the man, but I slipped by and flung myself on the ground in front of Judah.

"Please, Judah, you can't!" I sobbed wildly. "How can you do this to me? To Abi? What will Abi do?"

My brother looked at me in distaste. As he hauled me upright, I tried to press against him, pleading with him. "Be silent, you conceited, spying usurper," he hissed at me. "This will be the end of your dreams, and your wish to rule over us."

Strange rough hands pulled me toward the caravan.

"No," I said. "No! Abi! Abi!" I screamed. And then I sagged against the arms that held me, and I couldn't feel anything.

▲ ▲ ▲ ▲

We were moving again, I realized, as the sway of the camel beneath me roused me. Still unable to comprehend what had happened to me, I stared off into the distance, unseeing, the cold numbness still tight in my chest. I hadn't been able to eat, not last night or this morning. This was just a horrible nightmare and I would wake up soon and would be in my bed at home, Abi just a few steps away and everything all right again.

Because just over those hills was Father's encampment. I could see some of our sheep grazing on the hills. Father must have moved part of the flocks to this side. Ebed's flock most likely, now that Reuben and the others had gone to Father's land at Shechem.

No, not Shechem, I caught myself, Dothan. I had had to go the extra 15 miles, because they had relocated. They shouldn't have, not without consulting Father. I had to report to Father. He worried about my brothers at Shechem, afraid that the people there might attack them in revenge for sacking the city. I sat up straighter on the camel, knowing that I needed to report to Abi.

Then Simeon's eyes swam before me, and Judah's harsh voice rang in my ears. How could they have done this to me, their brother? How could they hate me that much? What had I done? They hadn't been that upset at my dreams. Instead they had laughed and shrugged and mocked. But I had seen hatred in their eyes. Hatred and rage. Where had that come from? And when?

Could it be they had deceived me? And Father as well? What if they really did believe my dreams? What had Simeon said? "May you die, and your dreams with you"?

I shuddered. No, that was just part of the dream, the horrible nightmare that wouldn't let me go so I could wake up. They didn't really feel that way. How could they? I was their brother. Surely they couldn't really want me to die.

I wasn't a Shechemite. I hadn't done anything to Dinah, or them, so I was safe—wasn't I?

My throat felt dry. Hamor and Shechem had believed my brothers too, and they were dead. My brothers had deceived them—and Abi as well—about their plans for Dinah. But surely they wouldn't trick Abi about me! Abi would have known if they hated me this much. He never would have sent me to check on them if he had realized how they felt.

No, this was just a dream. Besides, what could they possibly tell Father when I didn't return? They would have to say that I'd never found them, or that I was dead or something, and they would never do that to Abi.

Why had they kept my coat? It had lain right there on the ground. Why hadn't they sent it with me? They couldn't wear it. If they returned it to Father, he would ask where I was, and what could they say? They'd have to admit to selling me, or say that I was dead.

Suddenly I couldn't breathe again. With blinding clarity, I knew they would tell Abi I was dead. What would Father do? How would he feel? I knew he would die. He had clung to me ever since Mother died. And what about little Benjamin?

"They'll tell Abi I'm dead," I said out loud, trying to make myself understand. I had to wake up from this nightmare. I had to get to Abi and tell him that it was all a dream, that it wasn't real, that I was all right and still there and not dead. Otherwise, otherwise . . . I couldn't bear the thought of what would happen if Abi thought I was gone.

Well, I would just have to tell him myself that I was still alive. I would go right now. His tent was just over those hills. If I hurried, I could get home in time for supper, and everything would be all right.

Swinging my leg over the camel's saddle, I slid off. My ankles gave way when I hit the ground, but I didn't worry. I could still walk. I couldn't get my hands around in front of me for some reason, though. It didn't matter—not really. I could walk with them in back of me. Struggling to my feet, I started straight for the hills, my eyes locked on the sheep grazing there. I'd get home. Abi couldn't go on believing I was dead. It would tear him apart. I had to stop that.

People shouted behind me, but I ignored them and took some more steps. My ankles hurt quite a lot. I might not make supper, but I wouldn't be too late. It was just to those hills. One of the shepherds tended the sheep there. It looked like Ebed. He'd help, I knew. I—

A hand gripped my arm painfully and jerked me back, while someone yelled in my ear. I wrenched away, never taking my eyes off the sheep and pushed toward them again. Suddenly I was on the ground. Rolling to my side, I struggled up again, still staring at the sheep. "Abi, Abi, Abi," I said again and again, pushing my way toward home.

Out of the corner of my eye, I saw one man raise his staff to hit me, but I didn't care. I had to get to Abi, to tell him that I was all right, because if I didn't, he would believe I was dead, and it would break his heart.

Someone stood directly in front of me and slapped my face twice, once on each cheek. Shocked, I stared at him. No one had ever slapped me in my life!

He had a familiar-looking face with white hair, and his eyes bored into mine. Somehow I knew he was an Ishmaelite trader. Camels grunted and shuffled in back of me, and my ankles hurt so badly that I could hardly endure it, and this whole horrible nightmare wasn't a dream. It was real. Terribly, horrifyingly, achingly real. My brothers had actually sold me as a slave.

▲ ▲ ▲ ▲

"He deserved to be beaten," Mishma muttered sullenly.

"He would not have recovered sufficiently to be sold from the beating you wanted to give him," Jetur reproved, settling his body more comfortably on the rug floor of the tent. "We must protect our investment."

Mishma looked suspiciously at his father. "What other reason did you have?" he asked, curious now. "What is it about this one that makes him different?"

The older man remained silent for several minutes. "I have told you before of the time I accompanied my father Ishmael when he buried Abraham," he said at last. "I met Prince Isaac. He is a rich and powerful man. But even more, he is a gentle and considerate one. I was wary and ready to take offense at the man who I thought had wronged my father, but Isaac treated my father like a true brother. Soon I fell under his spell. I look a lot like him, you know."

A servant coughed discreetly at the tent door, and Mishma stepped outside. He returned shortly.

"The boy still cries," he said sourly. "At this rate he will weep the entire night."

"Let him." Jetur glanced at Mishma with shrewd eyes. "He is Isaac's grandson, and your second cousin."

"How did such a one fall into the hands of those ruffians?"

"They were his brothers, my cousin Jacob's sons," the older man said calmly.

"And you bought him?" Mishma asked, amazed.

"What would have happened if I hadn't?"

"They would have killed him," Mishma admitted.

Jetur nodded. "Yes, I think they would."

"I'm glad I don't worship their god," Mishma snorted in derision. "To tolerate such an act against your own blood! It is against all that is right."

"They don't worship any god," Jetur sighed. "Certainly not the God of Isaac. They have forgotten Isaac's God, and they'll pay for that someday."

Mishma looked again at his father with curiosity. "You sound as though you believe in their deity yourself."

"Maybe I do," Jetur said slowly after a moment of silence. "Isaac had a sense of certainty, of peace, of power. It comes from the touch of God. I have felt it in my cousin Jacob, and I wonder about this one we bought yesterday. It may be that it's there also."

"Then why don't you return him?"

His father shrugged. "His brothers would only wait for another chance. No, we will carry him beyond their reach. If Isaac's God is indeed with him, then He will take care of the boy, no matter where he is. I can do that much for Isaac's sake."

"And perhaps turn a profit in the bargain?" Mishma asked slyly.

Jetur chuckled. "There's that as well."

▲ ▲ ▲ ▲

I still cried, but I had emptied myself of tears. How could I face this calamity? How could I endure a life of slavery? I was a prince, not a slave, destined to rule, not serve. What was I to do? How could I live?

And Egypt? A wicked country, it had tried to kill my great-grandfather Abraham. Its gods were animals, and I knew no one there. Egypt was a place where people worshiped the dead and where monsters with long teeth swam in its only river.

Who knew what could happen to me there? I might be thrown into the river and torn apart by the monsters dwelling there. Or maybe I would be buried alive in the huge tombs I had heard of, or crushed under the foot of a huge statue. As a slave I'd have to work in the hot sun, without rest or water. Likely I'd get little to eat. I tried to swallow, but I could already feel the thirst consuming me, and fear wrapped itself around my heart.

No one would save me. I was alone. A dark terror seized my mind, and I shuddered. I could die—I would die. I was—I was—

"Remember, Joseph, you are never alone."

I caught my breath. Where had that voice come from? It sounded just like Grandfather Isaac! He always said those words to me after he told me stories, after he described his trip with Abraham to Mount Moriah and the feelings he had had as he lay bound on the altar and waited for his father to slay him as a sacrifice.

What else had Grandfather said? I must remember, for he had felt as I did. Something about El Shaddai. El Shaddai-jireh, that was it. God Almighty would provide. I clung to that thought. He had provided for Abraham and Isaac and protected my father Jacob. Maybe—maybe he would provide for me too.

More stories flooded my mind. My father at the brook Jabbok. Even as young as I had been, I remembered the fear we all had felt, wondering if Uncle Esau would kill us, or if father's presents and submission would appease him. Father still limped from that struggle at Jabbok, but he had been curiously unafraid after that. And El Shaddai had provided.

Uncle Esau had come, but in friendship, and he noticed me especially, since my hair was red like his. He had roughed it up and teased me about my blue eyes. I remembered how handsome he looked and how many scars he had. He told wonderful hunting stories.

What started badly had turned out well. El Shaddai had provided. Would he really do the same for me?

My father's God, El Shaddai. Shaddai, the strong immovable mountain, and Shaddai, the full overflowing breast, making Him El Shaddai, the Almighty One who nurtures as a mother suckles her child. I clutched the thought desperately, feeling my need of an all-powerful, comforting protector.

I could still see the expression on Grandfather Isaac's face when he told me about his decision to stay and be sacrificed if that was what El Shaddai required. And Father's face when he told me how it felt to cling to his God and beg for a blessing and assurance of acceptance. I would have to give El Shaddai all.

Not that I had much to give. I was a slave, with nothing but the undergarment I still wore, and even that would be taken from me eventually. Having seen slaves bought and sold before, I knew what happened.

For hours I struggled, remembering, fearing, hating, and hoping by turns. Dawn came, and the camp stirred to life. Still I agonized as thoughts whirled around and around in my mind. Would El Shaddai help me? Would he be with me as he had my father and grandfather and great-grandfather?

All I could give him was myself. Would that be enough? I had nothing to sacrifice. The sun beat down on the hot road as the caravan plodded on south to Egypt. I could not eat and could hardly drink. I suppose my ankles still hurt, but I didn't feel them.

Darkness came again, and I shivered with the chill. My hands were still bound, and I could not get comfortable. The battle within intensified until I thought my head would burst with the chaos inside. Battered by the swirl of fears and terrors, pain and grief that tore at my mind, I was lost, alone. I had nothing to cling to for protection, nowhere to go for relief.

By now I couldn't even cry, my sobs just dry wracking coughs that tore at my throat. The night grew darker, and the darkness pressed into me, invading my very soul. I could not bear this any longer. I would lose my mind to the terrible fear that clawed at it—the fear of the future.

Desperately, I hunched onto my knees. "El Shaddai-jireh," I whispered hoarsely, "I have no one else. I have nothing to bring, only the memory of the way You have provided for my family in the past. So I beg of You, provide for me. Although I am but a slave, I will serve and honor You all of my days if You will take me into your tents. I, too, am bound as Grandfather Isaac was on the altar. I am alone as Father was at Jabbok. My life also hangs in the balance as theirs did. Do with me as You will. Only do not reject me, or I shall die."

Shaking, I waited. I had cast everything in one throw. Was it enough? What would be the answer?

It started as a small prick in the center of my heart, a tiny glow of warmth and peace. As it grew and spread, the muscles deep inside began to unwind. My stomach unknotted, the painful twisting easing away. The warmth continued, rushing through me now, relaxing my limbs, and I stopped shaking. Tears of joy ran down my cheeks. El Shaddai, the Creator God, had welcomed me into His arms, wrapped me in his power and safety. I had given all, and it was enough.

Finally I dropped into the dark oblivion of rest.

CHAPTER 2

The next morning I woke up with God's peace still in my heart. Although shaky from lack of food, I felt awake and aware for the first time since Issachar and Zebulun had hauled me out of the pit. Curious, I looked around.

Fifteen camels waited with full loads. While I couldn't tell what was in most of the packs, from the smell I knew that they had once contained frankincense, myrrh, and balm. Out of habit I noticed the camels were all in good condition, and so were the donkeys. I caught a glimpse of the carpets carried out of the main tent. Their high quality indicated it must be a prosperous caravan.

Everyone was busy except me, and I felt conspicuous and out of place. Also I seemed to be the only slave. One of the traders walked over to me, and I hastily stood, remembering that now I must be respectful to everyone and keep my eyes on the ground as befitted someone in my position.

Untying my hands, he shoved some food into them, then waited impatiently. I ate as hurriedly as I could. After binding my hands again, he pushed me over to a camel. I climbed on the load and gripped tightly with my legs while the animal lumbered to its feet.

My ankles were still swollen, but not so painful. I noticed the caravan owner, the old man who had slapped me, as he went by. When he turned his head, I caught my breath. He looked so much like Grandfather Isaac that tears came to my eyes. Hastily I looked down, lest he spot me staring at him. He couldn't possibly know who I was, but he might be one of Ishmael's kinsmen.

The sun beat down all day, and the caravan plodded on. No one seemed in any particular hurry, but the pace never slackened, and everyone did their jobs smoothly. This master knew how to manage well.

That evening the same Ishmaelite who had fed me in the morning came again. Pulling me to my feet, he pushed me toward the main tent. Since he entered without pausing, he must be someone close to the owner. Probably a son.

Silently I stood looking down and waited to be spoken to.

"Mishma tells me you ate today," the old man said.

"Yes, master," I replied, the words feeling strange on my tongue. *Get used to it,* I thought wryly. *You only need to know two names from now on—Master and Mistress.*

"My name is Jetur. How do your ankles feel?"

I almost stared at him in surprise, but stopped myself in time. If he wished to inquire after my health, it was now his right. "They should be well in a couple more days, Master Jetur."

Just then an animal screamed. My head jerked up, eyes wide with amazement. Surely it couldn't be!

"What was that?" Mishma asked, puzzled. "It sounded like a donkey or something."

A lion roared, and the animal screamed again.

"Just a lion on the hunt," Mishma decided.

Without thinking, I started to contradict him, then hastily choked back my words. As a slave now, I had no business interrupting my master's conversation.

Jetur's eyes bored into me, and I flushed, wondering if he would have me beaten. "You don't agree?" he asked.

"I don't know for certain," I answered, trying to keep my voice from trembling, "but it may be a horse. I saw one several years ago, and it screamed like that when angry."

"A horse!" Mishma exclaimed.

"You are certain?" the older man pressed.

"No, Master. It's been several years."

"We must check," Jetur decided. "Mishma, get the men ready. If it is a horse, it will be worth half the goods I carry when we get to Egypt. Perhaps the Pharaoh himself will buy it. You know I have wanted to trade directly with the Great House. This may be my chance."

The Ishmaelites took spears and torches and followed the sounds into the night, forgetting about me. My heart beat faster. Here was my chance to get away. With everyone intent on capturing the horse and possibly killing the lion, no one paid any attention to me.

I wasn't that far from home, and in the darkness I could get far away before pursuit began, if it did at all. I wasn't worth that much I reminded myself as I ducked out of the tent. Which way should I go? I took two steps, then stopped. I had given myself to El Shaddai. What did He want me to do? But surely He couldn't intend for me to be a slave, for my dreams had said I would become great.

Egypt held nothing for me. In my father's tents I was a prince, a favored son, destined to rule. Then something Grandfather Isaac had once said to me came back to mind.

"I did not understand why I was on that altar," he had said in his gentle deep voice. "I did not see any possible way that I could serve Him by dying, but I knew that He had placed me there, and so I chose to remain."

But Abi! What about him? Could it be El Shaddai's will that my father believe me dead? Long I stood, fighting the battle in my mind. Surely it could not possibly be El Shaddai's desire for me to be a slave and for Father to grieve. I must take this opportunity to make my way home at once.

Then Grandfather Isaac's words rang in my ears again. "I did not understand. It did not seem possible. But I had submitted, and I remained."

What was I doing? Having given El Shaddai all just last night, I had vowed total submission to *His* will, not mine. And how dare I presume to tell Him what His will was! Shame flooded me, that my vow meant so little so soon.

I took a shaky breath. Although I couldn't see any earthly reason for staying, if El Shaddai wanted me elsewhere, He would see to it. Until then, I must remain. Maybe I was a fool, but I was going to be as faithful a fool as I knew how. Returning to my place, I lay down.

▲ ▲ ▲ ▲

"What say you now, Mishma?" Jetur asked, chuckling. "We arrive at the border tomorrow. Do you approve of my treatment of our investment?"

"I don't understand it," his son said, shaking his head. "He had every opportunity to escape in the confusion of capturing that horse, but he didn't."

"Not only that, but he remembered a remedy for the lion's wounds on the horse's hip," Jetur added. "If I don't miss my guess, they will heal without scars. I notice that you don't chivy him as you used to," he continued, glancing at his son out of the corner of his eye.

Mishma shifted uneasily. "There's no need. Since given the care of the horse, he has devoted himself to it. He's obedient and—" Mishma paused.

"Yes, he is," Jetur said with a dry chuckle. "He's obedient and properly respectful, but just the same, you wouldn't try to beat him as you did that first day, would you?"

His son flushed.

"Don't be embarrassed," his father said, suddenly serious. "You feel the mark of Isaac's God, for He has claimed him as His own. We will sell him, for I believe this is what we are meant to do. But I wish to keep my eye on him. I must decide carefully who we will offer him to. He will go far, this one. It is fortunate we have been kind." Jetur chuckled dryly again. "You don't believe me," he said with twinkling eyes, "but you will."

▲ ▲ ▲ ▲

Trying to shield my eyes from the glare, I squinted at the sand and rock that seemed to stretch away into eternity. We had crossed the border a day ago, but after leaving the fortress, we had seen nothing but desert and the occasional caravan. The variety of people traveling fascinated me. Syrians went by, Mesopotamians, and more Ishmaelites or Midianites. None of the caravans seemed as prosperous as ours, and all stared with envy at the horse, muttering among themselves about how much we would get for it in Memphis.

Jetur paused his donkey beside the cart where I rode, leading the horse. He would come by once or twice a day to check on things. I noticed he did that everywhere in the caravan.

"It is a different desert than our own, isn't it?" he observed.

"Yes, Master Jetur, very much so."

"The Egyptians call it Deshret, the Red Land. It is ruled by their god Seth and is the land of danger, misfortune, and chaos. Those of us who do not live in Egypt are outlanders and are always watched lest we upset maat—the way things are supposed to be. It is a thing to remember. The Egyptians do not like change or surprises."

"I will remember, Master," I said thoughtfully.

"We will camp in the uplands tonight," he continued. "And tomorrow we will descend into Kemet, the Black Land."

"Yes, Master," I said softly. Tomorrow I would see Egypt, the land of my slavery.

▲ ▲ ▲ ▲

She wanted to scream and run, but couldn't do either. What was happening? Why didn't someone help? Covered with sweat, she woke up and sagged back onto the bed. The cool night air of On in Egypt skittered through the window. In the moonlight, she saw the palms in the garden in back of the house.

That terrible nightmare! She hadn't had it in years. Why had it come back now? Getting up, she stumbled to the low table in the bedchamber and picked up the polished silver mirror, her most prized possession. The moon gave enough light that she could see her delicate face reflected in the mirror, and she shuddered.

She hated her face. And she shivered with the memories the dream dug from her mind, of that night so long ago. Of the handsome foreigner with trimmed black hair all over his face who had come to do business with her father, and the terrible things she had seen and heard later.

No one knew that she had crawled from her bed during the last hours of the feast to follow that fascinating foreigner to his room. There she had hidden and watched until Sumet had come. Sumet, with her pretty face and quiet, gentle manners.

Again shuddering, she covered her face, trying to drive the memories away. Sumet had died the next afternoon, still moaning in pain and calling on Isis and Mut to aid her. They hadn't, she remembered with bitterness.

Why had the dream returned now? Oh, yes. Her father had said at the noon meal yesterday that he needed to arrange her marriage. The empty feeling in her stomach wrenched clear to her spine.

As she looked into her mirror she saw the terror in her own eyes, just like what she had seen in Sumet's that night long ago. With shaking hands she put the mirror down. It wouldn't happen to her. She would be certain of that. After all, she was named for Neith, the war goddess who had invented weaving. Somehow she would weave such a web that no one would ever get her out of it. Gradually, she shoved her fear aside and sat there for hours, planning out her life. First, she would need someone to help her. Who?

Then she thought of Renseneb, the young scribe who had just come. He saw her as a child still. He shouldn't, since she was nearly 12, but for what she wanted, his perception of her would be useful. Now, what could she start with? After a long time, she looked down at what she clutched in her hands. She would have to start with her mirror, the only thing of value that was hers alone.

As tears welled from her eyes she hugged it to herself. It alone remained of her mother. No one had noticed when she carried it out of the room when the doctors pronounced her mother dead. Since then she had kept it hidden, for it was made of the White, and silver was of great value in Egypt. Her land had lots of gold but no silver mines. Although she couldn't bear to let it go, it was her only chance. Her father would remarry in a few weeks, and no one would pay much attention to her. The timing was perfect.

Forcing her fingers to let go of the mirror, she decided that she would speak to Renseneb tomorrow.

▲ ▲ ▲ ▲

The noise of the market place swirled all around me, accompanied by a bewildering array of colors and motion. I had never seen so many different people in my life. Syrians, I recognized, as well as some further away. I overheard Mishma mention Greeks, whom I had never heard of. A few Black men walked the market as well. I had seen them before at Shechem when a Kushite ambassador on his way to Babylon had stopped there.

Booths in the square offered foodstuffs fresh from the night's fishing, or from the ships down at the harbor. Farmers from the surrounding country crowded in to sell and buy. The stallion I held snorted with nervousness and pranced as I clung to the rope around his neck and murmured soothing words in Canaanite until he quieted.

"There he is," Mishma said quietly to Jetur. I looked at the man Mishma indicated. A frown of anger on his face, the Egyptian strode impatiently through the crowd.

"He is not the one I expected," Jetur said with a frown of his own.

"The previous overseer retired last year," Mishma explained. "This is his replacement."

"I don't know," Jetur hesitated. "He doesn't inspire confidence. What's his name?"

"Imenhet."

"You are certain he is Potiphar's chief herdsman?"

"That is he," Mishma insisted. "It'll be an easy sale. Potiphar needs a gift for Pharaoh, and a horse would be just the thing."

"How you find out these things, I'll never know, my son," Jetur sighed. "But you haven't failed me yet. Bring the man here."

Mishma moved off into the crowd, and I kept tight hold on the horse. The colors and sounds of the market began to sort themselves out. A rich lady entered the market, her attendants clearing the crowd for her to pass. I stared in shocked amazement at an attendant. Her dress did not cover her chest.

I blushed in deep embarrassment for her, but no one seemed to take any notice. Then I did not know where to look, for I suddenly saw that most of the people in the market were dressed just as revealingly. Fishermen carrying baskets of freshly-caught fish wore nothing at all. They must be slaves, I decided.

Heavy dread pulled at my heart, and shame flooded through me. I would just have to bear it when my turn came. The market became busier as more customers arrived. I kept my eyes down as much as possible.

"It is a different world," Jetur said, watching me. "They don't think the same as we do. There is no shame here in being uncovered."

"Then I will have to accustom myself to it."

"There will be a lot to which you must accustom yourself." His voice was sharp, but his eyes kind. "Remember, different things are important to them than what you have grown up with. This is a prosperous society, and very old. Older possibly than your own. Do not be afraid to learn and to change."

"Yes, Master," I nodded. Realizing that I might as well start to learn now, I forced myself to observe what went on around me. The market was full of people bartering for goods. Occasionally, I saw rings or pieces of copper or gold exchanged for goods, but that was rare. At a booth where some Greeks stood, a silent bartering session had begun. The customer selected an item and placed what he wanted to trade beside it. If the seller was not satisfied, he would point to more items, and the buyer would lay a few more on the table, then indicate what he thought the seller should add. This went on until both sides were satisfied with the goods laid out, and the sale was complete.

I soon became so engrossed in watching the people that I didn't notice when Mishma returned with Imenhet. An exaggerated cough from Jetur brought my attention back to my duties, and I led the stallion around for inspection.

The bargaining was long and involved with Mishma translating. I knew Jetur wanted gold for the horse, so his insistence on payment in goods instead puzzled me.

Jetur and Imenhet retired to a shady spot during the heat of the day and ate the midday meal. Mishma had me take the horse to water and rub him down, cleaning off the sweat. We attracted a lot of attention, and when the bargaining began once more, a small crowd watched. I could see that Imenhet did not like an audience, but he could not avoid it.

At last Imenhet announced, "What you ask is impossible. I cannot have that amount of goods available in just two days."

The old trader assumed a sad expression. "I am truly sorry, my friend," he said. "I understand your predicament. I wished to sell the horse here, but now I will have to try Memphis." Quietly he sighed.

Imenhet glanced up involuntarily at the mention of Memphis. "Do not be too hasty," he said. "Perhaps we could trade in gold."

"In gold?" Jetur said skeptically. "But I was expecting to find trade goods here to take with me to Memphis. I do not wish to lose my profits."

"But gold is easier to carry, and you can use it to buy on the way. That will be cheaper for you. By the time you get to Memphis, you will have your goods, and your animals will not have to carry them the entire route. Accepting gold will serve you well."

"I must consider this," Jetur demurred. "If you will excuse us a moment?"

He and his son conferred in low tones. Mishma kept shaking his head no, and I saw the creases in Imenhet's forehead deepen a little.

Eventually Jetur sat down again. "I will accept gold, although my son does not agree. He thinks I am too soft in my old age."

It took another hour to settle the amount of gold for the horse. Imenhet kept pointing to the partially healed wounds from its fight with the lion, and Jetur kept explaining how well behaved the animal was and how strong, since it had bested the lion.

He added that I had taken special care of the horse and that the wounds would obviously heal without scars, mostly due to my care. It didn't take long for me to realize that Jetur intended to sell me with the horse. My mouth went dry, and my stomach tightened from apprehension.

Imenhet looked at Jetur impatiently. "So you expect me to buy the boy as well? Why should I?"

"It will be a good investment for you, though I shall be sorry to lose him. He has already profited me greatly. But Potiphar is a friend of mine, and I would do him a favor when I can. The boy will assure the complete recovery of the horse."

A man stepped out of the crowd, laughing. "Jetur," he said in heavily accented Canaanite, "will you never stop? How much have you taken from my overseer?"

"Ah, Lord Potiphar," Jetur said, a smile of welcome on his face. "Your overseer drives a hard bargain. He even forced me to accept gold rather than goods."

Potiphar threw back his head and laughed. "That must have truly been a hardship," he replied, his eyes twinkling at Jetur. "And for what do I pay out my gold?"

After seeing the horse, Potiphar confirmed the bargain almost immediately. I could see a glint in his eye and knew that he had plans for the horse already.

Then Potiphar turned his eye on me. "The lad is to come with the horse?"

"He is a separate sale, I am afraid," Jetur said. "I am somewhat loath to let him go."

"The slave looks average. Why should you hesitate?" He motioned to me, and I glanced at Jetur questioningly.

"Give me your garment," Mishma hissed in my ear. "Let him look at you."

Stifling the urge to run and trying to stop my hands from shaking, I obeyed.

Jetur looked regretfully at me. "I might be tempted to sell for 50 gold pieces."

I suppressed my start of astonishment.

"Why so much?" Potiphar said testily. "His looks are nothing to notice, and his ankles appear a bit weak. It is entirely too high a price."

"His value lies in his knowledge," Jetur said smoothly, looking directly at me, giving me the impression that he spoke more to me than Potiphar. "He speaks well, can read and write, and has already increased my profits. But I paid dearly for him."

I couldn't suppress a glance of surprise. After all, 20 pieces of silver was minimum price for a slave.

Jetur continued. "I paid 20 pieces for him—in the White."

A gasp ran through the crowd, and Potiphar showed amazement. "You paid in the White? In silver?"

The trader nodded. Potiphar looked at me with respect, and the crowd regarded me with awe.

"All right, 50 pieces," Potiphar said. "Perhaps he will be just as profitable for me."

And so I became an Egyptian's slave.

▲ ▲ ▲ ▲

"It was your bright idea in the first place, so you should tell him," Simeon snapped, glaring at Judah.

"And what will Father think if I walk in alone with a bloody coat in my hand and ask if it's Joseph's?" Judah demanded. "We should all go."

"Why? As proof of our brotherly concern?" Simeon sneered.

"Precisely. You've been very careful so far to hide your hatred from Father. And you don't dare stop now."

"Why not?" he challenged.

"Use your head, Simeon. What do you think Father would do if he suspected what we've done?"

Uncomfortable silence settled on the group around the fire. They uneasily eyed Reuben, then quickly looked away. A flush spread under Reuben's tan.

Judah glanced at his oldest brother. "Father came near to having Reuben executed for fooling with Rachel's maid. What do you think he'd do if he found out we sold Rachel's son?"

"You should have thought of that sooner," Levi accused. "You always think you're so smart, Judah."

"Isn't that just what I told you?" Reuben broke in. "I kept saying not to harm him, but would any of you listen? I'm the oldest. What am I supposed to tell Father?"

"Oh, keep quiet, Reuben," Simeon snarled. "We all know you just wanted to rescue Joseph to get back into Father's good graces. You hate Joseph just as much as we do."

"At least I've learned better than to rile Father by selling his favorite," Reuben said hotly.

"That's why we've got to convince him Joseph is dead," Judah interrupted. "And it will be more convincing if all of us go."

Gad dug into the dirt with his toe. "What will Father do when we tell him? You know how he loved Joseph."

No one spoke.

"How do you feel about it, Dan?" Judah asked.

Dan stood. "I think we should have thought of a lot of things sooner," he said stiffly, then walked away.

Simeon snorted in derision, but when he looked down, his eyes were uneasy.

The closer they got to their home encampment, the slower they traveled. Everyone hung back, refusing to look at each other. At last, Judah sighed in exasperation and pushed his donkey into the lead. Best get it over with. They had dipped Joseph's coat in goat's blood several days ago, and had left it out at the edge of camp since then. Between the weather, the ants, and the animals, it looked convincingly battered.

Judah shuddered every time he looked at it. One patch of brilliant blue that exactly matched Joseph's eyes remained unstained by the blood and the weather. It brought the vision of his brother clutching at him, begging not to be sold, every time he saw it. He drove the thought from his mind.

Jacob met them at the edge of camp. "Have you seen Joseph?" he asked anxiously. "I sent him some days ago, and he hasn't returned. Did he arrive? Is he all right?"

Judah's stomach turned over. This was worse than he'd thought it would be. He'd never noticed how gray Jacob's hair had gotten, or how old his face looked, creased with worry.

Nobody moved.

"Well?" Jacob continued.

Slipping off his donkey, Judah walked back to the pack animal that carried Joseph's coat. He pulled the bundle off and walked back to his father.

"Here," he said brusquely, shoving the coat into Jacob's hands. "We found this on the trail and thought you might be able to tell if it's Joseph's or not."

In a daze, Jacob turned it over in his hands. "It is," he said hoarsely. "See, the blue that matched his eyes. And the green I ordered. The purple trim—it is. It is." He felt the coat, his hands moving faster and faster, as if frantically searching for Joseph somewhere in its folds. "Why is it so torn?" he choked out. "And the blood all over! It's Joseph's. Some wild beast must have attacked him. Joseph? Joseph!" he called, his voice rising in panic. "No, not Joseph."

Abruptly, his face went gray, and he sagged toward the ground. Judah sprang forward to catch him, his trembling arms hardly able to break his father's fall.

Clutching the coat to his chest, Jacob wailed, "Joseph! Joseph! Look at his blood. He's been torn in pieces. Some wild beast ripped him apart. Joseph! Joseph!" he cried, rocking back and forth.

As Jacob's lament continued, everyone from camp crowded around, asking what had happened. The word passed swiftly. "Joseph is dead. A wild beast attacked him. Judah and the others found his coat."

Ebed, the chief herder, pushed his way forward. "Attacked by an animal?" he asked softly, looking directly at Judah.

Judah met his gaze for a minute, then glanced away. "See for yourself," he said, gesturing to the garment his father clutched.

The shepherd looked around. "Here," he said to two others, "help Master Jacob to his tent." Gently they lifted the old man from the ground and supported him as he staggered to his tent. He refused to let go of the robe until Ebed forced his hands open.

"Don't take it, don't take it," Jacob sobbed.

"It's right here, Master Jacob," Ebed replied, keeping it where Jacob could see it. "It's right here."

On the way to the tent, he examined the torn and bloody robe thoroughly. In order for a wild beast to have done this, the tears should have the pattern of claws. And they didn't. Ebed frowned, glancing back at the sons following them to the tent. Surely they wouldn't have harmed their own brother. All the same, he couldn't forget the commotion he'd seen when that caravan had passed a couple weeks before. At the center of the disturbance had been a young man, and unless his eyes had faded with age, that young man had had red hair. Joseph's hair was red, like his uncle Esau's.

Placing the robe back into Jacob's hands, Ebed looked thoughtfully back at Leah and the maid servants' sons. Then he glanced at Benjamin, who was crying without knowing why. He had better keep the lad with him from now on, just in case.

▲ ▲ ▲ ▲

"Father, when will Grandfather Jacob stop crying?"

Judah winced and looked down at his youngest, Shelah.

"He's been crying for weeks and won't tell me stories anymore. And he won't let me sit with him. All he wants is Benjamin."

Judah swallowed the bile rising in his throat. "I don't know, Shelah," he said, trying to steady his voice. "Grandfather Jacob is very sad."

"I know. He lost Joseph. But he still has us. Why is he still so sad?"

"He loved Joseph very much. It is hard for him to lose him."

"I miss him too," Shelah said suddenly.

"Do you?" Judah asked, surprised.

The child nodded solemnly. "Yes. I liked him the best of all the uncles. He used to let me and Benjamin play with him. He laughed a lot, and he made Grandfather Jacob laugh too. Why doesn't he come back and make Grandfather Jacob laugh now?"

Judah felt his stomach twist into a tight knot. "He can't come back. He's dead. Go to your mother now."

As Judah watched little Shelah run toward his mother's tent, he suddenly wondered what he would feel like if a lion had torn his child into pieces. The thought sent him almost running into the night. But he could not go anywhere to get away from the sound of Jacob's mourning.

Covering his ears, he tried to blot out Jacob's lament. But his father's words, "I will go to my grave mourning for my son. Joseph! Joseph, my son!" constantly echoed in Judah's innermost thoughts.

CHAPTER 3

Master Imenhet's voice drifted through the early morning fog. "How many times do I have to tell you?" he shouted. "Keep the calves away from the river during the night!"

A crocodile must have snatched another calf, I thought, wincing. I'd been right about that part of Egypt anyway. Monsters lurked in the river, an ever-present danger.

I patted the stallion grazing at my side. His wounds were almost fully healed. In a few more days it would be impossible to tell that he had been injured at all. Raising his head, he nuzzled my arm and nickered. We had become good friends in this strange land of wet fog and mist. But even though the grass was rich and abundant, Master Potiphar paid a low rent for this grazing because it was on an island. The cattle had to swim across a fairly wide channel, and more often than not, crocodiles took some stock.

I shivered. The crocodiles were the ugliest-looking animals I had ever seen, slinking along the ground on their short legs, heavy tails dragging, and teeth bared in a rapacious grin. Even the stallion hated them, snorting and stamping whenever one was around.

Hazor walked toward me out of the fog, his face already swelling from Imenhet's blows, and his back sore again. The fog had muffled the sounds enough that I hadn't heard the beating.

"Is another calf gone?" I asked quietly in Canaanite, which we both spoke.

He nodded. Captured in battle, he was a large Syrian warrior. Such prisoners became royal servants, technically personal slaves to Pharaoh, but farmed out to anyone the king wished to honor or pay special tribute to. Hazor had worked for Potiphar for two years now, the last one under Imenhet, who seemed to delight in beating him.

Silently I thanked El Shaddai again that Jetur had mentioned he had bought me with the White, or silver. Hazor told me that silver was rare in Egypt. They had gold in abundance from mines in the desert, but no silver. In addition, Potiphar himself had made the purchase, and Imenhet dared not damage me too badly.

Although I was under Imenhet's supervision, Potiphar made it clear that my sole job was to give the stallion the best of care. It spared me the worst of Imenhet's temper since he knew what his master would do if anything happened to the horse. And I was the only one the horse would willingly let near him. While Imenhet had knocked me down once or twice, he never gave me a beating such as the Syrian suffered.

"Sometimes I think he gets up in the night and drives the kine to the river himself," Hazor muttered, feeling the bruises on his face carefully.

"Why do you say that?"

"Someone was around in the dark," he said bitterly. "And this morning another calf is gone."

"I doubt it's Master Imenhet," I said. "He has to give an accounting at the end of the year. But so many calves have been lost, I think he's afraid."

Surprised, Hazor looked at me. "How do you know that?"

I shrugged. "The free herders talk among themselves."

"You are picking up Egyptian fast," he commented, sharply eyeing me.

I lowered my eyes. That was becoming a habit. I'd discovered that my blue eyes made many Egyptians uneasy. They apparently associated the color with one of their many gods, or the eye of a god, or something. I hadn't quite figured it out yet.

What I had figured out was the list of animals Imenhet kept in his hut. I had been standing close enough to watch the first time Imenhet had Sekhmet, the scribe, record the loss of a calf. The incident reminded me of Jetur's comment that my value lay in my knowledge. I decided to learn as much as I could as quickly as possible.

It hadn't taken long to realize that the best way to become very valuable was to learn to read and write in Egyptian. Scribes kept track of everything all the time. Most were connected in some way to the local ruler's house and recorded taxes, which were paid in kind. A certain portion of every harvest and increase went for taxes, and the scribes were very exacting. I had already heard stories of the punishments meted out to the farmers and their families who could not pay their proper tax, but I didn't know whether to believe them or not. I'd have to wait and see.

The sun burned away the morning's fog, and I moved the stallion to another patch to graze. Gradually the cattle, mostly cows with nearly grown calves, emerged from the haze, feeding quietly. The rough reed kilt around my waist chafed a spot on my hip. I'd need to make another one soon and, hopefully, I could do a better job this time. I sighed. Reeds were better than nothing, but I now understood the reason so many commoners didn't bother with clothing. It was hot, and it got in the way.

The fishermen who plied the channels around the island hardly dressed at all, even though they were free men. There weren't many slaves, and the majority were royal servants like Hazor. Someone like me, who had not been captured in battle, was unusual.

The cow whose calf had been seized during the night bawled disconsolately, wandering the pasture as she searched for it. I swallowed the lump in my throat. Sometimes the longing for home was so overwhelming that I had to get away to hide my tears. I wondered especially about Benjamin. Once I'd promised to show him how to track a wolf when he turned 6.

My eyes filled, and I rubbed them with one hand, turning my thoughts away from home. I dared not think about Abi. The pain was too great to bear if I did that.

At noon, I went back to my mat, the small rectangle that represented home. Hazor already had the fire going and the noon meal mostly cooked. He had made a flat unleavened bread, baking it on the hearth, a low slab of limestone, and cooked a stew made with onions, lentils, and duck meat. A jug of beer sat on the ground. I picked it up and took a long draught of the thick, sweetish liquid. Hazor said it was made from barley and vegetables. I had been wary of it at first, for it was fermented, but I quickly found that it was far less fermented than the wine back home. It made an excellent food, and many commoners lived on not much more than bread and beer.

This had been one of the surprises about being a slave. I ate well. We had lots of food of a good variety. By now I had already acquired a liking for the varieties of green leaf called lettuce that everyone ate, and for a small sweet onion that I'd never seen before either.

As I looked around it was obvious that Sekhmet had taken the boat to the village and stocked up on supplies. The craft was a small affair, made of reed bundles lashed together. The Egyptians made most everything of reeds in the delta. My mat, the awning we used for shelter from the sun in the heat of the day, the kilt I wore, even the hobbles for the stallion consisted of reed fiber that I had braided into ropes. Of the 10 of us on the island, only Imenhet and Sekhmet wore linen—Imenhet because of his status as overseer, and Sekhmet because he was the scribe.

I envied Sekhmet his linen. My kilts regularly disintegrated, much to my disgust and Hazor's amusement. He couldn't understand my attachment to clothing.

I ate my fill of the noon meal, the big meal of the day. Then everyone drowsed in the sun until the heat of the day passed. When the cattle roused, standing and wandering into the grass again, we herders followed them, constantly on the lookout for snakes or anything else that might harm the herd. Kine were valuable. Most Egyptians had small cattle—sheep and goats. Only the rich had kine. As darkness fell, we bedded the animals away from the river, and I carefully hobbled the stallion.

A sudden roar jerked me from a sound sleep. I opened my eyes in the pitch darkness. The night was foggy and damp. Quickly I pushed aside the reed mat that lay over me, giving me some warmth and keeping the insects away. A cow bawled, and then another. Hazor raced past me, yelling a word I had not heard before. The others rushed after him, and I followed, stumbling in the dark.

As Hazor shouted, the stallion screamed. Recalling my special charge, I altered direction toward the horse. He screamed again, not in pain, but in rage. In moments I heard the pounding of his hooves. He must have broken the hobbles I'd made.

Another roar shattered the night, and I felt the ground shake under my feet. Imenhet shouted from across the way, and I finally realized that he wanted the kine driven to the other side of the pasture, away from whatever roared. The stallion screamed again, and I headed toward it. The fog made it impossible to see, and Hazor ordered in Canaanite for torches.

That meant he wanted me to bring them, and I raced back to the camp. Sekhmet was already lighting them and giving them to Kinen and Siamon, two other herders. Grabbing four, I headed with the others as fast as we could toward the source of the noise. Hazor's harsh shouts mingled with the stallion's screams and the roars of the beast they fought.

A squeal, another enraged roar, and the stallion screamed again. Hazor yelled encouragement. Breathless, the other herders and I arrived, holding our torches aloft, the smoky flames making an eerie glow in the dark fog.

For several moments I could only stare. A huge beast that resembled a gigantic pig faced Hazor and the stallion. It had a huge round body, great stumps of legs, no neck, and a head with monstrous jaws that gaped open. Four yellow teeth gleamed in the light. By its side was a smaller version of itself.

As soon as he could see, Hazor leaped in with a stick, threatening the little one. When the larger beast turned to him, my stallion would pound against its side with his hooves or bite with his teeth. Then when the creature shifted to face this attack, Hazor charged in again, shouting.

Waving the torch and yelling at the top of my lungs, I darted toward and then away from the animal. The others soon joined me, dancing around and making as much noise as we could. Soon the beast's little pig eyes whirled with confusion, and at last it lumbered toward the river, shaking the ground as it ran, followed closely by its baby.

"What was it?" I asked Hazor, panting, as we watched it disappear.

"Hippopotamus," Hazor said. "A river horse," he added in Canaanite in a low voice while the others excitedly discussed the incident. "They're very dangerous, coming out of the river to graze at night. This is the first one we've had this year.

"A friend of mine was killed by one," he said a moment later. "He was bitten, and then trampled." The Syrian turned away.

"I'm sorry," I said softly.

Hazor shrugged. "It's past. But I'm glad we leave soon. The crocodiles are bad enough. You did well," he added. "All those waving torches convinced it to run."

"Thank you," I stammered. For the first time since my brothers had thrown me into the cistern, I felt something besides grief and fear. I was pleased to have helped, and I hugged Hazor's compliment to my heart.

The stallion had calmed somewhat now, so I coaxed him to me and checked him over carefully. The horse hadn't gotten a single scratch and was obviously pleased with himself, snorting into the darkness in the direction the hippopotamus had gone.

"Yes, you were very brave," I said soothingly. "You chased away the beast. I believe you'll fight anything—lions, river monsters, or anything else."

My torch had almost gone out, so I extinguished it in the dirt and led the stallion back to the camp in the dark, holding onto his mane. I collected my reed mat and covering. With a sigh I decided that I'd have to spend the rest of the night by the horse. Tomorrow I'd have to make more hobbles—and a new kilt.

I must have proved myself by fighting the hippopotamus, because the other herders, led by Kinen and Siamon, dropped their former reserve. They talked to me now and helped me learn Egyptian words. But they always went off by themselves to eat, and I asked Hazor about it.

"We are not of the Black Land," he said. "They think Kemet is the center of the world, created as a place for the Pharaoh to live while he's in human form. We and our countries exist solely to provide Pharaoh with whatever he might want. Thus we are barbarians, not men. They won't eat with us. Besides, we have too much hair," he finished with a sly grin.

I didn't say anything more. Sometimes I had difficulty sorting out what Hazor meant by some of the things he said. What did my hair have to do with anything?

His comment brought hair to my attention, however, and I noticed that none of the Egyptians had beards. Kinen's and Siamon's hair was uncut, but they shaved every day. Imenhet and Sekhmet also shaved and wore wigs over their close-cropped haircuts. In addition, Imenhet used a scented hair oil.

Later that day, I looked at myself in a quiet pool of the Nile. My beard had thickened and begun to show. My coarse red hair was bushy and wild, falling raggedly to my shoulders and beyond. Even my face looked different. It had always been mismatched somehow, with no feature seeming to fit with any other, and with my disheveled appearance I looked almost frightening. Only my eyes were the same, but even they had a hooded, shielded look to them, quite different from the confident, direct stare I used to see in the water.

When I dropped my gaze, I laughed bitterly to myself. Now I couldn't even look directly at my own reflection. I'd never realized how much of my self-respect depended on the mere fact of my birth. It would have to depend on something else now. My birth meant less than nothing here. "Your value," I repeated aloud, "is in your knowledge."

Turning to my reflection again, I forced myself to gaze directly into my own eyes. "You must learn," I told myself. "You must learn everything you can, and you must serve well."

Glancing up, I saw a small boat heading down the channel. The two men in it looked around constantly. One spoke to the other, and they turned sharply toward the island. They would land not far from me, and I stayed very still, knowing as I watched that they would leave if they saw me.

Cautiously I crept toward the place where they had tied up. Neither tried to get out of the boat but just waited. I moved slowly in the grass, keeping the river reeds between me and the men.

Footsteps came from the meadow, and I heard Sekhmet's low greeting. For a second I almost stood up, but stopped myself, wondering why the men didn't come openly to the island if they wanted to see the scribe.

They spoke in low voices, and I wasn't certain of what they said, my Egyptian still quite patchy. But they were discussing the herd, and something about calves.

"Take the two," Sekhmet said. "That is enough."

One of the men asked something, muttering Imenhet's name,

and Sekhmet laughed. "He will blame Hazor," he said. "We leave next week."

The conversation continued a bit longer, and then the two men pushed their boat away. I waited, trying to make sense of what I had heard. The meeting felt wrong somehow, but I couldn't understand enough of the language to really be certain what had been said.

Frustrated, I moved and heard a startled exclamation from Sekhmet. Instantly I froze, looking around cautiously. Sekhmet called out and stepped toward the reeds, swishing the nearest ones around a little. Not liking the sound of his voice, I eased back.

He left after a little more searching, and I made certain he was gone before I showed myself. Looking down, I saw how obvious it was that I'd been in the reeds. Racing to the other side of the island where another reed patch grew, I hurriedly gathered a large armful and lugged them back to the fire, arriving late for the noon meal already in process.

Sekhmet watched me narrowly as I entered camp. Coming over to the fire, he asked, "Where did you get the reeds?"

Assuming a puzzled expression, I stood.

"The reeds," Sekhmet said, pointing.

I remained silent.

"Ask him where he got the reeds, Hazor," Sekhmet ordered.

The Syrian questioned me in Canaanite.

I replied, pointing toward the reed bed in the opposite direction from the place where Sekhmet had met the men.

The scribe looked at me sharply and then walked away. But I knew he didn't believe me. Later that day I saw him examining the fresh cuts in the reed bed. I pretended to be engrossed in the stallion and didn't glance his way.

We were busy now with preparations for the cattle drive from the Nile Delta to Potiphar's estate near Memphis. The harvest was near, and along with harvest came taxes. Potiphar would oversee the process for his estate. My Egyptian improved daily, with Hazor and the others helping me as much as they could.

Two days before we left, Kinen looked up from the noon fire and asked, "Can you swim?"

"No," I said. "Where I am from there is little water."

Kinen clucked his tongue. "You should know how to swim."

He demonstrated the way I should move my arms and legs in the water, and I watched closely.

"Tomorrow," he said. "We will put you in the water tomorrow."

I agreed, going back to my mat and reviewing what the herder had said in my mind. Sekhmet watched me. He had done so constantly since the day I'd overheard him talking to the strangers. His eyes made me uneasy.

The next day the scribe kept me so busy with packing that I did not have time for my swimming lesson. However, all the fetching and carrying provided plenty of time to get acquainted with the tools of his trade and to study the records that he had kept. Soon I had worked out that of the 14 calves born to the kine, four were missing, lost to crocodiles, and all of them within the last month. And it struck me as strange that the crocodiles waited until the calves could get along without their mothers before they ate them.

That night, I heard hesitant footsteps entering the clearing. Remembering Hazor's comments about someone being around in the night, I quietly got up to check.

Imenhet staggered into camp. Thinking he was hurt, I went to his side, but one smell of his breath told me he was drunk instead.

"Who are you?" he asked, blinking at me in the faint light from the moon.

"One of the herders, Master Imenhet. Come to your bed."

"One of the herders, is it?" he repeated, weaving on his feet. "You're the new one, the expensive one, the ugly looking, stupid one that tends that horse."

"Yes, Master Imenhet, that's me. Come to your bed," I repeated.

Imenhet draped himself on me. "Bed is a good place. I need to be in bed. What's your name?" he added.

"Joseph, Master Imenhet," I answered, helping him toward the small hut where he slept.

"So, Joseph," he said loudly, slurring his words a little, "do you like the Delta?"

"Quiet, Master Imenhet. Sekhmet is asleep."

"Shhhhh," Imenhet said immediately. "We don't want to wake Sekhmet. Sekhmet needs his sleep. He is a busy man."

"Yes, Master Imenhet, he keeps all the records."

"He does. He keeps them even before they are made!"

"Does he?" I asked, guiding Imenhet into the hut and trying to keep him from falling against the door frame. "He must be very talented then."

"Talented? Talented?" Imenhet opened his eyes to look at me. "He's not talented. I'm talented. I am Imenhet of Tanis! Did you know that I was the best potter in all my nome? Did you?"

"No, Master Imenhet, you never told me that."

"Of course not!" Imenhet nodded, half falling onto his bed made of reeds like I used. "How could I tell you when you weren't here? But I was. I still am, I think. Only someone smashed my pottery wheel. Smashed it to pieces," Imenhet said, starting to sob. "Ruined. It ruined me, and I had to sell myself to provide food for my family."

As I helped him settle on the bed on the floor I listened silently. I hadn't realized he was a slave.

"So," Imenhet went on, "does Potiphar put me back in the pottery shop where I belong? Does he? No. He makes me graze his kine on this miserable Delta. And why does he do this?" His voice rose in anger. "Because of Sekhmet, that's why."

"Hush, hush, Master Imenhet," I soothed. "Surely you are mistaken. Why would Sekhmet do such a thing?"

"He hates me," Imenhet said, closing his eyes. "He's always hated me. And now he will get even with me. Six calves, six calves gone, and Potiphar will be very angry. He will punish me for losing his kine. But how am I to know what to do? Am I a barbarian, to herd the animals? I am a potter! I make pots, jars, and bowls for the nobility, for their grave goods, for the nomarch's house to serve guests with! What do I know of animals?"

"Hush, hush, Master," I said, pulling his mat over him.

"Six calves," he muttered.

Ignoring the oil lamp on the low stand by the bed, I sat in the dark until he drifted off to sleep. He kept saying six calves, but only four were missing. Could this have anything to do with what I'd overheard Sekhmet tell those men? If it did, when would two more calves disappear?

During the swim across the channel, of course. What would be more natural than that crocodiles would seize two more during the trip?

Slowly I walked back to my bed, wondering what it all meant and what, if anything, I could do about it.

The next morning we began the drive to Potiphar's estates. The herders tied the calves to small boats, and the cows would follow along. In the confusion and shouting, two cows kept breaking from the herd and running back to the pasture.

Hazor, Kinen, and I ran after the cows for the sixth time, Hazor swearing in Canaanite, and Kinen in Egyptian.

Suddenly, I stopped. "Hazor," I said, "why do those cows always head toward the same place?"

The Syrian looked at me, puzzled.

Kinen stood panting. "They act like they are running to their calves," he said in disgust. "Their calves are back at the crossing."

"What if they are not?" I said in a quiet voice. It occurred to me that Sekhmet could best get those calves by taking them before the swim, not during. When the kine arrived at the other side, minus the calves, everyone would assume crocodiles had gotten them.

Kinen glanced at Hazor. "Maybe you did hear someone those other times," he said. "Let's go."

We followed the noise the cows made as they bawled by the reeds. There we found two men trying to keep the cows from the calves and get the calves aboard a boat. As soon as they saw Hazor and Kinen, they turned and ran, shoving the boat away from the island and paddling as hard as they could.

"Thieves," Kinen fumed. "Well, we don't have time to go after them. We have held up the drive long enough. Wonder who those two were?"

Although I would bet the men were the same ones Sekhmet had talked with, I kept quiet. I could prove nothing, and as a slave, I would need irrefutable proof before I dared accuse one of my masters. Even then, I might be risking a beating.

Now that they had their calves, the cows went easily enough to the crossing. I glimpsed the rage on Sekhmet's face, quickly suppressed, as we arrived with the missing kine. He didn't have time to do anything, however, since Kinen plunged the calves right into the river and the boats began to cross with the bawling calves behind. In moments the entire herd had plunged in and started the swim to the other side.

I returned to the side of the stallion, who pranced and danced beside me, snorting at the river. But when I stepped into the boat waiting for me, the stallion followed willingly enough and eased smoothly into the swim.

As we floated along I paid strict attention to my charge and kept an eye out for crocodiles.

"He swims well," Sekhmet said.

I glanced up in surprise to find that he shared the boat with me.

"Yes, he does, Master Sekhmet."

I scanned the river again. A large pleasure boat rounded the bend in the channel. Six rowers on each side propelled it smoothly through the water, and on the high stern deck I saw the noble owner watching our drive.

We reached midstream when Sekhmet suddenly sat up.

"There," he said pointing.

I looked. "What is it?"

"Crocodile, I think, and he has his eye on that horse!"

When I scanned the water, the sunlight winked into my eyes, and I couldn't see anything.

"There he is," Sekhmet said excitedly. "He's getting closer."

I looked at the stallion, who swam easily, seeming to enjoy the dip.

"Can you see it now?" I asked uneasily.

"I don't—yes, there he is!" Sekhmet replied, pointing.

I stood up to get a better view. "Where?"

"Right there." Sekhmet stood also.

As I looked, I felt a sharp shove, and the boat rocked. With a cry, I fell into the Nile! Water filled my mouth and ears and blinded my eyes. Panic made me flail my arms, and suddenly my head broke the surface. I gasped air, then panicked again as I started to sink. I heard shouts, distorted by the water as I went under.

Pulling my arms down, I felt myself rise. When I kicked my legs I rose more. Looking up, I saw the surface just above my head and kicked again. As I came up, I saw the stallion swimming toward me, his eyes full of curiosity.

I took a breath, coughed, and started to slide under the surface. Desperately I kicked and managed to keep my head above the surface for another breath. The stallion surged toward me, seeming to realize I was in trouble. As I went under again, my fingertips grazed his neck and tangled in his floating mane.

Grasping the mane, I pulled myself to the surface. Then I grabbed his mane higher on his neck with my other hand and hung on for dear life. Towing me, the stallion turned and started after the cows again.

"No," I gasped, in between coughs. "Take me to the boat."

But I couldn't get the stallion to change course, and he seemed determined to avoid the boat, for whenever it started toward us he turned away.

At last I had my breath back enough to think again and waved the boat away. As long as I had hold of the stallion I'd be all right.

Now that I no longer tried to get him to go somewhere he didn't want to, we made rapid progress toward shore. I remembered how Kinen had told me to move my legs and arms, and by the time the stallion struck the bottom, I could let go and swim the last few feet on my own.

Most of the herders were gathered around, yelling encouragement, and some had come down into the river to help me.

The stallion climbed up the bank, snorted at the men to clear himself some space, and shook all over, spraying water from his mane for yards around. The men scattered more and laughter drifted to us from the pleasure boat coming into the bank. Hazor helped me sit down and cough up the last of the Nile in my lungs.

"I thought you said you couldn't swim," he said in Canaanite.

"I couldn't—but I just learned."

"How'd you fall in?"

I hesitated. Had I really felt a push or not? "I'm not sure," I replied, truthfully.

"Why were you standing up to begin with?" Hazor continued.

"Sekhmet thought he saw a crocodile coming after the horse."

The Syrian cast a quick glance at the scribe's smooth face and said nothing more.

"If I had known what a show you put on swimming the kine, I'd have come in previous years," a hearty voice said.

The nobleman from the boat stood in our midst.

"Master Potiphar," Sekhmet gasped, suddenly pale.

Scrambling to my feet, I glanced around for the horse. The stallion stood a few feet away, ears forward, watching me with interest.

"Check him over, lad," Potiphar said, looking at me. "Now that you have dripped half the Nile onto the bank, look after the charge I gave you."

Hastily, I turned to the stallion and took up the rope hanging from his neck. I examined him, but he seemed fine, dancing under my touch and snorting at intervals.

"He is not hurt, Master Potiphar," I said.

"Nor are you, I see," Potiphar replied. "Well, Imenhet, how did it go this year?" he asked, turning his attention elsewhere.

The stallion snapped his head around to stare at the Nile, then snorted and lashed out with his front foot.

"What is it?" Potiphar asked, turning back to us.

"Probably a crocodile, Master Potiphar," I replied. "The horse hates them. He has given an alarm several times in the night when they came ashore."

The stallion was so restless that I led him away from the crowd and over by the boat I'd started across in. Sekhmet eased after us.

The stallion turned his head and flattened his ears, bunching the muscles in his hip.

"Careful, Master Sekhmet," I warned. "He's upset, and he'll kick."

But the stallion lunged, snapping his teeth instead. Sekhmet jerked back. But he didn't leave. He kept trying to go past us.

"Please, Master Sekhmet," I insisted. "Stay away for a bit until he calms down."

Reluctantly, the scribe drew back a little, but the stallion kept a wary eye on him and reacted if he tried to move closer. I puzzled over why the man didn't just walk away.

"Six!" Potiphar's voice rose in surprise. "That is almost half the increase."

Sekhmet's face blanched at the sound, and he sidled again toward the boat. The stallion snorted and lunged, almost dragging me off my feet.

And then I understood. The records. Imenhet's drunken comment about Sekhmet's records came back to me, and I knew that when Potiphar checked the records, six calves would be missing. But only four were, because we had stopped the theft of the last two.

"Get the records," Potiphar said, his voice annoyed. "If 14 calves were born and 10 are here, you are only missing four, not six."

At that moment Sekhmet lunged toward the boat, and the stallion let loose a blast of sound from deep in his chest. His head snaked forward, and he opened his jaws wide. Sekhmet tripped and fell, scrambling away.

Imenhet walked by the stallion and got the records from the boat without a word. The scribe got up and tried to clean the Nile mud off his linen.

"Sekhmet!" Potiphar shouted.

Swallowing, the scribe straightened his face into its usual mask and hurried over to Potiphar.

"How is it that we gained two calves?" the noble asked, his voice icy.

"It is but a slight mistake," Sekhmet said. "I must have written the wrong number when I copied the tally last. I only know of four calves missing. The crocodiles were very bad this year."

Another scribe behind Potiphar murmured something.

"Why were they only bad this last month?" Potiphar asked coldly. "You have been on the Delta for nearly a year. Why did the crocodiles wait so long?"

"The blessing of the gods, I suppose," the scribe said calmly. "It is a strange coincidence."

Potiphar looked thunderous, but remained silent. Sekhmet looked down, and a faint smile crossed his lips.

"Maybe it is not a coincidence, Lord Potiphar," Kinen said. "Perhaps these men can tell us something."

I glanced up to see two of the herders dragging the men we'd chased off the island toward us.

Potiphar heard Sekhmet's gasp of dismay, and his head snapped around in time to catch the look of fear on the scribe's face.

"Lord Potiphar," Siamon gasped, out of breath. "We found these two thieves down the river trying to load four calves with your brand on them into a boat."

"And I can witness that Hazor, Joseph, and I chased those same two men off the island earlier this morning," Kinen added grimly. "They tried to steal two calves before we crossed."

"Well, well, it seems I have regained all six of my calves," Potiphar said, his face a mask. "Imenhet, go into town and bring the Nubian police here."

Sekhmet almost fell to the ground.

"Not a word," Potiphar said, his voice harsh. "Your own records condemn you. Your case will be tried in the courts."

The scribe's glance of hatred felt like a blow as they led him away. I didn't look at him. I only prayed that I would not make my master that angry with me. The look in his eyes reminded me of Simeon's, and I shivered.

CHAPTER 4

Hazor, Kinen, and I worked closely together during the cattle drive to Lord Potiphar's estate. The greatest problem was keeping the animals out of the surrounding fields, but after a day or two the herd settled down for the most part. Several of the cows had already made this trip more than once.

Hazor could spot problems quicker than I did. Although I wondered how a Syrian warrior came to know so much about kine, I didn't want to ask, since it seemed so many of Hazor's memories were violent ones.

The third day out, I got a leech on me when I bathed in the Nile, and when Hazor pulled it off, he noticed the thin white scars on my right shoulder and down my back. They were almost invisible unless I had a tan and a person was examining me closely.

"Looks like something took a swipe at you," he said carelessly, after we'd started the herd moving for the day.

"A lioness," I said. "I was 12. If it hadn't been for a friend of mine, I'd have died."

"Sounds like quite a story," Hazor commented, prodding a cow back into line.

"It is, I suppose." I paused a minute, but found that I could remember the incident without too much pain. "We lived at Shechem. You know it?"

The Syrian nodded.

"Father bought land there. He wanted to be close to the temple to the God of the Covenant, and we went often to worship while we stayed. Anyway, Father heard that someone from Kush was traveling through, and he wondered why.

"I was quite curious. I'd heard that people from Kush had black skin. Father took me to the market place with him, and we learned the man was on his way to Babylon.

"Prince Hamor introduced Father to the Kushite ambassador. The ambassador had a son, who was much taller than I, and they did indeed have shiny black skin. The son was near my age, and by the end of the day we were fast friends, in spite of not being able to speak each other's language.

"I called him 'Kush,' and he called me 'Habiru.' That's what the locals called my great-grandfather's clan."

Hazor looked at me with quick attention. "I have heard of them," he said. "They are very rich. Your great-grandfather was Prince Abraham?"

I nodded. "Kush and I roamed the hills around Shechem and surprised a lioness in some rocks. Kush had the presence of mind to grab me and jump off the ledge. I was too frightened to move. Instead of killing us, the lioness only got in one swipe of her forepaw across both our shoulders and down my back. Fortunately the gashes weren't deep.

"Father was very thankful to Kush for saving my life, so he gave a feast after the lion hunt. They killed it. It was old and sick, which is why we had managed to surprise it in the first place. Prince Hamor and his son Shechem joined in the hunt. I think that same lioness had been a threat to the townspeople."

Hazor walked along in silence. The sun beat down, and the glare hurt my eyes. I kept squinting and rubbing at them. Come to think of it, that feast was probably when Shechem noticed Dinah for the first time. What a lot of trouble that had led to! I sighed.

"Is your father Prince Jacob?" Hazor asked abruptly.

"Yes," I said, swallowing the lump that rose in my throat.

"How did you end up a slave?" he continued, his voice harsh.

I pressed my lips together to stop them from trembling. "My brothers sold me," I finally answered.

"Your *brothers?*" he echoed in disbelief.

I nodded.

"They would be the same brothers who sacked Shechem not long after that feast?" he probed.

Again I nodded miserably.

"Why does your god allow this to happen? You said that your father worshiped in the temple all the time. Why didn't your god protect you?"

"I don't know," I answered with a sigh. "But I think he wants me here, now."

Hazor looked at me in disbelief. "You serve a very strange god. I'm glad my god does not expect such things of me."

"How did you become a slave?" I asked, changing the subject.

The Syrian laughed. "Strangely enough, because your brothers sacked Shechem. My wife's family is from there, and her father and brothers were killed that night. I left my home to become a soldier, so I could kill the men who took my wife's family away from her.

"While I was still in training, my captain unwisely decided to raid an Egyptian encampment. He was killed. I was captured."

"What does your family do?" I asked.

"My father is a successful merchant. I took to farming and herding, so I managed two farms that he had purchased."

Just then, Imenhet shouted at us to hurry along, and we stopped talking and pushed the straggling kine faster on the trail.

▲ ▲ ▲ ▲

I lay on the hard ground in the darkness and stifled my sobs. We would arrive at Lord Potiphar's estate in two days. I was stiff and sore from the trip south from the Delta, my eyes burned from the constant glare of the sun, and homesickness overwhelmed my mind.

I wanted to be home, away from the sand and the smell of the Nile. Home, where I understood what people said to me, and where Abi waited in his tent at the end of the day for my report of its events.

I didn't want to be here, exhausted, dirty, and ragged-looking, my skin peeling from sunburn, my hair matted and dusty, and my shoulder sore from the blow Imenhet had delivered because I didn't get out of the way quickly enough.

I was a slave. The bitterness and reality of it pressed down on my mind. Dust and heat and glare awaited me the rest of my days. I would work and sweat for someone else's profit, and have to humbly accept blows and curses with my food.

The rest of my life stretched before me in all its bleak darkness. I had made the wrong choice. I should have run back there in Canaan when I had the chance. I should have made my way home, not stayed with Jetur's caravan like a lunatic. I was a fool—a complete fool.

The next day, I could hardly drag myself up to take the stallion to the Nile to drink. He pricked his ears at me, nickering a greeting and nuzzling me. When I didn't respond with the usual petting, he shoved me impatiently with his nose, then looked at me with wonder when I slapped him away. Quietly he followed me to the river, laid back his ears at the ducks in the water, then stamped to make them go away.

When I got back to camp, Hazor remained silent. Although he left me alone, to my surprise he did my chores as well as his own. Even though I was grateful, my depression deepened. I had been a fool to think that El Shaddai cared anything at all about me. I was not important to him. Not anymore. I wouldn't get the birthright or inherit the promises El Shaddai had made to my fathers. Instead, I would live a bitter life and die alone, and no one would care.

Why did I serve El Shaddai anyway? Hazor's god cared for him better than mine did for me. The Syrian hadn't been sold by his brothers. He knowingly took the risk of enslavement when he chose to be a soldier.

I was innocent of every wrong, yet I suffered undeserved, malicious betrayal. Coughing from the dust, I swerved away from the track, trying to find a better place to travel.

The stallion snorted and pulled me back to the trail, right into the dust rising from the kine before me. I coughed again. It wasn't fair. I'd never done anything—anything at all.

The day dragged on, and later than usual that evening, I took the stallion down for his drink. He pranced and snorted and pawed and refused to put his head down. Growing more and more impatient, finally I walked out into the Nile and tried to pull him in.

Snorting in annoyance, he refused to budge. Suddenly, the stallion gave a heave backwards, yanking me toward the bank as I saw a movement from the corner of my eye. With a scream of rage, he rushed passed me, rearing and striking down into the water. Stunned, I turned to see the swirl of a crocodile and barely avoided a slap from its tail.

Kinen shouted from behind me and hands pulled me from the water. The horse kicked up a blinding spray, teeth bared as he snaked his head toward the surface. A crocodile raised his head, jaws agape. The stallion jumped, whirled, and lashed out with his hind legs, catching the crocodile on the nose. Hazor and Siamon rushed into the river, beating the monster with sticks and yelling.

The crocodile lashed with its tail, catching Siamon before he could move away. With a cry, he fell. Hazor grabbed him and pulled him back, but the beast had had enough, and it disappeared.

Imenhet towered over me, his face black with rage.

"Base-born vermin," he yelled. "How dare you risk that horse? It could have been killed, you stupid barbarian."

He raised his staff, and I hunched silently against the pain as he rained blow after blow on my shoulders and back. I lay still as tears squeezed out of my eyes.

I didn't sleep that night. I lay on the ground, aching in every bone, and contemplated my carelessness and stupidity. Obviously I wasn't as perfect as I thought I was. The maids' sons at their worst had never been this negligent.

Maybe I wasn't so innocent either. My mind drifted back to incident after incident. Why had I worn that coat Abi gave me at every possible occasion? And yes, Dan had been a bit careless with the herds, but his stock losses had been less than usual, as I well knew. He had done the job well, he just hadn't done it exactly the way I would have, and I was arrogant enough to resent that. My life suddenly began to appear in a very different light.

Now I realized how I had goaded my brothers and bragged to them and flaunted Abi's love for me in their faces. Of course they hated me. I had been hard to please and exacting, lording it over the maids' sons as if I were their master, not a brother. How could I expect them to care about me?

And then my dreams. I cringed inside, recalling the proud way I had recounted them. No wonder my brothers couldn't even speak to me—that they wanted me dead, that they would sell me into the pain and the struggle and the servitude of slavery.

I could look forward to nothing but more of the same. Black despair pressed against my mind.

"Am I a fool?" I whispered between dry lips. "El Shaddai, am I a fool? Did I make a mistake? Did I displease you somehow? Why has this happened?"

In the distance I saw the outline against the stars of the giant stone piles called the pyramids.

"Are those gods better to serve than You, El Shaddai-jireh?" I asked the night. "I must know. Tell me somehow. Give me back the peace of Your presence. Or am I just a fool whispering in the dark with no one to hear or care?"

The next morning I got up so stiff and sore that I could hardly bear to move. The stallion followed me to the river, walking daintily and obviously leaving plenty of slack in his line. He studied the river carefully before lowering his head to drink, and when he finished, he nickered softly and gingerly touched me with his nose.

"I'm sorry," I whispered. "I should have listened to you yesterday."

He pressed his head against me, asking for a scratch behind the ears. We walked back to the camp, and my heart ached a little less than my back.

Hazor stayed close to me all day and adroitly saved me many steps. Grateful, I wished I could do something to repay him. Siamon had a badly bruised leg and had to ride in a cart. At the noon meal, I served him myself, trying to say how sorry I was in my limited Egyptian. His gracious refusal to admit I had done any wrong to him brought tears to my eyes again.

Imenhet watched me closely, a concerned frown on his face.

Hazor chuckled. "He's worried," he said to me softly. "He knows he shouldn't have beaten you that badly."

A bit later Imenhet walked to me, and I struggled to my feet.

"Why are his eyes so red?" Imenhet asked Hazor, indicating my face.

The Syrian shrugged. "He has no kohl," he replied. "The sun's glare is bad for him. His eyes water much."

I suppressed a glance. Hazor was up to something.

The chief herdsman's frown deepened. "The kohl will help?"

"We could try and see, Master," Hazor suggested blandly.

Imenhet turned away, and a few minutes later Kinen delivered a small pot of kohl, which Hazor accepted with a straight face. "I will show him how to apply it," he said. Kinen nodded.

"What it is?" I asked.

"Eye paint," Hazor said in delight.

"Eye paint? That black or green stuff the Egyptians wear around their eyes?"

"Yes. Here, I will show you what to do."

I pulled away. "I can't wear that."

"Why not? It cuts the sun's glare. Why do you think the Egyptians wear it?"

"It will lessen the glare?" I asked, dubious.

"Try it and see," he urged. "Besides, it's for you. You have to wear it."

"But you won't object if I share?" I asked, amused.

"I wouldn't dream of it," he said with a smile.

Gingerly, I let Hazor help me apply the black powder under and around my eyes. When I looked around, I was astonished at how much easier I could stand the sun. It took some getting used to, but within minutes I was so grateful for the relief from the glare that I didn't care what I looked like.

"There are many things to which you must be accustomed," I muttered to myself. Jetur was right again.

The kohl did help the glare, but I'm afraid my eyes still watered a lot as I cried with the terrible ache in my heart and the black discouragement that washed over me.

Hazor dropped back to walk with me, coughing at the dust.

"Why don't you walk in front of the herd?" he asked in disgust.

"Because the stallion won't walk anywhere but here," I said. "Maybe he thinks the kine are his or something, but he won't go in front of them."

"They had a good harvest this year," Hazor said with satisfaction. "These are Lord Potiphar's fields. See, they are just starting to reap the wheat."

I looked up without interest. Off to my left, the reapers had harvested half a field. A wave of dizziness swept over me, and I missed a step, pulling the stallion to a halt.

Unable to swallow, I could only stare at exactly the same wheat field as in my dream! The reapers stood just as my brothers had with the harvest half gathered and the sheaves—*those short double-headed sheaves—lay on the ground* in piles around them.

Egypt? My dream was about Egypt?

"Joseph! Joseph," Hazor said, touching me. "What happened? Are you all right?"

Dragging my gaze briefly away from the sight, I muttered, "I'm all right."

"What do you see?" he asked, looking at the same field.

"Uh, nothing," I said hastily, coming to myself and shaking my head. I'd half expected those sheaves to stand up and bow. I started walking again, but my heart was pounding.

"Hazor, do they always cut the grain so short?" I asked after a little while.

"Yes. They use the straw to make mud bricks, so they leave as much as they can in the field."

Slipping away from my sleeping mat that night, I went to another field, touching the sheaves as they lay on the ground. In the moon's light, I saw the multiple ears on each stalk.

"Forgive me, El Shaddai-jireh," I whispered as I knelt. "I see now that you do care for me, after all. I shall not doubt you again. Every year at harvest, I will remember." I still did not understand how I could become great in Egypt as a slave. But El Shaddai must mean for me to be here.

▲ ▲ ▲ ▲

Standing, I looked at the measuring rod in the mud. The upper fields would be plowed today. Inundation Season was almost over. I stretched in the early morning sun, and my hand brushed my face. I hadn't shaved yet. As I turned back to the estate compound I caught a glimpse of myself in a puddle.

Yes, it really looked as if Sabestet, the barber, had finally tamed my hair. Even though most lower class Egyptians didn't, I elected to cut my hair. Sabestet cut it at chin length all around, the ends neatly flipped under. I looked down in satisfaction at my kilt. While only of a coarse grade of linen, old and stained, it was linen and a proper kilt. I tried to keep it as clean as possible, since when the washerman took it, I had to fall back on reed fabric again. Soon I hoped I could get a second linen one and dispense with reeds for the rest of my life.

Back at my place, I rubbed a bit of oil on my face and picked up the sharp flint razor. I used it carefully, thinking back on the year and a half I had worked here on the Memphis estate. My Egyptian was passable now, and I understood everything people said most of the time. Silently I again thanked Jetur for telling me not to be afraid to learn new ways. As the trader chieftain had said, this was an old and prosperous society. Their way of life worked very well. It wasn't what I'd grown up with, but I wasn't where I'd grown up.

Some of the other slaves thought I was foolish to want to learn so much and to adopt Egyptian customs. But putting kohl around my eyes had reduced the glare, and keeping my hair cropped and beard shaven was much cooler and a lot less trouble to keep clean. Egyptians placed great emphasis on personal cleanliness. I wanted to do everything I could to make my life easier and more secure.

I was almost whistling when I finished shaving. Yesterday I'd found out for certain that the status of slave was not nearly as bad as one might think. Much of the population was always restricted in some way. The peasants were tied to the land and its owner, whether that was a private individual, a temple, or the state, and were subject to the corvee, or state-required labor, and compulsory military service.

I, as a slave, might be bought and sold, but I could marry, own property, and earn my freedom. Since Potiphar had paid such a high price for me, I wasn't certain I could ever buy myself back, but I could build a reasonably secure life with possessions and maybe even a family of my own, provided I met a woman willing to marry a slave. Thinking of the possibilities gave me a more cheerful outlook.

As I walked out of the hut I slept in, I automatically glanced toward the field where the stallion had stayed. I missed him since he left. Last month, Lord Potiphar and I took him to Memphis. At first, the stallion refused to leave me, but when he got a whiff of other horses, especially the mares, he had finally let himself be persuaded to go.

Huy ran up to me excitedly as I walked toward the gate. "Joseph, did you hear? Lord Potiphar is wearing ear rings!"

"I had not heard," I said. "Is this important, Huy?" One of the house staff, Huy was tall, very excitable, and had a wandering right eye that gave him an odd, crazy look. Most of the other house staff ignored him, but I liked him and found him to be a reliable information source. He never tired of explaining Egyptian customs to me.

"Is it important!" he echoed. "It is the most exciting thing that has happened yet! It means Lord Potiphar received the gold collar from the Pharaoh!" Huy was almost bursting with excitement. "Only a few of the nobles at court can wear ear rings. None have served the Pharaoh as well as Lord Potiphar.

"And it has something to do with you," Huy went on, dancing beside me. "I heard Lord Potiphar say it was because of you that he got the collar."

I was about to tell him that he must have heard wrong, when Khay, one of the house boys, ran up with the message that Potiphar wanted to see me immediately.

Glad that I had shaved already, I headed toward the house. Walking through the walled outer court, I crossed the pillared porch and entered the vestibule. Ahmose, the porter, had already gone into the dining hall, the main room of the house, to tell Potiphar that I had arrived.

I glanced around. The dazzling colors never ceased to startle me when I entered the house. The mud brick walls were stuccoed and decorated with country and river scenes. Even the wooden pillars, supporting the ceiling, were painted bright colors. The gypsum floor felt cool to my feet.

Ahmose stepped into the room. "Master Potiphar will see you now."

Entering the dining room, I passed the first row of pillars and stopped in front of the large low table where Potiphar sat in a wooden chair. I bowed, kept my eyes on the floor, and waited.

"Joseph," Potiphar said, "I expect you have already heard the news."

"Huy mentioned that you were honored by Pharaoh, Master Potiphar. The house is very excited."

The noble laughed. "Huy doesn't 'mention' anything. He shouts everything to the skies. Did he also tell you that you were involved?"

"Huy mentioned my name, Master, but I thought he misunderstood," I said, flushing a little.

"He did not. That stallion you cared for turn out to be one of a pair that Pharaoh had purchased from Mesopotamia. It got lost during the trip here. Pharaoh was very grateful and pleased to recover his property, and in such good condition."

"Then it is fortunate that you bought the horse from Master Jetur," I replied.

"Yes, but your constant care allowed me to return Pharaoh's horse in better condition than any of the other animals in the stables. You are to be commended."

"Thank you, Master." I also silently thanked El Shaddai that my one slip at the river hadn't ended in injury to the stallion.

"You have indeed been profitable to me," Potiphar went on. "I wish to reward you. I have heard that you were of some assistance to Menneb during Harvest Season last year. He mentioned that you speak more than one language?"

"I can read and write in Canaanite, Master, and I have tried to learn as much as I could of Egyptian as well."

"You have succeeded remarkably. Would you like to work with Menneb all the time?"

"Yes, Master Potiphar, I would," I said eagerly. An assistant scribe to Snefru, Master Potiphar's chief overseer, Menneb oversaw the farming and herding aspects of the estate. Since I was familiar with both aspects myself, it was a perfect place for me.

"You will start today. Report to Menneb at once, and do whatever you can to aid him."

"Yes, Master Potiphar. Thank you." Bowing again, I hurried from the room. I would have jumped for joy if I hadn't been almost 20 years old.

▲ ▲ ▲ ▲

Pulling my feet out of the mud, I looked around. Planting was almost over, and the irrigation system to the upper fields was finally repaired. Every inundation of the Nile damaged something or other, and this last flood had wrecked a large section of the upper field's canal.

To my right, Khay shouted as he drove some sheep over the newly planted field to trample the seed into the ground. Further below, in the lowest fields, the plowing was almost completed. Tomorrow the field hands would sow seed by hand and then trample it into the dirt.

We could rest for a little after that, but soon the hot sun would dry the land enough that we must irrigate the upper fields. The constant chore meant carrying water from the Nile to pour into the canals that watered the field. I had done my share of it last Growing Season. The lower fields usually did not dry so soon, and their crops would not need irrigation.

Stretching, I headed toward the house. Menneb would be wondering where I was. The day's tally had to be made and records written of all the grain sown in which field and by whom. Already feeling the cramp I got sometimes from writing so much, I flexed my fingers. During the past year, I had learned to do the simple repetitive recording in the flowing hieratic shorthand used by the scribes. Menneb had been glad to push it off on me.

Kemi, the weaveress, hurried past on some errand and gave me a cheerful greeting. She had woven the linen of the kilt I wore. I had four of them now, one for best, one for worst, which I should have been wearing for the job just finished, and two for everyday. By my mat in the hut, I had a battered wooden box to keep them in. That box had been a lucky find, floating in the Nile.

"Wait, Joseph," Khay called, catching up to me and breathing hard from his run.

I waited, smiling at him. His eagerness to please and sunny smile reminded me of Benjamin, and he soon took advantage of the soft spot in my heart by forever tagging after me and asking endless questions, most of which I couldn't answer. He reminded me of Benjamin that way too. Oddly, it eased the aching homesickness that never seemed to leave me.

Menneb hadn't minded Khay's peskiness. He encouraged it sometimes, after telling me that Khay was an orphan and needed some guidance as he grew up. The scribe said I was the first person the boy had formed an attachment to since his parents died.

Although I'd taken Khay for only a boy, he was actually close to manhood. Menneb mentioned that the lad's family would have starved if Lord Potiphar hadn't taken them in. They were from Upper Egypt, in the south, close to Thebes.

"We have lentil stew for supper," Khay said, sniffing the air.

"Are you certain?" I asked, pretending to doubt.

"Very," Khay replied. "Want to bet?"

Having learned that his nose was never wrong, I shook my head.

"They put leeks into it," he added, delighted. "Did you know Lord Potiphar might be back today? If he comes there will be a great feast."

"And you will eat most of it," I teased.

"No," Khay said solemnly. "But I will try!"

Master Potiphar was indeed home and had brought his wife with him. Normally, Tanefret, or Lady Tanefret as I was instructed to address her, remained in the house in Itej-Tawy, the capital. She liked the bustle and excitement of the court.

As soon as Minemhet, Potiphar's cook and baker, heard that Lady Tanefret was here, he sent kitchen boys scurrying to find all the help they could, and he started three assistants baking bread. Within a couple hours, Khay dashed to the kitchen with the message that Lady Tanefret wished to give a dinner party in two days. Minemhet just grunted and kept issuing orders.

The next morning, Menneb met me in the courtyard, muttering in disgust. He'd had to give up his room in the house to Iteti, Lady Tanefret's overseer.

"What does Iteti oversee?" I asked, subtly guiding Menneb across the large courtyard to his house on the far side. He had the eye sickness and would soon be completely blind. It worried him, since he had no family to take care of him then.

"He has charge of all Lady Tanefret's property," he said sourly.

"A woman can own property?" I asked in amazement.

The scribe snorted. "Of course. Only you barbarians would think that a woman was unable to manage possessions. She has a large house in Thebes, where her family is from, and one in Memphis where her business is. Lady Tanetfret trades in dyes for linen. Iteti has plenty to keep him busy.

"And Lord Potiphar will have less time than ever to tend the estate, what with Iteti here as well."

"Why would Iteti report to Master Potiphar if he manages Lady Tanefret's property?" I asked, puzzled.

"Because Lord Potiphar manages her properties with his own," the scribe explained patiently. "Lady Tanefret keeps an eye on things, especially in trading for dyes, but leaves most of the care of her houses to Lord Potiphar. Still, while they are at the court in Itej-Tawy, Lady Tanefret manages the house there. And when she is here, she will concern herself with running this household, as if Snefru could not handle it himself," the scribe ended with a sniff.

He paused uncertainly several feet from the door to his house. "Have we gone inside?" he asked. "It seems so dim."

I looked at him in astonishment, opening my mouth to reply, then shutting it firmly. "Come and sit down, Master Menneb," I said gently. "With your approval, I think I would like to try handling all the records myself. Do you think you could allow me to do that?"

Menneb sat down on the one stool in the room with a tired sigh. "Tell me the truth, Joseph. The sun still shines, does it not?"

"Yes, Master," I whispered.

His lips trembled briefly, and he wiped his hand across his face. "It is dusk now for me, and soon it will be night. You had best tell Lord Potiphar that I can no longer serve him."

"That is not true," I said. "You know I do not have enough experience to handle this job on my own. I can do the writing part now, but you must still be here to make the decisions. For instance, Imenhet has sent a message that the grazing on the island is no longer sufficient for Lord Potiphar's herd. We must find another pasture, and I know nothing about how to locate more land to rent for grazing.

"Nebnufer sends a message for direction on where to build pens for the birds that will be captured on the hunt next week in the marshes. Hekamaat wants to know how he shall fatten the antelope caught last year when the supply of bread dough for force feeding has disappeared, and when will this year's hunt take place. And—"

"Enough, enough," Menneb put up his hand with a slight smile. "I see I shall have to remain to keep you from panic. Let us begin with Hekamaat. Tell him that Lady Tanefret is giving a dinner party, and the bakers have time only for that. In two days, he shall have more dough for the antelope."

Picking up the reed pen, I began to make notes. When I glanced out the door, I could see the baker's assistants kneading a huge basin of dough with their feet. Kemi, the weaveress, darted by the doorway, complaining about being behind with her work and having to interrupt it to heat her oven to help bake bread.

Menneb switched to Imenhet's message. He gave me the names of several officials who owned land in that part of the Delta and might have some to rent for grazing.

Minemhet's voice drifted to the house, chastising someone for putting sour milk into a large batch of bread dough. Khay trotted past the door for the fifth time carrying pots and jars from the potter's shop to the kitchens. Before long, Meru, the potter, went storming to the kitchens to demand some of his pots back, especially the ones he hadn't fired yet.

Close to noon, Hekamaat himself strode into the compound and demanded of the house porter where Menneb was.

"Hekamaat has come," I said to Menneb. "It sounds as if he is asking for you."

"Of course he is asking for me," Menneb said sourly. "I am the only scribe who will listen to his impossible demands."

"Shall I bring him?"

"You might as well," he sighed. "He will not go away until he sees me, and the sooner we get him out of here, the better."

Stepping outside the house, I crossed the courtyard.

"I tell you I do not know," Ahmose the doorkeeper repeated.

"You must know," Hekamaat shouted. "I need to speak to Menneb right away."

"Master Hekamaat, I can take you to Master Menneb," I dared to interrupt.

Hekamaat swung around, his large form even bulkier close up. "What's that you say?" he shouted.

"Master Menneb sent me to bring you to him," I repeated. "If you will come this way?"

With a look of disgust at Ahmose, Hekamaat turned on his heel and strode after me. I hurried to keep ahead of his long steps. He muttered under his breath until we got to the house.

Pushing past me, he started talking as soon as he walked in. "Menneb, I must have that bread dough. Lord Potiphar has particularly selected me to maintain the fatness of his herd here at the estate. How can I possibly do this if I am denied the basic necessities of my job?"

Leaving him to finish his tirade, I slipped out and walked to the kitchens. Catching Khay in mid-stride, I asked, "Where is Minemhet?"

"Arguing with Meru about pottery. They are in back of the kitchens."

"Khay, go get three donkeys and those old baskets you put in the storerooms yesterday. Meet me by the kitchens with them as soon as you can."

Eyes wide, the boy ran to obey.

I found Minemhet fuming as Meru sorted out the pots he hadn't fired yet. "We need them for bread," he protested.

"They may not be used," the potter retorted. "They are unfinished and unfit for use until fired."

"Master Minemhet, would it help if the pantries were emptied of the old bread?" I asked.

"Anything would help," he snorted. "I need anywhere possible to put the baked goods. Do you know how many people are coming? Over 50 so far, and I still hear of more—"

"Yes, yes, Master," I dared to interrupt for the second time today. "Perhaps you could store the bread in baskets. Didn't we have some in the storerooms? There are some fine colorful weaves there and maybe the bread could be served straight from the basket. That way Master Meru can properly finish his pots, and you will still be able to store the food for the feast."

The chief baker and cook looked at me. "Well," he said grudgingly, "it might work."

"Especially if the pantries are cleared," I said.

Meru whistled at a couple boys and started them carrying the unfinished pots back to the pottery. Minemhet walked back to the kitchens. Khay waited there with the donkeys and large baskets.

"I cannot use these!" Minemhet exploded. "They are too big and old."

"Of course, Master," I said. "These are only for the stale bread to be carried away in. Khay will empty the shelves into these baskets. The others are in the storeroom across from the large bakery."

As Khay began to load the big baskets with bread, I paused by him and said, "Load the ruined batch of dough while you are at it." Khay nodded and brazenly picked up a large pot for the ruined dough. I moved on and led Minemhet to the storeroom, opening the door. About 20 good-sized new baskets sat on the shelves.

"They will do," the baker admitted. He stuck his head out the door and yelled for help. I slipped out, checked on Khay who was almost done, and ran back to Menneb's house.

"Yes, yes, I hear you," Menneb's voice came to me as I ran up. "But with the party the bakery is fully occupied—"

"And if the beasts are not properly fattened, what will the guests eat?" Hekamaat shouted. "Lord Potiphar demanded a whole beef of me just two hours ago. I must be ready at all times to supply meat fit for his table, and to do that I must have bread dough to fatten them on!"

"Joseph!" Menneb called.

"I am here, Master," I said from outside the door. "I think that there may be some bread dough available for Master Hekamaat, as well as some old bread."

"I must have dough, not old bread!" the herder roared.

"Would it be possible to soak the bread and use it as dough?" I asked. "Just this once, of course, in case the dough is not enough. It would a be a big help to Lord Potiphar, since this is the first party for the year."

Hekamaat snorted in disgust, but didn't protest. I waited.

"Where is this bread?" he finally asked. "I will do what I can to help Lord Potiphar."

"Khay is coming with it now," I said hastily, catching sight of the boy leading the donkeys toward the house.

Pushing me aside, Hekamaat strode toward him. "Hold up there. It is not hard as rocks is it?"

"No, honored one," Khay said, holding out a half-eaten loaf. "Want some?"

The herder looked at the loaf suspiciously. "Looks fresh enough. Perhaps we could soak it." He grabbed the lead rope of the donkey and marched toward the gate, grumbling about having to do everything himself, and why couldn't the supplies just be delivered without his having to fetch them personally.

I glanced sideways at the loaf Khay ate. It still steamed from the ovens.

"Khay," I began.

"He didn't ask if this loaf was from the baskets, Joseph," the boy said innocently. "I would have told him it was not if he had. But he didn't."

I sighed. "I suppose if he soaks the bread, it will not matter."

"Want a roll?" Khay asked, holding one out.

"All right," I said, taking it from him. I was hungry.

He ran off, and I bit into the bread, almost breaking my jaw. The little scamp had given me a piece that was days old and hard as a rock!

CHAPTER 5

I should have kept my mouth shut about the bread for Hekamaat because by the end of the day I'd had to settle three other problems like it. With Snefru closeted with Potiphar and Iteti regarding Lady Tanefret's estates, no one else knew enough details to answer questions like the herder's.

But I had noticed all sorts of things while I ran errands for Menneb, going between the fields and the house several times each day. I remembered how Jetur used to visit all parts of the caravan at least twice a day, and I'd consciously tried to do the same around Potiphar's estate just to increase my own knowledge of how it operated and who was responsible for what.

Today I was either punished or rewarded for that habit, depending on how you looked at it. It didn't take long for people to get in the habit of sending Khay to ask me. What really surprised me, however, was that I had an answer more often than not.

Menneb snorted with impatience as Khay appeared at the door for the umpteenth time that afternoon. "Joseph," he panted, "Minemhet is all upset again. Do you know where the large jars of last year's wine are?"

"I thought I saw them in the cellar under the ladies' rooms." I said after some thought. "Check to be sure before you tell Minemhet."

The boy disappeared, eating another fresh roll, and I turned back to Menneb.

"You will be Potiphar's steward soon," he said abruptly. "I must train you well."

I was too astonished to say anything in reply.

Snefru hurried into Menneb's house near supper time, looking worried. "I heard Hekamaat," he said. "What happened? What did he want? Did you put him off?"

"I did not need to put him off," Menneb said calmly. "Joseph found dough for him and gave him the stale bread to soak and use for dough as well. He went away satisfied, if not happy."

The chief overseer looked at me with surprise. "Hekamaat accepted the stale bread?"

"He did it to help out Master Potiphar," I replied respectfully. "It was only a suggestion on my part."

His lips twitched. "I see. You would be Joseph, the one everyone has told me to ask about the location of last year's wine for Minemhet?"

Blushing deep red, I nodded. "Yes, Master Snefru. I told Khay to check the cellars under the ladies' rooms."

"Since I saw the jars being carried to the kitchens as I came over, I assume you were correct," he said. "Are there any other details I have missed while talking with Lord Potiphar?"

Menneb broke into a laugh. "You have missed half the details of the feast. I have been interrupted time and again by Khay dancing into the room, eating fresh bread, and demanding answers from my assistant."

I blushed again. "It is only that I noticed some things and remembered them," I started to explain.

"Mmm," Snefru said. "You remembered, did you?" With that, he turned and left.

I rubbed my hands nervously on my kilt. What if Master Snefru was offended? What if he thought I was trying to take over his place? I bit my lip. I shouldn't have answered so much. My impulsive behavior might have encroached on his responsibilities, and that wasn't my place.

Many times I'd already seen demonstrated the Egyptian resistance to change. It went against maat, the balance of things. Everyone had a position and responsibilities in society, and everyone kept to their place, since to leave it or change it would upset the balance and open a possibility for chaos to enter. And chaos was feared by all.

"Joseph, sit down," Menneb said. "We have three more messages to answer."

"Yes, Master Menneb," I said, taking a seat.

But instead of beginning on the messages, Menneb asked. "What is wrong, Joseph? You have done well today."

"I do not want to offend Master Snefru," I blurted. "What if he thought I was trying to do his job for him?"

"More than likely, Snefru was delighted to find someone who could remember what they were told," the assistant scribe said dryly. "Do not worry over it."

The next day was worse. Khay appeared at Menneb's door for the fifth time in an hour, asking, "Joseph, are there more fuel bricks anywhere?"

Since Egypt had few trees beyond date palms, wood was very precious. Fuel consisted of dried dung mixed with water and straw and molded into bricks to dry in the sun.

"Khay, Snefru is the one to ask about the fuel for the ovens," I answered. "He is the overseer. I am Menneb's assistant, and it is not my place to take over such responsibilities."

Khay waited patiently, chewing on some raisins, while I protested. Then he rolled his eyes at me. "Joseph, Snefru is the one who wants to know about the fuel."

I opened my mouth, then closed it.

Menneb chuckled beside me. "Answer the lad, and let us get on with our work."

"I saw some of the boys making fuel bricks down by the river," I said. "Were those bricks brought up to the kitchens or not?"

"I will check," Khay said, racing off.

The scribe chuckled again. "At this rate, you will be running the entire country before you are done," he teased.

Even I laughed at that.

The feast was a success. At least, that's what I heard. From my place behind the scenes, I didn't get to see any of it myself. I can say what a scramble the cooks and servers had to serve the food on time and make certain the guests had enough wine of various kinds. Snefru also sent me on a mad search for a lute for one of the musicians, who broke a string in the middle of the meal.

I did hear the music, though, and discussion about the quality of the dancing troupe, along with some comments about the way Lady Tanefret acted. I collapsed that night with only a vague memory of hastily apologizing to one of the serving women when I nearly ran her down as I hurried after some more dates for Minemhet. She gave me a rather odd smile.

The next morning, Snefru sent for me and told me I would be his assistant from now on.

▲ ▲ ▲ ▲

As the sun rose, I stood up from where I'd knelt in the wheat field. Yesterday had been the first day of Harvest Season, the last of Egypt's three divisions in the year. Inundation came first, with New Year's marked by the highest point of the flood. Then Growing Season, followed by Harvest Season.

As I had promised El Shaddai, on each second morning of Harvest, I came to the fields to touch the sheaves and remember His care for me. Glancing over my shoulder at the pyramids gleaming in the dawn's light, I thanked El Shaddai for my life and asked Him to care for my father and brothers in Canaan.

The homesickness bothered me most at this time. I still missed Abi painfully and did not even know if he was still alive. If my brothers had told him I was dead, and I couldn't see anything else they could do, his grief must have broken his heart. I remembered the way he mourned Rachel, my mother; the way he clung to me after she died, and how he told me that I was a comfort to him.

Now all that was left of the great love in his life would be Benjamin. I prayed every day that El Shaddai would preserve him from my other brothers' jealousies, so that Abi would have the comfort Benjamin alone could provide for my loss and for Rachel's. I wiped my eyes; the tears seeped from them in spite of all I could do.

I mourned here in Egypt for another reason as well. Menneb had died. We buried him in the desert, facing west, with a few possessions that the Egyptians believe he would need in the after-life. Though poor and dependent on Potiphar, he had served well. Potiphar rewarded him by promising to place a stone with his name on it in Abydos, up the river near Thebes, to preserve his name for eternity.

The Egyptian beliefs about death were very complex, and I had not had time to ask Huy much about them. I did not see how a stone at Abydos would help Menneb, but he had been so relieved when told about it, that I gathered it must be very important. It was part of the story of Osiris, one of the gods, whose burial place was Abydos.

The sun crept up, and the house below me started to stir. Snefru and I would be in the Memphis market today. Word had come from the capital, Itej-Tawy, that Lord Potiphar would be returning home in a couple days bringing Lady Tanefret with him, and there would be lots of feasts given until she left.

Lord Potiphar's allotment of foodstuffs from the palace in return for his labor as captain of the palace guard was such that most of what grew on the estate could be bartered for luxuries or paid out to work-men who were making Potiphar's tomb, a very expensive enterprise. Today, Snefru and I would barter for exotic foods for the feast Lady Tanefret invariably gave two days after she arrived at the estate.

Perhaps the market might have pomegranates. My mouth watered at the thought. Stealing a few more minutes from the day just to watch the sun rise and to worship not Ra, but the Creator of Ra, I asked that He would honor my efforts today to serve my master well, and that He would honor my master, who had treated me with consideration. Then I started back down the path to the house.

"Good morning, Joseph," a voice said breathlessly.

"You are up early, Aneksi," I replied in surprise, stopping in the path.

"I—I just happened to be up," she said, twisting her hands and blushing.

"Well, good morning to you also," I said, starting on my way once more.

Aneksi made me uncomfortable. I didn't know what to do about her. Minemhet's daughter, and a very pretty girl, hardly more than 12 or 13 years old, she "ran into" me often, and gazed at me with her large brown eyes as if I was the answer to all her dreams. I hardly knew what to say to her. Above all, I didn't want to upset her, for that would disturb Minemhet, and no one upset Minemhet when Lady Tanefret gave parties.

Minemhet was the best cook and baker in the nome. Lord Potiphar had increased the man's allotment of bread and beer three times rather than lose him to some other nobleman looking for a cook. I hurried down to the house. Why would Aneksi hang around me so much? Khay said she was in love with me, but I couldn't believe that. I was a slave and an ugly one at that. There must be some other reason. At least I devoutly hoped so.

Soon I forgot Aneksi in the complexities of bartering for luxuries in the market. With the amounts Snefru and I wanted, we did not barter for a simple in-kind exchange. First we converted the value of our needs into deben, a small copper piece used as the universal exchange medium. Then we would offer to barter an amount of goods we thought of equal value in deben.

The seller naturally thought our offer much too low in deben, and demanded more. We argued that the seller was valuing his goods too high. But I only saw Snefru buy with actual deben once, and that was from a Greek who demanded it because he sailed the next day.

As I waited for Snefru to finish a barter for some scented oils, I caught the smell of frankincense, and it reminded me of my first experience with Egyptian markets in Tanis. I smiled in remembrance of my ignorance, my arrogance, and my shock at the things I saw around me for the first time.

Jetur had had more wisdom than I knew, and I owed him much for the advice he had given me as a raw young man sold into a hard and alien life. To begin with, I had almost hated him for selling me away from all connection to my home. Now I knew I would have fared worse among the constant reminders of who and what I had been.

Straightening abruptly, I looked intently across the square. My eyes did not deceive me. It was Mishma, patiently trailing a potential sale, as he had done with Imenhet in Tanis.

Snefru joined me. "That robber!" he snorted. "Tried to take me for 30 deben a jar! As if I would even consider paying that much!"

"Master, didn't you say we needed olive oil?"

"Yes, and where we will find it, I don't know," Potiphar's chief overseer said. "I went to my usual source, but he had already sold out to Renseneb and will not have more for another 60 days, and we need that oil now. I will have to go begging from Renseneb and pay twice as much. I wish I knew who Renseneb acts for. He is an agent for a very shrewd buyer, and one with money. Twice in the past two years I have been forced to buy from him. Once I needed wine and once, myrrh. Now it will be the olive oil."

"Master, we only need five jars, don't we?" I asked when Snefru paused to catch his breath.

"That is right. But I will have to pay as much as for 10 from Renseneb."

"Maybe not, Master," I replied, watching Mishma and remembering that Jetur always carried a little bit of everything on his trips to Egypt. "What about antimony? Do we have enough to make kohl for the year?"

Snefru looked at me in surprise. "We should, but I suppose we could always get more. Everyone uses the kohl, and it goes fast."

I turned my full attention to him. "So you are somewhat willing to buy, but not especially interested?"

The overseer stared back at me. "I believe so," he said slowly. "Lead on, Joseph."

I had noted the alley that Mishma ducked into, and I led Snefru that way. As we passed the entrance, I paused, and asked, "Is that all we need, Master?"

"Most of it," Snefru replied cautiously. "There is just antimony left. We found most of what I wanted."

"Yes, Master," I replied.

"But perhaps you would be willing to make a small purchase?" Jetur's deep voice spoke from his place just inside the alley.

Snefru turned around with a start.

"Pardon," he said. "I did not see you there. Yes, I might be interested in a small amount of antimony. Do you have some?"

"I have a little left," Jetur replied. "Let us see if we can settle on a price."

"I would only want a few deben worth," the overseer warned.

I stayed in the shadows, watching Jetur, my eyes hungry for the sight of my own people. He had hardly aged at all, and he recalled Grandfather Isaac to me in a flood of pleasant memories. The way he moved his head, the lines of his face—I could easily imagine it was Grandfather there, not the Ishmaelite trader who had sold me in Egypt.

"No, no," Snefru said, bringing me back to the present. "What you ask is too much."

I listened for a bit, enough to determine that Jetur wanted to unload the last of his antimony onto Snefru.

"Perhaps the caravan master would add something into the bargain," I said softly to Snefru.

"Well," Snefru hesitated. "I really don't need so much, and there are other small things I wanted to purchase—" he left the sentence hanging.

Jetur responded as I knew he would. "Good man, I can see that you cannot pay so much for so little. What else would you like? Perhaps I can add something to the antimony to sweeten the deal for you."

"I don't know," Snefru hesitated. "We have most of what we need. Maybe some wine, or oil?"

"I have olive oil, the best to be had. A jar perhaps would be what you require?"

The overseer consulted his list. "There is plenty of oil on the market," he said. "I have a regular merchant for olive oil. I do not think—"

"But the regular merchant will charge you the regular price," the trader broke in. "Just this once, you could buy for a different price." He named an amount that was significantly higher than normal.

"Oh, no," Snefru said. "I get a much better price than that at my regular place." He quoted one far below market value.

I leaned against the wall in the shadows and listened as the bargaining went on. Jetur fought Snefru's price up a deben at a time, until Snefru reached a bit below the going rate on the market. From there he wouldn't budge.

Soon Jetur realized with a sigh that it was as much as his buyer was willing to pay. "For you," he said. "For you will I go this low. How much did you want?"

Snefru looked doubtful. "Would you have four jars?" he asked. "I know it is much to ask, but if I could buy the rest of what I need here—"

"Four jars? Come, what can you do with four jars? You need seven or eight jars. Olive oil is good for so many things."

Finally, Snefru let himself be convinced to buy six jars at below the market price, and concluded the deal for the antimony as well. Knowing Snefru, I believed that he was pleased with his bargain, and as for Jetur, I knew he was relieved to get rid of the antimony and not have to transport those jars of olive oil beyond Memphis.

The bargaining ended past noon. Jetur invited us to have a meal with him, and Snefru accepted. As I followed Snefru into the rooms where Jetur stayed, Mishma looked up and started slightly when he recognized me. With my red hair and blue eyes, I was quite distinctive. I set my scribe's tablet and pen down and seated myself behind Snefru as he and Jetur conversed while the meal was served at two tiny, but separate, tables.

I ate lightly and listened to the news that Jetur passed on about the political situation between Egypt and the powers to the northeast. It didn't take Snefru long to realize that the caravan master was worth cultivating as a supply source. He asked about spices and wood, things I knew he wanted, or that Master Potiphar would require for his burial and tomb furnishings.

"I am sorry, I do not have myrrh this trip," Jetur said. "I sold it all to a relative of mine in Canaan. He had recently lost two grandsons." I pricked up my ears. Jetur's family was sort of my family, no matter how distantly related. Who had died?

"It is a sad thing to lose sons," Snefru commented. "My sympathies."

"Thank you," Jetur replied. "He is a cousin of mine, named Jacob. Er and Onan, both sons of his son Judah, have died. The family needed spices for burial. What could I do? I could not refuse."

"No, you could not," Snefru agreed. "But perhaps next time?"

"Certainly," Jetur replied. "Where should I send a message?"

"To Lord Potiphar's Memphis estate," Snefru replied. "Tell me or my assistant, Joseph."

Jetur betrayed no reaction. "Of course."

I sat very still. Er and Onan both dead! They were my nephews, older than Benjamin. Little Shelah was very close to Benjamin's age. What had happened to them? How had they died? What a blow that would have been to Judah, both his older boys gone. *Now he knows what it feels like*, I thought. *He had lost a son just as he deprived Abi of a son.* Then ashamed, I turned away from the prick of anger in my mind, for I knew how much Judah loved his boys and how much he would grieve for them.

As Snefru and I returned to the estate, I wondered why Jetur had mentioned these deaths. I was grateful that he had, but it was a bit strange.

▲ ▲ ▲ ▲

"Was that the same one?" Mishma asked.

"It was," Jetur said with a smile. "And he has done well for himself. We sold him as a herd boy, and he is now assistant scribe to the manager of Lord Potiphar's proprietary estate. He has come far in three years. Isaac's God takes care of His own."

"He said nothing," the trader chieftain's son commented.

"He said plenty before they came," Jetur said with a chuckle. "Joseph bested me on that deal. They needed the olive oil, and I didn't see that until too late."

Mishma made an angry sound.

"Don't be angry. I have gained a valuable customer we can deal with for years to come. It's worth the loss of profit, for we will make it up in the future. And it will be interesting to deal with this one. He's shrewd and learns quickly. Mark my words, he will go far, that one. He has the mark of Isaac's God and will go far."

Jetur's son looked doubtful.

▲ ▲ ▲ ▲

"Well?"

Renseneb sighed. "I do not know. He found olive oil somewhere. Six jars of it."

"And you do not know where?"

"No, my lady."

"Watch this, Renseneb. Something new has entered the market."

"Yes, my lady."

▲ ▲ ▲ ▲

Judah sat in his tent and stared at nothing, his aching heart consuming his thought. Both gone. Both, and so suddenly. That woman! That cursed woman. Shelah quietly entered the tent and sat down beside him.

"Don't cry, Abi," he said. "I'm still here."

Reaching over and taking his only son's hand, Judah said, "I know you are, Shelah. But I miss your brothers very much."

"Like Grandfather Jacob still misses Joseph?" the lad asked hesitantly.

His father paled and swallowed. "Yes, Shelah," he said very quietly. "Just like that."

"Can I be a comfort to you like Benjamin is to Grandfather?" he asked next, looking at Judah with a clear direct gaze.

Judah looked away. Shelah had Joseph's look. That same directness, that same candor, only Shelah had gray eyes, and Joseph's had been blue.

"Yes, Shelah, you will be my comfort now. But go now. See how your mother is doing."

Quickly the boy left. Judah wiped his eyes. He had thought to be rid of Joseph by selling him, but everywhere he looked, everything he heard seemed to remind him of his brother.

Jacob was still bowed with grief, his once stalwart form bent under the load of sorrow that Judah dared not lift. Ironically, his father turned to him for the day-to-day management of the encampment. Judah had indeed gotten his wish. He had taken Joseph's place and was assured that he would get the birthright when his father died. His three older brothers accepted the decision without a protest, Reuben knowing his father would never forget his actions with Bilhah, and Simeon and Levi realizing that their slaughter of the Shechemites had barred them from the blessing.

Some days Judah felt almost insane from the irony of it. He had done the worst sin of all, selling Joseph, and Jacob had turned to him to take Joseph's place. The bitterness of his success almost choked him every day of his life.

As Jacob's grief went on and on, Judah had become more and more ashamed of the deed that had devastated his father. He had been impatient with his father's grief at first, then disgusted, then amazed. Finally, he had tried to ignore it, while taking it into account in his dealings with Jacob.

Now, at last, he understood it. How could he have done that to his father? What had possessed him? He had taken his father's son—had robbed his own father of the joy and happiness, of the companionship and comfort of a son! A son who had been devoted to him, who had loved him, who had deserved to stay with him more than any of the others.

Yes, Joseph deserved to be with his father more than any of them, for he had been the one who looked after Jacob when Rachel died. Joseph had been the one who cared about the family possessions, who tried to see to the affairs of the encampment, who asked after the welfare of the servants and the animals. He'd been annoying and a pest, true, but he'd only been 17 years old, and trying to do the job of a more mature manager.

No wonder Jacob had loved him more than the rest. He'd been the one who had tried to share Jacob's burdens. *And I deprived him of that,* Judah thought. The blackness of his crime almost overwhelmed him at night. Sometimes he tried to dredge up the old feelings of hatred and frustration that had driven him to the deed, but lately he had stopped trying to relive the past. He had to get through the present.

When Jacob had reached across the newly marked grave to comfort him at Onan's sudden death, Judah felt such a stab of conscience that he would have killed himself if he had dared. And now Bathshua was ill. Losing her two oldest boys would be her end, Judah knew. She had loved them despite the trouble and grief they had caused.

Judah hadn't done much to stop them. He had been rather proud of Er, his firstborn. Er was wild, as his father had been in his youth, but then Er got mixed up with his wife's people and started down the road to wickedness. He met his end quickly and decisively.

At least there had not been children, Judah thought with a shudder. Then he smiled bitterly. That was the rest of the problem. Tamar, Er's widow, had rightly come to him for a son, and Judah had instructed Onan to give Tamar a child so that his brother's name would not die out. And now Onan was dead also. It must be that Tamar was cursed. She had taken both his sons—

With a start Judah glanced up. Tamar stood inside the tent doorway, looking at him.

"What am I to do now?" she asked quietly, her large brown eyes wide with emotion.

But what emotion? Judah asked himself. Did she feel grief at Onan's death? How was she reacting to Er's death? He didn't know. She just stood quietly, and one never knew what went through her mind.

"Go back to your father's house and live there," he replied. It was the best thing. Get her out of here. She had taken two of his sons. That was enough.

"I have no son," she said, looking down, her form still lithe and slender beneath the robes she wore.

"I have no more sons to give you," Judah replied. Why couldn't she see that the best thing was just to go?

"You have a third son," Tamar reminded him.

Shelah! Now she wanted Shelah! Judah almost laughed, then stopped. She could demand her rights, and he could not deny them. But he would not let her have Shelah. She already had two of his sons. The third was his. Besides, Shelah wasn't old enough to marry yet, and wouldn't be for some time—Judah's thoughts stopped there. In time, who knew what would happen?

"I think it would be best for you to go back to your father," Judah said, looking full at Tamar for the first time. "When Shelah is old enough, I will send for you, and you shall have a son for Er by him."

"Do you swear this?" she asked.

"That is the agreement we will tell the clan. You shall have Shelah for husband."

"Thank you, my lord. Tomorrow, after you announce this, I shall return to my father's house as you request."

Judah nodded and Tamar left the tent. He stared after her sourly. She was too bold, and too smart. Oh well, it would be several years yet, and anything might happen.

CHAPTER 6

I put on a fresh kilt and walked from my room across the small courtyard to the door of the main house. As I passed the passage to the women's rooms I wrinkled my nose. The house boys had neglected to change the sand in the chamber pots again. Perhaps I should ask Snefru to speak to them. They never seemed to remember when I reminded them.

Quietly I went down the hall and through the dining room. The pillars here were my favorites, painted to resemble lotus flowers in bloom. Ahmose, the porter, had not yet taken his place in the vestibule. Outside the estate wall, I glanced toward the river. An early trader was getting under way, headed up-river for Thebes most likely, or maybe all the way to Aswan on the first cataract.

After a quick and chilly bath in the river, I started back to the house. Since becoming assistant to Snefru, I had a room in the house itself. He saw to it that I was properly dressed to serve in the house and that I had all I needed to keep myself presentable.

As I reentered the gate, I paused in amazement. Master Potiphar was here!

"Welcome, Master," I said, hurrying up. He must have traveled at night to arrive here from Itej-Tawy at this hour. I wondered what had happened. "Is all well?"

"All is well, thank you—Joseph," he said after peering at me in the faint light. "Is anyone else up?"

"Snefru will be up soon," I said. "May I serve you in any way? Did Lady Tanefret come also?"

"Lady Tanefret will be stopping here briefly," he replied in a wooden voice. "She will continue her journey early tomorrow."

"Yes, Master," I said, keeping my puzzlement to myself. What journey was Lady Tanefret making, and why had it started so early? Suddenly remembering the chamber pots, I said, "With your permission, Master, I will go see that Lady Tanefret's room is ready for her."

Potiphar nodded absently, and I hastily left, ducking into the rooms Lady Tanefret always used. Her chamber pot was filled with clean sand, but some others were not. I set them outside the house wall. Khay came sleepily around the corner, and I grabbed his arm.

"Khay, you were responsible to see that the pots were changed," I said sternly. "Why didn't you?"

"We did most of them, Joseph," he said, with another yawn.

"You didn't do the women's quarters."

"No need to," he said with a grin. "Lady Tanefret is not here."

"Well, she is now," I said, letting go of his arm. "I set the pots outside the wall. Get them emptied and refilled immediately. Did you check the master's room?"

"No," Khay said, looking uncertain. "Are you sure Lady Tanefret is—"

Losing my patience, I looked him right in the eye. "I just left Master Potiphar in the courtyard. Go get your work done, *now.*"

Khay swallowed and stepped back. He didn't say another word, just ran to do my bidding, casting an almost frightened glance over his shoulder.

I brushed my hair back impatiently and started for my room. Here I was chastising Khay for negligence, and I hadn't even shaved yet!

Huy fell into step beside me as I headed to the kitchens for breakfast. For once he was subdued and quiet.

"What happened, Huy?" I asked.

"What happened? Didn't you hear? It is a shame to us all."

"I have heard nothing, yet. Does it have something to do with Master Potiphar being here?"

"Something to do with it?" Huy echoed. "It has everything to do with it. Lord Potiphar caught Lady Tanefret alone with Lord Tawy's personal attendant in the middle of the night. Our Master is furious, and Lady Tanefret is in a rage as well. She says Lord Potiphar cannot tell her who to talk to and who not to talk to. Lord Potiphar says that she had better consider her position and reputation and not go running off after every man in sight."

Pausing, I turned to Huy, the pit of my stomach falling. "What will happen?"

He shrugged expressively. "Happen? Probably the same thing as last time, since they were only talking. Lord Potiphar will insist she stay at the small country house two days up the river. Then they will make up their quarrel, and she will go back to Itej-Tawy."

"This has happened before?" I asked, surprised.

Huy nodded. "Before, yes. Four or five times. She makes eyes at another man, and Lord Potiphar gets angry and orders her to stay at the country house."

"But why should she do such things? Lord Potiphar is a good husband to her and supports her well. I could understand if Lord Potiphar refused to supply her bread as Lady Senet's husband did, but Lord Potiphar keeps Lady Tanefret well and takes good care of her estates and everything."

Huy looked at me patiently. "Everything is not enough if there are no children, Joseph. Children are very important. They spent a lot of goods on doctors, but nothing helped, and they gave up." Huy hesitated. "I worry about this, Joseph," he said quietly. "Lady

Tanefret considers herself better than Lord Potiphar since her family comes from Upper Egypt in the south. She used to just flirt, but now it seems she is willing to go beyond that. Her maid said Lady Tanefret has been saying she could get a child if she married someone else."

I frowned. This might really upset things.

After eating, I reported to Snefru in his room. He looked at me absently. "You heard?" he asked.

"About Lady Tanefret, yes. Was there something else as well?"

"That is enough by itself. It is a bad time for Lord Potiphar to be away from Itej-Tawy, too."

"Oh?"

"The Pharaoh has not felt well the past couple months, and the co-regent needs Lord Potiphar available."

I remained quiet, realizing that I knew nothing at all about the politics of the country in which I lived. Not even sure where Itej-Tawy, the capital, was, I resolved to remedy my ignorance as soon as possible. With Potiphar holding an important position in the palace, I needed to be aware of what that meant.

Midmorning, Khay hurried into the room. "Snefru," he panted, "Lord Amony is on his way."

"Coming *here?*" the overseer exclaimed.

The boy nodded.

Snefru glanced at me. "Quickly, change into your best linen. We must be ready to receive Lord Amony when he arrives."

"Who is Lord Amony?" I asked Khay as I hurried to my room.

"He is close to the co-regent, as well as a Friend to Pharaoh, and Chosen of the Guard, thus allowed private audiences with Pharaoh. Not even Lord Potiphar is Chosen of the Guard."

When I presented myself to Snefru a little later, he looked me over carefully. "You will look all right," he decided. "But we must get you a wig." I noticed, then, that Snefru wore his. It fitted neatly over his head, completely covering his slightly gray hair.

Not certain that I wanted a wig, I couldn't imagine anything covering my red head.

Snefru looked at me for a little and then frowned.

"What is wrong, Master?" I asked anxiously.

"I had forgotten," he muttered. "You will have to keep your eyes down while Lord Amony is here. "

"May I ask why?" I said hesitantly.

"Your blue eyes," he said with a sigh. "Lord Amony is very su-perstitious. Your eyes will make him uncomfortable."

"Yes, Master." But I still didn't understand.

Snefru made certain I knew just how to act and bow when Lord Amony arrived, then waited in silence, nervously fiddling with his linen. When we heard the sound of a sedan chair in the outer court-yard, Snefru led the way to the dining room and stood waiting just out of sight.

I caught a glimpse of Lord Potiphar sitting in his usual spot, but I noted that he wore the gold collar from Pharaoh and his very best linen.

Ahmose announced Lord Amony, and my master stood to greet him, bowing slightly. Lord Amony returned the bow, and the two exchanged the obligatory courtesies before sitting down. The visitor wore a long outer skirt of the finest linen I'd ever seen, covering a very short inner kilt. He carried a fan and had bracelets with amulets dangling on both wrists. As the two men got to the real subject of the visit, I looked a silent question at Snefru.

"Lord Amony does our lord an honor," Snefru said very softly. "One of the very few who can wear the shendot, the royal short skirt, he carries his fan, symbol of his rank as Nearest Friend to Pharaoh. The amulets are charms against evils and sicknesses. Lord Amony is never without them."

Turning my attention to the low conversation in the room, I learned that the Pharaoh's agents had apparently picked up some ru-mors of a plot against either the king's life, or the co-regent's, I couldn't determine which.

I missed entirely the sign Lord Potiphar gave to Snefru, but I fol-lowed him into the room, keeping my eyes down as I had been in-structed. I bowed deeply when Lord Amony noticed us and sat behind Snefru, ready with extra writing supplies as he took notes on the decisions the two officials made.

I listened intently, but was soon bewildered by the plethora of names and titles that constantly peppered the conversation. My be-wilderment eased somewhat when I figured out that most everyone named had more than one title, but I had great difficulty making sense of it all. I would need to ask Snefru later.

Time passed swiftly, and Snefru sent me to the kitchens to bring food for the noon meal. Because of the content of the conversation,

Lord Potiphar did not want the regular house staff to be around, and I served by myself. Neither man ate heavily, so I managed nicely.

Also I chased Khay away from the doors more than once. He was insatiably curious to see Lord Amony, and finally I told him to wait in the front court where he could watch the man depart.

The discussion continued through the heat of the day, and Lord Amony finally took his leave close to dusk. As soon as he had gone, Lord Potiphar fell into bed, exhausted from his night journey and the extended conference.

Going to the kitchens, I asked Minemhet for something to eat. He grumbled at me a little, but pointed me to the fresh baking and told me where to find some raisins, dates, and the little sweet onions I liked so well.

After taking my supper, I walked out of the compound and up the path to the upper fields. The grain was growing well. It would soon be Harvest again.

"Is he gone?" a timid voice hissed at me from some bushes.

I stopped. "Huy? Is who gone?"

"The lord. Is he gone?"

"Yes," I replied, puzzled. "He has been gone for some time. What are you doing up here?"

"I am here because I always leave when he visits. He doesn't like me."

"Why do you say that?"

"I say that because it is true. He thinks I am bad, because of my eye."

"That makes two of us," I said with a sigh. "Snefru warned me to keep my eyes down. What is wrong with our eyes?"

"He is afraid an evil spirit is in mine, and he would be afraid of yours because they are blue. That makes them the eyes of Ra."

"Hazor said something about them being the eyes of Horus. Which is it?"

The man shrugged. "Which is it? Either. Horus, Ra, it is all the same."

"Just what is the eye of Ra or Horus?" I asked curiously.

"It is the sun, at least the right eye of Ra is the sun. The left eye of Ra is the moon. Horus, Ra, it is all the same."

"But Egyptians like and worship the sun," I protested. "Why would my eyes be a problem?"

He thought for a minute. "The problem is that the eye of Horus sheds light," he said slowly. "And when you have the eye of Horus, you can see things. Sometimes when you look at me, it is as though your eye sheds light inside. And I know you can see what I think."

I had to sit down for that one. "Oh," I said slowly. "And being a slave makes it worse, because slaves are not supposed to know what the master is thinking?"

Huy nodded eagerly. "Exactly."

"How does the rest of the staff feel about it?"

He shrugged. "They know that you have carried out your duties well and pleased your masters. You don't often use the Eye on them, and they know you like them and don't mean any harm. In fact, they are rather proud of it. They brag in the market sometimes that you provide protection for our house. Since you came, there have been fewer troubles, less sickness, and better crops than normal."

"I am a slave, Huy. Not a god. I don't work miracles."

He shrugged again. "Someone has," he said simply.

I opened my mouth to reply, but didn't say anything. After all, I had been praying that El Shaddai would bless my master's house. Was it possible that my God actually cared about me and my prayers enough to make this noticeable a difference? I didn't quite know what to think.

"Is this why Aneksi hangs around?" I asked suddenly.

Huy looked down and swallowed. "Yes, she thinks that if you marry her, she will be able to have children without fear they will die. She thinks your Eye will see the evil coming and drive it away. Not like me. She assumes any children that I gave her would have an evil eye like mine."

As I looked at him he trembled a little, his face white.

"How long have you loved Aneksi?" I asked gently.

"There! See!" Huy said explosively, turning to me. "You did it again. You looked and you saw what was in my heart." Turning, he raced up the path toward the desert.

Now what was I going to do?

▲ ▲ ▲ ▲

"You are certain you know what to do?" I asked Khay for the third time in as many minutes.

"Yes, Joseph," he said, a bored expression on his face. "I know what to do."

"Sorry, Khay," I said with a rueful smile. "I am nervous. This is the first time Snefru has sent me to the market alone, and I don't want to make any big mistakes."

"You won't with me around," the boy said brazenly. "I will tell you everything you need to know."

"I hope so," I muttered under my breath. We were extremely early, for I wanted to have Khay pick up the gossip before Renseneb arrived. Snefru and I between us had bested Renseneb three times in the past year, so we were one up in the quiet good-natured war we fought. I had come to share the overseer's curiosity about whom Renseneb acted for. I had deduced someone with good connections in the palace, but that was all.

Now I decided to turn Khay's energy and curiosity to good use and started him collecting information for me. He stumbled on the fact that Renseneb had outsmarted more than one household manager. Always the commodity was something needed immediately, usually for a big party just after an official and his wife returned from court. That meant that whoever Renseneb served knew just when someone left court and where the household would shop for supplies.

From my position at the entrance to an alley, I could see most of the marketplace and down the street toward the docks at the river. Suddenly I saw Khay trotting along the waterfront. How had he gotten down there? What was he doing? Then, as the marketplace filled, the sellers setting up their stalls for the day and a few early customers prowling around impatiently, I lost track of him.

Suddenly he appeared at my side, breathing hard. "There is a ship just in from Byblos and Tyre," he said urgently. "They carry the new dye, the one they call purple."

Before he even finished with the news I had started on the run. Lady Tanefret would be very pleased to get some of that dye. As Huy had predicted, the quarrel soon blew over, and Lady Tanefret was again in Potiphar's good graces and had returned from Itej-Tawy for a time to tend to her business. She had heard of the purple and wanted to try some on the cloaks that Kemi made. Remembering that fascinating color, I knew she would like it.

But we would have to pay well for the dye. The captain knew

the value of his commodity, but I figured Lady Tanefret would make more than enough profit selling dyed cloaks of the new rich color.

Khay and I met the captain as he came up the dock from his ship.

"Captain," I said, "I hear you have purple dye to sell."

The big man stopped and looked at me suspiciously. "What makes you say that?"

I shrugged. "If I am wrong, I apologize."

"I didn't say you were wrong. Are you a buyer?"

"I am. I am Joseph, of the house of Potiphar. My mistress, Lady Tanefret, deals in dyes. I would buy the purple from you."

"I am Neshi," the man said, looking me over. "Have a seat, and we will deal for a price."

"Name your price," I said quietly. "I think you will be fair with me."

The seafaring merchant looked at me in amazement as I stared back steadily at him. I had noticed how neat and well-kept his ship was compared to some of the others on the docks, and I'd sensed the general attitude of the men on board. His ship advertised the same kind of care and prosperity that Jetur's caravan evidenced. Here was a good man and a reliable one.

"What would you say to 10 golden deben a jar?" he asked.

"I would say that was a bit high."

Neshi grinned. "You would be right. One hundred copper deben each will give me a good profit, and you a good buy."

"How many jars of dye do you carry?"

"Four."

"What will you take payment in? I have barley, some wine, or gold amulets."

The captain considered. "Amulets, I think."

Reaching for the pouch of amulets I carried, I showed them to Neshi. We agreed on 10 of them as a fair exchange. I arranged for the dye to be picked up the next day and left after finding out the type of goods that Neshi usually carried.

We left the wharf just in time. As I looked back, I saw Renseneb hurrying toward the ship we'd just left and smiled to myself.

Lady Tanefret was delighted.

"The purple? Really?" she asked, a pleased smile on her face.

"Yes, Lady. The captain carried four jars, and you have it all."

"Wonderful! Now, how can I sell it?"

"Perhaps, Lady, you could use one jar to display it first," I suggested diffidently. "The fabric Kemi is weaving will take the dye well, and—"

"How do you know that dye will take to wool?" Lady Tanefret interrupted.

"I have seen it in my homeland," I replied, steadying my voice and rigidly suppressing my memories. "It produces a kind of glow in the fabric. A cloak in the evening from the new weave Kemi is using will—"

"Yes, of course," Lady Tanefret laughed. "It is perfect. Especially if the cloak has a border of gold. It is a pity Kemi has no help to weave."

"If I may suggest something else, Mistress?" I dared to say.

"Certainly."

"Kemi's weave is a special one and might only be suitable for the most honored ladies of your acquaintance. The others could, if they wish, bring cloaks of their own weave to be dyed if you still have dye available from your sample."

Lady Tanefret laughed again. "After which I can sell the cloaks Kemi makes for double what I would before. You have a devious mind. I like it. What is your name?"

"I am Joseph, my lady. I assist Snefru."

"Not for long, I should say," she said, studying me. "You have served me well."

"Many thanks, my lady," I said, taking my leave.

▲ ▲ ▲ ▲

"I was too late again, Lady," Renseneb confessed.

"How much was lost?" she asked, disappointment in her voice.

"All."

"All! Who bought it?"

"I could not find out."

"Our mysterious rival?"

The merchant nodded.

"Well, the new dye will show up somewhere. We will have to watch for it."

▲ ▲ ▲ ▲

"You sent for me, Master Snefru?" I asked, entering the room he used for his business, then halted and hurriedly bowed. "I am sorry, Master Potiphar, I didn't see you here," I added.

"Don't concern yourself about it, Joseph," Potiphar replied. "Snefru has told me about your work. And I heard from Lady Tanefret about the purple dye you purchased for her. As you probably guessed, everyone wants a purple cloak for the evenings. They are a great success."

"I am glad I could help, Master."

"Do you find your work with Snefru agreeable to you?" Lord Potiphar asked next.

"Why yes, master, I do," I replied, startled. And I did. The constant parade of people and problems challenged me, and I enjoyed finding my way through them to a solution that could satisfy everyone—or almost everyone. Hekamaat was rarely pleased with anything. "The house staff are willing and wish to serve you well," I went on. "That solves over half the problems by itself."

The chief overseer snorted. "The staff was not half so willing or agreeable until you started managing them. Khay may actually become a responsible agent, thanks to you, and Huy has not tried to hit anyone since you came either. Minemhet was actually whistling the other day, and Meru and Hekamaat have not quarreled for months."

I blushed furiously, trying not to fidget. "Please, master," I stuttered. "I have not done so much."

"Well, it is either you or your god," Snefru shrugged.

I looked up in surprise, my mouth open. Seeing Master Potiphar's amused eyes, I looked down again hastily. "Oh," I said weakly.

"You do go to the fields and pray to him every morning, do you not?" Snefru continued relentlessly.

"Yes, master," I said softly.

"And you ask him to honor and protect this house, do you not?"

I was terribly red now. "Yes, master. I mean no disrespect to your god, Master," I added to Potiphar.

Potiphar chuckled. "Your god appears to listen to you quite well. He has certainly added much to my house because you serve me. Let us see what he does when you are in charge of this estate."

I stared in amazement, glancing from Lord Potiphar to Snefru. "But what about Snefru?"

"He will be overseeing all my possessions, both personal and proprietary, as well as Lady Tanefret's properties," Potiphar said. "You will still report to him if necessary, but he will be gone quite a bit. He tells me you are well able to take over, and if we can keep all the women away from you, he says you will continue to do the excellent job you have been doing for some time now. You will begin today."

I couldn't help staring again. "Women, Master?" I asked in a weak voice.

Potiphar glanced at Snefru. "You were right. He hasn't the least idea," he said cryptically. "Tell him sometime." Then he left the room.

"Tell me what, Master Snefru?" I asked, pleading for understanding.

"Later, Joseph," he said with a maddening smile. "You will move into my room in the house. The day after tomorrow I will leave with Lord Potipher and will spend a great deal of time in Abydos, overseeing the building of his tomb. Work has not gone well, and we cannot determine why.

"Now, I have told my father, Chensu, to direct questions to you, and only if you are unable to answer them should they come to me."

"Yes, Master," I gulped. Chensu had charge of the small country house two days up the river. Lord Potiphar owned it personally, and it was his favorite retreat. The Memphis estate and the residence in Itej-Tawy went to whoever held the title of Captain of the Guard to Pharaoh.

When Snefru left the room, carrying most of his things, I sat down behind the low table shakily. My throat felt dry. I was chief steward of the entire estate with no one above me except Snefru and Lord Potiphar, and they wouldn't be here.

"Oh, El Shaddai, be with me," I breathed. "Help me to serve well. Honor my efforts, and cover my mistakes. Protect all that is under Potiphar's care."

Huy stuck his head into the room. "Is it true?" he asked breathlessly. "What I heard, is it true?"

A pleased smile spread across his face. When he got excited, his eye wandered even more.

"I guess it is," I admitted.

Huy vanished. "It is true," he shouted, running from the room. "It is true. Joseph is chief steward of the estate. Joseph is chief!"

From outside I heard the cheers and shouts of excitement that greeted the news.

"Well, Menneb," I said to myself, "you were right. Your eyes saw more clearly than mine, clouded as they were." I looked at my shaking hands and laughed at myself. Six years ago, I had ignorantly believed I was the best manager of my father's possessions that he had. Now, I was nervous and uncertain facing duties with which I was familiar just because I had received a title. I laughed at the callow boy with such presumptuous confidence in his abilities, knowing now that I had been more of a hindrance than a help most of the time. How much Abi had had to put up with! And he never once let on. He just did his best to teach me what I needed to know.

Finally I pulled myself together to make my rounds on the estate. When I walked out of the house, Khay waited for me in his usual spot with a huge grin on his face. He bowed deeply and said, "I wait to attend you, Master Joseph."

When I blushed, everyone around burst into laughter. Laughter led to cheers, and it took some time to get everyone calmed down again.

"Thank you," I said simply. "I want to do a good job for Master Potiphar, and I will need everyone's help. Ra is well on his journey across the sky," I said, indicating the sun. "With all the excitement, we are behind schedule. It is time to work now."

With good-natured jostling, the crowd dispersed. Trailed by Khay and Mahesa, a young scribe just out of school, I headed for the pottery where I always checked on Meru first.

"Joseph," he said when I first entered, "I know Snefru meant to get some more help in the pottery, but he has not done it yet. Could you please remind him that I cannot keep up with all the needs here for the estate? I have two wheels busy now, and another that I could use if I had someone to run it. With Lady Tanefret demanding fancy pottery, I have not time to keep up with the useful items that we all need. I—"

"Are you the only one who doesn't know?" Khay burst out. "Joseph is chief steward now. Snefru is gone."

The potter looked at me quizzically, rubbing the wet clay that stuck to his fingers. "Are you now? Well, would *you* see that I get some help?"

"Let me think on it today," I told him. "When I come tomorrow I can discuss it further. Do you need someone to do the household pots or the decorative ones?"

"I can do some fancy work," Meru said slowly.

"But you prefer the more useful items, do you not?" I finished for him.

He smiled in relief. "Yes, Joseph, I do. But where you will find a potter to do fancy work that is not already busy, I do not know."

"I will get back to you tomorrow," I said, realizing that Snefru had avoided the problem because Meru had put his finger on the problem. Any potter capable of decorative objects would already have a position somewhere.

A house boy ran up to Khay, handing him a message. Khay passed it to me. "Another complaint from Imenhet," he said wryly. "Likely the crocodiles are eating the calves again."

"They should not be, since Snefru rented pasture other than the island—" I stopped in mid-sentence. Imenhet! "Khay," I said, "remind me to discuss Imenhet with you later."

"Yes, Joseph," he said, looking at me sideways. The lad could read me well, and he knew that I had just thought of something.

We checked on Kemi and her looms, and Minemhet in the kitchens. From there I went to the granary and then outside the compound walls to check on Nebnufer and his ducks and geese. Last stop was the pastures and Hekamaat. He grunted when he heard that I was steward and looked down at me from under his bushy eyebrows.

"Maybe I can count on quick answers now," he said, returning to his flock.

Khay looked after him in amazement. "Was that a compliment?"

"I believe so," I said with a smile. We checked the fields next, and I decided to begin harvesting the next week. "The granaries are low," I said to Mahesa. "Make a note to fill them this year." The young scribe nodded solemnly and carefully made his notes. I bit my lips to hide my smile and headed back to the house.

Aneksi served my noon meal in the office. She had gotten over her crush on me and had married Meru's son Hefner. But every once in a while I caught a knowing glance from her, and it still made me uncomfortable.

"Now that you are steward, we must get you married," she said to me, setting down the basket of food. I stood up to help her.

"What did you say?"

"Married. You need a wife."

"Aneksi, I cannot support a wife."

"You will receive more from Potiphar than Hefner does," she reminded me, "and we have enough for two."

I didn't know what to say. I hadn't thought of what I would do with my increased rations.

The girl watched me, an amused smile on her face, as the idea she had planted struck home.

"I could not possibly," I sputtered. "I am a slave, Aneksi. Completely dependent on Master Potiphar's good will"

"And who among us is not?" she asked archly.

"But most of you are free," I protested. "As a slave, I could be sold at any time to the desert or the mines or just anywhere. No one would want to live with that."

"Oh, I don't know about that," Aneksi replied, giving me a long slow look that took me in from top to bottom. "You might be surprised at who would marry you. I would have." With that, she departed.

As I sank down onto the cushion on the floor I tried to swallow my astonishment. Just the thought of the look she had given me made me blush to the roots of my red hair. She had to be teasing me. I was a slave and not very good looking, as I well remembered. What she suggested was impossible. Determinedly, I put it out of my mind.

CHAPTER 7

I had barely finished eating when Khay appeared. "What about Imenhet?" he asked without preamble.

"Oh, yes. Khay, I want you to go to the Delta. If I remember correctly, Imenhet has a family. I want to know where they live and how they are. See if you can find out where he lived and worked before he sold himself to Master Potiphar. He mentioned Tanis one time."

"Imenhet is a servant, not a commoner?" Khay asked. "I never knew he had sold himself."

"I am not absolutely certain. Find out quietly if possible. I do not want to raise a fuss. Let me check something."

I turned to Snefru's records, neatly sorted and stacked in the room to one side. Quickly I found the record of how much bread and beer Imenhet earned each year. He received about the same amount I did when I first came to this estate. If he had a family to support, I assumed he had some other source of income. At least, I hoped he did.

Later, I took the time to go back through the records and check Imenhet's allotment. It had remained the same since the beginning. When I saw the original allotment made, I recognized Sekhmet's hand with the pen. Imenhet's drunken words rang in my ears. "He hates me. He always has." Not liking the way this situation shaped up, I was eager to hear what Khay would find out.

I missed him the next day when the supply caravan from Memphis arrived with Potiphar's allotment of supplies. Mahesa tried his best, but he just wasn't as quick as Khay, nor as active.

Finally I dragooned Huy into running errands for me and taking messages to various people on the estate. When he came rushing back, cringing behind me with Hekamaat shouting in his wake, I barely held onto my patience.

"What is that excuse for a man doing, telling me to come here," the herder demanded in his usual roar.

"Please, Hekamaat, you do not need to shout. I can hear quite well," I said calmly, deliberately looking him right in the eye. Everyone around me grew instantly silent, holding their collective breath.

The burly man stared back at me, startled. "Was I shouting?" he asked quizzically.

"Yes, Master Hekamaat, you were," I replied smoothly. "And you have frightened Master Huy half out of his wits. I sent him especially to you for I knew you wanted these new ropes immediately."

"Did I frighten the man?" Hekamaat said, even more puzzled. I glanced at him. He was truly perplexed.

"When you roar at him like a bull, he thinks you are angry at him," I said quietly. "He has been abused because of his eye, and he fears blows. It would help greatly if you would lower your voice."

"Oh. I had not realized. I have to shout to be heard in the fields."

"Yes, Master Hekamaat. But these are not the fields, and hearing your powerful voice so close can be hard to handle. If you speak to people as you do to your birthing kine, things might go better."

"I shall try, Steward," the herder said awkwardly.

The people listening looked relieved and began to return to their jobs.

Hekamaat peered at me. "Now, where are those ropes you said had come?"

"Right over there," I replied pointing. "Do you need someone to help carry them?"

"Huy might be useful. Come along, man, don't dawdle."

Looking very hesitant, Huy picked up two of the ropes and followed Hekamaat.

That evening as I sat in the office and recorded some final notes, the light from the oil lamp attracted Huy's attention as he passed by, and he came in. When I finished, I looked up and asked, "How did it go with Hekamaat this afternoon?"

"This afternoon it went well," he said, looking proud. "He said that I was a good help to him."

"What did you do?"

"Do?" Huy echoed. "He has several children. They are constantly running about the place, and with three kine about to calve, Hekamaat wished the children to keep away. He asked me to do something if I could. I took them to one corner of the field and told them stories and showed them some tricks. They liked it and stayed away from the kine all afternoon. Hekamaat said it was a big help."

"What sort of tricks?" I asked, curious.

The man shrugged. "Tricks I learned from a wanderer," he said, looking down.

"Would you show me?"

Huy had a small stone in his hand. He moved his hand, and the stone disappeared. I couldn't see where it went.

"It is gone!" I exclaimed, startled.

"No," he said, opening his hand, and there it was!

"Do it again."

Again that stone just vanished before my eyes.

"I can see why you succeeded in distracting the children. You have distracted me very well also," I confessed.

The tall man smiled shyly. "Did I?" he asked. Then he left, looking pleased with himself.

I went to bed very thoughtful that night. Although I had known Huy since the first day I arrived here, it was the first time I had ever seen him proud of something. It certainly changed him.

The next day was my normal market day since the supplies had arrived. But without Khay, things went slower than normal, and I was unable to get to Memphis to the market. So I was a day late and got a tardy start on top of that.

The market was very busy by the time I got there, and I discovered that Renseneb had been at it again. We had run out of flax for linen, and Kemi had specifically ordered some of the young flax for fine linen.

By the time I reached the market, I could not find any. Close to noon I realized that Renseneb had it all. I had never dealt with him personally before, and I doubted he knew who I was. It helped that I always wore my wig to the market. It hid my red hair.

"Master Renseneb," I greeted him. "I hear you have flax to sell."

"Yes. How much did you want and what grade?"

I described Kemi's needs, and Renseneb nodded. "Yes, I have some of what you want. I don't have enough to fill the entire order, but enough to supply your weaveress for a time. Whose house do you buy for?"

"Lord Potiphar's," I replied.

At Renseneb's look of surprise, I explained. "Snefru is in Abydos with Lord Potiphar. I am standing in his stead."

"This must have been sudden."

I shrugged.

We settled into bargaining, and I paid more than market price, but less than I feared I would have to. Pressed for time, I didn't try to beat Renseneb down as much as I might have otherwise. When we settled, I got the feeling he didn't think I was much of an opponent, which suited me just fine. Now that he had met me in person, I would have to be very careful in the future when I crossed his path.

I had some extras from my allotment with me, and I purchased a pomegranate. Sitting in the shade of an awning, I ate and listened to the gossip of the market. Two women were talking quite near me.

"Did you hear?" the first one asked. "Lord Nehere is dead, and his lady married already."

"Did you expect anything else?" the second woman commented. "Lady Kawit could hardly wait for him to die. She and her new lord are on a trip to Thebes, I heard."

"I heard he was quite a handsome man. What was his name?" the first inquired.

"Senamun," the second replied. "He was Lord Nehere's steward."

"Steward?" the first said, disappointment in her voice. "I thought he was a slave."

I stopped chewing, listening intently.

"Oh, he was," the second woman assured her friend. "But he was such a good steward that Lord Nehere freed him. That was only a year ago. And now he is married to his mistress and will be received in court, last I heard. You know Nehere was—"

My mind drifted away from the conversation and settled on thoughts of its own. A slave steward, just like me, freed for doing an excellent job. A tendril of hope sprang up in my heart. Maybe, just maybe, Master Potiphar would see fit to do the same for me someday. It was quite a thought.

▲ ▲ ▲ ▲

"What happened, Renseneb?"

"They had to buy at our price," he replied.

"Good," she smiled. "It has been a while since we bested Snefru."

"It was not Snefru," her agent told her, "But a young assistant. A barbarian slave if I mistake not. He is taking Snefru's place while the overseer is away. The man puzzles me."

"Why?"

"He seemed unskilled in the market, but I do not think he was."

She considered for a while. "Do you think he might be the change we have noticed?"

"It is possible," Renseneb replied doubtfully.

"In any case, I will enjoy besting him."

"Yes, Lady." Renseneb wondered as he had many times before what his lady had against foreigners and what she would think if she knew his own background.

▲ ▲ ▲ ▲

A week later Khay returned, so angry he could hardly talk. He brought with him a woman that looked to be mostly bones and carrying a bundle of rags that turned out to be a child.

As soon as Aneksi took the woman and child off his hands and called her father to send out some food, I motioned Khay to come with me to my office.

"Who is it?" I asked once we were inside.

"What is left of Imenhet's family," he said between clenched teeth.

I closed my eyes and sat down, feeling sick. "How did this happen?" I asked, although I had a feeling I already knew the answer to that.

"His wife cannot give me a coherent answer. She has some story about refusing some man and the man playing crocodile and eating calves for revenge or something. I cannot make head or tail of it."

"Did she mention a name?" I asked grimly.

"Sekhmet, I think."

"What about Imenhet?"

Khay sighed. "I got a curious story there also. It seems that Imenhet, if it is the same man, was a potter at one time and a very good one. Somehow he lost his shop and job. He sold himself to Lord Potiphar in order to win bread to support his family. But it seems that Lord Potiphar kept him on very short rations and sent him out to herd kine, of all things!

"It makes no sense," Khay burst out. "Lord Potiphar took in my family when he had no cause to and treated us well. Why would he do differently to Imenhet? And why would he waste a potter herding kine?"

"I don't think he ever knew about Imenhet," I said quietly. "I imagine Sekhmet saw to that."

"Who is Sekhmet?" Khay asked. "Was he a scribe or something?"

I nodded. "Imenhet's scribe in the Delta. He got caught stealing calves from Lord Potiphar."

"So Sekhmet put Imenhet on short rations and saw that he stayed there?"

"Apparently. Did Imenhet come also?"

"I am afraid I didn't stay to talk with him," Khay said sheepishly. "I got so angry over the condition of his family that I left a message with a neighbor and brought them to you."

I jumped to my feet. "Imenhet will be frantic. We must send a messenger immediately."

"To where? The drive back to the estate has already started. Taxes are due soon."

"We have to try," I said firmly. "We cannot just run off with a man's family and not tell him. Get someone reliable on the trails immediately, and tell Aneksi I want to see her."

"Yes, Joseph," Khay said, disappearing out the door.

Aneksi arrived shortly.

"How are they?" I asked.

"Filthy and starving," she replied. "They have not had a decent meal in so long the child doesn't know what food looks like. Imenhet must be the worst husband on earth," she added fiercely. "When I find him, I will give him a piece of my mind, you can be sure."

"It was not his fault. His wages have been hardly enough for a dog, let alone a family. That can be remedied soon enough. In the meantime, do whatever you need to see that they are properly cared for and housed. And if Imenhet turns up, send him to me immediately."

Aneksi nodded. "I told his wife you would see that things were made right, but she seems frightened out of her wits."

Two days later, Hekamaat sent word that the herd had arrived from the Delta. I hurried out to the pastures, wondering how I would explain Khay's highhandedness to Imenhet. I didn't have to, since the herd had arrived without him.

"Who brought them in?" I asked Hekamaat.

"The Syrian fellow, Hazor," the chief herder said. "If I do say it, the kine are in better condition this time than any other. Hazor must know his business."

"Could you work with him?" I asked.

"I would rather work with him than Imenhet, if you must know. Imenhet knows nothing of kine and cares less."

"Why do you care about them?" I asked. "Most of your fellows must look down on you for it."

"They do," he admitted. "But I don't let it bother me. I am only half Egyptian anyway. My mother was a Syrian, like Hazor."

That solved one puzzle that had nagged my mind. Most Egyptians would not go near a herder if they could help it. It probably also accounted for Hekamaat's belligerent attitude sometimes.

I went out to the herd, and Kinen and Siamon greeted me

with real warmth. They congratulated me on my new job and asked after my health. Hazor saw me and came over to hear the news as well.

"You have done well for yourself," he said in Canaanite when the others had left. "I wouldn't have known you except for your blue eyes."

"El Shaddai has honored me," I said to him. "Where is Imenhet?"

Hazor shrugged. "A messenger came to the grazing land just after dawn one day, and we have not seen Imenhet since. Kinen knew when we were supposed to leave the graze, and when Imenhet did not return, he decided to start the drive. He and I have worked together on this."

"Good. I want you to continue to work with him. I am putting you in charge of the herd that we move each year. Hekamaat has a great deal of respect for your judgment, and so do I. Among the three of you, I expect the herd will improve greatly."

Hazor stared at me for some time. "Can you do that?" he asked finally.

"As chief steward, I can do pretty much what I want," I said with a smile. "And I want you in charge of the herd. You understand kine a lot more than Imenhet does, and you care a lot more than Kinen, who is content to follow orders and just draw his rations.

"I will make the increase in your rations effective from the beginning of this drive. And send your scribe to me later in the day. I will need to go over the records with him."

Hazor blinked a couple of times, then slowly straightened. "I will. I'll do just that." As he walked away I could sense his back straightening more with every step.

The sound of Khay's running footsteps and shouts from the courtyard woke me from a sound sleep in the middle of the night. Jumping from my bed, I hastily threw a kilt around my hips and ran from the room toward the front court.

"Where is he?" a drunken voice shouted. "I'll kill him. I'll kill him, I tell you. He took my family. Lord or no lord, I'll stab him to the heart. He makes me graze his miserable kine on that miserable Delta, and then he takes my family.

"Let me go, you oaf," the voice continued. "Where is Potiphar? I'll murder him in his bed for this!"

Torches flared in the court, and I saw Imenhet standing in the light, swaying, with a knife in his hand. Ahmose hurried from the house, his kilt awry and his wig on backwards.

"What has happened?" he shouted. "Is Lord Potiphar all right?"

"Lord Potiphar is fine, Ahmose," I said firmly. "Go back to bed."

I motioned to Khay to escort the porter back to the house. Taking a torch from one of the men, I approached Imenhet.

"Master Imenhet, you need to be in bed," I said to him quietly.

"Bed?" he shouted. "I came to see Lord Potiphar. He took my family, what few I had left!"

"Lord Potiphar did not take your family. Khay did. And your wife and child are peacefully sleeping in the house next to Aneksi and Hefner. We tried to send a message to you, but the messenger could not find you to deliver it. Now, you need to be in bed."

Imenhet peered at me. "Who are you?"

"I am Joseph. You remember, don't you?"

Imenhet swayed a little more, frowning. "Well, now, do I remember or not? Joseph."

He stepped toward me, almost falling.

"Set the knife down, Master Imenhet. I don't want you to hurt yourself with it."

"What knife?" Imenhet asked, looking around in a daze.

"In your hand. Put it down, and we can get you into bed with your wife, where you belong."

"My wife? Is she here?" Imenhet appeared puzzled.

"In the house next to Aneksi and Hefner," I repeated, stepping closer. "Here, let me hold the knife for you."

"Good idea," Imenhet said, trying to figure out which hand to hold out to me. "Good idea. I don't want to drop it."

"No, I will take care of it for you." Taking the weapon, I quickly passed it to one of the others.

Imenhet draped himself over my shoulder as he had the first time I had helped him, and said, "Where am I?"

"At Lord Potiphar's Memphis estate. The herd arrived in fine shape. We were worried about you, though. You had disappeared."

"Trying to find my wife. She ran away. Probably because of that thrice-cursed son of a crocodile, Sekhmet."

"Come to bed, now, Master Imenhet."

"You are Joseph, that stupid, expensive, red-haired slave," Imenhet said triumphantly. "I remember."

"Yes, and very well, too. Come now."

It took some doing, but I got Imenhet into the house with his wife before he collapsed on the floor. I arranged him as comfortably as I could and left him to his sleep.

Imenhet was predictably ill the next day, and I decided to interview him after he felt better. The following morning, I sent Khay after the man and prepared for the delicate situation of being over my former superior.

When Imenhet walked in, he glanced worriedly around. "Where is the steward?" he asked me.

I stood. "I am Master Potiphar's chief steward."

"You are?" He stared in disbelief.

"Yes, Imenhet, I am," I repeated.

The man swallowed a couple of times and looked down. "You—you sent for me?"

"I wanted to discuss your situation," I told him. "Khay found your wife and child in Tanis and brought them back here. Unfortunately, he neglected to tell you what he had done. I apologize for his carelessness. I am sure it must have been quite a shock to you to hear they were gone. And I doubt anything less would have induced you to leave the herd as you did."

Imenhet looked at me as though he couldn't understand a word I said. "The herd?" he said. Suddenly he looked sick. "The herd! I will go back immediately."

I lifted a hand and silenced him. "The herd is fine and arrived here safely before you did. Hazor and Kinen brought them along without any problems. I have placed Hazor in charge of them from now on and—"

"Master, you cannot!" Imenhet cried, dropping to his knees in front of me. "You cannot! How else will I earn bread? My family must eat. You cannot turn us out. Please master, let me stay with the herd."

I closed my mouth and bent to help Imenhet to his feet, angry at myself for my clumsy handling of the situation.

"Imenhet, I am not turning you out."

He refused to get to his feet. "What will I do? Lord Potiphar will take away my place. What will I do?"

"We need another potter. I wanted you to work with Meru. Will you?"

"I can do whatever you tell me," Imenhet said, still not taking in my words.

"I need another potter," I repeated.

"A potter?" The man finally looked at me.

"Yes, a potter. Meru cannot keep up with the demand. And he needs someone to do the decorative objects. Will you help him?"

"Pottery? You are taking away the herd and want me to do pottery?"

"Yes, Imenhet, that is exactly what I want. Will you do it?"

The man searched my face for long moments, not believing I was serious.

"Yes," he finally answered. "Yes, Master Joseph, I will. I will."

"Good. Then it is settled. Khay, take Imenhet to Meru and get him started."

The lad entered the office and managed to get Imenhet off his knees. "Come, Imenhet. Meru is beside himself waiting to see if you are really Imenhet of Tanis, and if you will really make pots in his shop."

As Khay led the dazed Imenhet away, I turned back to my records. With taxation time coming I would have to report to Master Potiphar, and I wanted to be ready.

CHAPTER 8

Potiphar sat back in the low chair and stretched. I knelt on the floor across from him, my records and supplies scattered on the table. Snefru sat beside me, checking up on one last record.

"It is amazing, but correct," he told Potiphar. "In this year, the Memphis estate has more than doubled its profits. The taxes are paid, and even the commoners have more than enough to carry them through the year. The storehouses are full as well. The draw for corvee was light this year, which helped."

"That will not last for long," Potiphar sighed. "With Pharaoh enlarging the temple for Ra at On, the corvee will be heavy for the next few years. How many free commoners do we have?"

"Only two or three," Snefru answered.

The lord of the estate frowned. "Well, there is no help for it. The Pharaoh will have his projects completed." He leaned back in the chair. "Still, I cannot complain. You have done very well, Joseph."

"Thank you, Master," I said, finally allowing myself to believe that I had managed to make it through the year. I expected to be dismissed, but Lord Potiphar fingered the scarab seal ring he wore and looked at Snefru. The overseer kept his eyes on the table.

"Well?" Potiphar asked.

"My father calls for me, and Joseph is ready," Snefru said. "But I will serve you as you wish."

"You always have, Snefru," Potiphar replied kindly. "And it is time you had a rest. Also your father needs you. I noticed that Joseph has managed the country house for the past six months."

The overseer nodded. "My father, Chensu, was ill."

"Very well. You may go to the country house tomorrow."

"Thank you, my lord," Snefru replied, unable to hide his smile.

"Joseph, I will need to consult with you first thing in the morning, in the dining room," Lord Potiphar said to me. "As you are now steward of all I possess, we will need to get an early start. I am worried about the work on my tomb. It goes even slower than last year, and I must consult with you about it."

"Yes, Master," I said, not really taking in what he had just told me.

Potiphar's lips twitched. "Make him understand, will you?" he said to Snefru. "And if you have not told him about the other item yet, do so."

"Yes, my lord," Snefru answered as Potiphar walked out of the room.

I looked at my master's overseer. "Shall I have Khay call you in the morning?" I asked.

"What for?" Snefru replied. "I am going to retire to the country house. My father is very old and will not live much longer. Lord Potiphar will let me manage his country house so that I may be near Chensu until he dies."

"But what about all the rest?" I asked, a slight panicky feeling rising in my stomach.

"I assume that is what Lord Potiphar wants to discuss with you tomorrow," he replied, smiling.

"*Me?* But I don't, I mean I could not possibly—he doesn't really mean me, does he?"

"He said he did."

"But, Snefru, I don't know enough," I protested, a sense of despair filling me. "I am only beginning to learn about politics, and etiquette, and all the other things that go with officials and the Pharaoh's court. I will not be able to—"

"You will do just fine. I have taught you all I know, and when I took the job of Great Chief Steward of Potiphar's affairs, he knew that I was not able to adequately fill the position. I was only a placeholder until you could take over. I have no children living, Joseph. I had hoped to pass my position on to a son, as my father did it to me. But sickness took them years ago. Being childless created a bond between Lord Potiphar and me, which made him tolerate my limited skills."

I started to protest, but Snefru raised his hand.

"When I saw you, as Menneb's assistant, handling the house with greater wisdom than I ever had, I knew you were the one to manage Lord Potiphar's estate as it deserves. I have taught you all I could. I hope you do not mind, but I have looked on you as my son since I called you to assist me. Old Menneb knew how I felt; that is why he let you go so easily. You were a son to him also, and he wanted to see you rise as high as you could.

"Lord Potiphar also has no son, and he takes a keen interest in your career. He has watched you closely. Never has he given anyone as free a hand as he has you, and you amply repaid him by turning this estate into a very profitable enterprise. Even Lady Tanefret's business has increased. Our master is proud of what you have done. It will not be long before your skills will be wasted on Potiphar's estates. What will happen then, I don't know."

"Thank you, Snefru," I said humbly, near to tears. "I am honored to be your son. But it is not me. I don't know nearly enough to be all that you say I am. It is—" I stopped.

Snefru waited. "Say it," he told me. "Do not hide."

"It is El Shaddai, my God, honoring my efforts that has produced such success," I confessed. "Alone, I can do very little."

The overseer looked at the records still scattered on the table. "Maybe you are right. It is amazing what you have done in so short a time. I have this to say to you: Cling to your god. He is taking you somewhere. Somewhere great."

Levering himself to his feet, he left the room.

I managed to hold back the tears until he had gone. Then stumbling to my room, I threw myself on the mats of my bed. "Oh Abi, Abi," I sobbed. "If only you were here now."

▲ ▲ ▲ ▲

Judah looked up as the messenger entered the tent. "Yes?"

"Master Judah, my master Hirah asks if you will come to Timnah for the sheep-shearing this year."

For a moment Judah sat thinking. Shelah was old enough to handle things here, and with Dan and Benjamin helping Reuben, he need not stay because of Jacob. Bathshua had died, so no one waited for him.

"Tell your master that I will," Judah decided.

"Will Shelah come as well?" the messenger asked. "My master's son wanted to know."

"No, he will stay here."

The messenger nodded and left the tent.

Judah moved uneasily. Shelah had grown into a fine young man, and Judah feared to let Tamar near him. What if he died as Er and Onan had? He didn't want to lose his son, as Jacob had lost Joseph . . . Roughly, Judah pulled his mind away from that. It didn't matter, really. Tamar was well cared for by her father. She didn't need a son.

Shelah's entrance into the tent distracted him from his unprofitable thoughts.

"Are you going to Timnah?" he asked eagerly. "May I go also?"

"Yes, I'm going," Judah said. "But I want you to stay here and take care of things while I am gone. You're old enough now."

"I was old enough for that last year," Shelah said slowly. "I'm old enough to marry, you know."

His father winced. "There's plenty of time for that," he said noncommittally.

Shelah looked at him for a minute. "It's Tamar, isn't it, Abi?" he asked softly. "You are afraid to let me near her, aren't you?"

Before Judah could answer, his son ducked out of the tent and hurried away. Slowly Judah sat back down. So much for trying to be subtle. He shivered slightly. Those gray eyes of Shelah's, they saw things. Just like Joseph's blue ones—

He stifled the thought. Why did everything have to remind him of Joseph? Hadn't he been punished enough by now?

▲ ▲ ▲ ▲

"Well, how goes the shearing?" Hirah asked with a grin as Judah walked up to him.

"Very well. So well that I need to celebrate. Want to come with me to Timnah?"

"Not today," Hirah replied regretfully. "I have to supervise one more afternoon. Don't celebrate too well, then we can both go tomorrow."

"Fine with me," Judah said.

The flock had done well, Judah thought as he walked down the road. Better than he expected. He'd have to be certain to get the same graze next year. Maybe he ought to see the owner yet today and seal the bargain for another year or two.

Ahead, he saw a woman sitting by the side of the road. She sat with her face covered and watched him approach her.

Judah slowed a little. It had been a long time since Bathshua died. Perhaps the woman would be willing to celebrate his good fortune with him.

"You must have had quite a celebration," Hirah said jokingly when Judah finally returned to the sheep-shearing camp. "Looks like you celebrated so much you forgot some things. What happened to your signet ring and staff?"

"I didn't lose them," Judah said. "I gave them as a pledge. I met a woman on the way to town and convinced her to help me celebrate. I said I'd send her a kid from my flock, and she wanted surety for the exchange."

"Was she agreeable?" Hirah asked with a wink.

"Very," Judah replied, smiling. "Would you be willing to take the kid back to her and get my things?"

His friend shrugged. "Sure. Where was she?"

"On the road to Timnah. That open place before the hills. Come on, I'll show you which kid to take."

The Adullamite returned at dusk.

"What took so long?" Judah asked. "Did she celebrate with you too?"

"No," Hirah said sourly. "I couldn't find her. I led that kid all over the place and even asked some of the locals. No one knows anything about her."

"But she sat right there by the road," Judah said, astonished. "How could they miss her?"

"I don't know, but they all have," Hirah said, sitting down with a sigh. "I'm tired."

"But she's got my seal," Judah protested.

"If you want to search for her, you can. But I don't think you'll find her. You look a little odd without your staff, you know."

Judah started to pace. "What am I going to do? Hirah, do you think someone might be playing a joke on me?"

"Why would anyone do that?"

Judah grimaced. "Well, since my brothers betrayed the Shechemites, some of the townspeople have been against our family."

Hirah snorted. "Do you blame them? That story has been recited from one end of the land to the other. I'm just surprised the surrounding towns didn't rise up and kill all of you."

"Sometimes I can't understand that either. But do you think someone might be playing tricks on me now because of it?"

"Old sins have long shadows?" Hirah asked. "Maybe."

"Let's just forget it," Judah finally decided. "I'll have to get another seal made, but there's no help for it. If I go running after a woman that way, I'll be the laughing stock of the country."

"Maybe you already are," Hirah muttered under his breath, rubbing his aching feet.

▲ ▲ ▲ ▲

Judah stood in the field watching Shelah help check the donkeys' hooves. He really should speak to him about getting married. After all, he was ready.

Tamar's face rose in his mind, and he hastily shoved it away, then smiled at the way he'd fooled Hirah three months ago about the real reason he hadn't wanted to parade around the country looking for a woman. He hadn't wanted Tamar to hear he was in the area. She might have demanded that Shelah give her a son.

But then she had every right to do so, Judah admitted to himself, though why should he risk his last son's life on that woman? Didn't he deserve grandchildren? His son was so alive, so full of fun and laughter. Just as Joseph had been.

He ground his teeth. Everything, everywhere brought him back to Joseph. Joseph in Shelah's eyes, Joseph in Jacob's voice, Joseph on Benjamin's lips. Couldn't everybody just *forget Joseph*?

Rage flooded him, such as he hadn't felt in years. *Always, everywhere in everything it was Joseph. Well, Joseph was gone and would stay gone. So just forget him. Forget all about him. He'd had silly dreams anyway, and—*

"Master Judah," a voice interrupted him.

"What is it?" he asked savagely, whirling around.

Hirah's messenger dropped to his knees. "Forgive me, master."

"Get up," Judah said sourly. "What is it?"

"Master Hirah sent me to say that Tamar, your daughter-in-law, is with child," the man replied in a shaking voice.

"With child?" Judah roared, his anger at last finding an outlet. "How did she come to be with child?"

"No one knows, master."

"Well, I know," Judah said viciously. "She's been playing the harlot. Bringing shame to my house and name. Pretending to be a proper widow. She's been unfaithful, has she? Tried to deceive me? Let her see how I'll deal with that!"

On the way to Tamar's home, Hirah tried to calm him down, but Judah nursed his rage, deciding how to deal with the shame she had brought upon his name. She had always been too bold and too smart, daring to force him into promising Shelah to her. Well, she needed a lesson, as did the rest of this area. They needed to know not to cross Israel, or any of Israel's sons. This time she'd slipped up badly, and he could be rid of her forever.

Word spread rapidly that he had come, and a crowd gathered. *Let them gather,* Judah thought grimly. He would soon teach them a lesson.

"Bring Tamar to me," he commanded.

Looking as if she'd been waiting for him, Tamar came out of the house and walked toward him, followed by one of her servants.

Her composure irritated him, as it always had. How dare she be so calm? She wouldn't be, not when she heard what he had planned.

"You have brought dishonor on my house because of your unfaithfulness, Tamar," he declared. "Because you have played the harlot, getting a child by harlotry, you shall be put to death. You shall be burnt until you are dead."

The crowd gasped, but Judah refused to take notice. He knew he could require Tamar's life, and he meant to do it. How dare she bring such shame to his house and name. It had to be erased, and her blood would do it.

Tamar didn't move. She waited until the crowd had quieted.

Judah shifted uncomfortably, trying to ignore the looks of the crowd and the dislike and resentment hidden in their eyes. Didn't he have the right to pass sentence? Why should they complain? His name had been dishonored, not theirs.

He looked at Tamar, so still in front of him. Why didn't she say something? Defend herself or beg for her life? What was that woman thinking behind those cursed eyes of hers? Didn't she fear his rage? Joseph had. His brother had begged—Joseph! All over again, Joseph!

Judah's rage flamed afresh. He would grind Joseph out of his life no matter what it took to forget.

Calmly she raised her head. "Greetings, Judah. You come in anger, hearing I am with child. It is true. I am with child." She reached behind her, and her maid handed something to her.

As Tamar walked toward him, carrying a staff in one hand and a seal on a cord in the other, Judah froze, his hot anger iced over with the sudden sickening thought of what those things might be.

"My lord," Tamar said clearly, "by the man to whom these belong, I am with child. Look at them and tell who owns this staff and this seal and cord."

Judah couldn't move. He could only stare at his own seal. Tamar—Tamar had been the woman by the road to Timnah. She had known he never intended to give her Shelah. So she had taken by guile what was rightfully hers, what the law required he give.

And he had sentenced her to burn. His own hypocrisy rose up and choked him. Tamar had not brought shame on his name. He had done that himself, again and again.

His daughter-in-law stood motionless in front of him, holding his staff and seal, simply waiting. Next to him he heard a man choke and knew that he had recognized the seal, and that the truth could never be buried. Suddenly he was sick of pretending, sick of telling himself what he deserved, sick of lying to himself about the kind of man he was.

Reaching toward her, he took the seal from her, slipping it over his hand. A collective gasp ran though the crowd. He held out his hand for the rod.

Hesitating a moment, looking into his eyes searchingly, Tamar handed the rod to him.

"These things are mine," Judah said clearly, "as the child you carry is mine." A murmur ran though the crowd. "You are in the right, and I am in the wrong," he added when the crowd quieted. "I refused to fulfill your rights when I withheld my son Shelah from you in the place of my firstborn, Er, who was your husband. Take now what is rightfully yours. When you are ready, come back to your place in my tents."

Turning, Judah walked away, waiting to hear the laughter of the crowd at his defeat at Tamar's hands. But he heard only silence.

▲ ▲ ▲ ▲

Judah? Bested by a woman? I could hardly believe my ears. The two Ishmaelites chuckled over the story for some time, and I had to smile as well. What a scene that must have been! Part of me wished I could have seen it, and part of me sympathized with Judah's humiliation. It must have been a very bitter pill to swallow. And from a woman!

I had settled in the shade of an awning in the market to eat the noon meal while I watched for Mishma to return. Quite by chance, I overheard the two Ishmaelites talking and listened in, hungry for the language of my country.

The story was half told before I realized it was about Judah. So, Shelah was old enough to marry. That meant Benjamin was too. It didn't seem possible. What did he look like now? Was he even alive, or had my brothers disposed of him as well?

And what about me? Would I ever marry and have sons?

Shouts of excitement from across the market drew my attention, and I smiled. Huy was a big success. After he had entertained Hekamaat's children so well, I had taken him to the market with me and prodded him into doing some of his tricks. The children loved him, and he soon worked his wandering eye into his patter by telling the children that his eye was so curious it just had to look for the things that disappeared from his hands.

Now, he came nearly every day. Constantly trying to use his eye had improved it, and when he wasn't doing a show, the eye wandered much less than before. Self-respect turned him into a steady, cheerful man that the whole city recognized, and gave him a regal dignity that went well with his tall frame.

He became another of my information sources, rapidly becoming conversant with anything that went on in Memphis, and he had told me that Jetur was in Memphis again.

Khay had blossomed also. He did a very good job as steward of the Memphis estate. I had no idea how he knew things—his sources of information were his own—but he could find out almost anything I needed to know in the Delta region.

The smell of myrrh drifted past my nose, and I breathed deeply. Mishma entered the market, and I watched him closely. I wanted ivory, and I knew Jetur carried it. I would have to be very careful, for Renseneb had a man watching me, and I didn't want to tip my hand about my connection with Jetur.

The thought made me smile again. Renseneb and I carried on our war very quietly, but it had gotten more and more intense. We were about even on victories here in Memphis, but I could beat him in Tanis because of Khay, and he could beat me in Thebes since I had very few sources of information there and had to deal long-distance.

We rarely spoke to each other, but we respected each other a great deal. I had not yet found out whom he acted for, and he had not discovered how I bested him here in Memphis. It was because of Jetur and Neshi, of course.

Neshi's connection with me was well-hidden. Normally he sent items he got for me overland from Tanis, using Khay's network.

It hadn't taken long for Jetur to notice our battles, and he entered fully into the spirit of the thing with all the delight of a connoisseur.

I still had somewhat mixed feelings for the old caravan owner. His resemblance to Grandfather Isaac brought both pleasure and pain. He had never acknowledged a blood relationship to me, but I suspected he knew that I was descended from Abraham. Often he spoke of conditions or events near Bethel, where my father lived, but always so casually that I never could tell if he realized how much I longed to hear of it. I would go home afterward and torture myself with thoughts of Abi and home long into the night.

There—Mishma had ducked into the alley just to the right of

Huy. I knew that one. A trader's wife tended a stall there that sold pomegranates, and I usually bought one from her. Easing out into the crowd, I worked myself toward the stall.

Renseneb's man kept me in sight as I bought the pomegranate and stood to one side to peel it and eat the seeds. I reached for a cloth to wipe the juice from my face just as a loaded camel went lumbering by. Immediately I slipped into the alley and found my way down it.

Jetur's man stood outside a door and let me by with hardly a glance. The trader looked up from his cushion and smiled. "You are late today. Renseneb is hampering your movements."

I shrugged. "For now," I admitted. "Have you had a successful season?"

"I make some, I lose some."

"Mostly you make some," I commented, and Jetur laughed outright.

"And how do you know?" he chuckled.

"Your carpets," I said, digging my toes into the one I stood on. "Every time I come, they are thicker and softer."

Jetur laughed again. "What do you come for today?"

"Ivory. I only need a little, and the price in the market is much too high."

"How little?"

"Only some as big as my little finger. Aneksi heard it will ward off evil spirits from her child, and she must have some immediately. I promised I'd get her a little for an amulet."

Jetur looked at me for a minute. "And since you have told me all this, and thus told me just how much I can charge you for the ivory, there must be another reason for your visit."

"There is, Master Jetur. I have come to feel you are a reliable man, and I have a favor to ask."

Jetur straightened. "You do me an honor. Sit down and we will eat."

After a light meal, and a sweetmeat after it, Jetur settled himself on the cushions. "Now, tell me how I can serve you."

"Just recently Master Potiphar promoted me to be his Great Chief Steward. I will be traveling to Abydos tomorrow, and I will be gone for some time. I know my master is worried about something, and I know it concerns the Pharaoh. I am afraid that rumors about attempts to assassinate the Pharaoh have some substance to them. Would you, as a favor, send a message to a man I will tell you of, if you hear anything involving threats to the Pharaoh?"

The trader sat for some time in silence. "I will do this," he said finally. "I will give you this favor."

"Thank you, Master Jetur. It will relieve my mind."

I told him where to find Lord Potiphar's agent in Memphis, then took my leave, following Jetur's man down the twisting alleys until I could reenter the market place without Renseneb's agent seeing where I had come from. After that, I hurried openly toward the estate. I must be ready to leave on the morrow, and my ankles were hurting. They did that, lately, after a hard day.

▲ ▲ ▲ ▲

"He is a man," Mishma said as his father entered the room.

"Yes, he is a man," Jetur agreed. "An uncommonly shrewd one, he is now my master."

"What?" Mishma exclaimed. "How can that be?"

"He has beaten me at my own game," Jetur said with a chuckle. "Do not worry, my son. I go to defeat willingly, for I shall be very, very rich."

"What did he offer you?"

"He offered me the chance of a direct connection to the Great House. That one, he divined that my life's ambition was to trade directly with the Great House, and he came here with an offer I could not refuse. If I cannot turn this opportunity into profitable trade with the Great House itself, I do not deserve to be a merchant. I have looked for a crack in the wall around the Great House for years, and he just showed me where one was. For that, we shall owe him for the rest of his life."

The merchant was thoughtful a moment. "I pity Renseneb. He will fall also, as I have done."

Mishma looked annoyed.

"Look happy, my son. Because of this, you will die a much richer man than I, and I will soon be much richer than I am now. Without doubt, those 20 pieces of silver were the best bargain I ever made!"

▲ ▲ ▲ ▲

"I was so close, Lady, but I lost him in the market," Renseneb reported.

"So it is someone who comes periodically," she mused, running her delicate fingers along the arm of the chair.

"Yes, Lady," he replied. She had changed so much since he had first known her. From a frightened child, she had matured into a beautiful, shrewd woman with an instinct for weaknesses in others that she exploited ruthlessly.

He still could not believe what she had accomplished. She owned three estates, two of them in the south, and one right here in On under her father's nose. In addition, she kept two separate caravans busy with trade all year round, and yet she had never once left her house.

Her step-sisters despised her and thought her a half-wit. If she left her rooms, she always wore her clothes wrong and kept her hair always messy. Her manners were clumsy and awkward. How she managed to hide her beauty, he did not know, but she always looked such a misfit whenever her father saw her, that he was more than glad to forget her the minute she left. In private, however, she became as graceful as her mother had been.

The woman intrigued Reseneb. He wondered what had driven her to live as she did. When she had first approached him, years ago, he had been hard put not to laugh in her face when she solemnly asked him to trade in the market for her. But when she handed him that mirror, made from the White, he had not laughed. It had taken him years to learn that the distant closed look in her eyes covered a fear so sickening she dared not admit to it, and yet he knew nothing of what caused it.

He understood now that she had planned ahead—far ahead. She had woven a web of informants and sources that served her so well she could stay hidden in her rooms and yet keep abreast of the commerce in the markets and the political twists of the court.

Renseneb watched as she studied the situation in her mind. From past experience, he knew she put together personalities, bits of gossip, and information gleaned from her sources, with information he delivered, to fill out a picture of her problem.

Poti-Phera was a fool, he thought for the hundredth time. A harsh, thoughtless man bent on political power, he aspired to the office of Tate, second only to Pharaoh. *If he had the sense of an ibis, may*

Thoth forgive me, Renseneb decided, *he would let his daughter manage his career, and he might end up as Pharaoh.*

"May the gods pity us if he succeeds," Renseneb muttered, thankful that Poti-Phera's daughter understood her father's character well. It was bad enough that he had been appointed Great Vision of Ra, the high priest's title and the most sought-after priestly position. How Poti-Phera gained it puzzled everyone, except possibly his daughter. Renseneb would bet his life she knew how her father had arranged that appointment even if no one else did.

"It must be a caravan owner," she said, breaking into his thoughts. "And his trade centers in Memphis. I suppose getting anything in Tanis is hopeless?"

"Yes, Lady," Renseneb sighed. "We have lost Tanis. But we still have Thebes."

"Then dig into Memphis. We must learn who trades for him, or we shall lose both."

"Yes, Lady Asenath."

CHAPTER 9

I settled down on the cushions on the high stern deck of Lord Potiphar's transport ship as the boatman pushed us away from the dock. I loved my job, but I hated this thick, heavy, hot wig. If it hadn't had to cover my red hair, it wouldn't have been so thick or so hot. But it did, and I hated wearing it. After we passed the country house, I would take it off and leave it off until we arrived in Abydos, 250 miles south.

I enjoyed traveling. The scenery constantly changed, and the traffic in the river interested me. I could sit and relax, and after the first three days off my feet, my ankles wouldn't hurt at all.

Mahesa, the scribe, accompanied me as chief of my staff, but I kept work to a minimum, knowing that both of us needed the time to relax. We would be busy enough in Abydos, where I must stay for some months, overseeing the building of Lord Potiphar's tomb. Master Potiphar was greatly concerned about this, since during the last three years progress on the tomb had steadily declined.

Snefru had been unable to determine why Superintendent of the Work Hutor was no longer doing the job with the same efficiency as in the past. Potiphar was very worried, since his holdings now provided enough income to complete the majority of the work. It might not in the future, and above all else, Potiphar wanted a tomb ready for his and Lady Tanefret's burial.

I understood more, now, of how important it was to him. From Khay, Huy, and Mahesa I had learned about the dead and why it had been so important to Menneb to have a pillar set up in Abydos with his name on it.

In Canaan, our family buried the dead knowing that all would become right when the promised Seed of Abraham arrived. In the grave one had no knowledge, no feeling, no connection with the living at all.

But in Egypt! My head whirled sometimes just thinking of it all. The Egyptians believed in an afterlife, a time when the life force, or Ka, of the dead person went to the West and continued living. The Ka needed a place to stay and preferred its old body. It was, therefore, of absolute paramount importance that the body not decay or be destroyed in any way, else the Ka would have no place to live and would eventually perish. This meant the loss of the afterlife and was the worst possible thing that could happen to an Egyptian. They called it the Second Death.

Potiphar had given detailed and specific instructions to me the very first thing about how his body was to be embalmed after he died. Pharaoh had granted him a full royal embalming when he had attained the title Chosen of the Guard not long before. After the 40 days of embalming, a funeral barge would take the mummy up the river to Abydos, where it would be carefully put in the stone sarcophagus and the inner tomb sealed to prevent anyone from entering it and disturbing the body or the things in the tomb.

Potiphar had chosen to be buried in Abydos instead of Beni Hassan where many nobles had tombs because he wished to be close to his father who was already interned at Abydos. Only a tomb near the Pharaoh's pyramid near the Fayyum might tempt him away from Abydos. But knowing Potiphar's attachment to his father, I doubted it.

Mahesa joined me on the high upper deck in the stern of the boat. The breeze tugged at our hair, and I finally took off the wig. It was just too hot. Mahesa had lost his fear of me, and we got along well together.

"You will have to put it back on as soon as we land," he said. "As Potiphar's Great Chief Steward, you must preserve the dignity of the office."

"I know," I sighed, "but right now the breeze is too enticing to ignore."

Mahesa smiled. "It is nice," he admitted. "I have been thinking, Great Steward, about transportation in Abydos. I think you should have a sedan chair. It befits your station, and it will save your ankles."

"Is it that obvious?" I asked ruefully.

"Most people would not notice," he assured me.

"Is it necessary? After the trip up the river, they will be much better."

"All the more reason to hire the chair. They will stay better."

"Are you sure?"

"Yes, Great Steward. I think it would be best."

I yielded the point. I had come to trust him on questions of propriety and etiquette. Mahesa had come to Potiphar's estate from the school for scribes in the capital city. It was the most prestigious school to attend, next to the palace school itself.

"What was it like, the Capital School?" I asked curiously.

Mahesa thought for a moment. "I had a hard time, Great Steward. My father is a merchant in Thebes. I went to the school at age 10. Up to then, I had had a very free life, helping my father. I could have gone to the House of Instruction in Thebes, a day school, which would have been easier, but my father wanted the best, and he sent me to Itej-Tawy.

"At the school, everything was regimented. We learned reading, writing, ethics, practical philosophy, etiquette, math, and science. Swimming also. I was good at that already. It was the only subject I was good at to begin with.

"After the noon meal, we worked at practical things, and when I was good enough, I would assist a regular scribe at his work. When I completed my studies, Lord Potiphar took me to his estate as he promised."

"Oh?"

Mahesa nodded. "His recommendation got me accepted in the Capital School. My mother is related to Lady Tanefret. He promised to employ me when I finished. It is a great favor. I could have started as a public scribe, doing contracts, letters, and business correspondence from the street for whoever needed it, but beginning in a secure position will push me along much faster. And, of course, the position carries prestige already because of Lord Potiphar."

"How much prestige?"

A puzzled expression crossed his face.

"I am a slave from Canaan," I explained. "I know little about these things, and I must learn as fast as I can."

"It seems you have learned a lot already, Great Steward," he said with a smile. "Lord Potiphar is very high in the government. As captain of the Palace Guard, he is responsible for the safety of the Pharaoh. His last couple years at the Palace School coincided with the first ones of the co-regent.

"Lord Potiphar's father worked in the Palace Guard as well. Since Lord Potiphar does not have a son to pass his position to, another one of the members of the Palace School will get the job when Lord Potiphar retires or dies. Most of the high officials of the palace attended the school. It provides the co-regent with a pool of skilled officials that have formed a loyalty to him, making it easier to choose administrators when he becomes Pharaoh.

"For Lord Potiphar to hold the position of Captain of the Guard, he must be trusted by both Pharaoh and the co-regent. He is in daily contact with both, and they rely heavily on him. More than ever now that the Falcon is soon to fly."

"What does a falcon have to do with it?" I asked, puzzled.

Mahesa looked pained. "The falcon is a symbol of Pharaoh, Chief Steward. When the falcon flies, the Pharaoh goes to the West to join his father, Osiris."

"He dies," I translated.

Mahesa looked uncomfortable. "If you must say it that way."

As we traveled, I asked Mahesa about everything. He taught me about the 24 nomes, the political divisions of Egypt. A nomarch ruled each one and its people worshiped its own god. Some of the nomarchs were so powerful that they were almost independent of the Pharaoh. Many had a permanent fighting force and were rich enough to do what they pleased. Most of these were in the South.

Mahesa explained about the strict twofold division of the central government. It had two of everything. One for upper Egypt, the south, the more prestigious part of the country, and one for lower Egypt, the north, the under-civilized part of the country originally conquered by Menes more than 1,000 years ago. Egypt had two Houses of Silver, two Houses of Gold, two Houses of Cloth—two of everything.

I listened with wonder as Mahesa recited hundreds of years of history, explaining how Menes had unified the land and enforced order and government. He told me of the Pyramids; of Abydos, the city of Osiris; of Memphis the ancient capital. The scribe spoke of the Land in Front, the first nome of Egypt, the southernmost nome at the first cataract of the Nile, and the pride of its people that they guarded Kemet, the Black Land, from the forces of Deshret or chaos.

Mahesa described the expansion of Egypt above the first cataract to the second, and that there, at the forts of Semna and Kumma, special scribes kept record of the rising and falling of the Nile, so that they could inform the Pharaoh whether there would be feast or famine in Egypt. The annual Nile flood washed the land and laid down a rich layer of silt in which to grow crops for the next year. However, too low a Nile inundation meant not enough water to raise crops. Too high meant the river receded too late to plant.

By the time we arrived in Abydos, I had acquired a fairly good understanding of the political and social structure of Egypt. Upper Egypt was very different from Lower Egypt. The southern people were generally taller than northerners, and they looked at themselves as being the Egyptians. They considered the north an annex of sorts, and only grudgingly granted northerners status as Egyptians so long as they kept to their place. Also upon arrival at Abydos, I understood Mahesa's gentle insistence that I wear a wig and have a chair litter.

Courtesy and etiquette were important in Lower Egypt, but in Upper Egypt, they were absolutely paramount and treated accordingly. After dealing with Huy, Khay, Kemi, and the rest of Potiphar's house staff, meeting with Hutor, Superintendent of Work at Potiphar's tomb, was a revelation.

Hutor was somewhat at a loss to know how to treat me, since I was a barbarian—and thus not one of the human races—as well as a slave, putting me on the lowest rung of society; and yet I was Lord Potiphar's Great Chief Steward, and thus his superior.

Our first meeting was quite formal. Hutor met the boat at the docks, but waited for me to disembark before greeting me in the most correct manner imaginable.

"I pray the gods granted you a good journey," Hutor said, after introducing himself.

"They have indeed," Mahesa replied smoothly. "The wind was constant, and our sails were always filled. They smile on the work to be done to honor them and our Lord Potiphar."

"I am glad to hear of this," Hutor said. "Arrangements have been made for you to rest. A house is prepared in town."

"You honor us," Mahesa said. "We shall certainly stay. And now, Chief Steward Joseph requires a chair litter. Is this arranged?"

The request put Hutor in a quandary. During the preliminaries he had cast little arrogant glances at me. I had let Mahesa take over, realizing in just these few minutes that I would have to learn an entirely different way of behaving, and I needed the scribe to point the way.

Now, Mahesa's question informed Hutor that he may have been negligent on a point of etiquette. To do less than required for the Great Chief Steward of his lord's estate was a serious breech of courtesy. In his mind I was a slave, yet the scribe treated me as a high-ranking Egyptian steward.

I turned to Mahesa.

"Yes, Great Steward?" he asked immediately.

"We have been sitting for some days. I would like to walk for a little to see the town. If the chair could meet us in a little while, I would be pleased."

Mahesa turned to Hutor. "Great Steward Joseph wishes to exercise after the confinement of the journey. He wishes the chair litter to meet us."

"Of course, Great Steward," Hutor said, his mixed emotions playing across his face. "I shall so instruct the bearers." As he turned away, I knew he felt grateful for the honorable way out of the situation, and yet angry that any situation had arisen at all and that I had been the one to point the way out of his dilemma.

Mahesa's face darkened as Hutor left without taking proper leave. He started to speak, but I stopped him. "One thing at a time, Mahesa."

After waiting while the crew unloaded our things, I then walked from the wharf with Mahesa guiding me toward the town market.

Everywhere I saw evidence that Abydos was a city for the dead.

Funeral barges lined the docks. Osiris figures were on sale all over. Hawkers sang about the services for tombs and funerary cults that their masters provided. Temples abounded to Osiris, to his sister/wife Isis, and to their son Horus. The city existed to serve the dead, and it took the job seriously.

The market was busy, stalls of food and goods were there, as in every market on earth, but the atmosphere was much more restrained than in Memphis. Priests, completely shaved from head to foot, were everywhere representing every god in the Egyptian pantheon. Three funeral processions went by in the short time it took us to walk from the dock to the market, the mummies carefully drawn through town by oxen, the processions following into the desert for the rituals of the tomb.

By the time Mahesa directed me to the chair litter, I longed for the simple ceremonies and beliefs of my own people about the dead. All this seemed such a waste.

That evening, I sat in the small garden of the house provided for me for the next few months.

"The house should be bigger," Mahesa complained, dissatisfied. "Your position requires it."

"It will do," I said. "I may be Master Potiphar's Chief Steward, but I am also a slave. I gather already that here in the south keeping a good balance in things is very important."

The scribe nodded. "It is, perhaps here more than anywhere else. We are an arrogant people. I learned that in the Capital School. It did my Ka good to see Hutor uncomfortable on the dock today."

"Oh?"

"He always looked down on my father—and on me. Hutor is related to the Nomarch's family, as is my mother, but he scorned my father's wish that I be a scribe. And when Lord Potiphar gave us the recommendation for the Capital School, he said I would never succeed."

"Well, I am here now," Mahesa said in a low voice, his eyes gleaming with a fierce light. "And I shall continue to rise."

I glanced at him. Mahesa turned to me, and I caught his eye. One glance was enough to read the bitterness and anger of wounded pride that raged in his soul.

Instantly the young scribe looked away and stepped back, breathing hard. "Forgive me, Great Steward."

"I wish you would remember one thing, Mahesa. I do not ask

you to forget whatever bruises your soul. But I do ask you to remember that the best way to take satisfaction from the situation is to go beyond it.

"We are here to serve Master Potiphar. Take the energy your feelings produce and do just that to the best of your ability. In so doing, you will prove Hutor wrong in the one way that he cannot deny. Do not stay to argue with him. He will defeat you. Go beyond him, and become the best scribe Lord Potiphar ever had."

Mahesa remained silent for some time. "I had never considered it that way, Great Steward," he finally commented. "I will think of what you have said. Now, I will bid you good night, if there is nothing else you require," he finished.

"Not until morning. I will need to go to the tomb then."

"I will see to the chair," he promised. "It will be ready as soon as you have eaten."

"Thank you, Mahesa. Good night."

The next morning I rose early and was on my way to the tomb at sunrise. We traveled some distance into the desert, and I felt sorry for the chair bearers by the time we arrived. At the same time, I felt extremely grateful that I hadn't had to walk all that way myself.

When we arrived at the work site, no one quite knew what to do with us.

"Is the Superintendent of the Works here?" Mahesa asked.

"No, scribe," a worker ventured to reply, taking his cue from the pen and papyrus Mahesa carried. "But Inspector of the Works Teti is here."

"Please tell him that Lord Potiphar's Great Chief Steward has arrived to inspect progress," Mahesa announced impressively.

After one startled look, all the workers bowed respectfully to me and the one who spoke rushed into the tomb itself to bring Teti.

In moments the official came hurrying out. Teti was a tall man with large hands and a sharp, sure look about him that impressed me. I wondered how he got on with Hutor.

He also bowed. "Please forgive us for lack of a formal welcome, Great Steward. I am not properly dressed or prepared to escort you. If you are willing to wait—" he left the sentence hanging.

Mahesa turned to me, clearly signaling that I should address my remarks to him.

"The formal welcome can wait for another time," I said. "Today

I am here for a brief inspection. I do not wish to interrupt important work any more than necessary. Please have your men continue as usual."

Mahesa told Teti what I had just said, and the Inspector of the Works thanked Mahesa for my consideration. I saw in Teti's eyes his frustration at the interruption and required formalities as he urged his men back to work.

Stepping down from the chair, I walked toward the entrance of the diwar, or chapel, of the tomb. Mahesa followed me, as did Teti, looking startled.

The chapel was just taking shape, though still in rough form. Sitting in place was the block of granite that Potiphar's statue would be carved out of, and the sculptor was hard at work.

He jumped when he saw me watching and hurriedly bowed.

"You have made good progress," I said. "Master Potiphar will be pleased."

"Thank you, G-Great Steward," he stuttered, having heard my title hissed at him by Teti. Again he bowed, and I glanced around the small room. Four pillars supported the ceiling, and in the middle of the back wall was the door to the harim, the secret part of the tomb, where the mummy would rest.

I walked in to be greeted by the usual riot of colors and pictures that decorated Egyptian houses. Two walls were completely painted. The third had grid lines and outline drawings waiting to be filled in, and the fourth was blank. In the center stood the sarcophagus, every inch covered with text in hieroglyphics, listing the formulaic answers to all the questions the Ka must respond to in the Hall of Truth.

Teti stopped the painter and brought him to me. "This is Chief of the Painters, Great Steward," he said. "He has worked hard on the walls."

"I see that," I replied. "Master Potiphar told me only one and a half walls were done, but you have already completed another half wall. This is very good indeed."

The man beamed, rubbing his paint-stained hands on his kilt. "Lord Potiphar is generous with his praise. I will remember it gratefully."

"Continue your work," I said. "I will need to study the walls so that I can report to my master."

With a bow he returned to his wall.

I walked to the first wall, and Teti raised his torch so I could see the judgment scene. The deceased stood in the Hall of Two Truths, presided over by Osiris as King of the Dead. Forty-two demons represented the sins that the deceased had to deny. In order to see if the deceased had lived a righteous life, his heart was weighed in a balance against the feather of truth, taken from the goddess Maat. Ibis-headed Thoth, the scribe of the gods, recorded the result of the weighing, and if the deceased passed the test, Horus escorted him to Osiris to be received into the afterlife. If the deceased did not pass the test, the destroyer of souls, Amemait, a monster part crocodile and part lion with the hind quarters of a hippopotamus, waited to devour him.

The next wall was the scene of Lord Potiphar's house in Memphis. The painting was crowded, for it must include a complete inventory of everything in the estate. All the workshops, the kitchens, the fields and pastures, house staff, possessions, servants and slaves—absolutely everything. In one corner, I saw a miniature depiction of the country house with its walled garden and small fields.

All this must be there in order for Potiphar's Ka to be able to use it in the afterlife. If it wasn't on the wall, it would not be available for the Ka if he needed it. This applied to people also. They must have both arms, legs, hands, feet, and shoulders. It would never do for Lord Potiphar's Ka to be minus one hand in the afterlife. In addition, the painting provided an alternate dwelling place for the Ka should anything happen to the mummy or the statue in the diwar.

The wall in progress was a river scene, with Potiphar on his pleasure boat hunting fowl in the marshes assisted by Lady Tanefret. Again, every detail must be present, so that it would be there for eternity.

The fourth wall would be a scene of Potiphar honoring the gods to prove his piety and readiness for the afterlife.

Outside I heard a commotion and with a hasty bow, Teti disappeared. I followed him. It was a small tomb, but it would cost Potiphar a large percentage of his life's earnings to complete it for himself and Lady Tanefret. In addition, he must furnish the tomb with everything the Ka could possibly want, and that was my next stop, to check the progress on furnishings.

Hutor stood outside the tomb, berating Teti for paying the workmen an extra bottle of beer for work done. As I listened, I thought back to the records I had brought with me. The figures Hutor quoted and those I remembered did not coincide.

"Mahesa, note down that I must check on the payments to be made to the workmen," I said quietly.

Nodding, he scribbled a note to himself.

Teti said something to Hutor and then sent a scribe scurrying to get something. The scribe returned with a tablet, and both Hutor and Teti consulted it.

"I want to see that tablet," I said to Mahesa. "Could you bring it?"

While everyone's attention was on Hutor and Teti, Mahesa quietly walked up and stopped to the side of and slightly behind Hutor.

I could not quite hear what Hutor said, because of the noise of the work in the tomb, but I could see Teti's reactions. His face did not change, but his back tensed, and his hands clenched into fists. As Hutor continued to speak, Teti's chin jutted out, but he remained silent.

Hutor thrust out his hand with the tablet in Mahesa's direction, who deftly took it, then immediately slid behind Hutor. I stayed in the shadow of the tomb's chapel as Mahesa handed me the tablet, a badly copied list of the payments due each worker. I had difficulty making out what the proper amounts should be. I passed it back to Mahesa.

"What do you make of this?"

He studied the tablet for some time. "Someone who could barely write tried to copy it, Great Steward. From what Hutor was saying, he took the minimum possible figures, and Teti opted for the higher ones, which, I might add, are more in line with regular payment schedules."

"Hutor is very strait-laced, but I do not think he is dishonest," I commented. "Why would he berate Teti for making this decision?"

"If he thought Lord Potiphar would be displeased at the cost of the labor, he would feel honor-bound to do anything he could about it," Mahesa said thoughtfully. "That might account for it."

"Let us assume that is the case. Now, I think it is time to go."

As I walked from the tomb, Mahesa respectfully followed me. Hutor had only now noticed the chair litter and swung around, looking for the person to whom it belonged. He stopped short, seeing me.

"Inspector Teti," I said, walking toward him, "Master Potiphar will be well pleased with the progress you have made. Please compliment the workmen and see that they are suitably recompensed for their hard work."

"Yes, Great Steward," he said, relaxing a trifle.

"Superintendent Hutor, I will be inspecting the funerary furnishings next, and I must request your attendance. Shall we go?"

Without waiting for an answer, I turned and started to the chair litter, which the bearers waited to pick up. Beside me I saw the faint, satisfied smile on Mahesa's face and guessed that I had handled the situation to his approval.

The rest of the day we spent in the workshops of the craftsmen making the funerary furnishings for the tomb. When we finished, I told Hutor that I would expect to meet with him the following day to discuss further plans.

By the time he came in the morning, I had decided on the manner in which I would approach him. I met with him in the dining room of the house and had him sit across from me at the low table. Electing not to sit in the chair, I chose instead to use a low stool like the one provided for Hutor.

"Superintendent Hutor," I began, "I feel that I can now discuss intelligently with you progress on Master Potiphar's tomb, since I have seen all that pertains to it.

"When I became Master Potiphar's Great Chief Steward, he sat with me several times, giving me detailed instructions about what was to be done. He charged me with the job of finishing the tomb as soon as possible. I shall need to depend on you extensively to fulfill this obligation."

Hutor looked a bit surprised at my words, but straightened a little. "Yes, Great Steward."

"Now, you are to be commended for finding such a man as Teti to be Inspector of the Works. He has a good rapport with the workmen and has gotten much done since Snefru was last here.

"I am glad to see that you give Teti a free hand," I went on.

Hutor turned a bit red at that remark, but remained silent.

"This plan is working well. However, I noticed that the funerary furnishings are not coming along as quickly as Master Potiphar would wish. Have you also noticed this?"

"Yes, Great Steward. I have done my best to push the craftsmen to greater speed, but they do not always do so."

I watched his eyes as he glanced around the room, then

reached for some figs on the table. His hand hesitated, then crept forward a bit more until his fingers found the dish, and he fumbled a fig from it.

"Yes, I can imagine they do that," I said. "Here is a list of the items that should be attended to immediately." I held out the tablet to Hutor, and he reached for it, again moving his hand slowly forward until I placed the tablet in his hand. He held it in front of his face a moment, then set it down, almost missing the table when he did.

"Now, Hutor," I went on, pretending to notice nothing, "I am authorized by Master Potiphar to do all in my power to fulfill his wish to complete the tomb. There will be more workers added to the project for you to supervise. Next time you come, you must bring your personal scribe, for there will be many notes to keep track of."

"Many pardons, Chief Steward, but my personal scribe is sick at this time. He will not be able to attend."

"But this is terrible," I protested. "You must have a scribe. It is essential. I will appoint one to attend you for as long as you need him. He shall be paid by the estate with the rest of the workers and shall answer to you for this project."

For some time Hutor remained silent. "As you wish, Great Steward," he said softly, his shoulders relaxing their tense posture.

After our conference, Mahesa returned from ushering Hutor out. "Anything I should note, Great Steward?" he asked, sitting down with his pen ready.

"Yes," I said. "See about hiring a reliable scribe for Hutor. He must have one. I wish to interview anyone you find before assigning him to Hutor, though."

Mahesa looked startled. "Pardon my questions, Steward, but should we add this expense? Hutor can both read and write."

"Hutor has been unable to read and write for some time," I said quietly. "His eyes have nearly given out, probably from the constant glare of the sun, although it could be the eye sickness. That is why I wish to interview whomever you find. We will need someone strictly honest."

Mahesa sat back in amazement. "Blind?"

"Almost. He has hidden it well, probably fearing to lose his job if it is known. But I would imagine he could recite everything on that tablet he left on the table, since I went over it item by item with him."

"He probably wrote this payment schedule then," Mahesa said, taking the tablet we'd gotten at the tomb.

"Most likely. If he no longer fears for his job, he will go back to the efficient supervisor he used to be. I think you will be surprised if you go back through the records on this project. Hutor saved Master Potiphar a great deal on more than one occasion with his shrewd, careful management. I came here knowing something was wrong because I had gone over all the records myself before starting the trip. The last three years have been one disaster after another, and I now know why."

"He should be fired," Mahesa said. "If he no longer does his job—"

"Hutor is still the same shrewd, efficient person," I interrupted. "He just needs someone to see for him. That is something I can easily arrange. Let me know as soon as you find a candidate."

"Yes, Great Steward. I will begin the search tomorrow."

CHAPTER 10

I spent only three months in Abydos, instead of the intended six. Mahesa found a young public scribe named Sheshon to work for Hutor. Sheshon was more relaxed than Hutor, but understood the older man and worked with him well. It didn't take long before Hutor was back to his old efficient self.

With Master Potiphar's tomb problems out of the way, I checked on the funerary endowment for Master Potiphar's father. If the priest had kept the tomb according to contract, Lord Potiphar wished me to arrange an endowment for himself.

I visited the land donated to support the priest, and the scribe presented up-to-date and complete records detailing its usage and profits, all of which supported the tomb. Then I met with Heqanakht, the priest who tended the tomb, and he impressed me as conscientious. A lector priest as well as a funerary priest, he could read the tomb's formal hieroglyphics. He provided food in the diwar chapel for the Ka twice a day and assisted anyone who came to make requests of the Ka or bring offerings. Also he saw to it that grave robbers left the tomb alone.

After examining the items ordered for Master Potiphar's tomb, I understood the temptation to rob tombs. The jewelry, dishes, and everyday objects—most made from gold, as Potiphar was rich—would tempt anyone. Although some of it was clearly not intended for human usage, it could be melted down or reused in another form.

Satisfied with what I found I made the preliminary arrangement for another piece of land to be donated upon Potiphar's death, the profits of which would support his tomb.

"I shall see that his name is not forgotten," Heqanakht assured me after the arrangements were made and the contracts signed. "I will protect the living place of the Ka and preserve its life through remembrance as long as I shall live. My son trains to follow me, and he will do as I have done." His sincerity impressed me. Clearly he truly believed in what he did.

"Thank you, Heqanakht. Master Potiphar will be most pleased."

I wrote out a report for Master Potiphar, assuring him that his father was well and richly supplied with all needs. It seemed so odd to report this when his father was no longer alive. Perhaps someday I would understand. I also placed before the statue in the diwar chapel the sealed letter which Lord Potiphar had written to his father and given to me to deliver.

Before I left Abydos, I found the temple to Thoth where the pillar with Menneb's name had been erected. I walked between the huge stone pylons and into the walled courtyard. It resembled a town with houses, workshops, and sellers' stalls lining the huge enclosure. The people who lived here worked on the temple's lands and tended to the needs of the priests and the corvee workmen when they came to enlarge and repair the buildings under Pharaoh's orders.

As this was a temple to Thoth, god of scribes, they had a school and a House of Life, a library with hundreds of scrolls on subjects ranging from funerary texts to science to history and literature. Mahesa told me that temples soon became rich, even when small. Being an extension of Pharaoh's personal household, they received goods from Pharaoh's storehouses. Thus, anything they grew or manufactured could be sold to the populace or put on the market, as they held trading concessions from Pharaoh allowing them to do so.

I did not go into the temple itself, for I had seen one in Memphis, and they were all the same. The first hall would be followed by a smaller, darker room, and then the smaller and darker chapel of the god. To each side were chapels for the god's consort and son. Further back was the small, sealed room with the god's statue. Every morning, the priests would unseal the door, dress and place food before the statue, then seal the door again until the next day.

The morning ritual in every temple in the land echoed the ritual in the palace when the Pharaoh, as a god in human form, was wakened, dressed, and given the first meal of the day. Such ritual also re-created the universe and kept chaos from destroying it.

I approached a Wab Priest, the lowest order of the priesthood, and asked directions. He checked the records, then pointed out the correct courtyard. In it, I located the small pillar with Menneb's name on it, surrounded by scores of others.

As I stood there, looking at that pillar, I began to understand the Egyptian attitude toward the dead. Seeing Menneb's name brought back so many memories. He lived again in my mind, and thus, although dead, he was not gone.

Menneb had taught me so much. I was what I was today because of the things he said and did. I understood, now, Mahesa's comment on the boat about the Egyptian concern with the past. He had said that without it, the present would not be what it was. Without Menneb, I would not be what I was. I was tied to the past, indebted to it, and I saw how the experiences of my life had rooted me to this land of my captivity.

Silently, I bowed my head and touched Menneb's name on the pillar. "El Shaddai," I whispered, "I give thanks now for the benefits brought into my life by Menneb. He knew much, and he taught me many things.

"I do not believe, as those here do, that some part of Menneb is alive, but I feel it is well for me to honor him in memory. Thank you for providing this man and all that he did for me."

In Thebes, Mahesa left me for a few days to visit his father and mother, the merchant Chety and his wife Nofret. Quickly I missed Mahesa's ready advice and social explanations, but I got along as best I could, knowing enough now to hold my own in my meetings with Iteti, Lady Tanefret's chief scribe.

"You have kept excellent records, Iteti," I said, when we had gone through the last of them. "This review is the easiest I have done. I think we can increase the allotment for the commoners you mentioned and for the potter, but you might wish to keep track of the weaveress for a while before increasing her pay.

"I noticed that a washerman was lost to crocodile attack last year. What happened to his family?"

Iteti thought for a minute. "The wife entered domestic service in the house, then left for service in the temple to Amun. It is a small one, but very busy."

"Iteti!" Lady Tanefret called, coming into the room. "I wanted to talk to you about buying—" She stopped and stared at me.

I bowed again, having hastily risen when she entered the room. "Greetings, Lady Tanefret," I said, looking down.

"Greetings," she replied. "I didn't know you were here. What brings you to Thebes?"

"I am receiving Iteti's report. Master Potiphar made me Great Chief Steward of his possessions."

"So he did," Lady Tanefret replied slowly. "I remember now. He mentioned that you would bring him luck."

"I serve him as best I know how. I am glad he is pleased with me."

Lady Tanefret continued to stare at me, and I began to feel uncomfortable.

"Lady?" Iteti said. "You wished to speak with me?"

"Oh, yes," she said, breaking her gaze. "I did."

"I will excuse myself," I said. "I have much to do."

Lady Tanefret did not reply, but her eyes followed me out of the room.

The next day, Iteti took me on a tour of Lady Tanefret's estate in Thebes. It resembled Master Potiphar's Memphis estate, and I found nothing to criticize. However, I did make one or two suggestions for Iteti to take to Lady Tanefret for approval, and he seemed enthusiastic about them, immediately grasping how Lady Tanefret would benefit from them.

After this, I had only one more thing to accomplish in Thebes. Needing an agent in the markets for Master Potiphar, I decided to check out Mahesa's father. I walked further than I expected to a modest house on the outskirts of Thebes.

Mahesa was scandalized when the porter announced my name, and Chety was distressed that he didn't have a proper welcome prepared for me. His wife Nofret flew around sending attendants to all corners of the house to provide anything I might want.

Smiling wryly to myself, I thought of how often I had done the running for just such requests. I was beginning to understand the meaning of prestige.

"Please, Mahesa, is all this necessary?" I asked. "Could you make your father understand that I have not come on a formal visit, that I wish to just talk to him?"

"But we could not possibly do that without the proper setting," Mahesa replied, eyes round. "What would people think if we did not honor you as befits your station? You will be given time to wash and refresh yourself, as my parents will also, and then after a suitable meal, you can talk."

We left the next morning, Mahesa having sent for my chair litter during the night so that no one would know I had walked here. Chety agreed to act as Lord Potiphar's agent in Thebes. He seemed eager to try his skill against Renseneb, who was well known in the markets. I felt very pleased with my visit south.

▲ ▲ ▲ ▲

"You were right, Lady," Renseneb reported. "Our rival has moved into Thebes. He has a new agent there. I am working on discovering who it is."

"Let someone else handle that for now. I have word that Lady Tanefret is returning to Memphis soon. Here is what we will do."

▲ ▲ ▲ ▲

I had barely returned to Memphis when word came that Lord Potiphar and Lady Tanefret would arrive and had planned a large dinner party.

Khay and I settled easily into our normal working partnership, and, as usual, I ran into Renseneb in the market during my quest for spices for the wax headdresses for the guests. At any feast, each guest received a cone of spiced wax to wear in their hair. The wax slowly melted, providing a sweetly scented hair oil as the feast continued.

But the spices Lady Tanefret wished to use for this feast were not to be found in Memphis. Renseneb had bought them up during the past two days.

That puzzled me. How could he know of Lady Tanefret's preference before I even got the message that she was planning a party?

After conceding victory to Renseneb and buying from him at a horrendous price, I returned to the estate and plunged into the details of the feast. Khay had most of the routine under control, so when Master Potiphar sent for me, I hurried to the dining room immediately.

"Come in, Joseph, and sit down," Master Potiphar said as soon as he saw me.

I sat across the table from him in my usual spot.

"I just got a report from Hutor," he said. "I don't know what you did, but he is making rapid progress again. At this rate, most of the work will be done in another three years. This is very good news."

"Thank you, master. Superintendent Hutor just needed a bit more help."

Master Potiphar looked at me and smiled. "I think there is much more to the story than that," he teased. "But I will not ask."

Flushing slightly, I looked down. Since making me his Chief Steward, Master Potiphar had treated me with ease and affection. I was a slave and he had no obligation to like me. But he did, and that made my life significantly different from what it could have been. In return, I did my absolute best for him. He wasn't my Abi. No one ever could be. But I loved him for the kindness he showed me, and the patience he had with me as I learned the difficult twists and turns of Egyptian social etiquette and political protocol that my position now demanded I grasp.

"I am very concerned that this party go well," he confided to me. "Many of the guests have not been here before, and they are relations of Lady Tanefret. Her family is from the south, around Abydos and Thebes."

"Mahesa mentioned she is related to the nomarch of Thebes."

"She is related to three southern nomarchs," Lord Potiphar said drily. "In addition, she has relatives holding six high court positions, one of whom is Lord Amony."

My eyes opened wide, but I nodded. I understood now why Potiphar treated her as he did when she caused him trouble. With those connections, he would have to be very circumspect.

"This feast must be perfect. There must be more than enough of everything. The music and dancers must be the best." Potiphar paused. "I don't suppose you could find something unusual for this feast?" he asked wistfully.

"Let me think about it, Master. I will try my best."

"Find anything you can. Spend whatever you need to. This feast must be talked about for the next year at least!"

I left the room sometime later. For the first time, Master Potiphar was nervous and apprehensive about a party. I went to Khay and asked for the guest list. He handed it to me with a wry grin, and as I read it, I looked at him in wonder.

"These are Lady Tanefret's relatives?" I asked.

"Not all of them, just the most important ones."

I looked back at the list. Lord Amony held the highest rank, but all three nomarchs and their wives were coming, as well as 15 other high officials from the court with their wives. With three nomarchs from the south, etiquette must be letter-perfect, and with Lord Amony, we would have to be careful not to cross his numerous superstitions. And Master Potiphar wanted something special for the entertainment!

Outside, I heard the children shriek with joy as Huy arrived from the market.

"That's it!" I exclaimed. "Mahesa!" I yelled, running from Khay's office. "Mahesa!"

"What is it?" the scribe called, from somewhere in the house.

"Mahesa, come at once! I need you."

In moments he materialized by my side. "Mahesa, I need to know everything you can possibly dig up about these people," I instructed. "I want it on my table tomorrow morning. I don't care who you have to see, or what you have to do, but I need to know the foibles and preferences of every person on this list." Then I shoved the guest list into his hands.

"What do you mean?" Mahesa asked, aghast.

"Like Lord Amony's superstitions. What are these people known for? What do the commoners whisper about them? What are their favorite colors? What do they like to eat?"

"But—" he started to protest.

"Just do the best you can. But I need something about every one of them by tomorrow."

As I went back into the house, thinking hard, I almost ran into the dining room, where Master Potiphar still sat, looking over accounts.

"Master?" I said.

He looked up. "Yes, Joseph?"

"Master, can Lady Tanefret delay her return home for one more day?"

"I suppose. She hadn't finalized on the day after tomorrow, and the invitation for the feast was for the day after she arrived."

"I need one more day to prepare."

Potiphar looked at me. "I can tell from your expression that you've thought of something, didn't you?"

"I might have. While I do not know if it will work out, I would like the time to try."

"You have it," Potiphar said. "I will write a message now, and you can send it by the Pharaoh's special messenger to Itej-Tawy."

"Thank you, Master," I exclaimed, then rushed out, forgetting to bow. I heard his chuckle as I went.

Looking up in surprise as I entered his room, Huy jumped to his feet. "What is it, Joseph?"

"Huy, can you do something for Master Potiphar?" I asked.

"Something? Anything," he said eagerly. "Lord Potiphar has never needed me before, but I will do whatever I can."

"Huy, would you provide entertainment at the feast when Lady Tanefret comes home?"

His face fell, and he paled. "Joseph, I—I just don't—"

"This is a very important feast to Master Potiphar," I said gently. "He wishes so much to impress his guests, since many of them are Lady Tanefret's relatives, and they have never been here before. Because of that, he asked me to find something different for entertainment, and I thought of the tricks that you do in the market for the children."

The man looked his amazement.

"They fascinated me. And I think they will other people as well. Here is what I want." I went on to detail just the way I desired him to do his tricks.

When I finished, he drew a deep breath. "If it will be like you said, I think I can. But what about Lord Amony? My eye disturbs him."

"Your eye is much better, and I think if you go to him last, it will be all right."

"If you say it will be all right, I will do it," Huy decided. "Now,

I must practice. Some of the things you want will mean I need to do my tricks another way."

The next morning, Mahesa presented me with a list that he had obviously been up all night compiling.

"This is perfect, Mahesa," I said, glancing at it. "Thank you. Go get some sleep."

Rushing out of the house, I headed for the market. Fortunately, Jetur was back in town. I chuckled with anticipation at what he would say, and what Renseneb would feel if I managed to pull this off without letting him know that I had.

As the guests for the feast started to arrive, I silently prayed for the hundredth time that all would go well. Last night I had hardly slept at all, wondering what would happen if things didn't work out, and I got up this morning a nervous wreck. Out in the fields as the sun rose, I pleaded again that El Shaddai would provide for Master Potiphar.

Now, as the guests arrived, I was in despair. How could I have thought that my idea was so wonderful? It would fail. I knew it would fail. And then Khay hissed at me, and I was too caught up in the rush of arrivals to think anymore.

"Do we have plenty of wine?" Khay asked a little later.

"Three large jugs more than normal, why?"

"Lady Wernero just announced that she intends to get good and drunk today. And she can drink a great deal."

"We have enough," I said with a sigh. The Egyptian attitude toward overindulging in food and drink still puzzled me. Eating and drinking to the point of illness commonly occurred, and a host might consider his feast a failure if no one became ill.

Shaking my head, I looked over the guests. The serving women, who had put beads in their hair and decorated their wrists and ankles with henna, showed them to their places. No one made a mistake. Those who ranked chairs were seated in them, those who rated stools had them, and the rest sat on the floor.

The musicians were playing already, and large bowls of food went past from the kitchens. Minemhet had outdone himself with bread this time. And he had cooked two whole oxen, not just one. Wild fowl, quail, and goose after goose went by. Figs, dates, raisins, cucumbers, lettuce, onions, fresh berries, and honey cakes were equally distributed around the room so that every guest could choose what he or she wanted most. The first jar of wine brought several exclamations of pleasure, and Master Potiphar beamed.

After the guests had satisfied their first hunger, the dancers came out. I tensed up, for after the dancing, Huy would arrive. Behind the scenes, I saw Khay handle one or two hitches in the food service. None of the guests noticed a thing, and Lady Wernero was true to her word, drinking cup after cup of wine with definite purpose. I saw that Khay already had a woman with a basin near by to help the woman when she got sick, so I ignored her thereafter.

Glancing around, I caught a signal from Lady Tanefret and made my way around the edge of the room to her.

"You are looking well, Joseph," she said in a low voice.

"Thank you, Lady Tanefret. Was there something you wanted?"

"Yes," she said, looking at me from lowered eyelids. "I would like something very much, but I don't think you would give it to me."

"I will do whatever I can, Lady," I said, puzzled.

"We shall see. Khay is waiting to see you. You should go."

"Thank you, my lady," I said, returning to Khay.

"What did Lady Tanefret want?" he asked anxiously. "Is everything all right?"

"I don't know. She mentioned she wanted something, but said I wouldn't give it to her. Do you have any idea what she was talking about?"

He stared at me. "Do you?"

"No," I admitted. "As far as I can see, the feast is going along perfectly."

Choking a little, he echoed, "The feast? Yes, the feast seems to be fine. Oh, Aneksi is signaling." Then he disappeared.

I didn't have time to puzzle over Lady Tanefret's comments because I saw Huy enter the room. He certainly didn't look as nervous as I felt.

Huy carried a small table and wore a cloak as he wandered into the room and stopped beside some guests. While the other guests talked and laughed, unaware of his entrance, he knelt by his little table, and in moments the guests gave him their attention. When he left the table, their cries of delight didn't attract much attention in the general noise.

Approaching another table, he set down his own little one again. The guests there soon quieted, watching intently, and the first table of guests whispered and pointed and tried to see. An adjoining table soon went silent as well.

Again Huy left quickly to cries of delight, and drifted over to my side of the room. I watched him set up and start making things appear and disappear. Before he left, he had pulled from the air little gifts for each guest at the table. The gifts were tailored to the individual, each one receiving something different, but appropriate for their likes.

Lord Potiphar noticed something unusual now and looked quite startled to see Huy in the dining room. Frantically he glanced around for me. When he caught my eye, I shook my head no and motioned for him to watch Huy.

After two more tables, Master Potiphar thoroughly enjoyed the sensation that the entertainment caused, growing more and more pleased. I breathed a sigh of relief. Only one more hurdle to go.

Finally Huy walked past me, his face set and slightly pale as he headed for the last table, the one with Lord Amony at it. But he went smoothly into his act. As I watched, I wondered if Mahesa had instructed Huy in southern expectations of etiquette. He performed flawlessly, never crossing the line, yet taking liberties no one else would have dared.

Huy left Lord Amony for last. Bowing to the lord, he then went into an elaborate ritual that clearly indicated that this gift would be something very special. I held my breath as he revealed a miniature scarab beetle amulet carrying the winged sun disk in its horns and made from the White, pure.

As Lord Amony stared in shock, Huy faded away silently. The other guests at the table gasped, then broke out into frenzied clapping and shouting. Everyone demanded to know what Lord Amony got, and he finally stood up and held the amulet for all to see.

"You honor me," he said to Lord Potiphar. "You honor me very much."

Lord Potiphar stood up and raised his cup. "I wish to bring honor to all my guests. Drink now, for there is plenty more!"

The guests clapped and shouted for more food, which streamed from the kitchen in endless bowls. After the last guest left, Master Potiphar sent for me, receiving me at the table in his bedchamber. I had never been in this room before.

"Joseph, you are a miracle worker," he said soberly. "You cannot possibly understand what you have done for me tonight."

"I am glad you were pleased," I said, with relief. "Huy did a masterful job."

"Yes, he did, and I will thank him personally for it. But you thought of it, and you convinced him to do it, and you—" he stopped. "Who is your God?" he demanded suddenly. "Who is this God that you pray to every day, and who listens to you and honors you so much?"

I gulped, not knowing what to say. "His name is El Shaddai," I finally said. "In my language that means the Almighty God who nurtures and provides. I believe He created the world and all in it. He is a loving God, who cares for and loves those who serve Him."

"How do you know these things?"

"Because El Shaddai has spoken to my fathers. He declared Himself to them and promised to be their God if they would be His people."

"How did He speak? In a dream?" Potiphar asked curiously.

"To my father, yes, in a dream. To my grandfather Isaac, He spoke in an audible voice in the daytime to save my grandfather from death. To my great-grandfather, He came in human form and shared a meal, and then warned my great-grandfather that He would destroy a wicked city. And my great-grandfather pleaded with Him to save the righteous people of the city, and El Shaddai listened, and saved them while He destroyed the rest."

"Tell me of this," Potiphar continued.

And there I sat, in my master's bedchamber, and talked until dawn, telling the old stories that I had heard as a child. And my master listened with bated breath as I told of the history of my family. Of Lot and Sodom and Gomorrah, of the birth of Isaac and the sacrifice and the ram. Of my father and the brook Jabbok and reconciliation with my uncle. And there I stopped.

"And what of you, Joseph?" Potiphar asked. "You are a slave. What of you?"

"I do not know," I said. "But I know that El Shaddai wishes me to be here." Hesitantly, I told of seeing his wheatfield in my dream, how everything was the same even to the positions of the reapers and the sheaves.

Master Potiphar stayed silent for a long time. "I think you are right, Joseph," he said at last. "Your God wants you here. And because you are, He honors me. How can I thank this God? Where is His temple?"

"He does not need one," I said. "El Shaddai is wherever you need Him to be. Even in your bedchamber. Just speak His name, and He is there."

"Thank you, Joseph," Potiphar said finally. "I will think deeply about what you have said. You may go now."

I bowed myself out of the room.

CHAPTER 11

The afternoon after the feast, Lady Tanefret sent for me. I found her in the dining room.

"Yes, Lady?"

"There you are. I wanted you to go over some accounts from the estate in Thebes," she said, indicating the table that had some scrolls on it.

"Yes, Lady," I said, examining them. "What is puzzling you?"

"I'm not certain Iteti has these numbers straight," she said with a sidelong glance. "Would you check them?"

"I would be happy to, my lady."

While I checked Iteti's addition, Lady Tanefret hung over my shoulder, almost touching me. It made me uncomfortable, but I tried to ignore it.

"The records are quite correct. Your estate is doing very well."

"Because of the suggestions you made," she said with a smile. "Yes, Iteti told me about them, and I am glad that he followed them."

"I am pleased to have helped you, Lady. Is there anything else?"

"Not today, Joseph," she said, touching my arm. "But maybe tomorrow."

Lady Tanefret sent for me often in the next few days about little things, and I couldn't understand their importance.

I took my puzzlement to Khay one afternoon. "Can you help?" I asked him. "I have to get the records ready for tax time, and Lady Tanefret is constantly asking for me to see to something or other. You could easily handle it."

"No, I couldn't," he replied. "Only you will do."

"But why?" I burst out in frustration. "I don't understand."

Khay regarded me sardonically for some time. Then he sighed. "You really don't, do you?"

I shook my head in bewilderment.

"Come along. I guess you are the only one in Memphis who doesn't know."

"Know what?"

"Know that you are the best-looking man in the whole of Kemet," Khay said matter-of-factly.

I laughed. "You are crazy," I said, when I could talk. "I know what I look like. My face never did fit together. Judah, now, or Uncle Esau, they are good-looking. I am the ugly one of the family."

"You *were*," he said, leading the way outside. "You are not anymore."

He led me to a pond, completely still in the afternoon's heat. "Take a look."

"Khay," I said, "I know what I will see."

"Look in the water," he commanded.

Reluctantly, I did. I had not paid any attention to my face for years, other than to concentrate on my beard when I shaved. Now, I looked at my face, not my chin.

I could not say a word. Slowly, I took off the wig that I wore all the time now, and gazed at my reflection in the glassy water. My face wasn't anything like I remembered it. No longer were the features mismatched and clashing. Somehow they had grown together into a face that combined the incredible beauty of my mother, which I well remembered, with the rugged masculine lines that had attracted women to my Uncle Esau.

I was horrified.

"Khay, what am I going to do?" I groaned. "This is terrible!"

"Terrible?" he echoed in amazement. "You have a face like Ra himself, and you call it terrible? You are the crazy one. Haven't you noticed every woman on the estate falling all over you?"

I blushed furiously. "Well, I did observe that they always seemed happy to do what I asked," I said lamely.

"Seemed happy?" Khay howled with laughter. "They have been holding contests to see who could get the most attention from you. Each of them has plotted and planned and schemed to find a way to get a kiss from those 'divine lips' of yours, and you have been oblivious all this time? If they find that out, they will be furious, every one of them. Even though they have done everything but steal you away in the night, you still haven't noticed!"

"Khay, please," I pleaded. "This is a disaster. What am I going to do?"

"Enjoy it. What I wouldn't give to be in your place! Why not have some fun? You want a wife, don't you?"

"Well, yes, but I am a slave, Khay. What woman would want to marry me under those circumstances?"

"Any of them who have seen you," he chuckled. "You don't know how gloomy the women around this place become when you are gone. One would think that Ra had refused to bring light."

"But now it is Lady Tanefret who has noticed me," I said soberly.

Khay instantly reflected my own mood. "Yes, that is a problem. I would tell you to just be discreet, but I don't think that would suit you."

"It would not. Lady Tanefret belongs to Master Potiphar. It would be wrong of me to steal her."

"She is perfectly willing," Khay said, eyeing me.

"What difference does that make? It would still be wrong."

"What do you mean wrong?"

"It would be a sin against God," I said in surprise.

"What do the gods have to do with it? They don't care. All you have to do to keep them happy is give sufficient offerings to the temples, and honor them during festivals, and stuff like that. Your life is your own."

"No, it is not. It is Master Potiphar's," I reminded him acerbically.

"You know what I mean. The rightness or wrongness can easily be fixed. If Lady Tanefret wants to marry you, she can have you freed, then divorce Potiphar and live with you. She will be happier than she is now, which is all to the good. With her connections at court, there won't be any problem from Pharaoh."

"What does Pharaoh have do to with it?"

"Everything," Khay said in surprise. "The whole thing could be arranged with a minimum of fuss, and so long as nothing upsets things in court, Pharaoh will say it is right. Then it is."

"Do you mean that Pharaoh decides right or wrong?" I asked incredulously.

"Of course. Right is what Pharaoh loves, and wrong is what Pharaoh hates. If Lady Tanefret divorces Potiphar before marrying you, what should be the problem?"

"But I would have stolen my master's wife!"

Khay shook his head. "She left him. Then she is free to do whatever brings her the most pleasure. That is what life is about. Enjoy yourself and don't get hurt. You have to be reasonable about it, of course. Do your job and respect those who deserve respect. Once you marry, it is better to stay with your wife if you have children. Just be well-mannered, and pleasant to everyone and do the best you can for yourself when the opportunity arises. What else is there?"

"What about Master Potiphar? He will get hurt. Khay, he loves her."

Khay shrugged. "If Pharaoh says it is all right, what can he do? But he will find another wife, and live just as happily with her, if not more happily. Lady Tanefret is always threatening to run out on him."

I had to sit down. "Aren't there any set laws of right and wrong that always apply?"

"Why should there be?" he replied, puzzled.

"Because in my country, and for my God, there are. El Shaddai tells me to respect Him above all else, and to respect others as I wish to be respected. That means it is always wrong to kill, to lie, to steal, to take another man's wife."

"That is a very hard way to live," he said, sitting down beside me.

"Not really. It means being content with what you have, and leaving the things that belong to others alone. And you do that all the time, not just when it suits you. What about your family, Khay? Didn't someone steal from them?"

His face hardened as it always did when he remembered his past. "Yes," he said shortly.

"How much better would it have been if the people who stole from you had respected your family and left them alone? If they had been content with what they had, no pain would have come to your family."

"I see your point," he said after a short silence.

"It seems to me that the best way to have a pleasant life and avoid trouble and pain is to follow the way El Shaddai has marked," I said quietly. "Even Egypt believes that life is best when you obey maat."

Khay shrugged. "Come on. It is time to eat."

I may have been right in my conversation with Khay, but clinging to my decision to stay away from Lady Tanefret had certainly made my life hard.

It had not been too bad, at first. I carefully avoided Lady Tanefret as much as possible. Since she lived in the capital most of the time, I found it quite easy to begin with. In addition, I took frequent trips up and down the Nile to handle responsibilities for Master Potiphar. I could, and did, stay out of her way for months at a time.

But the past few months had been one long nightmare, for Lady Tanefret came to the Memphis estate to stay. Lord Potiphar had been relieved with her decision. She had been especially troublesome, and he hadn't had the time to deal with it, since the old Pharaoh had taken ill.

Knowing how much Master Potiphar needed to be at the capital, I determined to handle the problem myself. I immediately set out on a trip to Abydos, but she soon followed, arriving in Thebes, saying she had to check on Iteti's work. Mahesa got a message to me in time to leave Abydos before she arrived to inspect the tomb. The progress on the tomb was the only good thing so far. In spite of all the trouble, Master Potiphar's tomb had been finished just a couple weeks ago. I knew he would be very happy.

After my trip to Abydos, Khay got caught in the middle. As Master Potiphar's wife, Lady Tanefret was responsible for the house. When she had lived at Itej-Tawy it was not a problem. But now that she had established herself here, Khay didn't know whom to obey. Me, as Master Potiphar's Great Chief Steward, or Lady Tanefret as Mistress of the House.

When it first became a problem, I tried to have a meeting with Lady Tanefret every morning and work out between us the details of what should be done that day. Before long I realized that I must have a third party in the room at all times, and as soon as I did that, Lady Tanefret lost interest in the meetings. She would agree to anything I suggested, but would later contradict my orders and substitute her own.

Finally Khay sent a message to Lord Potiphar, asking outright whom he should answer to. It was the first Potiphar knew of any trouble. He made some decisions and wrote to Lady Tanefret, Khay, and me. Lady Tanefret read her letter and exploded with fury. Khay read his and sighed with relief. And I read mine and winced.

Master Potiphar wrote that Lady Tanefret was in charge of her business and small house in Memphis. If she chose to live at his proprietary estate instead of her own house, she could order meals and direct her personal maids. Absolutely everything else was mine, even management of her estate in Thebes. Then he made it clear that he saw no reason why he should be bothered with any further details.

Lady Tanefret refused to speak to me for a month, much to my relief. Then she caught me alone in a storeroom one day.

"Joseph," she said, looking into the room, "I have been hunting for you."

"I have been quite busy," I replied, "and can be hard to find."

"Especially for me," she said, studying me up and down.

"I am sorry, Lady."

"No, you are not," she said, pouting. "You do your best to avoid me."

"I must serve Master Potiphar as best I can," I said, edging toward the door. "I try to keep myself from distractions."

Her face lit up with a smile. "So I distract you? Good. I want to distract you. I want to say I am sorry for being angry at you. It is not your fault my husband is so tiresome."

"I do need to go, Lady," I said, moving closer to the door. "I—"

"I have not finished talking to you. You must stay and listen."

"Yes, Lady Tanefret," I said, looking down.

"I feel badly that I was angry with you," she went on. "I want to make it up to you. Why don't you come with me, and we can discuss what I can do."

"Come with you where, Lady Tanefret?" I asked warily.

"To my bedchamber. I am sure we can come up with some way I can apologize."

Well, there it was, the invitation I had avoided so long. I swallowed. She was a very good-looking woman, and no one would mind, but—she was Master Potiphar's wife, and I would not betray him as Reuben had done Abi.

"Lady Tanefret," I began in a steady voice. "Lord Potiphar is your husband and my master. He trusts me so much that he doesn't even know what he owns anymore except the food put in front of him. My master made me equal to him in authority and treats me like a son, not a slave. He trusts me with everything except you, because you are his wife.

"It would be evil for me to betray that trust. How can I do such great wickedness against him, and give such offense to the gods as well?"

She laughed. "The gods? What do the gods care? Give them some offerings, bow to them on festival day, and they will not care what else you do. As for Potiphar, leave him to me. I will divorce him, and that will be the end of it. It has been done before, you know."

As I looked at her I remembered the story of Lady Kawit and the freed slave, Senamun, whom she married.

"It would be so easy, Joseph. Think of it. You would be free, and I am rich in my own right. With you in charge of my business, we would soon be very wealthy. You would have a steward instead of being one."

I looked down. Free. And rich. And able to do a lot of good. What about my dreams? I could become great and rule. With Lady Tanefret's connections, a nomarchy was not impossible. But—

"I—I must go, Lady," I said, ducking out the door.

But it hadn't ended there. Every time I saw her, she reminded me with her eyes of her wishes. If we chanced to be alone, she brought it up again. And I told her—again and again I told her—that I could not betray my master in such a fashion, that I could not offend her gods that way. But she would not listen. Finally, I told her I would not offend *my* God that way. She just laughed.

But at night, I lay on the mat and fought with myself. She was a very desirable woman and wanted to marry me. Divorce provided a perfectly acceptable way for us to marry. I would be free and on my way to greatness. Besides, couldn't this be El Shaddai's way of leading me?

I grew more and more tired, and Lady Tanefret smiled more and more often, sure that I would give in at last, certain that her allure would wear away my loyalty to Master Potiphar. The other house staff smirked at me and pretended to notice nothing. Only Khay watched gravely, wondering what I would choose.

One night, I heard someone in the garden in back of the house, and I went to the gate of the garden to see who it was. Lady Tanefret sat beside the pool there. I drew back into the shadow of the house, my heart pounding. All I had to do was walk out there. She would be glad to see me—very glad—and I could be my own man again. It would be so simple. Potiphar would soon find another wife, as

Khay said. My hands turned sweaty, and I took a shaky breath. I—I wanted to walk out there. I wanted to be free and rich and able to do good with the money and time. And that beautiful, desirable woman out there would be mine. My slavery would be over. And, really, what would the gods care?

The gods? What was I thinking? I didn't serve the Egyptian gods! I served El Shaddai! Long ago I had given myself to Him, vowed to follow His leading and do only what He commanded. No matter what I tried to tell myself, I should not steal my master's wife, even if she did want me to. It would be a betrayal of Master Potiphar's trust, and I had promised to serve him as best I could. Silently I went back to my bed, resolved to follow El Shaddai in everything.

But I would have to leave. I had the perfect opportunity to do so, for Master Potiphar wanted some quality turquoise. The next day I scheduled a trip to the mines west of the Red Sea, the one place I *knew* Lady Tanefret would not go.

"You are looking solemn today," Khay greeted me the morning after I returned.

"I feel solemn," I said. "Being at the mines reminded me of how easily I could have ended up there instead of here. It is a sobering thought."

"I can see how it would be. Did you get the turquoise?"

I nodded. "Some very fine rough stone. It is at the jewelers for polishing. They were quite surprised at the quality. Usually stone of that grade only comes from the mines in the Sinai."

"I am eager to see it. Are you ready now to go over the reports?"

"Yes," I said, feeling a strange sense of urgency. "I want to see how well my assistant has done!"

Khay smiled. Once Master Potiphar had delineated lines of responsibility, I began intensively training him to take my place. He was easily capable of doing it, and I felt compelled to provide my master with another steward should anything happen to me.

"When does harvesting begin?" I asked, walking into his office.

"This morning," he grinned. "And it is the best harvest yet."

With that, we plunged into the details of another tax season.

Early the next morning, I watched the dawn in the same field I came to each year. I knelt, touching the sheaves as I did every year, and feeling the thankfulness flow out of my heart.

"El Shaddai," I said, "You have provided so much for me. I could have been working in a mine, or laboring in the fields for a temple, or still herding kine on the Delta. But instead you have granted me honor before my master and given me work that I love. I have learned, and You have rewarded me.

"It has been 10 years since my brothers sold me," I continued, pausing to steady my trembling lips. "And I have become a man. There is trouble ahead with my mistress. I ask You, El Shaddai, to provide a way of escape.

"Honor Master Potiphar as he is by the side of the new Pharaoh, Amenemhet III, who has just come to the throne because of his father's death. It has been a trying time for my master, and I ask that you will deal kindly with him.

"Thank you, El Shaddai, for listening to my prayer."

I left the field feeling settled and secure. But instead of returning to the house, I headed straight for the marketplace in Memphis.

Afterward, pleased with the victory I had scored against Renseneb over a matter of wood from Byblos, I did not at first notice the silence of the house. But when I did, I stopped and listened for a moment, then started down the passage toward the women's rooms, looking for someone, anyone.

As I glanced into the small halls, I heard a sound behind me and swung around.

Lady Tanefret stood in the hall, smiling, blocking my way. "So Joseph, you come to seek me after all," she said, approaching closer.

I swallowed. "I was looking for anyone in the house. It is so quiet in here."

"It is very quiet, because no one is here but you and I. I will have you listen to me, Joseph. You will not avoid me, or run away from me, or any of the other silly things you have done."

I felt my heart begin to pound. This was real trouble. "Lady Tanefret," I said formally, "I am willing to help you any way I can. If you will allow me to get my tablet and a pen, I can attend you better."

She laughed. "You cannot do anything I want with a tablet and a pen, and you know that already. I want you, Joseph. I want you as I have never wanted anything in my life. What would be so bad about living with me? Don't you think I am desirable?"

Again I swallowed and stared straight in front of me. I could feel the sweat run down my back. The dress she wore was of court-grade linen and very sheer. And suddenly I did want her. Very much. So much that I started to shake.

But she was my master's wife. I must hold onto that thought. She was Master Potiphar's wife. Not mine. I had already decided this issue.

As she moved closer she watched my face, knowing how I struggled.

"I could be yours," she said softly. "I could be yours anytime you wanted. Don't worry about Lord Potiphar. He never deserved me, or he never would have insulted me as he did."

A warning sounded in my mind, but I couldn't hang onto the thought.

"He will soon be content with another woman after I divorce him," Lady Tanefret went on. "I will get you freed, Joseph. I can do it, as you well know. You will be free, your own man, and my husband. Together we can go back south and have children and live on my estate in Thebes. You can manage it and soon will have enough to buy land and a house of your own."

I clenched my teeth and my hands. The way her eyes wandered over me made my whole body burn. I'd never known that a man could feel this way.

"You will be rich and free and have me all at the same time, Joseph. What is so wrong with that?" She looked beautiful and alluring, and offered me everything I had ever dreamed of having.

Then I closed my eyes, and in my mind I saw my father's face when he found Reuben with Mother's maid, Bilhah.

The pain, the betrayal, the loss poured into my memory. If I were to take this woman, I would bring that kind of sorrow and betrayal to Master Potiphar. I would not do it. I would not bring to my master, whom I loved, the same shame and betrayal and humiliation that had so wounded my beloved Abi.

"No, Lady Tanefret."

At first she didn't believe what she heard. "You cannot mean to say no." Her voice rose as I simply shook my head. "You must, Joseph," she said, walking toward me. "I want children. I want Potiphar to realize— I will not take no for an answer," she ended fiercely and threw herself on me, wrapping her arms around my neck, trying to kiss me.

"You want me. I know you want me."

Although I reached up and tried to loosen her arms, she clung to me. Finally I forced her to let go and pushed her away from me. "No, Lady Tanefret," I repeated.

"You will," she insisted. I slipped by her and started away. She came after me, and I ran, but she moved quicker than I expected and caught hold of my kilt. I wrenched away from her grasp and fled, leaving the kilt in her hand.

My first thought was to get away, and my second to get to my room and put on some clothes. Thankfully the house was deserted and I hurriedly dressed, but as I did, Lady Tanefret suddenly screamed and cried for help.

Automatically, I started to go to her, then stopped uncertainly. What should I do? I heard hurried footsteps in the passages from the courtyard, so I stayed put, worried about what was happening. Memories of the first time my clothes had been ripped off me by my brothers flooded my mind. Cold, leaden dread sank into my stomach. What would happen to me this time?

Lady Tanefret's screams gradually subsided, and the staff moved about the house. Huy glanced into my room and saw me, then backed away hurriedly and ran. In moments, Khay came rushing to my room.

"Joseph, what has happened?" he panted. "Lady Tanefret says you tried to rape her!"

I felt all the blood drain from my face. "She says what?" I choked.

"She says you tried to rape her. She has your kilt to prove it and great bruises forming on her arms. What happened?"

My knees gave way, and I landed on the floor. This was worse than I imagined.

"Joseph, you didn't, did you?" he asked in an anxious voice.

"No," I blurted out instinctively, then hastily shut my mouth.

"She says you ran from her when she started screaming, and that is how she got your clothes."

"What else does she say?" I asked in a tight voice, knowing I had to hear it all.

Khay looked at me for some time, then entered the room. "She says you came to her and mocked her because Lord Potiphar cannot give her children. She says you tried to force yourself on her, and when she screamed, you ran, and she grabbed your clothes."

Covering my face, I started to shake.

"But it was the other way around, right?" he asked. "She tried to force herself on you, and you ran from her, and now she is having her revenge. What are you going to do?"

"What can I do, Khay?" I groaned. "If I deny the charge, Master Potiphar will believe me, you know that. That will put him in an impossible position. He cannot brand his wife a liar, bringing public shame and condemnation down on her. Her relatives would never forgive him for that.

"They would break him, Khay. They would see to it that he loses everything, and then where will you and the others be? You know this estate is a proprietary one. If Lord Potiphar loses his position, he loses this estate with it. With all the political maneuvering in the palace since the old Pharaoh died, Lord Amony would jump at gaining control of the office of Captain of the Guard. How do you think supporters of Lady Tanefret would treat everyone here?"

He blanched at the thought.

"If I say one word," I continued, "I will ruin Lord Potiphar's life and bring about the destruction of this entire estate. I cannot do that, Khay. I don't dare say a single word that will force Master Potiphar to choose between his wife's story and mine."

He stood silently for a few minutes and then sat down. "I see what you mean. But what will happen to you?"

"I am a slave, Khay," I reminded him softly. "He can do anything at all."

"At least he cannot kill you."

"He cannot legally have another *Egyptian* killed. What about me, Khay? Would anybody protest if I died from a beating? Or just disappeared? Who would ask questions? Master Potiphar is a high noble with an important position in the palace."

"It is not fair," Khay said savagely. "Why should you be punished because you stayed faithful to your master? Surely there is something you can do! Or something I can do—or something!"

"There is nothing, Khay, and we both know it," I said, having regained some control over myself. "I will bet Lady Tanefret has already sent someone to fetch Master Potiphar from the capital."

Khay nodded miserably. "The very first thing."

"How long do we have?"

"About three days," he whispered.

"That is time enough," I said. "If we start work this afternoon, we can have the entire review of the estate finished by the time he arrives. That will give you a good start on my job."

For a second he started to interrupt me, then shut his mouth. "Yes, Joseph."

I saw no one but Khay. He brought all the records to my room, and we worked there.

The estate was strangely silent. Khay reported that everyone worked, but no one talked. Minemhet turned out some of the worst meals he ever cooked, but no one complained. Lady Tanefret looked a little scared when she was alone, Khay said, and she stayed mostly in her room.

I just nodded grimly and plowed on, grilling Khay relentlessly on the business of the estate, making certain that he thoroughly understood every detail. Then I outlined a course of action for him to follow for the next five years.

I had considered this previously, and since I could hardly sleep at night, I had plenty of time now to work out the details. Although I had to modify it a little, allowing for my absence, all in all it worked out well.

Those three days were the swiftest and the slowest I ever lived through. Just after noon on the third day, Master Potiphar arrived.

CHAPTER 12

He is here," Khay said as he breathlessly entered my room. "El Shaddai, please provide for me," I whispered. "I have done nothing, but my master will not know that."

"I won't let it happen," Khay said, his lips tight. "I will tell him myself. I—"

"Khay!" I said sharply.

He looked at me.

"You will be silent," I said sternly.

"Joseph, he may kill you," Khay said wildly. "He might—"

"That does not matter," I interrupted. "You will not say a word. We will leave this in El Shaddai's hands."

"Joseph—I, I cannot," he said, tears streaming down his face. "I lost everyone. I had no one until you came, and you took me under your wing and you taught me everything. You made me what I am today, with an honorable job, able to support a wife and family, and now, now—"

"It is in El Shaddai's hands," I said again. "Khay, the only thing you will do if you speak is lose what you have worked so hard to gain. You cannot help me. I must know that you will be here to take over for Master Potiphar. His tomb is finished. You can easily handle the rest. Promise me you will do this."

Unable to speak, Khay stared at me. Then he did the strangest thing—he knelt. "That which you command is that which will be done," he whispered, his lips pale.

I left him there and walked down the hall. My life lay in El Shaddai's hands. I was in dire danger, but no more so than Grandfather Isaac on the altar, or Abi meeting Uncle Esau. El Shaddai was able to provide. I had given myself fully to Him, and He would decide my fate. I had done the best I could for my master, had been as faithful as I knew how. Now it was up to El Shaddai.

Just hearing Master Potiphar's voice told me he was tired and upset. I swallowed and walked into the dining room. He looked more exhausted than I had ever seen him, his face lined with the strain of the old Pharaoh's illness and death. I sensed his impatience, his resentment at having to make this trip when he was so needed at the capital.

Lady Tanefret rushed in. "Oh, my lord, I am so glad you have come," she gasped, throwing herself into his arms.

"What is it? What has happened?" Lord Potiphar said, as she clung to him, practically sobbing. She caught sight of me and gasped again, shrinking away, but I noticed the worried expression in her eyes. It vanished when she looked at Potiphar.

"It was terrible," she said. "I have never been so frightened in my life."

"Frightened?" Lord Potiphar said. "Tanefret, what has happened?" He took her arms to disentangle her from him and she winced. Potiphar looked down and noticed the bruises fitting neatly under his hands.

"Tanefret!" he exclaimed. "What happened? Tell me at once."

She started to cry. "It was that Habiru you brought into this house," she said. "Three days ago he—he found me in the women's rooms, and—and he came to me." She stopped, casting a quick glance at her husband.

"Go on," Potiphar said. "What happened?"

"Oh, Potiphar, he mocked at me because you have given me no children. He said he could give me children, and then—and then, he tried to rape me!"

I stood frozen in place. If I had not known what had really happened, I would have believed her myself. I swallowed. Could things get any worse?

"Joseph? Joseph tried to force you?" Lord Potiphar asked incredulously

"He did. He did," Lady Tanefret said hysterically. "Look at my arms, where he grabbed me. See the bruises? And I screamed. I screamed and screamed, and he got frightened and ran. But I knew, I knew I would have to convince you, so I grabbed at him and—and caught his kilt.

"But he pulled away, and left the kilt right there in my hands. And here it is," she sobbed, holding it out to him. "He said terrible things about us. He would have forced me. I was so frightened!" She broke out into fresh sobs, and Potiphar slowly took the kilt from her hands.

He stared at it for the longest time, and then at me. I said nothing, as I had planned. Tired, worn out with the worry of his job, and totally unprepared for something like this, his rage simply exploded.

"How dare you!" he shouted, striding toward me. "You cur, you son of urine, you thought to force your mistress? You thought to have my wife? After all that I have done for you?" The next thing I knew I lay on the floor, with my head ringing.

"How dare you? How dare you attack my wife!"

I shook just from the sound of his voice. I had only heard that ice in it once before, when Sekhmet had been caught stealing the calves. The sound of it twisted me up inside, reminding me of Simeon's voice when he cursed me. I saw the pit yawning under me all over again.

Potiphar reached down and grabbed my hair, pulling me to my knees, forcing me to look into his face. Mirrored in his eyes was that same bewildered hurt that had so tortured my beloved Abi. I could not stand to look at it. He hurt just as Abi had. I would take anything if it would ease that torment.

"You would force yourself on your mistress," he said, still in that icy tone. "I gave you everything, and you repay me like this?" Suddenly he heaved me up and threw me to the floor. "How could you?" he cried, his voice carrying the anguished rage burning in his soul at my seeming betrayal.

Grabbing me again, he jerked me to my knees, his knife against my throat. I could feel the blood pulsing in my vein against the edge of the knife. "I should cut you into pieces and throw your live flesh to the crocodiles," he raged. "Mock her about children, would you? Leave great bruises on her? You crawling barbarian wretch! How could I have ever trusted you?" His face was set and hard. He had made his decision. I would die. Here. Now.

I heard a choking sob. The house staff crowded around the doors, wide-eyed and scared. But Master Potiphar didn't notice them. He looked at Lady Tanefret. She had stopped sobbing, and watched with a slightly smug look in her eye. It quickly vanished, to be replaced by fear.

Lord Potiphar caught sight of the others. "Get out," he shouted. "All of you, get out of this house!" They ran from the room. Potiphar manhandled me to my feet, then threw me down on the low table, still keeping his knife at my throat. "Leave us, Tanefret," he said in a thick voice.

His wife hesitated, worry fleeting across her features.

"Leave us!" Master Potiphar raged at her.

She hurried away, for all the world like a scuttling rat.

"El Shaddai, give me strength to keep my silence," I prayed silently. I didn't know what to do with my hands as I waited for the final slash, finally clenching them at my sides. I wished I could stop trembling. Briefly I wondered if Grandfather Isaac had trembled as his father stood over him with a knife.

"How dare you interrupt me!" Potiphar shouted.

Surprised that I had them closed, I opened my eyes, heard a gasp, and then tablets and papyrus leaves spilled all over the table next to me. Footsteps hurried away, and I wondered why on earth Khay had come in.

Potiphar's grip on me tightened, and I hoped he would get this over with. His rage might at least give me a quick, clean death. If he had time to debate, he might really feed me alive to the crocodiles, and I was afraid.

But Potiphar didn't move. His hand holding my hair started to shake. Again I fought with myself. I could still speak. I knew that he did not want me to die. He dropped me, picking up one of the tablets. I dared to roll over onto my face and froze, waiting for whatever would come next, begging El Shaddai for strength again and again in my mind. I still couldn't stop trembling.

"What is this?" he demanded, hauling my arm backward until I was on my knees again. He thrust a tablet in my face.

"It is part of this year's tax records, Master," I said, only able to manage a whisper.

"And this?"

"The same, Master."

"When did this get done?" Potiphar snapped.

"Khay finished it just this noon," I replied, keeping my head bowed and still trembling.

"Did Khay also finish this?" Master Potiphar asked sarcastically, shoving the papyrus leaves into my hands.

I glanced at them, then carefully set them down since I could not hold them steady.

"Don't bother to deny it, Joseph," he added. "I would know your hand anywhere. I will be a very rich man if Khay follows what you have outlined here."

The knife tip dug into my chin, forcing me to look up. "Look at me, Joseph," Master Potiphar commanded. "I will have an answer, and I want to see those Horus eyes of yours while you speak. Did you attack Lady Tanefret?"

Frantically, I sought for an answer. Above all, I could not put him in a position where he must choose between my story and Lady Tanefret's. The knife dug deeper into my skin, starting a trickle of blood. I could smell the blade, so close to my face.

"I have served you as faithfully as I know how, Master," I said slowly. "And I will continue to do so until—" I had to stop and take a breath "—until I die." I wished my voice was steadier.

Potiphar searched my face for some time, then removed his knife and turned his back. "And that is all you have to say?" he asked in a strange tone.

"Y-Yes, Master."

"You would have let me kill you, would you not?"

I didn't reply.

"Answer me, Joseph!" he commanded, his voice grim.

"I am your slave, Master."

"So you are. Those bruises," he muttered to himself, "right under my hands as I moved her away. And she hates Memphis." He remained silent for a long time.

"Khay," he shouted suddenly. I jumped, and the man appeared so fast I knew he had been waiting outside the door.

"Yes, Lord Potiphar?"

"Bring the two Nubians waiting outside in here."

"Yes, Lord Potiphar." After a worried glance at me, he disappeared.

"Even your successor worries about you," Potiphar remarked. "Put your face between your knees," he snapped.

I obeyed instantly and heard the Nubians enter the room.

"Take this man to the House of the Prison in Memphis," Lord Potiphar said coldly. "He is to remain there until I decide what will be done with him."

"Yes, Lord Potiphar," a strange voice answered. "What is the charge, Lord Potiphar?"

"He thought to attack my wife," Potiphar replied, sounding as if he discussed a particularly unpleasant type of insect. "Treat him accordingly."

"Yes, Lord Potiphar," the voice said, and then I gasped as someone twisted my arms behind my back, then tightly tied them at the elbows, pulling my shoulders back and toward each other in a very unnatural manner.

"Oh, that is quite enough," Potiphar said impatiently. "Get him out of here."

"Yes, Lord Potiphar," the same man replied.

Once again, I found myself begging El Shaddai for strength as the Nubians dragged me away.

▲ ▲ ▲ ▲

At least the tears waited until the darkness before spilling out of my eyes. I didn't want to move. Every square inch of me ached. One eye was swollen shut, and I had bruises all over me, with a few cuts as I lay on the cold stone of the prison cell, my wrists and neck bound to the wall. I kept my teeth clenched so I would not scream from the pain in my ankles. The ankle bonds were so tight my feet were swelling.

And this might be only the beginning. Once again I fought that raw fear, the same fear that had invaded my mind while I lay in the cistern in Canaan. Only this time, I was 10 years older. Ten years wiser about the possibilities that might lie ahead. I shivered uncontrollably. What if I was sent to the mines somewhere?

The thought of what I had seen at the turquoise mine made me sick, and I knew that the gold mines far to the south in the Nubian desert were 10 times worse. Egypt did not kill the most dangerous criminals—it just sent them to those mines.

What would happen to me? As Captain of the Guard, Master Potiphar was powerful enough that anything he wanted done to me would happen—very quietly. I could suffer beatings, dismemberment, any kind of horrible death at his whim. Even though sobs shook me without restraint, that total terror could not overwhelm me. I was not alone, and that held back the final blackness.

I clung to the thought. Deliberately, I remembered the stories that Abi and Grandfather had told me. So much had happened in the past 10 years that I had forgotten much, so I had to dig deep for them. I whispered the stories to myself, the act of telling them bringing more and more details to my mind.

Gradually my fear subsided, and my pounding heart eased. They would not kill me immediately. Time might be on my side, for as Master Potiphar's temper cooled, he might think of some way to soothe Lady Tanefret and not damage me too badly. He might just send me away.

That thought brought the mines to mind again and with it the fear. I fought it down, clinging to the family stories I remembered all during that long, long night.

That night presaged many more to follow. At first I suffered so much pain that I could barely eat the food brought to me. I could only tell night from day because in the daytime the blackness around me turned a bit gray.

My feet were red and swollen, and then they were blue and swollen, and finally they were black and swollen. The guard who brought my food took a good look at them on the fourth day when he touched them, and I screamed. He brought the keeper of the prison, and the keeper ordered the bonds on my legs removed.

As the guard worked over the bonds, I strained against those on my wrists until I thought I would pull them from the wall. I managed not to scream, but I was exhausted and drenched in sweat when the ordeal was over.

The guard later returned with some beer, which I gratefully drank. He left without saying a word, but I took comfort from his gesture of kindness. Then the coldness returned.

▲ ▲ ▲ ▲

"He is in prison, Lady," Renseneb reported. "Soon after he bested us on the wood from Byblos, he was taken to prison."

"Where?" she asked in amazement

"They took him to the Pharaoh's prison in Memphis."

"But why?" she demanded, bewildered.

"He tried to rape his master's wife," he replied. Her reaction caught him completely by surprise.

She cried out, then wrapped her arms around her midsection and bent over, her face dead white.

"Lady?" he asked, approaching her.

"Don't touch me," she almost shouted, jerking away.

Renseneb stepped back and waited.

It took her a long while to calm herself. "You said he was handsome?"

Puzzled, Renseneb nodded. "Yes, he is the best-looking man I have ever seen."

"And a barbarian," she added softly, looking sick. "Leave me, Renseneb."

He went quietly away.

▲ ▲ ▲ ▲

The endless succession of grayness and blackness continued. I got used to the silence, the darkness, the bonds on my arms, the rigid collar across my throat, and my nakedness against the cold stone. I hardly noticed the coldness seep deep inside and slowly creep up my legs from my feet. It came down my arms, taking over my body and bringing a strange numbness in my mind that dragged at me. I repeated El Shaddai's name endlessly. Otherwise I would sink into the cold, yawning pit that waited just at the edges of my sight, and I knew that I could never be pulled up from that one. But it got harder and harder to keep myself above the abyss waiting to swallow me. As the coldness insinuated itself into more and more of my body, I slipped closer and closer to the blackness waiting to suck me into it. Although I tried to pull myself back from the edge, inexorably I slid further and further down into the abyss waiting below.

Then the door to my cell opened unexpectedly and I squinted in the torchlight.

"By the gods, what have you done to him?" Khay's voice roared in the confines of the cell.

I gasped, the noise hurting my ears.

"Get the Keeper, and get him now!" my friend added savagely. The guard scurried away.

"Joseph? Joseph, can you hear me?" he asked urgently as soon as the guard had gone.

It took me a while to figure out how to answer him. "Yes," I whispered hoarsely. I could hardly make my mind work through the coldness inside of me.

"What have they done to you?" he demanded in a hard voice. "Don't you get anything to eat?"

Again I had to struggle for words. "Maybe. Generally not hungry."

"Generally not hungry?" Khay echoed incredulously. "Oh Joseph, Joseph, only you would come up with a comment like that!" he moaned. "You looked dead when I first saw you. I have never been so frightened in my life."

"Not yet," I said, trying to sit up to reassure him. But somehow I couldn't move very well.

"I am not so sure about that," Khay replied grimly. "You may be alive, but I think your Ka has died."

The Keeper arrived with another torch.

"Get this man out of these bonds," Khay commanded.

"But—but Steward," the Keeper protested, "Lord Potiphar, the Captain of the Guard himself, ordered him put in them. How can I take him out? I cannot possibly remove them without his permission."

Khay swung around to stare at the Keeper. "Lord Potiphar is at court. And since I am his Great Chief Steward, I speak for him. *Get him out of those bonds!*"

"Yes, yes, Honored Steward. Right away, Honored Steward,"

the man stammered. "Well, go get the tools," he told the guard. "You heard the man."

"How long has he been here in the dark?" Khay asked next.

"Since he first came. Lord Potiphar said—"

"I know what Lord Potiphar said," my friend reminded the man. "I heard him say it, and I distinctly remember hearing him say that this man was to be kept until he decided what to do with him. Now, Keeper, what do you think Lord Potiphar will do if he finds out that this man has died before he gets the chance to punish him?"

"Well—well, he will be very angry," the prison official sputtered.

"He will be more than angry," Khay warned. "He will be furious."

"Yes, Good Steward. Here is the guard with the tools, Steward."

The bonds were soon off. I was so grateful to Khay that I could have cried, but all my attention was taken up figuring out what to do with my arms. They didn't seem to know where to go, and I honestly couldn't remember what to do with them. I kept expecting the collar to jerk against my throat, and my muscles would only move my head so far.

Muttering under his breath, Khay knelt down on the stone floor and slipped his arms under me. I tried to decide how to protest that I was much to heavy for him to lift, when he stood up easily and carried me out the door.

That was very odd, I thought. He must have gotten a lot stronger lately.

"But where are you going?" the Keeper sputtered behind us as Khay carried me down the passage.

"I am taking him to your room," Khay said icily. "I cannot clean him up in that cell."

"My room?" the Keeper squeaked in horror. "But he is filthy! He is sick, he is—"

"And whose fault is that?" my friend retorted. As he turned a corner the passage suddenly got lighter. I shut my eyes, able to figure out how to do that much at least.

Khay stopped in the guardroom, eyeing a huge cooking vessel. "Fill that with hot water," he ordered.

"Steward? You are not— surely you are not going to—cook him?"

"No, but I am seriously considering cooking you if you keep questioning every single thing I say to you. Fill it with very warm water, if you cannot get your mind around the concept of hot."

"But—but why, honored Steward?" the keeper said, completely bewildered.

"Because it is the only way I can think of to get this man warm," Khay shouted. "He feels like a corpse in my arms. *Get the water!* You may feel capable of standing up to Lord Potiphar if this man dies, but I do not!"

"Yes, Chief Steward. Right away, Chief Steward." The official rushed away to order water heated.

I wanted to talk to Khay, to ask him why he had come and what had happened after I left the estate, but I felt as if an invisible barrier of icy emptiness separated me from the rest of the world. If I opened my eyes, I could see things, but they didn't have any meaning, and I knew they should have. Of course, opening my eyes hurt, so I kept them closed most of the time.

"Don't die on me," Khay kept repeating.

I could not make myself respond. Suddenly, I felt warmth. I heard someone groaning and wondered who was hurt. But I felt warm. So very warm. Hands rubbed me all over, working the warmth into my body. Someone talked to me. I faded in and out.

"Hold his head up! Get him back in quickly. We almost lost him again!" Khay snapped.

I blacked out again, but then felt that warmth return all around me.

"How long has he been sleeping?" someone whispered.

"Hours, and he will sleep hours more if he wants to," Khay retorted sharply, his voice weary. "Bring more water. What is here is cooling."

In moments a tingling, wonderful feeling spread all around me.

"Feels good," I murmured with a sigh.

"Did you say something?" Khay asked with suppressed excitement.

I tried to nod.

"Don't move your head."

"Sorry," I apologized.

"How do you feel?"

I thought about that. "Warm," I said in surprise. "How did you—" Leaving the sentence unfinished, I slowly opened my eyes. I sat in a huge pot, immersed up to my chin in water! Khay sat beside the huge tub, grinning at me happily.

I looked around. The walls were high and rough, but light slanted through the doorway, coming in from somewhere above the room.

"I'm still in the prison," I said. "What are you doing here?"

"Joseph, talk to me in Egyptian so I can answer you," he pleaded.

I thought about that. *Hmm. Egyptian.* I tried again.

Khay laughed softly. "I am keeping you warm," he said with a chuckle. Then he sobered. "If I had come one day later, I doubt you would have lived. You almost left me as it was."

I looked down at myself and didn't recognize anything I saw. Where I expected my body to be lay a wasted thin skeleton with every bone showing.

"What happened?" I asked in amazement.

"You tell me," Khay replied.

"I don't know. How long have I been here?"

"Almost six weeks. I came yesterday."

"You shouldn't have, Khay," I protested weakly. "Lord Potiphar will be angry with you."

"Use Egyptian, Joseph," he reminded me.

I repeated my comment.

"Lord Potiphar is at court, and as his Great Chief Steward, I can do pretty much what I want."

"I vaguely remember something like that," I said, trying to laugh. Then my thoughts wandered to the past few weeks. "It was the oddest feeling, looking at life from behind an icy void. I could not find my way across again."

Khay's eyes snapped angrily. "When I get done with that Keeper . . ."

"Don't, Khay. It's not his fault I couldn't eat."

"Joseph!"

I switched to Egyptian.

"Locked up there dying from cold and darkness, I don't blame you for not eating," he flared. "That man should have known better!"

"He only did what he thought Master Potiphar told him to."

"You are impossible," my friend said in disgust. "Let's get you out of there and see if you can eat now."

Later, I sat at a table, supported by every cushion the keeper had and well wrapped in a linen coat and a woollen cloak. Khay patiently fed me, since I didn't have the strength to eat by myself. Only then did I realized how close to death I had come. At the same time, I wasn't certain that I wanted to live. But I would have to think about that later. I didn't have the energy to deal with it now.

And I didn't have the energy for many, many days to come. I had, inadvertently, almost starved myself to death. For the first week, Khay came every day until he convinced himself I wouldn't die if he turned his back.

By that time, he had the keeper of the prison so afraid of what would happen should I die, that the man hovered around me like a mother hen with only one chick.

About two months after Khay rescued me, I opened my eyes one morning feeling as if I had suddenly awakened from a dream. Looking around, I saw that I lay in an alcove off the guardroom, with a thick mat of reeds for a bed. They needed changing. A box with no lid held two linen kilts and a comb. I raised my hand and felt my bristly beard. It itched.

I moved into the guardroom. The Keeper of the Prison looked up.

"Good morning, master," I greeted him respectfully. He was a rotund little man with a harried expression and worry creases between his eyes.

He stared. "Good morning," he replied.

"Did you provide the clothing I found in the box, master?" I asked.

He nodded.

"Thank you. It was very kind of you."

"Are you feeling all right?"

"I think so. I rather feel as if I am awake for the first time in a long time."

"Keeper Setne," one of the guards said, "there is a scribe here to see you. She has found another mistake in the records."

"Another?" Master Setne asked, his voice shrill. "How can there be another? Where are those records? Where did Tehuti put them?"

"I do not know, Keeper," the guard answered. "Tehuti did not come today."

Moaning in distress, Setne scurried away, his kilt flapping untidily about his knees. He returned with a mass of tablets and papyrus leaves. "Why did he have to stay away today of all days?" he muttered, squinting at the records. "He knew this would happen. Tehuti stays away just to distress me. What shall I do? The scribe has come, and I know not how to explain."

I knelt out of the way by the low table, glancing over the records spilled on it. They were in a terrible jumble, but I could see a few orderly categories among them.

"Well, Setne, what has happened this time?" a woman's voice spoke from the doorway.

"Truly, I do not know, honored scribe," he began, wringing his hands. "I cannot find any errors in the records."

"You never do," the woman replied. "You were supposed to receive 10 pieces of tanned leather last month, and I have no receipt for them. But I do have record that they were sent. Where are they?"

"But honored scribe, good scribe Hetepi, they might be anywhere. Please allow me to send for Tehuti. Tehuti keeps the records. He will know exactly where these pieces of tanned leather are. But he is not here today. No, he is not here. He stayed home. Why, I do not know. He did not tell me, and so I do not know. So, please let me send for him, or perhaps you could come back another day?"

There, right in front of me, sat the record for the leather. The notation beside it indicated that the leather had been inspected, and two pieces had been returned as unsuitable. The others had been put in the storeroom. It did not say which one, however.

Hetepi sighed. "Where are your records, Setne?" she asked in a pained voice.

"I have them out. I brought them as soon as the guard said you were here. I got them from Tehuti's room. Surely you want to talk to him. I can send for him. He can tell you all about the leather. I—I have so much to keep track of, I can do nothing else. I must concern myself with the prison. I do not have time for leather goods." He nodded his head emphatically, wig bobbing about his ears.

I picked up the tablet, and when Hetepi walked over, held it out to her, keeping my eyes down.

"Who is this, Setne?" she asked.

"This? He is a prisoner, what else would he be? He is a prisoner, of course. Does he look like a guard?"

"Have you been ill?" Hetepi asked me.

"Yes, Scribe Hetepi."

"Look at me," she requested.

Raising my face, I glanced at her quickly. Of medium height, she possessed the grace and lines of a noble lady. Her dress was well cut, but of midgrade linen.

"You are a barbarian. Where are you from?"

"Canaan, mistress."

"Why do you keep your eyes lowered? Look at me."

I gazed directly into her rich brown eyes for a moment, then lowered mine again.

"Ah, the eyes of Ra," she said, shifting uneasily. "I can see why you keep them down. This is the correct tablet I needed. Do you read?"

"Yes, mistress, and write."

"Since Setne is incapable of finding anything I need, would you help?"

"Certainly, mistress, if Master Setne is agreeable."

"Agreeable, agreeable?" the Keeper said, fussing with his hands. "If it will prove that I have done nothing, I will be very agreeable. Let him find whatever you wish in Tehuti's records. If Tehuti will not come to work, then he should not complain if someone else has to sort through his records to find what I do not know. That much is plain."

I noticed that the woman hid her smile at his indignant comments.

"Setne, if you will bring the rest from the desk?"

The prison official vanished and soon returned with his arms full of more tablets and papyri. Tehuti's writing was a bit difficult to read, and it took some time before I had everything sorted out. What bothered me was that none of the records specified which storeroom things went to.

"Master Setne," I said.

"Yes, yes, what now?" he replied anxiously.

"How many storerooms are there for this prison?"

Hetepi looked up alertly from where she compared her neatly written records with Tehuti's scrawls.

"There are five. There have always been five. Ever since I came here, we have had five storerooms. Mind you, they are not big. I do not have room to spare for anything, but we have five."

"Thank you, master," I said.

"What made you ask?" Hetepi inquired.

"I would find it a bit difficult to locate anything from these records. I wondered if anyone else had the same trouble."

"Chronically," Hetepi commented. "What is your name?"

"Joseph, mistress."

I thought she caught her breath when I spoke, but her face was still and calm when I glanced at it.

"Setne, come here," she requested.

"Yes, honored scribe," he answered, hurrying to her side.

"You will need to provide me with a complete inventory. These records are such a mess, they cannot be straightened out. I will be back in one week, and I expect to have the inventory by then."

"An inventory? What inventory," he protested, waving his hands helplessly in the air. "Can I do an inventory? Do I write like a scribe? Does Tehuti come to work? What you ask, I cannot do. No, I cannot do. Tehuti, now, he can do this. You must ask him. But is he here to ask? Is he? Of course not. Tehuti is never here except when it suits him to be."

"But this prisoner can both read and write," she reminded him. "He can do it for you. After all, he will be here all day and will not be able to leave. You can have him do the work, and you will not need to depend on the unreliable Tehuti."

The Keeper brightened up at once. "That is so. Yes, that is so. And he cannot refuse to come to work." He chuckled with the joke. "No, he must be at work every day. Ah, honored scribe, you are very wise to suggest this. I will do it. I will do it immediately. When you come in two weeks—"

"One week," she corrected him.

"—two weeks," Setne repeated, "you will find everything done, everything ready. There will be an inventory," he finished happily.

Hetepi sighed.

"One week," she said to me.

I nodded. "Yes, mistress."

CHAPTER 13

I stretched, glad to feel well again. All the fetching and carrying and lifting and sorting of the past seven months had provided just what I needed to regain my strength. Since I was a slave and a prisoner, Setne saw no reason to provide any help, so when the supply caravans arrived I unloaded, transported, and stored the heavy sacks and jars alone. I didn't mind, since it gave me something to do. In the process, I discovered the prison had eight storerooms, not five. Master Setne was overjoyed to hear of the other three.

Hearing him enter the guardroom, I stepped out of my alcove. "Good morning, Master Setne," I said, bowing respectfully.

"Good morning, Joseph," he replied with a delighted smile. "Do you know what happens today? I will tell you what happens. Today honored scribe Hetepi comes. And do you know that I do not care? That I am not worried? That I am not troubled in any way? Why not? Because of you, good Joseph, wonderful Joseph.

"You have things in such order, such organization, such tabulation that I know Scribe Hetepi will find nothing amiss. Not one thing," he beamed at me. "I do not know how you do it. But I do not want to know. I just want you to continue. It is so much better with you than with that miserable slacker Tehuti, who never came to work except when it suited him. And it never suited him, as I have told you before."

"Yes, Master Setne." I had worked closely with Hetepi the past months to organize and restructure the prison system and records. Between us, we had finally cleaned up the mess.

The guard greeted Hetepi, and she entered the guardroom with a smile.

Setne bowed and bobbed, his face one big smile. "It is good to see you, Honored Hetepi. I have come to the accounting. I will sit here, like a grand noble, and you will go over my records, and you will find nothing wrong. I will tell Joseph to answer any questions you have, and he will answer them." With that, he sat down to one side and waited eagerly, mopping the sweat from his face.

It didn't take long for Hetepi to do the inspection. She went over my records, glanced into the storerooms, and came back. "Just one question. What happened to Tehuti?"

"I do not know," Setne said, frowning. "And I do not want to know. He has not come back, and I do not want him back. He can rot in the Nile for all I care. The trouble he caused me! Days of inspection were the worry of my life! But with Joseph, I do not worry. I do not worry at all."

"Thank you, Setne," she said. "I only have a couple small questions for Joseph. You may go now, if you wish."

"Thank you, honored scribe Hetepi," he said, his kilt flapping as he left.

She watched him go with amusement, then turned to me. "And how long will it be before you see him again?"

I shrugged. "A week, maybe two."

"So you take care of everything now?"

I nodded. "Yes, mistress."

Hetepi looked around; we were alone in the room. "Why do you call me mistress? You know my name."

"Yes, mistress. But I am a slave, and I dare not forget that."

"Could I make you forget it?" she said, looking at me.

"Do you wish to?" I asked slowly.

"You know I love you," she said matter-of-factly.

"Yes, mistress."

Silence, then, "Is that all you have to say, just 'Yes, mistress'?"

"I am a condemned man, Hetepi," I replied softly. "Master Potiphar may decide to have me killed at any moment."

"I would guess he has forgotten all about you," she interrupted.

"Then to remind him would not be wise. He cannot let me go. To do so would mean shaming his wife. He put me here and forgot me. It is the best he can do."

"And you sit here with your talents and knowledge wasted on an eight-storeroom prison," Hetepi said bitterly. She took a deep breath. "Do you love me, Joseph? Please tell me the truth."

I looked into her calm face. She went very deep, and she had had enough pain in her life to know the value of truth.

"No, Hetepi, I do not think I do. I admire you, and am more grateful than you know for your kindness to me and concern about me. But respect and gratitude are not enough for what you want. You already know this."

She sighed. "Your Horus eyes see too deeply," she complained. "But I guess I needed to hear someone else say it."

I smiled.

"Don't do that," Hetepi said with mock despair. "You will be the death of me, flaunting what I cannot have!"

"I am sorry, mistress," I said, with another smile.

"Unrepentant wretch."

"So someone else shares my opinion?" Khay's cheerful voice boomed from the door.

Hetepi turned around to see who was there, and Lord Potiphar's steward stopped in his tracks. His eyes widened in surprise as he grabbed the lintel for support.

She flushed scarlet, the first time I ever saw her anything but cool and assured.

"Great Chief Steward Khay, may I introduce Scribe Hetepi?" I said. "Hetepi is Inspector of the House of the Pharaoh's Prison in Memphis. Chief Steward Khay is Lord Potiphar's overseer."

He nodded without saying a word, and Hetepi looked down, confused.

No one said anything, and I almost laughed. "Khay," I finally said, "did you want to see me?"

"Huh?" he said, waking up. "See you? Oh, yes. Yes, I did." He recovered his poise quickly. "I needed to ask you about the mine you got the turquoise from. I cannot find record of where it is."

"If you need to consult, I will go," Hetepi said hastily, then fled from the room.

He looked at me with a hint of amazement. "Who was that?"

"I told you, she is Inspector of the House of—"

"I heard that," he said impatiently. "Who is she?"

"That you will have to find out for yourself."

"With someone like that around, I might be willing to get thrown in prison myself."

I chuckled. "I doubt it. Now about the mine. I don't think I ever had the chance to record the location. But I can tell you easily enough."

Khay pulled his mind back to his duties. He had one or two other quick questions, but that was all and soon left.

And that was just the point. Everyone left.

That night I got up, unable to sleep. Prisons in Egypt existed to keep criminals until trial and judgment. They were not for punishment. People came and within days left. Few stayed longer than two or three weeks. Some were shipped to the mines, some were killed, most were punished and returned to their lives.

I stayed and never left. I was in this pit with no way out. Bitterness flooded through me. I had done nothing to be here, yet here I was. Restless, I wandered into the guardroom that formed the central hall, with passages to cells, storerooms, and living quarters for the Prison Keeper going off it. I had been down every passage, seen every cell, room, and cranny, except one.

Through the doorway, I saw the moonlight on the floor. For the first time, I went into the anteroom that led to the outside. Above my head, moonlight shone through the grillwork in the ceiling. Across from me was the passage that led up to the outside world. I would never walk that passage. I was a forgotten man.

As I stood under the grill, staring up at the moon, I turned my anger against El Shaddai. *How could you do this to me!* I screamed at Him in the silence of my mind. *I've done nothing! I was faithful, I served well and refused to go against Your commands, trusting that you would protect me. No one understood why I didn't just give Lady Tanefret what she wanted, even though it was an offense to their gods as well. They just shrugged. Their gods are easily satisfied, easily served.*

But You? You demand absolute obedience! You tell me I must deny my body, my ambitions, my wants. You tell me I must endure betrayal by my brothers, that I must let Abi grieve my death, that I must submit to slavery!

Moving restlessly in the moonlight, I felt bitterness welling from my eyes in silent tears. *And I did these things,* I told Him. *I did them. I trusted You. I gave myself to You. I believed that You would provide for me, that You would be my God. You were supposed to protect me. You were supposed to prosper me. There on the table with Master Potiphar's knife at my throat, I lay on the altar like Isaac, waiting for Your salvation.*

And did You save me? You put me in prison! I shook my fist at the moonlight, then fled to my alcove. But my bed brought no rest. I stuffed a rag in my mouth so that I could cry without alerting the guards.

Why should I serve You? I demanded silently of my Adversary. *Why didn't You let me die in the cistern in Canaan if all You planned was for me to exist in a hole like an animal? What good can I possibly do here? Any reasonable person can govern this place, even Setne, with his constant chatter and scattered brain.*

For 10 years, I served Potiphar. What have I done that mattered? If I hadn't been there, someone else would have. I trained Khay, but someone else could have done it. I gave Jetur a chance to trade with the Great House itself, but he could have found a way without me. I treated a horse's wounds, but any herder could do the same.

And now, I straightened out a mess of records for this prison, and Hetepi could have easily done it herself. So tell me, El Shaddai-jireh, just what have You provided for me? A life of boredom? Without the light of day? Do you expect me to spend my days receiving and storing and recording goods and prisoners like an ox on a treadmill?

I am a man, not a beast.

Pounding the mats beneath me with my fists, I shook with anger and hurt.

Hazor's god takes better care of him than You do of me. Khay's gods have served him better than You have done for me. Why should I serve you anymore? You have done nothing but tear me from my family and play with me like a cat does a mouse, feeding me with hope and promise, only to knock me down into despair.

How could You? How could You betray me like this?

▲ ▲ ▲ ▲

"I have found word," Mishma said, entering the room where Jetur sat.

"Ah, good. What has happened to our investment?"

"Apparently his God deserted him," the younger man said somewhat maliciously. "Some months ago, the Nubians dragged him away from Lord Potiphar's house, and took him to the Pharaoh's prison in Memphis."

Jetur's face revealed his surprise. "What had he done?"

"He tried to rape his master's wife. What do you think of those who follow Prince Isaac's God now?"

"How was he punished?" Jetur asked heavily.

Mishma frowned. "That I could not find out. I heard several rumors, but I could not go beyond that."

"Odd, that," Jetur said. "Such a crime demands a very public punishment." He fiddled thoughtfully with the tassels on the cloth over the table at his side.

"What shall we do?" his son asked.

"Wait," Jetur decided.

▲　▲　▲　▲

The days passed, dreary, dull, and empty. I received prisoners from the Nubian police, then released them for trial or punishment. Receiving goods from the state storehouses, I distributed them to where they needed to go. And I recorded every detail of every transaction of every day as did every other scribe in Egypt while silently burning with rage against my God who had wrongfully condemned me to this.

Khay rarely came, having taken my place as chief steward smoothly, and he did an excellent job. Hetepi checked my records, knowing she wasted her time, and shyly told me about her growing attraction for Khay.

Setne puffed himself up with importance on the rare occasions he visited the prison. He told me, and anyone else who would listen, about his great wisdom in choosing me to run the prison, and told the joke about my being unable to leave my work until everyone was sick of hearing it.

As I looked down the long years of my life I shuddered with the terribleness of it all.

One day I penned the date on the records and paused. I had been here for 11 months exactly. Then putting the documents away, I went to my alcove where I sat on the bed, looking at the lidless box that held an extra linen and a comb. That was the sum total of my possessions. Two cast-away kilts, and a comb missing three teeth.

Reaching up, I pulled the tie from my hair. Oh yes, don't forget the yard-long piece of rawhide I bound my hair back with. Throwing it into the box, I just sat there. Why hadn't Khay let me die?

▲　▲　▲　▲

I awoke, then a sudden restlessness drove me to my feet, and I stepped into the guardroom. All was still. As I looked into the anteroom, the moonlight streamed down, casting the pattern of the grill above on the dusty floor. Slowly I walked into the light, drawn by a strange compulsion. I looked up.

"Joseph, you must trust Me."

I looked around in surprise, but no one was there. I swallowed. Was I losing my mind?

"Joseph, give Me your anger."

I started to shake. "W-who are You?" I whispered.

"I am the God of your fathers, the God of Abraham, the God of Isaac, and the God of Jacob. Your wounds cry out to Me from your darkness."

Terrified, I dropped to the floor, sure that He would slay me.

"Do not be afraid, Joseph."

"W-what do You require of me?" I stammered.

"Give Me your anger, Joseph. It is too much for you."

"It's all I have left," I sobbed. "There is nothing else."

"You have never been alone, Joseph."

Sitting bolt upright in bed, shaking and drenched in sweat, I stared around at the stone walls of the alcove. A dream! I scrambled up, stumbling into the guardroom and through the door to the anteroom.

Throwing myself down on the hard stone floor, I buried my face between my knees. "My Lord, I have sinned," I cried silently. And there in the middle of the night, I let El Shaddai take away the rage and hurt I had held onto for the past year. As I had another night, 11 years before, I gave myself to Him. But this time, I knew more of what that meant. And as it had all those years ago, El Shaddai's peace glowed in my mind, warming me and quenching a thirst I hadn't known I had.

"You look worried, today," I said to Master Setne the next morning when he unexpectedly arrived at the prison.

"I am worried. There is much to worry me. Surely you have heard of the trouble in the palace? It is bad—it is very bad. With the trouble about the court, what shall I do if anything happens? There will be prisoners sent here. Important prisoners. How are we to treat them? I ask you? Do you know? Do I? If they come, I cannot offer them sweet food and soft beds. This is a prison. If they are killed when they leave, that is no matter to me. But if they are set free, they will remember how I have treated them, and they may be angry. I do not know what to do."

Setne quivered with anxiety, twisting his hands, sweat streaming from his round body.

"But Master Setne, it will not be you doing it. It will be me," I said gently. "If anything happens and prisoners come here, it will be me they meet. You will not have to see them at all."

He looked up at me. "Do you think so? Yes, yes, that may be so," he brightened. "It will be you, not me. And what can they do to you? You are already in prison. They will be able to do nothing. Yes, that is best. We will do it like you say. You will meet them, and I will be gone. I will go now."

With that, Master Setne's short legs trotted him out of the room. I made a wager with myself that I wouldn't see him again until the trouble in the palace had been resolved. Yet, I fretted with frustration that I did not even know what the palace turmoil was about.

Just then, the guard announced another prisoner, a bewildered young goldsmith named Senptah, accused of stealing part of the gold given him to make a necklace. I set about recording his arrival and the details of the charge against him. Then I made sure he had an appropriate cell, checking that the chamber pot had fresh sand and that the reeds for the bed were not rotten.

That afternoon, I found him sitting, dazed, by the table in the guardroom.

"What is the matter, Senptah?"

He looked up at me. "Are—are you the Keeper?"

"I can get something if you need it," I said, noting his vacant stare.

"I want to go home. They didn't let me tell my wife. She will worry if I don't come."

"Shall I send a message to her?"

He looked at me again. "Is that permitted?"

"I will permit it."

"Please tell her where I am. She will worry so if I don't come home. We just got married, you know. She chose me from all the other young men who wanted her. She chose me."

"I will send a message right away," I told him. I called Ptahhotep, the Inspector of the Guards, and had him send the message I wrote.

Senptah looked so lost that I started talking to him. At first he spoke as in a daze, then seemed to sort of wake up and began to talk intelligently. Avoiding anything about why he was there, I finally asked about any news he might have heard.

"All I know is just what everyone knows," he said, puzzled.

"But I hear nothing at all. Anything you know will be news for me."

"Well, there are the rumors from the palace," he began hesitantly.

"What is happening?" I asked, suddenly starved for information about the outside world.

"They say there has been an attempt on the Pharaoh's life. I guess there was poison in some food, or wine, or there was going to be poison, or something. Anyway, there is a big investigation going on. The palace guard has been here in Memphis. They took some officials from their houses in the capital and even took some merchants from the markets here in Memphis.

"I thought, at first, that is what I was taken for. But no, it is about the gold. I don't understand," he said tearfully. "I used all the gold he sent. I didn't take any of it."

"Tell me about it," I suggested.

It took a while, for Senptah was so afraid that he dissolved into incoherency more than once. When he had finished his story, I thought for a moment.

"You mentioned you were working on another commission at the same time?"

Senptah nodded. "Another necklace, with 11 weight of gold."

"And the necklace you worked on was for 15 weight, correct?"

"Yes."

"Did you send the wrong order back to the lord?" I asked. "You are charged with stealing four weight of gold, and that is the difference between the two orders."

His face lit up. "Maybe I did."

A guard came in. "Joseph, there is a woman outside wailing and weeping about her husband. Ptahhotep wants to know what he should do."

"Is it Dedi?" Senptah asked.

"That might have been the name," the guard replied.

"If it is, tell her Senptah is fine," I instructed. "Also tell her to go home and see if she can find the order for a 15-weight necklace and bring it here."

By that evening we had the whole thing straightened out.

Senptah had indeed sent the wrong order, and he waited impatiently for his court date in two days. Again and again he thanked me for helping him. In return he told me anything he could think of about life outside. The harvest had yielded little this year. But most nomes had sufficient reserves to carry them through to the next harvest. He did mention that the nomarch of the fifth nome, in the south, had not provided well for his people and now had to buy grain at extremely high prices.

I knew Master Potiphar's people would not suffer. All the granaries on every estate were full to overflowing. I went to bed that night feeling that I had done something good, a feeling that I hadn't had in a long time.

As I stared at the square pattern of the moonlight on the floor, the moonlight made my skin look white.

"Joseph!"

"Yes, Lord?" I asked, bowing to the floor.

"Joseph, I am the God of Abraham, Isaac, and Jacob. I have seen your trouble, and I have remembered you. Look now, I have given you sight and understanding. Your eyes shall see what is hidden and make plain to you what is dark. I will reveal to you the secret thing, and you shall glorify Me."

"It shall be as you wish, O Lord," I replied.

Again, I woke up in bed. Rolling to the cold stone floor, I knelt but said nothing as my soul fed on the words my God had said to me. "I have remembered you."

The Creator of the world had remembered me, the forgotten man. The glory in my soul welled up and spilled over. El Shaddai remembered me. What else had I need of?

The very next morning, Ptahhotep came in with great excitement. "It has happened," he said. "They come from the capital with two prisoners. It is the Chief Baker and the Chief Wine Steward. They are accused of trying to kill the Pharaoh."

"Send them in," I said, going for a papyrus leaf to write on.

Six palace guards, commanded by the Assistant Captain of the Guard, brought the prisoners into the guardroom. The men had been hurried away in the middle of their work, and they looked frightened and disheveled.

"Names?" I asked the Assistant Captain.

"Manakh, Chief of the Bakers to Pharaoh, and Tahsit, Chief of the Wine Stewards to Pharaoh," he replied.

"What charge shall I record?"

"Conspiracy against the Pharaoh's life."

I nodded.

"I and my men will remain to add to the guard as long as these men are here," he went on.

"As you wish. The prison has only one entrance. Have your men go down each passage if necessary. Perhaps it would be more convenient for you to remain outside the entrance. The anteroom is quite small."

After assuring himself of the truth of my statements, the Assistant Captain took my advice and stationed his men outside. I settled the new prisoners in the cell next to Senptah, and soon the sociable goldsmith told them everything they never thought they would need to know about how a prison operated. The gist of his statements was that whatever problem they had, or whatever they might need, apply to me.

They were dubious until I arrived with salve for the cuts and bruises the guards had inflicted on them and also brought some bread and beer. I treated them respectfully, then left them alone, drawing Senptah away also, for the two were obviously upset.

Not long after, Khay came striding in. "Where is the Chief Keeper of the House of the Prison?" he asked cheerfully.

I looked up in surprise to see his teasing grin.

"I was instructed to deliver this to the Chief Keeper. It is about the prisoners," he added.

Giving him a disgusted look, I held out my hand, and Khay put the message in it. Then he sat down, waiting for me to read it.

When I looked at the papyrus I almost dropped it. I knew the writing intimately. It was from Lord Potiphar's official scribe.

Khay chuckled. "Lord Potiphar told me to deliver it personally. He didn't want it to get lost, or something."

Breaking the seal, I read the message. In it Lord Potiphar instructed the Chief Keeper how to treat the two prisoners. He specified the type of food they were to have—better than we normally served—and that while they were not to be bound, they were to be kept in a locked cell at all times. He also instructed the Chief Keeper to assign me as a personal attendant to them both.

Setting the papyrus down, I looked at Khay.

"Lord Potiphar has remembered me," I said slowly.

"Lord Potiphar has never forgotten you, and neither has anyone else," my friend replied softly. "Who do you think sent me the first time I came? Why do you think I was so afraid you would die?" He shuddered. "I have never been so frightened! I don't think I could have faced Lord Potiphar if I had to tell him you were dead. It was bad enough as it was, with you so ill."

"Why did you tell him that?" I asked somewhat bitterly.

Potiphar's steward grinned. "I was here for more than two days, Joseph. You cannot imagine the state Lord Potiphar was in when I finally did get back. He literally pounced on me, demanding to know why I had taken that long for a simple inquiry. I could hardly keep him from murdering Keeper Setne after he learned what had happened to you."

I stared at him in amazement.

Khay chuckled. "You have been far from forgotten. Lord Potiphar was so overjoyed to see that first report you wrote up in this prison, that he came back to Memphis and threw a quiet party for some of his friends."

"He had a party?" I asked, stunned.

A nod. "He didn't tell anyone the real reason, but he went to the northernmost wheat field and buried that report, along with two gold earrings, as an offering to your god. And he has not worn earrings since."

Realizing which earrings he'd buried—the ones he'd received for returning that stallion—I did not know what to say. Potiphar had given my God the ones that symbolized the gift of the golden collar from Pharaoh. Khay waited for me to gather my wits.

"What about Lady Tanefret?" I asked.

His face hardened. "Lord Potiphar has neither seen nor spoken to Lady Tanefret since that day. After a month on the Memphis estate with every person there avoiding her, she moved to her house in Memphis and then to the residence in the capital. Lord Potiphar does not go the residence when she is there. He sleeps in the palace."

"What about her relatives? Have they made things hard for Lord Potiphar?"

He chuckled again. "When someone asked about the incident, he told them that he had personally attended to the matter and then left it up to their imagination to figure out why you had so suddenly disappeared. I have heard six separate rumors about the horrible death you suffered. Her relatives are quite satisfied," Khay ended with a laugh.

"What about later? Do you think Master Potiphar will take me out of here?"

He sobered and avoided my eyes. "I don't know, Joseph."

"Khay," I said, in a tone I seldom used.

He looked up quickly.

"Tell me the truth," I insisted.

"I don't think so, Joseph," he sighed. "You know Lord Amony is related to Lady Tanefret,"

I nodded.

"What you don't know is that Lord Amony is leading the opposition to the new Pharaoh. It has been very quiet, but Pharaoh finds it very hard to do anything that the most powerful southern nomarchs don't like. They pressure him for trade concessions, permission for larger personal armies, more support for the temple of Amun in Thebes, and other things. It causes problems. Pharaoh finds it difficult to attend to the needs of the northern part of the country and the Delta. Anything he wants to do, he finds the nomarchs in his way."

"I don't remember this being a problem a year ago."

"It wasn't. The old Pharaoh knew how to play one nomarch against another. His son is not nearly so skilled, and the nomarchs are taking advantage of it. Now, with this conspiracy against Pharaoh's life—" He stopped.

"It is very troubling," I commented.

Khay nodded. "He is a good ruler, Pharaoh," he said softly. "He and his father both have truly been a father to this land. They care about us. Not all Pharaohs do. This year the people are not starving until the next harvest because the old Pharaoh insisted on all the nomes storing grain. He kept maat, the way things are supposed to be. This young Pharaoh is struggling to keep the balance also, but—"

We sat in silence for some time.

"There is one thing more," Khay said, breaking the quiet.

"Yes?"

"Lord Potiphar asked for you to attend these prisoners, hoping you would do something for him."

I felt a shaft of resentment flash through me. Hadn't I done enough for Lord Potiphar already? Then I pushed the thought away.

Master Potiphar had been in an impossible position. I myself had told Khay that the only way to minimize trouble was to sacrifice me. How could I blame Potiphar if he did what his way of life dictated? At the same time, I admitted that my resentment rose from my own cultural understanding that people should be accountable to a set standard of right and wrong.

But I couldn't expect Master Potiphar to live by my ideals. He obeyed his own. What would El Shaddai want me to do? Suddenly I knew without really asking.

"Lord Potiphar wanted your opinion on whether the prisoners were guilty or not," Khay said.

I cocked an eyebrow. "My opinion?"

He reddened. "Er, yes."

"Just what did Master Potiphar really say?" I pushed.

"Unedited version?"

"Preferably."

"He said, 'Send them to Joseph. Tell him to use those Horus eyes of his to read their souls. Then we will know.'"

"How am I to do that?"

"I asked him that. Lord Potiphar told me that your god would take care of it."

I looked down. "I will do what I can."

That night I visited the anteroom again. As I gazed up through the grillwork I prayed that El Shaddai would aid my master in his task of defending Pharaoh, the first time I had done that since coming here. Shamed, I humbly asked forgiveness for my selfishness. I had not been forgotten by anyone, and my master did everything he could to ease my situation. When enough time had passed, maybe I would be away from here again. The possibility gave me hope for the first time since I had come to this place.

The days passed without any word about the political prisoners, making them more and more uneasy. I tended to them each morning and again in the evening, while keeping up my other duties. When I received a message from Setne saying his wife was ill, and that he would not be at the prison until she got better, I smiled to myself. It was the first mention I'd heard that Setne had a wife. Perhaps he did. I'd have to ask him when he returned.

Two holidays passed and still no message from the palace. Tahsit and Manakh did not know what to think. They had been tried in the special court appointed by Pharaoh, and were awaiting a final decision and sentencing. Normally, decisions were given and sentences carried out on holidays, so the delay was unusual and unnerving.

Three days before Pharaoh's birthday, I came to Tahsit and Manakh's cell at midmorning. The delivery of goods from the state storehouses delayed me, as I had to attend to that first thing. The instant I walked into the cell, I sensed something wrong. They both appeared frightened.

"What has happened?" I asked. "You look afraid."

They glanced at me, then down. "Come, I am here to serve you. Tell me what has upset you so."

Tahsit hesitated. "We had some dreams last night," he finally said. "Both of us. They were very strange, and we don't know what they mean."

"I don't like them," Manakh said. "They worry me."

"Interpretations of dreams come from the gods," I reminded them. "Tell me the dreams. Perhaps my God, El Shaddai, will reveal to me what they mean."

Tahsit looked at Manakh again. Manakh shook his head. "You start," he said.

The chief wine steward cleared his throat. "In my dream I saw a grapevine in the ground. It grew while I watched and put out three branches. The branches put out buds that turned into blossoms and then grew into clusters of grapes. After they ripened, I picked the grapes and crushed them, putting the juice into Pharaoh's cup. Then I took the cup to Pharaoh and gave it to him."

I was silent for a moment, not to search for the meaning of the dream, for it was perfectly plain to me as he told it, but to marvel at the mercy of El Shaddai in honoring me in such a fashion after I had turned against Him.

"El Shaddai has shown me what your dream means, Master Tahsit," I began. "The three branches on the grapevine are three days. In three days, Pharaoh will bring you into his presence. He will give you back your position, and you will serve the Pharaoh's wine as you have before you were sent to prison."

"Are you certain?" Tahsit asked, clearly not wanting to indulge in false hopes.

"I am certain. You will be freed and will serve Pharaoh as before."

A huge grin lit up his face. "Only three more days. Oh Joseph, how can I thank you?"

"Remember me," I blurted out. "If you wish to thank me, remember me and speak to Pharaoh about my situation. I was—" I paused "—was stolen from the land of Canaan, and here in Egypt I have done nothing to be put into this prison. Please, when you are with Pharaoh, please tell him about me."

"Of course, Joseph," Tahsit said eagerly. "I will be happy to."

"Thank you, Master Tahsit. It will mean much to me."

"What about my dream?" Manakh demanded. "Can I tell you mine, now?"

I tried to quiet the pounding of my heart and listen. I might be free. In a few days, I might be free as well. I could quietly disappear back to my own country. Surely that would be best for all involved. I could hardly keep my attention on Manakh as he started to talk.

"My dream had three of something too," he explained. "I walked along carrying three baskets on my head, piled on top of one another. In the top one, there were all kinds of breads and baked goods to give to the Pharaoh. But I was very vexed, for the birds kept swooping down and pecking at the bread and eating it. I could not shoo them away. And that was the end of my dream. What does it mean?"

Suddenly sick to my stomach, I looked down. I knew now which man was guilty of conspiracy against Pharaoh. But I did not want to interpret his dream. How could I condemn him to the worst thing that an Egyptian could imagine?

"Do the three baskets mean three days?" Manakh asked.

I nodded, suppressing my horror. "Yes, the baskets are days. In three days, Pharaoh will bring you also into his presence. But you will not be given your position back. You will be condemned to death. Beheaded, your body will be hanged in a tree, and the birds will eat your flesh."

His face drained of blood, and he swayed. "Eaten?" he choked out. "My body destroyed? But my Ka will die! There will be no afterlife. I will die the Second Death!"

Tahsit helped him down to his mat. He, too, was pale at the terrible thing that I had foretold.

"It cannot be! It cannot be!" Manakh moaned. "Tahsit, what will I do? I knew it was a bad dream. I knew it was!"

"Manakh, I don't know what to do," he said helplessly. "But perhaps the dream means nothing at all."

"Is it just a dream, or does it really mean what you say?" Manakh asked.

Remaining silent, I just looked him directly in the eye.

"It is true," he wailed. "You see with the eyes of Ra. I shall die, and my Ka will perish. There will be nothing, nothing." He broke into terrified sobs.

CHAPTER 14

I sat down to compose the message for Master Potiphar. A dozen times I picked up the reed pen and then put it back. What was wrong with me? I had never shirked a report before. Why now? Suddenly there flashed through my mind the look Dan gave me when he walked out of Abi's tent after I had complained to Father about his handling of the herds. I remembered the bitterness and distrust and hurt. Dan had never spoken to me after that. What a fool I had been! When my brothers accused me of spying on them for Father, I denied it, but now I saw that they were right. Even though Abi had asked me to check on things, that didn't mean I handled the situation in the best way—or even in the right way.

What about now? To be blunt, Master Potiphar had asked me to spy on the two prisoners. Should I? I knew, now, who was guilty. God had revealed it to me. Why should I not tell him what I knew? Because they trusted me. They felt safe with me. Was it right for me to betray that trust? On the other hand, Lord Potiphar trusted me also.

For hours I wrestled with the problem. To hold my tongue might mean the life of the Pharaoh. To speak betrayed a trust. Which was the right thing to do? I went to my bed and knelt on the floor.

"El Shaddai, show me what I ought to do," I pleaded. "I do not know what is right. I have seen what betrayal does, and it is evil. I am here because of betrayal. But to take life is also evil. My Lord, I do not know what to do!"

And then, the answer was there in my mind. I ran to the guard-room, and in the dim light of the last torch, hastily wrote out a message to Master Potiphar. I didn't even put in the usual greetings and courtesy phrases. "To Lord Potiphar, Captain of the Guard for Pharaoh. My God, El Shaddai, has marked the man who is guilty of conspiracy against Pharaoh."

I did not sign the message, for someone might see it, endangering the secret of my existence. Sealing it, I sent it immediately to Khay.

Setne celebrated the Pharaoh's birthday by bringing some pomegranates to me. I distributed them among the few prisoners we had. Tahsit and Manakh had gone back to Itej-Tawy yesterday. Impatiently I waited for word from Tahsit. The excitement of the holiday might distract him, and he might not speak to Pharaoh until a couple days had gone by. But I should hear something within two or three weeks.

My heart pounded every time I thought of it. Anticipation made me so tense that I could hardly keep my mind on my work. I would be free, and surely Master Potiphar would see that the best thing would be for me to really disappear—back to Canaan. I might even see Abi in just a few weeks. I was so excited that I couldn't even eat.

Every night I prayed; every morning I waited for word. Soon now it would come.

It didn't.

▲ ▲ ▲ ▲

After tossing on the mats, unable to sleep, I wandered into the dark guardroom, following the light coming through the grill above the anteroom as I had on so many restless nights. I stood looking up through the bars. I had been in prison for exactly two years. The word setting me free was not going to come from the palace. Tahsit had not spoken to Pharaoh, and I knew now that he would not.

Discouragement flooded my soul. Was there no one I could depend on for justice or help? Was I all alone? Blinking back the tears, I sat down in the floor in the moonlight. I never came into this room during the day. To see the sunlight through the grill was too much to bear. To remember what the days had been like, the breeze of the

Nile, the mud in the fields after Inundation, the misty mornings of the Delta—to know I was denied all that was too much for me to handle.

But at night, in the quietness and darkness, the moonlight seemed just enough. I could come and remember just a little of freedom, as the moon gave just a little light. What of Abi? And Benjamin? What had happened to Tamar and her child? Was Judah a grandfather by Shelah? Had Dinah ever taken a husband?

What of Ebed and the sheep? Did that cunning old wolf still harass the goats? Or had Benjamin learned to track him without me and finally killed him? One by one I remembered them, my brothers, Leah and Dinah, the servants and their families. And last of all, Abi.

Whom did he tell stories to? What children sat and listened with open mouths to the sacrifice of Grandfather Isaac, the wrestling match with El Shaddai on the Jabbok, and the reconciliation with Uncle Esau? Who heard about Lot, and Sodom and Gomorrah, and Great-Grandmother Sarah laughing at the thought of having a child? Or was Abi dead, brought to the grave by sorrow and loss, never to know that I had not died, that I lived and thought of him often, and prayed for El Shaddai's blessing upon him?

And what of me? What of *my* dreams? How could a slave forgotten in a prison ever hope to become great? Why was I here? Why had El Shaddai led me to this place? What good was my life? Was it worth it to serve El Shaddai?

The questions beat upon my mind and I could not answer them. "There is darkness all around me," I whispered. "How can I see?"

"Look up."

"There is nothing there. I have no answers. I do not know anything of all the things that I wish to know. I cannot do what I wish to do. I have nothing, and I am nothing. Why do You preserve my life?"

"Look up, Joseph."

"I cannot see," I whispered.

"I did not ask you to see, I asked you to look up."

Too overwhelmed with discouragement to think straight, I argued with the other voice I heard.

"There are only stars."

"How many children did Abraham have?" the voice asked.

"One, of promise," I replied.

"Yet Abraham counted his descendants like the stars, Joseph. Did Isaac know what would happen on the altar?"

"No, Lord."

"When I came to Jacob at the brook, what did he do?"

"He fought. I am like my father—I fight."

"And at the last, what did your father do?"

"He clung to You," I said slowly. "He refused to let go. He risked Your anger to plead for a blessing as Abraham risked it to plead for the lives of the Cities of the Plain."

"And in the end?"

"They were blessed, Lord."

"Remember, Joseph, you are never alone."

The moonlight left the sky, and I gazed at the stars. They were uncountable. With all the tabulation and counting and recording that was part of my life, I had never counted the stars.

El Shaddai did not ask me to understand. He asked me to obey. Would I?

Hours passed. As I looked back over my life I remembered my dreams and desires. But now I saw no glory ahead of me, no ruler-ship over my brothers, no greatness among humanity. I was a slave, imprisoned and inconvenient to remember.

What was left for me? The gift that El Shaddai honored me with—to see the hidden thing and interpret dreams, a gift with which I could serve.

The people who came here to this prison were not the great rulers of the earth, humbly begging for my attention. While they did include a few nobles, mostly I served the commoners, the lesser officials, and everyday people who got caught in events big-ger than themselves, or who made choices that Pharaoh hated. They tried to live as best they could, and sometimes they got caught. When they came here they were worried and anxious and afraid. And they needed a kind word, a pleasant smile, and a respectful manner.

Some died, some were beaten and released, some were sent far from home, but all of them looked to me while they stayed here. I could ease their pain, or I could make them afraid. I could be a fa-ther to them, or I could be their enemy.

And what of *my* dreams?

I stood up, looking at the paling stars through the grillwork. "I do not understand, El Shaddai, but I no longer need to," I said. "I place myself, my dreams, and my future in Your hands. It is my place to serve, and it is Your place to lead. I will follow where You take me. As Abraham trusted, so will I trust."

The first time I had given myself to El Shaddai, I had done it from terror. The second time I had done it from desperation. This time I did it from choice. I would receive no earthly glory, I knew, but I would share in the friendship and glory of the Creator God. Nothing was greater than that.

One more time I looked through the grill. There above me in the heavens was the exact same configuration of stars that I had seen in my second dream. The irregular line twinkled above me, the same star in the middle pulsating brighter than the others. I knew if I stayed to watch, they would make their obeisance, but I had no need. Turning away, I smiled my assurance of El Shaddai's care.

Then, as I entered the alcove that held my bed, I paused. "But, please, El Shaddai, keep me from boredom!" I added.

I will never, ever pray such a prayer again. Suddenly it seemed that this was the only prison in all of Egypt, and any person of any rank who was waiting for trial or sentencing, landed in my lap.

Master Setne was first appalled, then frantic, then ridiculously pleased with the importance that followed. He came to the prison to solemnly receive any important personage, instructing them to notice the place's efficiency and informing them that I was the person to go to for any question they might have. Then he would turn to me and charge me with the care of said personage.

Many times I struggled to keep my composure, but I knew how genuinely Master Setne worried over whether or not he fulfilled his responsibilities. Since I had taken over, he paid more attention to the details and could now run the place reasonably without me if he had to. He preferred, however, to play grand noble in his own inimitable way.

Several times Khay brought special instructions from Lord Potiphar, and I listened and learned what I could about the prisoners indicated. If anything puzzled me about them, I told Khay, and he took it to Lord Potiphar. Twice, my suggestions led to acquittals, and once to a conviction.

As the months passed, I learned to deal with the differences in needs and mannerisms between the northern and southern parts of the country. The Delta made a class by itself. Gradually, I worked out the smoothest ways to handle and interact with prisoners from each section. People from the Delta were generally easiest to deal with. They were glad to just stay dry. Those from Memphis to somewhat north of Abydos were usually easygoing and required little to satisfy them. People south of Abydos were reserved, resentful, and demanding, depending on how far south they were from. Prisoners from the first cataract and above could be unreasonably arrogant and self-interested. Many of them brought their own attendants and tried to insist that I let them serve them. I could not permit this, of course, and had to learn to be bland, but immovable.

From the higher social classes I picked up insights into the political and social scene in the country, and from the officials, crafters, commoners, servants, and slaves, I learned the basic survival worries of the majority of the population. Records of case after case passed through my hands, and I gained an understanding of the effects and uses of power. Power used well produced justice and equity for all concerned. But more often I saw firsthand the suffering and anguish caused by power employed for selfish and thoughtless concerns.

Through it all, everyone talked about the new Pharaoh. No one dared to openly disagree with anything he did, since his person and actions were sacred and not to be questioned. But silence spoke volumes if one knew how to listen. What Khay had told me was true. Many things could be done to improve life for those in the north, but the south manipulated the Pharaoh and the political and economic situation to its own advantage. The southern nomes were becoming rich and powerful at the expense of the rest of the land.

The south used bribery with the northern nomarchs to get their way. The nomarchs around Abydos and Thebes were the worst, since they could control to some extent where people could be buried, and how soon ground was available for tombs to be built, etc.

Witnessing a fascinating mix of opinions and viewpoints, I sorted them all out and considered what I would do if I were in command. I occupied myself working out tentative solutions to problems, and eagerly waited to hear from someone how Pharaoh had actually responded to the situation.

Sometimes I thought my ideas were better, and sometimes I admired what the king devised. It gave me a view of Egyptian life and culture that I could have acquired nowhere else, for prison is a great leveler and opener of tongues. People talk, sharing and debating opinions. Complaints abound, and wishes are everywhere.

Six months before my third anniversary in prison, the news rocked the land that the Tate had died. The Tate had the second most important position in the land. Only Pharaoh was greater. All the nomarchs allied themselves on different sides, each pushing their own choice to be appointed the next Tate.

The most powerful nomarchs from Upper Egypt wanted Lord Amony to be the next officeholder. Those in Lower Egypt who had not allied themselves with Upper Egypt worked desperately to keep Lord Amony out of the position. They wanted someone more open to trade with Syria, Mesopotamia, and the countries on the Great Green, the sea to the north. Believing that the South had quite enough trade concessions, they felt that the lower part of the land should be awarded some benefits.

Many in Lower Egypt backed a young lord named Sety. Although inexperienced and arrogant, he was connected to the most powerful nomarchs of Lower Egypt, and the only one they could agree on.

From Khay, I learned of the anxiety in the palace as the Pharaoh delayed appointing a Tate. Yet, he got some decrees written and established by dangling the office of Tate in front of first one, then another, of the parties struggling for control. The people from one end of the land to the other waited tensely to see whom the king would pick.

▲ ▲ ▲ ▲

Once again the moon shone through the grillwork, and once again I stood beneath it and stared at the sky through it. I smiled to myself. I was a condemned prisoner—unique in Egypt, surely, for I might never leave this place except through death—but I was content. El Shaddai had honored me with His companionship and mercy, and I found it to be all that I needed.

In my hand I held the message from Khay that he and Hetepi were getting married. There would be a feast, and then Hetepi would move her things into Khay's house. They would live on Master Potiphar's Memphis estate, since her husband-to-be used it as a base of operations just as I had done. The match was a good one, for Hetepi would steady Khay's exuberance and impatience, and Khay would spice up Hetepi's life in several ways.

My smile broadening I asked El Shaddai to honor them, then

wrote out a note giving them my best wishes. They could be very happy together, but I shuddered to think of what their children might be like!

"El Shaddai," I whispered, "I thank you for my life. It is not what I dreamed of, but I have found in You the glory that I sought. You have become friend, mother, brother, and father to me, and I am honored and grateful for Your regard. I am content, my Lord. I am content."

▲　▲　▲　▲

Several months later, Master Setne arrived one morning in a dither. "It has happened again," he said, trotting into the guardroom. "And what may happen, I do not know. It—"

"What is the matter, Master?" I interrupted, knowing I didn't have time to listen to a long explanation.

"It is the court. They have come to Memphis and are at the old palace—the Tate's palace. It is only for a time, you know, but they are here. The Pharaoh is here. Sometimes he comes to Memphis and stays for a while. What if there should be an inspection? What will we do?"

"Why would there be an inspection?"

"Because the Pharaoh is here," Setne repeated. "And when the Pharaoh is here, people inspect. It is done, that is all. If they should inspect here—"

"They will find everything in order," I ended for him. "I have kept it in order. Scribe Hetepi has checked every season, and all is in order."

The worried frown disappeared from between Setne's eyes. "Yes, yes, that is right. I had forgotten for a moment. But you are here, good Joseph, wonderful Joseph, and you have kept everything in order. I do not need to be concerned. Let them come and inspect. I shall invite them to inspect. They shall see what an efficient official I am, and how I have made a wise decision to entrust everything to you. Yes, perhaps I shall be rewarded. Maybe it will be so. I hope they inspect. I hope they come. It would be a good thing."

And having completely reversed his opinion, Master Setne trotted away with his kilt flapping as usual about his knees. He beamed in delight at the guard bringing in a prisoner, and the guard didn't know how to respond. Hiding my smile, I settled in for another day.

▲ ▲ ▲ ▲

Amenemhet III paced the room just before dawn, frowning to himself after finally having driven the guards and courtiers from his presence. He could hide no longer the troubling dreams that tormented him night after night. They nearly drove him out of his mind. Always the same, always as chilling and foreboding, they made him awake in a cold sweat, fear choking his throat. The gods were sending him a message, but what was it?

He told no one at first. As a son of the gods, a god in human form, interpreting dreams from his fellow gods should be child's play. Only he didn't know what these dreams meant, just that they represented something very, very important that he had to know. The fact that the dreams had come in two different ways indicated that. The gods always sent the important messages twice. But this one eluded him.

After struggling to interpret them for two weeks, he had visited the temple of Ra at On. He spent two nights there, abasing himself before the god, pleading for understanding of the message. None came. If anything, the dreams were more vivid and frightening, and he left oppressed with his helplessness. It should not be! He was Pharaoh! Son to Ra. Why wouldn't Ra answer?

Thinking Ra might not have sent the dreams, he discreetly summoned the Great Among Craftsman of the temple of Ptah in Memphis. The consultation with Ptah's high priest left him no wiser, and the dreams persisted.

Amenemhet stopped his pacing for a moment and stared at the paintings on the walls. The idealistic life of a nobleman in the country stared back. Pharaoh jerked away, irritated. Why couldn't he find the meaning of two simple dreams? Interpreting dreams was a primary duty of any priest, and he was the true high priest for every god in the land. He resumed pacing.

It gave him little comfort to discover that none of the other priests could interpret his dreams either. Just last week he had summoned every high priest from every temple in the area. In a private audience he had revealed the dreams, stating their supreme importance and subtly offering them a chance to explain them. Strangely, the priests gave him no interpretation at all. They couldn't even tell him for sure which god had sent them, though some suggested Hathor, the cow-headed goddess.

His frown deepened. Normally, any dream given to priests garnered a dozen interpretations at least, and left the priests arguing for hours. But not this time. Still, the dreams continued, sometimes coming twice in the night. Some terrible disaster hovered over his land. The gods were warning him, but he could not understand! He beat his hand against the pillars in the room in frustration, only stopping when the pain became too great to bear. His duty as Pharaoh required him to know these things. Why didn't he?

Two nights ago he had awakened to find the bed coverings torn off the bed as he had tossed and wrestled in his fear and frustration at the dreams. Again he summoned the priests from the nearby temples, all of them, any of them. Once more he told them the dreams, describing them in detail. And as before, they put forward not one explanation. Each priest stood in abashed puzzlement, unable to make sense of anything he said, other than the fact that it had something to do with seven.

Why did the dreams resist interpretation? Amenemhet nearly went wild tormenting himself about it. They meant something. And they were urgent messages. He knew it, could feel it. *But what did they mean?*

By now, of course, the entire court had heard of the dreams and discussed them. He sent Tahsit quietly to listen to what they had to say. The king smiled bitterly to himself. He was so desperate he would consider anyone's interpretation. Anyone at all. But Tahsit returned with no information whatever.

Then tonight! Amenemhet stopped pacing to swallow the terror that rose in his stomach. This night the dreams had blazed across his mind, possessing him, filling him with such panic that he had cried out again and again, and he awoke to find his room crowded with guards and courtiers trying to determine what was wrong.

Unable to keep still, holding his head, wanting to scream with the agony *of not knowing,* he paced back and forth. Then a sound made him look up. Tahsit knelt in the doorway, holding a cup of spiced wine. He could smell the grapes and the spices. "Come," he said peremptorily.

The cupbearer approached, kneeling again to hand him the wine, and he drank half of it in one draught.

"O Great One, may your servant speak to you?" the man almost whispered.

Amenemhet looked down at the wine steward. Since he had proved useful in the past, it could not hurt to listen. Besides, he needed something to take his mind off those terrible dreams.

"Speak," he said shortly.

"My lord, do not be angry with me for speaking so, but you are troubled about your dreams?"

Pharaoh glanced sharply at the man, bowing before him. Then smiled grimly. Why not admit it? Everyone knew it.

"Yes, Tahsit, my dreams trouble me," he said wryly.

The wine steward looked up, encouraged by his change of tone.

"My lord, I have done wrong. I made a promise in the past, at the time I was put into my lord's prison when you were angry against your servant."

The king looked at Tahsit again. "Yes?" he said, suppressing his impatience.

"I promised I would mention to you what had happened while the Chief Baker and I were in the prison under the Captain of the Guard. We each had dreams one night. They troubled us very much, and we could not understand them. Strange dreams, they frightened us."

Tahsit paused, and Amenemhet waited, his attention caught.

"My lord, in the prison a young slave of the land of the Habiru attended to us. He asked us why we were upset. My lord, we told him our dreams, and he interpreted them immediately. His interpretation came true exactly as he said it would and exactly when he said it would, down to the last detail. In three days, as he said, you brought us both into your presence. You restored me to my position, but you had the Chief Baker executed and his body destroyed by the birds, as the young slave told us would happen. I promised to mention him to my lord, since the Habiru claimed to have done no wrong."

Amenemhet smiled slightly. Every prisoner in the land claimed to have done no wrong. But if this Habiru had interpreted dreams, he should investigate. "Tell me about this slave," he encouraged Tahsit.

After questioning him closely about the Habiru slave, Amenemhet sighed. "You have done well to tell me this," he told the steward. "I will consider this further."

"Thank you, my lord," Tahsit said, backing away. "May Ra bless his son, and grant peace to—"

Turning away, the king ignored the empty phrases that continually rang in his ears. Two years, he thought bitterly. How ironic to learn after two years of a prisoner who could interpret dreams easily and accurately! Undoubtedly the Habiru was either dead or at the mines by now. And if half of what Tahsit said was true, this slave must have considerable administrative ability. But he must have committed a major crime to be in prison instead of just suffering a beating and returning to work.

Nekhty, his personal scribe, arrived in the anteroom, and Amenemhet sternly contained his frustration. The attendants would be here momentarily to dress him and give him his first meal of the day. He would have to wait—but no.

"Nekhty," he called.

The scribe answered immediately, entering the room and bowing low. "Yes, my lord?"

"Send an immediate inquiry to the records for the Pharaoh's prison in Memphis under the Captain of the Guard about a Habiru slave. Tahsit can give you his name. I wish to know where he is."

"Yes, my lord." Nekhty withdrew.

Amenemhet sighed. At least one courtier did not ask questions.

Some time later, as Amenemhet finished eating his meal, the scribe returned.

"Yes?" the king asked.

"My lord, the young Habiru you inquired about is still in the prison under the Captain of the Guard."

Amenemhet's hand halted on its way to his mouth. "How is this? He has been in the prison for two years, and nothing has been done with him?"

"Apparently so, my lord."

"Thank you, Nekhty," Pharaoh said thoughtfully.

The scribe withdrew.

As Amenemhet sank into thought he soon found himself pacing again. When Nekhty entered he whirled around in annoyance. "What is it?" he snapped.

"My lord, it is time to open the court," the scribe said diffidently. "The courtiers wait in the small throne room."

"They can wait until I chose to appear," Pharaoh said shortly, turning away.

"Yes, my lord." For the second time Nekhty left.

Amenemhet sighed. He could not put off facing the court for long, and he dared show no weakness. He must compose himself. Until yesterday he had managed to keep up a front of simple inquiry about the dreams without giving away how desperate he really was. He could hide it no longer.

Shuddering, he held his head in his hands. He felt desperate about so many things. The trade concessions, the needs of the North and Delta, the nomarchs in the South, the necessity to appoint a new Tate, and now these dreams.

He would have to interview this prisoner in the court. Now that the courtiers knew of the dreams, he dared not risk excluding them by holding a private audience. Needing every possible support against the power of the nomarchs following Lord Amony, he could not afford to offend even a single courtier.

At the same time, dare he seek counsel from a barbarian prisoner? That in itself was an admission of weakness, unless the man was truly gifted in some way. If he wasn't, if this interview did not bring some information at least, he refused to think of the political position he would find himself in.

Irritation rose again in his mind. Why should he have to seek help from a barbarian? He was Pharaoh, the greatest ruler in the world, the most powerful man on earth. Why should he need a prisoner from the dungeon? Son to the gods, he was—

He was a man, and he knew nothing. Amenemhet leaned against the pillar, shaking with a knowledge that he could never, ever admit to anyone but himself. He was only a man with no special communication with the gods. Although he did not know what to do, he realized that he had to do something.

"I do not even know which god sent the dreams," he whispered to himself. Why had no one come up with any interpretation at all? Surely some of the priests who dealt with dreams could find something to say about his. Why had they remained silent? Surely the god who sent the dream wanted it understood.

Unless a foreign god sent the dream. Amenemhet nearly collapsed under the implications of the thought. Surely that couldn't be true. What foreign god could be more powerful than Ra? Egypt and her gods had defeated all the other nations around and their gods with them, proving their power and supremacy.

Could there be a strange god powerful enough to touch Egypt? To touch him? Is that why no one could interpret the dreams, because a foreign god had sent them? But why? What non-Egyptian god would care? Or was Egypt about to be destroyed, and the unknown god was announcing that fact? Is that what the devouring meant in the dreams?

He had to know so that he could prepare, so that he could protect his land and his people. His nation was vulnerable. The nomarchs, preoccupied with power and riches, thought only of themselves. He could not command them as he ought to keep his land from the rule of Seth. Now, was some barbarian god also threatening his land and his people?

This prisoner Tahsit spoke of was a barbarian. He would know about other gods. Maybe he could at least tell which deity threatened the land. Amenemhet straightened up. If he knew even that much, he could rouse the people and gods of Egypt to defend themselves. Therefore he would have to take the chance and send for this slave at once.

"Tahsit!" he called.

The wine steward appeared immediately.

"Send Lord Potiphar to me," he commanded.

"Lord Potiphar has taken a short trip to his country estate, Great One."

The frown on Amenemhet's face deepened. "His wife?"

"Yes, my lord," Tahsit said, unable to hide his surprise.

Amenemhet laughed shortly. "Do not think that because I am Pharaoh, I am blind, Tahsit. I see what everyone else does. A pity her relatives are so powerful."

Pharaoh paced the floor between the brilliantly painted pillars. He dared not wait until Lord Potiphar returned. He must see this prisoner immediately.

"Nekhty!"

"Yes, my lord?"

"Send to the prison in Memphis for the Habiru slave. I wish to see him at once."

"Yes, my lord."

▲ ▲ ▲ ▲

Ptahhotep rushed into the prison. "Joseph, it is a message, very urgent, from the palace," he panted. "The messenger is waiting out—"

But the messenger himself strode into the room, glancing around swiftly. "I am here to find someone named Joseph," he said brusquely. "Bring him to me."

"Joseph?" I asked in amazement.

The messenger nodded. "He is an Habiru, from Canaan, I understand. I am to bring him to the palace at once! Where is he?"

"I am Joseph."

The messenger seized my arm and started toward the door to the anteroom. Ptahhotep watched with wide eyes.

"Master, please," I said, "what do you want of me?"

The guard turned to me impatiently. "What do I know of that? I am ordered to bring you before Pharaoh without any delay whatsoever. Let us go."

"Before Pharaoh?" I cried, stopping again.

"Yes, Pharaoh," the messenger repeated, reaching for my arm again. "Now. The matter is very urgent."

"You are to take me before Pharaoh, the ruler of Egypt, in person?" I asked, trying to make sense of what I heard.

"Yes, yes, that is what I said. And without delay. Let us go at once."

"But I cannot possibly appear before Pharaoh looking like this!" I exclaimed. My hair was long and ragged, my beard full-grown, bristly, and uncut, my linen stained with ink and threadbare.

The messenger looked me up and down. "You are a foreigner. Pharaoh will not expect much. Let us go."

"Absolutely not," I said quietly. To appear before Pharaoh in my present state was unthinkable.

The Egyptian opened his mouth to protest, but I flashed him one glance and turned to Ptahhotep. "Go, quickly, and find the barber who sits in the main market by the spice shop. Sabestet is his name. Bring him here immediately," I commanded.

Ptahhotep jumped to obey. I turned to another guard. "Find Master Setne." With a nod he ran out the door.

I sat down at the table, trying to think of where I could get some decent linen. Khay appeared in the door with his usual grin.

"Nearly got run down twice getting in," he said. "What is the big occasion?"

"I have been called to go before Pharaoh," I explained, still a little dazed. "The guards are looking for a barber and Master Setne."

Khay's eyes opened wide. "Pharaoh?" he choked.

I indicated the messenger.

"Is this true?" Khay asked.

The messenger nodded, watching the two of us. "About an urgent matter."

"Do you know anything of this, Khay?" I asked.

"I don't think so. But you know how rumors fly. It is whispered in the marketplace that Pharaoh is especially troubled about something since he came to Memphis, but that is all that I have heard."

That didn't help much. I brought my mind back to practical matters. "Khay, I need some decent linen. Where can I get some?"

The barber came in, hurried along by two guards and looking frightened out of his wits.

Potiphar's steward took over. "Good barber, this man needs a haircut," Khay said, pointing to me. "The Pharaoh has sent for him, and he must be presentable. Begin immediately, and I will make it worth your fright in getting here!"

The barber gulped, set down his tools, and looked me over. "I used to do someone like him."

"That was me," I told him. "Cut it the same way you did then."

Without a further word, the barber went to work.

Master Setne rushed in. "What is this that Ptahhotep has said?" he wailed. "Pharaoh has sent for you? Why? What can this mean? You cannot go away. If you go, what will I do? I do not wish you to leave."

"You will have to let him go, Keeper Setne," Khay said without regard for Master Setne's feelings. "Pharaoh has spoken, and we must all obey. To Pharaoh Joseph goes as fast as we can make him ready. Perhaps all the Pharaoh wants is to see this marvel that has done so much with your prison."

"Do you think so?" the Keeper brightened. "It could be. I made a wise choice when I put Joseph in charge. Has the fame of it reached even to the palace?" Master Setne was so amazed that he could say no more.

"It may be," Khay said with a straight face. "But the Pharaoh did not say why he wanted Joseph. He just said he wanted him now."

"Well, then, you must hurry, Joseph," Setne admonished me. "You cannot keep the Pharaoh waiting. It is essential that you go quickly. But you will come back, surely. And then you will tell me all that you saw in the palace and what the Pharaoh was like and how the rooms were decorated. I must know, for my wife will ask."

I didn't answer, but I did note the second reference to a wife, so maybe he really was married.

"Khay, linen," I said urgently, knowing that I had to have something more than what I possessed to wear to the palace.

The messenger paced the floor, glancing at the barber frequently and fretting that it took so long.

Master Setne sputtered about linen, and I gave a beseeching look to Ptahhotep who nodded in sympathy and then skillfully maneuvered Setne out of the room. Now that he knew I was leaving for the palace, the Keeper was more hindrance than help.

Khay disappeared as the barber finished shaving me. Someone handed me a small bronze mirror. After a quick glance at my hair I decided that it would do. I didn't have a wig, and this was next best, with the hair cut as before at chin length and the ends turned under all around.

Excitement began to surge through me. Excitement and dread. What could this mean? Was it good or bad? Was I being sent for to be freed or executed? Now that I was leaving, I realized how comfortable I had become in this place, and how much security its walls provided. I left now without knowing if I faced death or life when I reached the palace.

Khay handed me a linen, and I slipped into the alcove to put it on. I hadn't the faintest idea where he got it, but it fit well and would suffice. At last I felt presentable. As I came out, the messenger glanced my way.

"Can we go now?" he asked sarcastically.

"Yes, Master."

He grabbed my arm and started out of the guardroom. I didn't even have time to say goodbye to anyone. As I went by I observed that Khay seemed to have been wiping his pens on his linen. I hadn't noticed it when he came in.

The messenger kept his grip on my arm and made me run. Outside in the courtyard waited a chariot! Stunned, I almost fell as the palace retainer hustled me into it and gave the word to the driver. We started with a jolt, and I didn't have time to think of anything else but staying upright as the horses charged out of the prison complex. I made a wager with myself that my return would be much quieter, assuming I was still alive.

CHAPTER 15

O nce at the palace, the messenger didn't give me time to regain my balance from that incredible ride. He practically lifted me from the chariot and ran me up the steps to the porch. A kaleidoscope of colors and shapes rushed past as the man pushed me through the wide central waiting area and down a maze of halls.

Finally he opened a door and shoved me inside in front of him.

"It's about time," an official said. "What took so long?"

"He insisted on a shave, haircut, and proper clothing," the messenger replied.

The official looked me over thoroughly. "Wise of him. But I think a wig will be required. Wait here."

I tried to catch my breath while the messenger shifted impatiently. The official returned with a neatly crafted wig, large and heavy enough to fully hide my red hair.

"I will tell the Pharaoh all is ready. He will receive you in the lesser throne room. Take him there now."

Without even another glance at me, the official hurried away. The messenger took my arm again and propelled me out the door and down some more hallways, through rooms, and past people who all stopped to stare as I hurried by.

At last we came to a room full of people. The messenger paused a moment before entering, and he stayed near the door. Gratefully I rested beside him. From the looks of the room, it was a gathering of highly important government officials. My linen was quite respectable, but it was the shabbiest here. Two men wore gold collars, and one had earrings. Gold bracelets and ornaments abounded. A group of priests stood to one side, completely shaved, discussing something among themselves, and I soon realized that everyone in the room was trying to hear whatever they said.

The doors at the far end of the room opened, and we waited

among the pillars as the others preceded us into the next room. I caught a glimpse of the colors around me, then the messenger urged me toward the door.

We walked into the next room, and every eye riveted on me instantly. I felt the stares as the messenger escorted me toward the raised dais with its simple wooden chair overlaid with gold. Beside it stood a small table with some fruit and wine in golden dishes. On the chair sat a man about my age, with the royal head covering and the golden circlet of the cobra Uraeus around it. I didn't have time to see more before the messenger stepped aside, and I knelt and kissed the ground before the ruler of all Egypt, as was proper for someone of my station to do.

Then I stayed on my knees with eyes lowered until Pharaoh should speak to me.

"Rise," he said, a hint of curiosity in his voice.

I stood up, feeling the man's eyes on me and flushed slightly.

"Let me see your face," he commanded, and I looked at him, heart pounding. This man could either free me or execute me. Which would it be?

He was a young man with an old face. His mouth was firm and closed, his face laden with the cares of his people. I saw little laughter there, for the concerns and problems of the mightiest nation on earth had driven it away. Glancing into his dark eyes, I recognized the intense worry, the desperation, and the half-frightened hope that raged in this man's soul despite his calm demeanor and still form.

I realized then that I was here to serve, not to be freed or executed. Pharaoh needed something, and he thought I could help. I waited.

"I have had a dream," Pharaoh said, his voice resonate and easily filling the room. "No one has been able to tell me what it means. I have been told that you can interpret dreams."

The simplicity of the statement took my breath away for a minute. This man wasted no words. He did not try to impress with high-sounding titles, or forward his need with flattery.

Glancing around swiftly, I analyzed the situation as best I could. Tahsit hovered in the background. That explained how Pharaoh had heard about me. A dream accounted for the presence of the priests. But Pharaoh was a god in human form and the true high priest of every god in the land. For him to ask subordinate priests for an interpretation of a dream would be highly unusual.

Even more so, he had also sent for me, a prisoner and a barbarian, and brought me publically before him to ask me to do what he was supposed to do for himself! What could possibly be so fearful that Pharaoh would ignore maat, upset the balance, in this manner?

Only moments had passed. Once again, Pharaoh's eyes revealed the urgency filling his mind.

Suddenly I knew, beyond a shadow of a doubt, that this was why I had received the gift of interpretation. This moment was the reason for my journey to this land, to stand here before Pharaoh and answer his need. All my excitement and nervousness disappeared. I was here to glorify El Shaddai.

Pharaoh reached idly for a fig from the table beside him.

"Of myself, I cannot interpret any dream, Great One," I said.

His hand paused momentarily.

"But El Shaddai, the God whom I serve, will send you an answer of peace. Tell me the dream."

Amenemhet looked at me sharply, and for the first time since I came to this land, I stared directly back. Pharaoh's eyes widened, and he dropped the fig from his hand. He met my gaze squarely, and I watched the astonishment and curiosity turn to respect, then a wild, desperate hope.

"I dreamed I stood on the bank of the Nile," he began, his voice giving no hint of the emotions I saw raging through him. "Seven fat, sleek kine came up out of the river and began to feed in the meadow beside me. And then, seven thin bony kine rose out of the water. I have never seen such starved kine in my life. The thin kine walked over to the fat kine, but instead of feeding on the grass, the thin kine began to devour the fat kine. They ate them all, but they did not grow any fatter. They remained as thin and bony and weak as before. The dream was so disturbing that I woke up and realized that I had dreamed it all."

Out of the corner of my eye, I saw the looks the priests gave each other. Clearly they wondered what I, a slave and a barbarian, would make of this dream. Just as clearly, they had been unable to decide for themselves what they thought of it.

I pulled my attention back to Pharaoh. "Go on, my lord," I said respectfully.

Pharaoh raised his eyebrows slightly, and a quick smile of amusement flitted across his face. He continued.

"I fell asleep once more, still thinking about the dream. I stood now in a wheat field. A stalk grew near me with seven fat heads of wheat on it. The grains were full and plump, the best wheat I had ever seen. Then, while I watched, right next to it grew a second stalk, and it too sprouted seven heads of wheat. But this grain was withered and dry, scorched by the wind from the desert. The heads of dry withered grain reached over and devoured the heads of full plump grain, but they remained as withered and scorched as before. Again I woke.

"I called my wise men and priests to help me understand these dreams, but no one has been able to explain them."

I swallowed. The calamity that swiftly approached Egypt appalled me. The entire land could die. I must emphasize the danger.

Pharaoh watched me narrowly, reading the concern that crossed my face. The priests waited also, some with smirks on their faces. The courtiers and nobles remained silent, waiting to see what would happen.

"The two dreams you had are actually one," I said. "El Shaddai has showed you what He is about to do. The seven fat kine and the seven fat heads of wheat are seven years of plenty. The seven thin kine and the seven scorched heads of wheat are seven years of famine.

"The dreams have the same meaning. El Shaddai wants you to know what is to come so that you can be a true father to your people and prepare for what is about to descend on this land."

The priests whispered to each other, and Pharaoh held up his hand for silence. When the room quieted, I went on.

"There will be seven years of plenty. Seven years of harvests such as Egypt has never seen. These seven years will be followed by seven years of famine so severe that no one will remember what the years of plenty were like. The famine will consume the land as the thin kine and scorched grain consumed the fat kine and plump grain. All of Egypt will suffer. There will be no food to eat anywhere.

"The warning was given to you as a double dream because it is certain to happen, and it will happen very soon."

The lines around Pharaoh's eyes deepened, and the courtiers murmured among themselves. From the tone of the voices, I could tell that they believed what I had said. The expression on Pharaoh's face indicated that he did also. I breathed a prayer of thanks to El Shaddai.

While the anxiety in Pharaoh's eyes had left now that he knew the interpretation of his dream, it had been replaced by a heavy concern for what he could do to prevent the disaster from destroying his land. He glanced at me, and I took that as permission to speak.

"Perhaps Pharaoh would look for a capable man to set over Egypt," I said, surprising the others with my suggestion. "Let this man appoint officials over Upper and Lower Egypt to collect a full one-fifth of the grain harvested during the years of plenty. This grain should be stored in the cities in the name of Pharaoh and kept until the time of famine comes. Then when harvests fail, and the regular stores of grain are gone, it can be distributed to the people and thus the land will be saved from death."

Pharaoh's eyes lit up, and he almost smiled. "You suggest one-fifth, in my name, not the nomarch's?" he asked.

"Yes, my lord."

He looked at the others in the room for the first time. "Can we deny that the Spirit of his God is in this man?" he asked.

"No, my lord," the courtiers and priests answered.

"I must consider what you have said," the king continued. He nodded to the messenger who had brought me here, and the man came forward. We bowed, and he took me out of the room.

As soon as we left, the official the messenger had reported to pounced on us. "What happened?" he demanded of his fellow Egyptian.

Walking further among the pillars, I noted the faded paintings on the walls and the places where plaster had chipped or fallen away. Sand collected in the corners, and dust lay undisturbed on the floor. Behind me the messenger and the official whispered together. I wished I could sit down. That chariot ride had been very bad on my ankles, and they hurt for the first time in a long time.

As time dragged on, I wandered to the other side of the room and eased down behind an old scribe's table. It didn't look like I'd get back to the prison until late. I hoped that Master Setne had the sense to see that everyone got fed tonight.

▲ ▲ ▲ ▲

In the small anteroom behind the throne room, Amenemhet III paced back and forth, playing with the idea that had popped into his head when that barbarian slave outlined for him the perfect plan of action to avert the disaster bearing down upon his land. He smiled sardonically. One-fifth? A tax of one-fifth? How wide the nobles' eyes had opened at that!

Pharaoh sighed. He couldn't even collect the taxes due now, let alone a tax of one-fifth. Pharaoh he might be, but Lord Amony held him practically helpless, the powerful coterie of nomarchs following Amony blocking him at every turn. Taxes were only one example. The nomarchs managed to get their own right on time, but if he remembered correctly Lord Peun of the sixteenth nome was a year behind in royal taxes, and Lord Meritifi of the twelfth nome two years. The rest were somewhat up to date, but never sent quite as much as they were assessed. Ironically, only Lord Mose of the first nome sent punctual taxes, but then the man hardly deigned to notice him as Pharaoh when he came to court.

He sighed. If he insisted that Lord Meritifi pay up, the routes to the porphyry quarries by the Red Sea that began in his nome would suddenly be without guards and patrols. The price of porphyry for tombs and statues would skyrocket since Meritifi held the concession on trade in porphyry, and the entire nobility would rise in anger. Worse was the sixteenth nome, for Lord Peun could raise the price of land for tombs, which was already higher than usual, and Amenemhet knew very well what would happen if he threatened the afterlife of the nobility. He would have armed revolt on his hands, and he didn't have the treasury or the men to fight. Egypt would descend into chaos.

But one-fifth! On the other hand, did he have a choice? Famine played no favorites. Everyone died.

For a moment he paused to wonder why he had no doubt that the extraordinary interpretation of his dream was correct. Maybe because of those intense blue eyes that gazed into his and read his soul. He had seen the eyes of Ra now, and he knew this man saw and said the truth. He shivered with the feeling that came over him as he remembered looking into those eyes. More than humanness had gazed back at him.

Somehow he couldn't shake the feeling that this man was the answer to his prayers, not just to avert the disaster that had just been foretold, but to stop the other one that he witnessed every day, the neglect of the people by the nomarchs, the ever growing power of the nobles who cared only for their own riches and glory and nothing for the people they were supposed to rule and protect. Maat was threatened either way—by the nomarchs, or the famine. Whichever happened, Egypt would die.

He simply did not know what to do, which was the real reason he had not named a Tate. If he appointed Lord Sety, the man's inexperience and vanity would have the entire country in an uproar, and if he chose Lord Amony, he might as well give him the throne and be done with it. Several times he had almost named Lord Amony, since at least half of the country would be cared for, but he had always held off, hoping that some impossible chance would throw the balance of power his way for just long enough.

Might this be it? He needed someone loyal to him alone, someone who would share with him his burden of caring for the thousands upon thousands of people dependent on the maat he kept between order and chaos, between the north and the south, between the nobles and the commoners.

Could it be that the gods had sent him this man? He was a prisoner, so presumably he had done something wrong. And he was a foreigner, so how could the gods have chosen him? As a slave, how could he have governmental and organizational skills? What did he know of the differences that existed in Egypt, of the demands of economics and justice and diplomacy?

Amenemhet shook his head. As overlord of the world, how could he possibly consider appointing a barbarian slave as Tate? Because his back was to the wall, that was why, and Egypt faced destruction. Because he cared for the people who would suffer and die in the wars of the nomarchs or of the starvation of famine. Because he was Pharaoh, and must protect the land of the gods. And because he couldn't get away from those eyes and the uncanny light in them that spoke of the Spirit of a God.

He had been right. A strange god sent had his dreams. But who was this El Shaddai God that the slave spoke of? This God must be powerful enough to send a dream to someone who did not worship Him. If He could dispatch those dreams, surely He could make them true, for what god ever warned of something he could not accomplish?

Vainly, he wished he could talk to his father. But this decision he must make alone, and quickly, before the shock of the impending disaster wore off and the nobles went back to fighting for the highest place. He had no one he could talk to, for each of his advisors urged him to name someone different as Tate.

But the man was a slave, a captive. How could his god be powerful if he couldn't even keep his servants from slavery? Unless—

A shiver went down Amenemhet's spine. If this god was powerful enough to touch lands and people that did not worship him, *to touch him even though he was Pharaoh,* maybe this god was so powerful that it didn't matter if his servants became slaves. Perhaps this foreign god was so powerful that he could work even through slaves to do his will.

Those eyes had read his soul. The slave's God had looked back at him from them. They were not the eyes of Horus or Ra, they were the eyes of—of—what had that slave said his God's name was?

Ceasing his pacing, Amenemhet faced the door to the throne room. He needed a god right now to save his land from famine and from its rulers. The man who had been brought to him was a barbarian slave, but a barbarian slave possessed by a god. Amenemhet knew this chance would never come again. When he clapped his hands, a door instantly opened.

"Yes, my lord?" the attendant bowed.

"Send for Scribe Nekhty."

The attendant vanished. Amenemhet looked thoughtfully again toward the throne room. Either he had just saved Egypt or destroyed it. Only time would tell.

▲ ▲ ▲ ▲

Someone hurried in, and I looked up. An attendant went to an official and said, "The Pharaoh requires you, Scribe Nekhty."

Nekhty hurried away, only to quickly return and tell the messenger to bring me into the throne room. I wondered what hour of the day it was. Maybe after Pharaoh spoke to me, I could find the outdoors through the maze of rooms in this place.

Once again all eyes watched me as the messenger led me to the Pharaoh, and once again I bowed to the floor.

"Rise," Pharaoh said to me, and I stood up. "Scribe Nekhty tells me your name is Joseph?"

"Yes, my lord."

"Your plan is a good and wise one. Is it not so?" he asked the nobles and priests in the room.

"It is so," they assented. Approval and respect echoed in their words.

"Where is there a better man than one with the Spirit of God in him?" Pharaoh continued.

"We will not find one anywhere," one of the lords spoke up, and the others murmured their agreement.

"It is decided then," Pharaoh announced, standing and turning to me. "Because your God has shown you what will come in the future, you have greater wisdom and insight than any man in my kingdom. I have decided to appoint you as Tate. You shall be in charge of all of Egypt, and all of my people shall obey whatever you say."

A gasp went through the crowd, quickly silenced by Pharaoh's hand.

"Only when I sit on the throne will my authority be greater than yours. I now make you Tate, Governor of Upper and Lower Egypt."

Stepping down from the dais, Pharaoh came toward me. I couldn't move or breathe. Surely I was dreaming. I must have fallen asleep in the anteroom, there at the scribe's desk, and I would awaken soon.

Nekhty followed his king, carrying linen and gold.

Pharaoh removed the ring off his finger, and taking my hand, he placed it on mine. Then the scribe brought a golden collar that Pharaoh placed around my neck. Next Nekhty helped me into a fine linen robe so sheer it was all but transparent. After guiding me back to the throne with him, Pharaoh faced the court and said, "I am Amenemhet, Pharaoh of Upper and Lower Egypt. No one in Egypt shall lift hand or foot without your permission, Joseph. You shall be known as Paanekh, meaning 'This one lives.'"

From beside me Scribe Nekhty cried out, "Bow the knee," and the entire court obeyed instantly. "That which you command is that which shall be done, Sovereign and Lord," everyone assented with one voice.

If Amenemhet had not been standing right there beside me, I would have fallen. Those words were the same ones Khay had said to me when Lord Potiphar returned home to send me to prison. Amenemhet steadied me, with a look of dry amusement on his face.

"My—my lord?" I managed to whisper, completely bewildered, confused between what had happened here and what Khay had done three years before.

"I just made you second ruler of the land," Amenemhet said back in a very low voice. "Now we will go outside, and I will introduce you to the people. Any objections?"

I tried to bring enough air into my lungs to clear my head, or wake myself up, or something, but nothing seemed to work.

"But my lord, I am a slave," I said, still not understanding. "I am a prisoner."

"Not anymore," Amenemhet said, nudging me off the dais and walking me down the throne room toward the door. "I just freed you and gave you a full pardon for whatever you did wrong. Any other objections?"

"But my lord, this is so sudden," I stammered as we headed out the door.

"Bow the knee," Nekhty cried again from beside me as we walked into the anteroom, now filled with more courtiers and officials. They all quickly obeyed, and I looked over a sea of backs as we walked into a hallway. "That which you command is that which will be done, Sovereign and Lord," the people in the room recited.

"Yes, it was sudden," Amenemhet said. "But sometimes it behooves a ruler to move suddenly. Anything else?"

"My lord, I—I—" I stuttered to a halt as we took a sharp turn and I saw the light of day from the end of the hall.

"Well?" Pharaoh prodded.

"All of Egypt?" I said, still dazed.

"Kemet and Deshret, north to south, and Delta included," he replied with quiet amusement as we walked out into a porch. "Don't let the nomarchs intimidate you. You can have them executed if you wish."

"No, my lord. Yes, my lord. I—I—don't know what to say, my lord," I finished, still feeling as if I wandered around in someone else's dream.

"Since I am Pharaoh, and the only person in Egypt greater than you, just say, 'Yes, my lord,' 'Whatever you say, my lord,' and 'I will do it at once, my lord.'"

Two chariots, both overlaid with gold, waited by the porch, and people jammed the courtyard.

"Bow the knee," Nekhty cried again, and everyone dropped to the pavement.

"I am Pharaoh," Amenemhet said beside me, making me jump.

His voice echoed across the courtyard. "Be it known that this day I have made Paanekh, This One Lives, second ruler of the land. He shall be Tate to me from this day forward."

"That which you command is that which will be done, Sovereign and Lord," the crowd roared back.

The people began to cheer, shouting my new name, and Amenemhet shoved me toward the second chariot. I got in mechanically, then had to grab the handhold as we started with a jolt. We hurled through the streets and squares of Memphis, the news seeming to spread faster than we traveled. People flocked to see Amenemhet in the first chariot and myself in the second as runners went before us shouting "Bow the knee!" It was the wildest, most bewildering, most amazing ride of my life.

I remember none of it.

It is a complete blur of starts, stops, announcements, faces, noise, and backs of every imaginable variety.

▲ ▲ ▲ ▲

To be perfectly frank, I didn't know what to do, so I just stood there in the room, holding the linen, the collar, the ring, and the wig. My guide had just left, and the other service staff had not yet arrived at my rooms. I was supposed to sleep in the bed next to the wall with the garden scene painted on it. A dyed linen curtain divided the room, and the bed had a wooden frame with a soft stuffed mattress supported by a rope. Dusty coverings waited for me to climb beneath them.

I tried to wake up and looked at each individual item in the room, calling it by name to myself, and describing it to myself. The large jar in the corner. The colored curtain. The tables and chair, the fruit in a bowl, the pillars painted like lotus flowers, the beautiful inlaid chest that held more linens, the two feet standing beside the box—

Startled, I looked up. A guard stared at me oddly.

"Is Lord Paanekh here?" he asked.

I glanced around vaguely, trying to understand who he asked about.

"Are you new here?" the guard asked curiously.

I nodded. That one I knew the answer to.

"Shall I show you where the attendant's room is?" he asked.

Suddenly, I wanted very much to be back where I was familiar with everything. "Yes, I would like that." The things I had in my hands weren't really mine, they were for Lord Paanekh, and I knew what to do with them if I was a slave once more. I needed to fold them and keep them until Lord Paanekh wanted them again.

"There's a door at the back of this room, beyond the curtain," the guard said, gesturing. "When you have put your master's things away, come down the hall to the cross-hall. Go left and across the courtyard. The kitchens are there, and you can get something to eat."

"Thank you," I said.

The guard nodded and left.

After I went to the back of the room and through the door I looked down at a familiar reed bed, a battered box for linens, and a pitcher for water, now empty. All familiar, all normal, all connected with my life. I put the linen, gold, and wig on a small scribe's table in one corner. Suddenly, I had to sit down. Dropping to the floor right where I was, I stared at the gold winking at me in the flickering light of the oil lamp.

"Tate?" I whispered. "El Shaddai, You made me Tate?"

I just sat for some time, then I got up and took the ring from the pile. Folding the linen and settling the gold collar on it neatly, I covered them with the wig. Then I tucked the ring into a fold of the linen I wore, the linen that Khay had found for me a year ago this morning, and went back into the large room.

No other staff had arrived, so I explored the room, looking at the furniture and dishes in it. All were dusty and quite old. Obviously this place had not been used in some time. I moved a wall hanging in a corner, sneezing from the dust. My eye caught the wood of a door lintel, and I pulled the hanging away. Another door led somewhere.

It took some force before it grudgingly opened. A tiny forgotten garden met my eye. A very small pool in one corner flowed quietly from under one wall to under the other. Overgrown and neglected plantings met my eye, but the air was fresh, and the stars twinkled above me like familiar friends.

Out in the night, with the stars and moonlight, I found myself again. I was familiar with the moon and the stars. Sitting again, I tried to remember what had happened this morning—in the prison where I lived. Tonight, I was in the palace, where I lived. I couldn't take it in, even yet.

"El Shaddai, what have you done with me?" I asked, shaking my head. "How was this possible?" And then, I remembered for the first time what old Menneb had said to me that day, when everyone came running to me for answers about the feast. "At this rate, you will be running the entire country before you are done!"

How I had laughed. And how Menneb would laugh if he were alive now!

Snefru's words came back to me also. "Cling to your god. He is taking you somewhere. Somewhere great."

Bowing my head, I wiped a hand across my eyes. "I never imagined this, El Shaddai," I whispered. "Not even in my wildest dreams."

Only then did I begin to believe what had happened to me this day. Only then did it make sense, did it seem to have actually happened to me. I was free. I wasn't a slave anymore. Pharaoh himself had said so. I was not a condemned man, forgotten in a prison, but Lord Paanekh, Tate of Upper and Lower Egypt, Second to Pharaoh, Ruler of the Black Land and the Red Land, Chosen of the Guard, Nearest Friend to Pharaoh, Chief Advisor and Great Councilor, Friend to Pharaoh, Chief of the Judges of Sasat—and whatever else I had been called time and again today.

For the third time, my life changed in a matter of hours. First when my brothers sold me, second when Lord Potiphar put me in prison, and now as I gazed at a tiny pool in the palace that, if I remembered correctly, I now owned. I even had a new name. Throwing back my head, I laughed until I could laugh no more. Pharaoh had called me "This One Lives," and it was true, for in spite of my brothers, and Sekhmet, and Lady Tanefret, I was very much alive.

That night I spent sleeping comfortably in the attendant's room, which also had a door to the tiny garden. I rose early and followed the guard's directions to the kitchens. The baker took some bread from the oven as I walked in. He tossed me a piece, and I breakfasted on bread and fruit.

The guard who had showed me my room the previous night entered. "Ah, you are up early," he said. "My name is Chaf. What is your name?"

"Joseph," I said without thinking, then felt surprisingly relieved that I could cloak myself in the familiar manners of a slave for a little while yet.

"You serve Lord Paanekh, don't you?" the baker asked, curious.

I nodded. "Yes, and he will need some kohl. Where can I get some?"

"I can show you," a serving girl said shyly, blushing furiously when I glanced at her.

"Thank you—?" I paused.

"Abana," she filled in.

"Thank you, Abana."

I followed her to a storeroom and obtained kohl and hair oil. Also I picked up a razor and a battered bronze mirror.

"The mirror isn't very good," the girl commented.

I shrugged. "It will do for now. Thank you for showing me around." I hurried back to the Tate's rooms and quickly shaved, putting on the wig again first thing. The heavy, full piece completely covered my red hair. Then I opened the box of linens and shook some out. Finding one suitable to wear, I wrapped myself in it and put on the kohl, which I would need now that I would be outside more, and debated on the hair oil. I decided to skip it today. I had a little bit of trouble with the fastener on the collar, but at last I got it closed. Slipping the signet ring on my finger, I headed for the door.

Chaf stood outside. He bowed when I came out.

"Lord Paanekh?" he asked.

I nodded.

"I have been assigned to escort you. I am to take you to Pharaoh."

Again I nodded, and Chaf led the way through the maze that was the old Memphis palace. We passed through halls, rooms, and three courtyards on the way to Pharaoh's rooms.

Chaf announced me when we got to our destination, and Scribe Nekhty jumped up from his table to bow when I entered.

"You rise early, my lord," he said. "Pharaoh has not finished his morning meal. Please wait, and I will tell him that you are here."

He disappeared into a room and came back almost immediately. "Pharaoh wishes you to enter at once."

I faced the door. In that room was the most powerful man in my world, and he had just chosen me to save his land from destruction. One of us had to be crazy. Or else El Shaddai was.

CHAPTER 16

Amenemhet sat by a small table, finishing a pomegranate. I bowed deeply.

"Thank you, Nekhty," Pharaoh said, dismissing the scribe, who left the room, taking the other attendants with him. Pharaoh looked at me. "Sit down. I like to be relaxed whenever I can."

"Thank you, my lord," I said, sitting in another chair.

"You slept well?" he asked next.

"Yes, my lord," I said with a smile, thinking of where I actually had spent the night.

"Tell me of yourself," he commanded.

I groped for words. Suddenly everything about my life seemed unimportant.

"Tahsit said you were a Habiru?" Amenemhet prompted.

"Yes, my lord, I am Habiru, from Canaan. I was stolen from my people and sold as a slave. I became Chief Steward of my master's estate and then was accused of a crime and placed in prison. I was there when Tahsit and Manakh were brought there and the rest you know."

Amenemhet smiled. "Very concise, very brief, and very modest. There is much more to your story, I assume."

I flushed slightly. "It is not important, my lord."

Pharaoh chuckled. "Maybe. You intrigue me. Are you wondering why I named you Tate?"

"I would assume, my lord, that you needed someone loyal to you. Neither Lord Amony nor Lord Sety are attractive choices."

The king stopped chewing. "Oh? What do you know of Lord Amony and Lord Sety?"

"I do not know anything of Lord Sety except by hearsay," I admitted. "But Lord Amony I have met, and he appears to be a man who looks after himself very well."

Pharaoh laughed outright. "He does, does he? That is the best summary of Lord Amony I have heard in years." From there, the conversation ranged throughout many subjects. Amenemhet asked me questions about trade, business, diplomacy and military strategy, government and rulership.

I did not know how much time passed, but when Amen-emhet leaned back in his chair and sighed, I knew that I had pleased him.

"The gods truly led me to you," he said. "How a man of your education and talents ended up in my prison in Memphis, I do not know. If anyone had told me I would make a barbarian slave my Tate, and be glad of it, I would have called them touched by Seth. I feared I would have to teach you the responsibilities of your office, but I see that I will not.

"Now, how do you plan to save my country?"

"When is next Harvest?"

Pharaoh looked at me oddly. "Harvest is just ended."

"Pardon for asking, my lord," I explained. "In prison, seasons do not mean much."

Amenemhet looked thoughtful. "I can see where they would not."

"I will start by building. We must have storehouses ready for next year to hold the grain. Special care must be taken in the Delta to keep the grain dry and usable. I will need staffing and buildings to work from."

Pharaoh held up his hand. "Go to Nekhty for that. As for administrators, appoint whomever you wish. After talking to you today, I see that I can leave everything entirely in your hands."

"My lord," I said hesitantly, "what I have in mind may, well, rearrange the country somewhat."

Again Amenemhet laughed out loud. "How soon?"

"Not right away," I hastily replied. "But when the famine comes, there must be a system in place for efficient and swift distribution to every person in the land, and—"

"Will it really be as bad as you say?" he asked abruptly.

"Yes, my lord," I said soberly. "This will be the worst famine anyone has ever seen."

He stared at me for several seconds. I looked back.

"Do whatever you wish," he decided. "I place every person in this country at your disposal. That includes the nobles, nomarchs, lords and ladies down to the smallest official on the smallest estate. You are Tate. Your word is law, and you have the power of life or death. I must review any sentence of death, but I cannot imagine you giving a death sentence that was not deserved. The country is yours to command, Lord Paanekh."

I bowed my head briefly. "I am a newcomer and a foreigner," I said softly. "There will be those who object."

"And they shall come to me," he said with a wry grin. "And I shall send them to you. Understand me, Paanekh. I require but one thing of you. Save my people."

"Yes, my lord," I said, watching him. He had something else on his mind, I could tell, but I wondered if I should acknowledge my awareness of it.

"Is there, perhaps, something more?" I finally asked.

Amenemhet smiled wearily. "I have one other wish, but I do not know any who can give it to me."

"What would that be, my lord?"

"The desire of my heart is to control the nobility, especially the nomarchs," he said softly. "They have grown too powerful, and they are ignoring the needs of the land they live off of. But there is nothing I can do. It left even my father frustrated, and he was wiser than I. I am very afraid of what will happen to this land if the nobility is not restrained." Again, I saw the old face on the young man, reflecting his deep concern and heartfelt anxiety over the trouble he saw coming and could not avert.

I stood and bowed formally. "My lord, you have taken me from the prison and brought me to the highest office in the land. I will remember your wish."

Pharaoh gave me a tired smile. "Thank you. Where will you begin?"

"I must take some time to plan and learn what I have to work with," I decided.

"Every decision you make, I am more pleased with my decision to elevate you," he said. "I will send Nekhty to you tomorrow. He will be able to answer most any question you will have. How long will it take you to organize?"

"If I have good information, a week should give me a good picture of things."

"I will stay in Memphis until you are settled. Then I will return to Itej-Tawy. May the gods go with you," he added.

I walked out, to find Nekhty with several lords waiting to see Pharaoh. They stared at me briefly before bowing. I had to rigidly suppress my instinct to bow deeply in return. A slave no longer, I need bow only to Pharaoh.

As I walked the halls, followed by Chaf, I found myself wanting to move aside whenever anyone approached. I would have to watch myself carefully, for such behavior would not help me establish the authority and order I would need to successfully store enough grain in the next seven years.

The first time I walked outside, I stopped, startled. The sun was setting! I had spent the entire day with Pharaoh.

Returning to my room, I changed into the linen I wore yesterday, put away the collar and wig, and tucked the signet ring in my clothing, and reminded myself to keep my eyes down as befitted a slave. Then as I walked out, Chaf winked at me. With a grin and a wave, I headed for the kitchen and supper.

While I sat in a corner on a pile of sacks and ate, I listened to the gossip. The staff sent to attend me had searched half the night when they did not see me in my rooms, then decided that I had gone to the Memphis residence. Learning of that residence reminded me that I should find out how much property I controlled. Probably a lot.

I tucked away as many names as I could while the discussions went on. Faces I would have to match up later. I picked up quickly that the court was sharply divided. Those who had been in the throne room when I interpreted Pharaoh's dream either supported my appointment or were neutral toward it. But those who had not been there were angry and dissatisfied, demanding to know what would happen to the country with a barbarian slave upsetting maat.

That evening I spent helping about the place. Abana stayed close to me, and I welcomed her pithy comments on the lords and ladies that she served. She had a sharp eye for personalities. I picked up undercurrents among the staff and learned their opinion of Lord Sety—a silly wastrel—and Lord Amony—feared for his power, but despised for his lack of care for his people.

▲ ▲ ▲ ▲

"There is a new Tate," Renseneb reported.

Lady Asenath looked up in surprise. "Whom did he appoint? Lord Amony or that mincing Lord Sety?"

"Neither. He elevated a foreigner."

She stared at him in disbelief. "A foreigner? Someone from the Kap school for the sons the subject kings sent as hostages?"

"I do not know, my lady. I do not think so. There are stories going around that he came from prison, but I have not heard of any who attend the Kap school in the palace being in prison."

"You must have been mistaken, Renseneb. But in any case, with a new Tate, we must pull back a little. If he is truly a foreigner, we must wait to see what he will do with Pharaoh's trade. Whether he will open it up or close it down remains to be seen. We may have to get new concessions from the palace to continue."

"Yes, Lady."

"For now, let us concentrate in Beni Hassan. Most of what we do there does not require royal concessions."

"Yes, lady. I will go there tomorrow."

"Thank you, Renseneb. I will want to see you the minute you get back."

"As you wish, Lady."

▲ ▲ ▲ ▲

The next morning I ate early in the kitchens and then went back to Lord Paanekh's rooms to prepare for Nekhty. He arrived in good time, and I soon had him scrambling to supply answers to the questions I had for him. At first, he covered his condescension with polite and useless answers, but when I started reading the papyrus leaves in front of him for myself, he snapped alert.

I grilled him all day, breaking briefly for a quick meal at noon. He looked exhausted when he left my rooms, and he would have to work half the night to find the answers to what I wanted, but he no longer viewed me as a figurehead to placate and shuffle aside. Pharaoh had given me an order, and I meant to carry it out, one way or another.

Sighing, I shed the fine linen, collar, and wig. I looked around the room and shrugged, thinking I might as well sleep in the bed tonight. But first I wanted something to eat. As I stepped out of the door, someone ran into me. Grabbing the person, I saw Abana's frightened face.

"Oh, Joseph, I don't know what to do," she gasped.

"What is the matter, Abana?"

"I overheard Tais talking when I was out in the courtyard," she blurted out. "Does the new Tate stay here? I did not understand what they were saying but I think something bad is going to happen."

I looked at her intently. Pale and shaking, she was very upset by whatever she had overheard.

"Tell me the whole thing," I said quietly, pulling her back into my rooms and shutting the door. "Sit right here and tell me everything."

Wiping her eyes, she sat down. "Who sleeps here?" she asked again. "Is it Lord Paanekh, your master? You must warn him, Joseph."

"Yes, these are his rooms. I will warn him just as soon as you tell me what this is all about," I assured her.

Nodding, the girl took a deep breath. "I was resting out in the courtyard for just a minute, sitting under the flowers by the fountain where I usually go to eat. Someone started talking just on the other side of the wall and I recognized Tais' voice." She stopped, clenching her hands.

"What did they say, Abana?"

"The stranger asked where the barbarian would stay tonight, and Tais gave him directions and described where the bed was. Then Tais said, 'Where's the payment?' and the stranger said, 'I have it. Feels good to get paid for revenge, doesn't it?'

"And then Tais said, 'What is this? I was promised the White!' and it sounded as if they would argue so I crept away as quietly as I could. I remembered the directions Tais gave and they led me here," she said, her eyes huge.

"I didn't know what to do," she continued. "But why would Tais get paid in the White to say where the new Tate slept unless they want to kill him?" She burst into tears. "You have to save your master, Joseph. It has only been two days, but Pharaoh is cheerful again and he is confident that the new Tate can help us survive the famine. None of us want to die from starvation. You must save him!"

"You did the right thing, Abana," I soothed her. "I will take care of this."

After asking Chaf to escort her to the kitchen, I went slowly back into my rooms, needing to think. Going to the tiny garden I sat on the bench and leaned back against the small tree that grew there.

Abana was right. Why would anyone pay to find out where I slept unless they wished to harm me? And in the White? That certainly indicated murder as a possibility. But the comment about revenge puzzled me. Tais was a sullen young man, a baker's son, who kept to himself in the kitchens. He seemed very bitter about something. No one complained about his work—they just left him alone. Why would he want revenge against me? He didn't know me, and I had only been Tate for one day. It didn't make sense.

However, someone was upset over my appointment, and the obvious suspects were Lord Amony and Lord Sety. But such precipitous action did not fit Lord Amony's style. Highly cautious, he would know better than to trust anyone who would discuss anything where someone might overhear it. What little I had learned of the men supporting Lord Amony led me to believe they were just as careful. I couldn't imagine Lord Amony making a move until he had studied me thoroughly and decided that he couldn't use me himself.

No, this sounded like a reckless, impatient youth—Lord Sety, in fact. I thought it over for some time, but taking revenge did not make sense from that angle either. The only clear thing was that someone might wish me harm. And only one way to know for certain. I stepped out the door into the hall. Chaf had returned.

"Chaf, can you find six trustworthy guards?" I asked.

"Yes."

"Bring them here very *quietly.*"

He nodded.

Before long Chaf knocked lightly on the door, and I opened it for him and his companions.

"There may be some unwelcome visitors here tonight," I said. "Hide yourselves in the room, and we will see what happens."

The soldiers quickly took up stations about the place. I marveled again at what having power could do. I was thought to be only an attendant of Lord Paanekh, but everyone still obeyed me without questions.

Silence settled on the room, and we waited. At first, tension kept me awake, but as time passed and nothing happened, I relaxed and soon had trouble staying alert.

The door opened so silently that I didn't notice it at first. Stealthy footsteps headed for the bed, I heard a soft thud, and someone asked, "Did you trip over something? Where is a light?"

Chaf's torch blazed up, and the palace guards pounced on the two men standing, stunned, by my empty bed.

I had been successful beyond my dreams. Lord Sety himself

gazed in bewilderment at the soldiers holding him, and his companion still held the knife he had stabbed through the empty coverings. I suppressed a start when I saw the face of Lord Sety's accomplice. If he was the one who had talked to Tais, I now understood the remark about revenge.

"Bring Scribe Nekhty," I said to Chaf, turning away briefly to control myself. "Bind him," I added, indicating the accomplice.

Lord Sety recovered from his surprise and jerked his arms out of the guards' grasp. "Do you know who I am?" he demanded furiously.

"I do, Lord Sety."

"How dare you detain me like this! I shall speak to Pharaoh about what you have done!"

"Someone will certainly speak to Pharaoh about this," I replied. "How do you propose to explain your presence during an assassination attempt?"

"This is no assassination attempt," Lord Sety said disdainfully. "It is a quiet meeting between friends, and that is all. How you came to be here, I do not know."

I looked at him thoughtfully. In his position, he should know better than to speak at all.

"What sort of meeting?" I asked.

"One which better people than you attend!" Lord Sety snapped. "Lord Amony meets with us and talks to us about how best to serve the gods and Pharaoh. He exhorts us to keep the land of Egypt clean and pure for the gods—and for Pharaoh."

"How does he suggest you do this?" I prodded him, marveling at his arrogant indiscretion.

"He explains the importance of maat, that anyone who moves out of his place may upset it and threaten the good of the gods, putting more burden on Pharaoh to keep the balance. Lord Amony says that those from outside of Kemet should be strictly controlled and kept subordinate so that they do not bring chaos and destroy maat. When he hears that some barbarian son of offal such as you has dared to interrupt a meeting, he will deal harshly. Maat must be preserved for the gods and Pharaoh."

Before I could reply, Nekhty appeared, without his wig. He bowed to me. "What do you require, Lord Paanekh?" he asked.

At the sound of my name, Lord Sety's mouth fell open. He

stared at me, then down at my hand where Pharaoh's signet ring flashed back at him. Then he nearly fainted. "As Tate to Pharaoh, I am convening special court for a trial," I said, then turned to Nekhty. "If you will take note of what is said and done here?"

Eyes wide, the scribe found writing materials and moved the table to a convenient place.

I turned to the guards. "If you will witness to Scribe Nekhty what has happened here tonight."

The soldiers told their simple story, and Nekhty recorded it. As the evidence was witnessed, the knife recorded, the slash in the bed-clothes noted, Lord Sety grew whiter and whiter until he shook from fear. His companion remained defiantly silent.

"Search him," I ordered, pointing to the silent man.

Chaf carefully examined the accomplice. Finding something on the back side of the kilt in a fold of linen, he brought it to me. It was a seal.

"Where did you get this?" I asked the assassin, holding out the seal.

A flash of puzzlement crossed his face before he looked away, re-fusing to answer.

I rolled the seal on a tablet and read the strange name, sur-rounded by the royal cartouche. "Are you familiar with this?" I asked Nekhty.

The scribe shook his head, his face pale.

"Have you ever heard of any name like this in the past?" I pressed.

"No, my lord," Nekhty replied.

As he wrote down the name, I pondered the significance of a royal seal with a Pharaoh's name that no one had ever heard of.

I turned back to the two men. "Take the assassin to the prison immediately," I directed four of the guards. "Pharaoh will review my recommendation in the morning."

The assassin looked at me with hatred in his eyes. He knew the only kind of recommendation that would require Pharaoh's ap-proval. I waited for him to speak, but he remained silent.

Lord Sety's knees gave way as the four guards led the man away.

"What do you have to say?" I asked, after the door had shut again.

His shoulders started to shake. "My lord, I know nothing of a plot to assassinate you," he choked out. "You must believe me. I re-ceived a message to come here for another meeting, and I came. This other man waited in the hall, and we entered. Then the guards sprang at us. That is all I know, my lord. You must believe me!"

"Who gave you this message?"

"My personal attendant found it in my rooms. It could not be wrong, for Lord Hernofret's sign is on it as always," he said, his lips trembling.

"Do you have it?"

"Yes, my lord, we are required to bring the message to the meetings. Lord Hernofret takes them from us."

Chaf quickly found the small papyrus leaf and handed it to me. It stated the time and place of the meeting and had been stamped with a signet. Under that, but separated into two parts, were the same hieroglyphics as the seal I had just taken.

"What of the signs under the signet?" I asked.

Lord Sety looked bewildered. "They are always there, my lord."

Walking up to him, I jerked his face up to see his eyes and held his gaze. Silently I searched his eyes. He tried to turn away, but I held his chin firmly in my hand and would not let him look away. For a moment he struggled, then submitted as I bared his soul.

He was a vain, frivolous puppy, arrogant, unfeeling, and ignorant of what he was involved with. That was all.

When I let him go, he collapsed on the floor, unable to hide his sobbing.

"Take him to his rooms, and see to it that he leaves the palace by dawn," I ordered.

"Yes, my lord," the guards saluted.

"Lord Sety, you will return home," I commanded. "You are not to appear in court again until you know what it means to serve your people as nomarch."

The guards hauled him to his feet and took him out the door.

"My lord was merciful," Nekhty commented, his voice slightly disapproving.

"Maybe," I said coldly. How could I tell anyone that Lord Sety reminded me of myself just 13 years ago? That same disregard for others had blinded me to so many things, as it had done him. He was rich and spoiled and thoughtless, as I had been. But the core was sound.

"Lord Hernofret is Amony's son, correct?" I asked.

"Yes, my lord."

"Bring Lord Amony here immediately."

While I waited, I turned over in my mind what I had learned. Amony held meetings for young nobles about preserving the purity of Egypt for the gods. Lord Sety received a regular invitation to a meeting that no one else showed up for. An assassin carried a strange royal seal in the oddest place I'd ever seen, and he hadn't known he had it.

I sighed. Clearly, Lord Sety was supposed to take the blame for this assassination. That raised the question of who would set Lord Sety up, and that pointed to Lord Amony. The fact that the message came from his son tied in neatly. What did not make sense was what Lord Sety was doing attending meetings held by his political rival, or what business Lord Amony was up to in inviting him.

Unfortunately, Lord Sety had said that his attendant found the message, so I could not assume that Lord Hernofret had actually sent it. Anyone could have left it in the room. However, not many people would have a copy of Lord Hernofret's signet. I'd have to check and see if that was Lord Hernofret's signet, but I rather thought so.

A disturbance outside the door heralded the arrival of Lord Amony. Furious at being gotten out of bed and escorted by palace guard to the rooms of the Tate, he walked in and barely nodded his head, a breach of courtesy that Nekhty duly noted in the record.

"Nekhty, please acquaint Lord Amony with what you have recorded," I instructed.

When Nekhty finished reading, Lord Amony turned to me in disgust. "What do I have to do with this puppy and his man?" he asked angrily. "He is no friend of mine."

I raised my eyebrows.

"I have nothing to do with any assassination," Amony protested angrily. "It is a disgrace when a noble of my standing can be dragged from bed at the whim of some—"

When I raised my eyebrows again, Lord Amony choked off his next words.

"Do I understand you deny having anything whatever to do with these men and their action?" I asked.

"I do deny it."

"Yet you routinely invite Lord Sety to meetings to discuss the good of Egypt? He is your political rival, Amony. Why did your son pass word to him of a meeting to be held in these rooms? I find this very strange."

"I did not call any meeting," Lord Amony ground out between his teeth.

I handed him the papyrus leaf. "That is your son's signet, I believe."

Lord Amony glanced at the leaf, then his mouth dropped open.

"I thought so," I said. "Let me summarize for you. Your son lures your greatest political rival to my rooms at the exact time an assassination attempt is made. If the attempt had succeeded, Lord Sety would undoubtedly have been blamed. And with Lord Sety executed for treason and myself dead, you would almost certainly be made Tate."

It took him a while before he could respond. "Surely my lord does not think that I would be party to such an enterprise!" he finally managed to say.

So I was "my lord" now. "I have the sworn testimony of a noble that you called a meeting here and that you have very definite views about what is fitting for Egypt and what is not. I have the invitation with Lord Hernofret's signet. I have the assassin, his weapon, and the nicely placed slash in my bed clothes. What else am I to think?"

Sweat streamed down Lord Amony's body. Knowing that more than one noble had died because of far less evidence than what I had, he struggled to find something to say.

"I—I did not call a meeting," Lord Amony almost whispered. "I can only say to my lord that I know nothing of what went on here tonight, that I did not plot against my lord's life. I ask my lord to be merciful and to believe what I say."

"Lord Hernofret is your son?"

Lord Amony almost fainted. "Yes, lord," he admitted, clenching his hands.

"Send him to me," I said. "If he is a likely youth, I shall find a place for him."

"Yes, my lord," he said, head bowed.

"You will leave court immediately and return to your home estate, remaining there until you receive permission to leave."

"Yes, my lord."

"Your answer is inadequate, Lord Amony," I said coldly.

"That which you command is that which will be done, my lord," he said from trembling lips.

"Pharaoh will be very pleased. You may go."

Blindly, Amony turned to the door and stumbled through it.

Dismissing Nekhty, I sank into thought. None of this made any sense. In spite of the scenario I had painted for Amony, I knew he had not arranged this attempt. That meant a third player on the stage, one who had access to Lord Hernofret. I wondered just how closely Lord Amony kept track of his son. I was under no illusions about relationships between sons and fathers. My own experience had taught me that.

I tossed the seal in my hands, the only clue I had to the third player. I had a feeling it was the key to the entire plot.

"Show me the way, El Shaddai," I whispered. "The cartouche means someone plots for the throne, not just the office of Tate."

If only I had Khay to help me.

Pushing the thought away, I turned my attention to the assassin. Reluctantly, I wrote out the order of execution, fulfilling my responsibility as Tate and condemning Sekhmet the scribe to death. He had hated me since the day Lord Potiphar caught him stealing calves, but I had forgotten all about him. How had he found me now? Perhaps he saw me when Pharaoh escorted me through Memphis in the chariot, and knew whom to contact for a chance to kill me. I would never know.

CHAPTER 17

The next morning, Chaf brought my meal to my room. He set it on the low table beside the chair I sat in and then kissed the ground in front of me.

Startled, I looked at him. "What is it, Chaf?"

"I must ask my lord's forgiveness," he said, clearly afraid. "I have not given my lord the respect he is entitled to, and I—"

"Chaf, I am not upset," I interrupted. "You have served me well, and I am grateful for that. Had I wanted you to know I was Lord Paanekh, I would have told you."

The man didn't move. "Does my lord wish me beaten for my disrespect?" he finally asked.

"No, Chaf," I said, feeling a bit exasperated. "I do not. Get up. I am pleased with you, not angry."

Slowly he rose to his feet. "I have served my lord well?" he questioned.

"So well that I want you to be my personal bodyguard. You will go to the Captain of the Guard and arrange for whatever you need to fulfill that duty."

He continued to stare at me. "I, my lord?"

"You," I replied.

"Yes, my lord. Right away," he gulped, and vanished.

He had no more than left when Amenemhet himself strode in, his face white. "What happened?" he demanded.

"A rather clumsy attempt on my life," I answered uncomfortably, after bowing.

"That does not look clumsy—it looks quite accurate," Pharaoh retorted, indicating the slice in the bed coverings right where my heart would have been.

"There was no danger, my lord. I do not sleep in that bed."

He looked at me astonished. "Where do you sleep?"

I blushed, recognizing my mistake. "It doesn't matter, really. The assassin is in prison, and I have here the recommendation for punishment for you to review."

Amenemhet read it swiftly, then held out his hand for his signet which I hastily gave to him. As he stamped the tablet, it dawned on me that Pharaoh himself could do nothing unless I handed over that ring. His comment that only in the throne was he greater than I was not an empty phrase. It was reality. He returned the ring, gave the tablet to Nekhty, and sent him to deliver it in person.

Slipping the signet on my finger, I watched the tablet go out the door. I hoped I would never have to condemn someone again.

"How goes the work?" Amenemhet asked.

"I will know what I need by the end of the week."

He smiled. "Fine. I will continue to hold audience until then. After that, the people will need to see you. Limit the time you give to them, and have responsible officials screen those who come. Otherwise you will get nothing done."

"Yes, my lord." How I wished I had Khay at my side, or Mahesa. I could use them both.

"Oh, there is someone coming that you must meet," the king

said as he walked out the door. "He has been at his country estate these past two days and will return tomorrow. It is the Captain of the Guard, Lord Potiphar."

Fortunately Pharaoh did not wait for a reply. I had been so overwhelmed with my new duties and station that I had not had time to consider my former master. Nekhty arrived at that moment, catching me staring at the empty door. He had two helpers with him today.

I spent the morning assimilating the information the scribe had collected and acquainting myself with the procedures of legal justice as it related to the office of Tate. Egypt had three lower courts in addition to the courts established on estates of any reasonable size. In the estate courts, the lord of the estate settled disputes and dispensed justice.

Outside of the estates the Kenbet heard cases. Difficult disputes could be referred to the Great Kenbet and finally the highest court, the Sasat. However, any accused could appeal to the Tate, and I must review such cases and hand down a decision from which there was no appeal.

Nekhty informed me about the backlog of cases, since the previous Tate had been uninterested, and nothing had been done at all since he had died. I noted that I would need to take considerable time at first to handle this aspect of my position.

Afterward I ate a late supper in the little garden by myself. Only then did I have time to consider my up-coming meeting with Lord Potiphar. I did not have much time to think, however, for I heard Chaf calling my name. I rose and went back into my rooms.

My bodyguard bowed. "Pharaoh requires your presence."

"I have just heard that Lord Amony and Lord Sety are both missing from court," Amenemhet said as soon as I walked into his room. "This troubles me. Lord Sety is a young upstart without the brains to be a threat, but he could be used very easily. Lord Amony is very different. His absence is not good."

"I sent them both away, my lord."

He stopped and stared.

"You *sent* them away?"

"Yes, my lord."

"And they went, just like that?"

"Not quite that easily, my lord, but essentially, yes."

Amenemhet stared at me for the longest time. Then his lips twitched. "Pray tell, what is Lord Sety going to do with himself?"

"I believe he decided to devote himself to the governorship of his nome."

"And Lord Amony?"

"He will be making an extended stay at his estate and so will be unable to attend court for some time," I said blandly. "His son will be joining my personal staff in the immediate future."

The king sat down, still staring at me. "I find you in a prison, appoint you Tate, and in two days you send the most powerful noble in my kingdom hyng for home and hold his son hostage? By all the gods, how did this happen?"

"Because a serving maid was outside by a pool," I replied. "Was there anything else, my lord?"

Pharaoh studied me for awhile. "My father, may his Ka prosper, once told me that there are some things it is best for a Pharaoh not to know. But someday, I will ask you to explain this miracle."

"I will do so, if I am able," I stated with a straight face.

"You are a miracle, Paanekh," he said softly.

I shook my head. "Not I, my lord. El Shaddai wishes your people to live, and He is making certain that they will."

"Maybe that is so," he commented.

The next morning, I wondered why it was that for the third morning, no service staff had come to my rooms. Not that I needed any. Between myself and Chaf I got along fine, but someone should have shown up.

Nekhty greeted me in the hall. He had found an ideal suite for me to work in with a room for me with a private chamber in back, an anteroom for himself and his aides, a small reception room with waiting room, and a large reception room should I want it. I thanked Nekhty, and we settled in to work and broke for the noon meal much later than usual.

Shortly after I finished eating, Chaf entered. "Lord Paanekh, Lord Potiphar begs to know if you still wish to see him today. He continues to await on your presence in the anteroom off the third garden," he said hesitantly.

I looked up. "Still? Has he been waiting?"

"Yes, my lord, since early this morning."

I was horrified. "Why did no one tell me? Who sent him to this garden room?"

Chaf's face paled. "Your steward, Reret, my lord."

"What steward?" I demanded.

"Reret is steward of my lord's Memphis properties. He served the former Tate for years. Lord Potiphar went to him for an appointment and was told to wait there. I was walking by, and Lord Potiphar asked me to request information from you about what he should do."

Who was this Reret? I fumed, hurrying to my bedchamber. I would have to deal with him later. Right now, my first priority was with Lord Potiphar. I could not imagine what he must be thinking. To keep a lord of his rank waiting so long was a grave insult.

I took a minute to settle my stomach and started down the halls to the third garden. What should I say to him?

I stopped outside the door to the anteroom. Lord Potiphar paced back and forth inside. Closing my eyes a moment, I reminded myself that I was a slave no longer, but it would be a while before I would stop tensing up when a lord got upset. Especially this lord. Even though my mind knew I was no longer in his power, my gut still hardened with apprehension at the sound of his pacing, and my mouth felt dry.

Taking a couple of deep breaths, I quietly opened the door. Light from the courtyard garden lit the far end of the room. I started the apology I had planned when I caught a glimpse of Lord Potiphar. His face was pale with anxiety. He raised a shaking hand to wipe the sweat from his forehead, and I noted his quick, heavy breathing.

Something very wrong must have happened. Worried, I started toward him.

When he looked up and saw me, for an instant he froze, then every bit of expression left his face, and he sank to his knees.

I missed a step. Everything I had planned to say ran right out of my head. Lord Potiphar feared me! I didn't have the least idea how to approach this situation. Then as I looked down at him, anger exploded in my chest. I had served him well, and he repaid me with prison. The anger rose to choke my throat.

"My lord, I beg your mercy—" he began.

As I stepped forward quickly, my hands clenched into fists, and Lord Potiphar choked off his words and just waited. I paused, looking down at myself. What was I doing? This was not what I wanted. I fought my anger to a standstill and then banished it. That part of my life was over, and I wanted to get on with what came next.

"Please do not fear, Lord Potiphar," I said.

Lord Potiphar refused to rise from his knees, his breath catching in his throat every time he inhaled. "I am your servant," he said, bending toward me. "What do you wish done to me?"

"I wish to say thank you," I replied gently, putting my hand on his shoulder. I felt his muscles trembling under my fingers.

"Do not mock me," he whispered.

"I have never mocked you, Lord Potiphar. I owe you more than I can ever repay." I held my hand to him and waited to help him stand.

At last, he accepted my hand. "I do not understand. I have wronged my lord deeply. Why does my lord show mercy?"

"Because I owe you a debt of gratitude."

Potiphar looked up, startled.

"El Shaddai guided me to you when he sent me to this land," I explained. "And you treated me with kindness. I was your slave, and you treated me like a son. Do you think I can forget that?

"You put me into prison, yes, but El Shaddai wanted me there. I had much more to learn, and it was there El Shaddai fully prepared me to serve Egypt in this time of need. And in the prison I interpreted the dreams of the Chief Wine Steward and the Chief Baker. That is what caused Pharaoh to send for me to interpret his dreams.

"There is a great famine coming, Lord Potiphar, the worst this land has ever seen. That was the meaning of Pharaoh's dreams. We have seven years to prepare, and then there will be seven years of great want. You made it easy for me to learn what I had to know to govern this land. Allow me to say thank you."

Once again, Lord Potiphar searched my face, hardly daring to believe that I would pass up the opportunity to pay him back for the imprisonment he had forced upon me.

"Please, Master Potiphar, believe what I say," I pleaded, slipping back into my old form of address. "When I was taken from my country, I lost my father. I have tried to please you as I would have tried to please him."

Suddenly tears spilled down Lord Potiphar's face. "Even if you take my life, I could not be prouder of you than if you were my blood son," he confessed.

"If you live until I take your life, your Ka will never see its tomb," I replied, blinking through my own tears. Then I took the ear rings I had picked up in my room and with shaking fingers fastened them in Lord Potiphar's ears.

Then I backed up a step and bowed respectfully as I used to. "I am grateful, Master Potiphar. Thank you."

Lord Potiphar bowed back to me. "And I am honored. I will treasure your gift, Lord Paanekh, for the rest of my life. I shall wear them always. I—I lost the others I had."

"I do not think you will need to offer these as a sacrifice," I said. "El Shaddai has answered your request."

Potiphar flushed and shifted uncomfortably. "How did you know?" he couldn't resist asking.

"Khay," I said simply.

Lord Potiphar smiled ruefully. "Nothing can be kept from that man." Then he straightened up and bowed again formally. "If I may point out something to my lord Paanekh?" he asked.

"Certainly," I replied, also formally.

"It is unwise of my lord to pass over the wrong done to him. If my lord is to be effective in his office, he must prove himself willing and able to judge and punish where it is necessary. The wrong done to you will become known, and it demands redress."

I sighed. I did not want to consider Lord Potiphar's argument, but he was, unfortunately, correct. "I must admit your wisdom, much as I hate to."

A gleam of approval appeared in Lord Potiphar's eye. He bowed to me again. "What is my lord's wish?"

I turned my back and closed my eyes, calling on El Shaddai for insight and wisdom. And then the answer came.

"Where is Lady Tanefret?"

"She is at the country estate, my lord," he answered immediately.

"She shall remain there for the next three years."

"That which you command is that which shall be done, sovereign lord," Potiphar said, standing very straight.

"As for you, I will require from you Khay, your Great Chief Steward, and Mahesa the scribe. You shall be stripped of your proprietary estate, and it shall be given to Khay. You shall assist Lord Khay in his duties for me in whatever way he shall need and shall provide training for him as necessary so that he can take your place as Captain of the Guard. At that point, you will move to your country estate and shall not appear at court unless commanded to do so."

Silence.

I swung around to find Lord Potiphar looking at me with the oddest expression in his eyes. I maintained a straight face, while he adjusted to the notion that I had just sentenced him to do what he wanted most in the world—to train an able successor and leave the court. The only twist was the proprietary estate.

"Well?" I asked.

"That which you command is that which shall be done," he repeated, still dazed.

"That should suffice, I believe."

"If I may point out something to my lord?" Potiphar asked.

"Of course."

"If I continue to function, but Khay is given the proprietary estate of the Captain of the Guard, there will be confusion about who holds the office."

"Yes, I believe there will," I said blandly.

After several seconds, Lord Potiphar began to laugh.

I left him to his amusement. He had figured out that I needed Khay to provide me with information. Confusion breeds opportunity, and, as Lord Potiphar had just pointed out himself, it was next to impossible to hide anything from Khay to begin with! People would assume he had the royal office and tell him all kinds of things. He had already demonstrated his ability to gather information among the lower classes, and as a lord with a rich estate, he would now be part of the upper classes and able to garner information there which I would need.

I had spent more time than I planned with Lord Potiphar, and I worked Nekhty and his assistants relentlessly into the evening. I did not break off until another knock at the door revealed a very frightened attendant sent to bring me to Pharaoh.

"What is the matter?" I asked as we walked swiftly down the halls and through the courtyards.

"I do not know," the attendant answered, "but the Great One is raging."

I quickened my pace. What could have happened?

The scribe who had filled Nekhty's position looked up in relief when I appeared. He pointed to the other door, behind which I heard shouting. I took a deep breath and walked in.

The shouting stopped when I appeared. I bowed and waited.

"What is this you have done?" Amenemhet asked, starting in a low voice and ending with a roar. "What is this I hear, that the one man I know I can trust, the one man who is unquestionably loyal, is being stripped of his office? Are you touched by Seth? Whom do you think you can replace him with?"

I glanced up. Amenemhet's face twisted with anger, and Lord Potiphar stood by helplessly.

"I am alive because of this man. My father lived a long life because of this man. He is friend to me. What do you think you are doing by removing him from me? Would you strip me of my protection? Leave me open to my enemies? Is not Tate enough for you? Do you plan to take the throne as well?"

Pharaoh turned away, pacing like an enraged lion in the confines of the room. "What do you think you have done, Paanekh?" he shouted.

This was not the time to talk. I slipped the signet from my finger, unfastened the collar, and stripped myself of the royal linen I wore over the kilt Khay had found for me in prison. I put them on the floor, backed away, and bowed to the floor as was proper for a commoner, which I now was.

Lord Potiphar's eyes opened wide with disbelief.

Amenemhet turned back to me. "I should send you back to that prison where I—" He stopped, staring at the collar and ring on the linen. And then Lord Potiphar added the ring of his office to my pile and knelt down beside me. The stunned silence stretched longer and longer.

"What is the meaning of this?" Pharaoh snarled in a strangled voice.

"I have not pleased Pharaoh," I said quietly. "Let Pharaoh give my position to someone more worthy."

"And you?" Amenemhet grated out, turning to Lord Potiphar.

"I cannot stand by while Pharaoh throws away his own life," he said in a steady voice. "Perhaps another can make up what I lack."

"I will not let you leave," the king said between clenched teeth.

"Then I beg my lord to listen to what Lord Paanekh has done," Potiphar said. "If I have pleased you, Lord Nimaatre, then grant my request."

Pharaoh sat down. The use of his personal name instead of the royal one acted like a slap in the face.

I caught a glimpse of the smile that crossed Lord Potiphar's face, and I remembered that he had gone to school with this man and so knew him well.

"You are a disgrace, Lord Potiphar," Amenemhet said in a testy voice.

"Yes, my lord," Potiphar agreed, unable to keep the smile from his voice.

"Oh get up, both of you," Pharaoh commanded, annoyed.

We rose.

"Put on the ring, Paanekh," Amenemhet said.

"It is not fitting that I should, my lord," I said.

Another silence stretched dangerously.

"And why not?" he inquired in a hard voice.

I looked at Pharaoh, again locking eyes with him. "I can save the land from famine, or I can placate its ruler, but I cannot do both. It is most fitting that Pharaoh should choose which he wishes done."

Lord Potiphar gasped, and his face went white.

I looked down again.

Pharaoh rose from his chair, and I waited for the order sending me to death. Amenemhet turned his back. "He would make a fine son to you," he said to Lord Potiphar sourly. "He too, insists on telling me what I need to know but do not want to hear. Bring me the ring."

Lord Potiphar picked up the ring from the floor and gave it to him.

"Hold out your hand," Amenemhet commanded me.

I obeyed, and Pharaoh again slipped the ring on my finger. "Do not make me do this again," he warned.

"I will do my best, Great One," I said meekly.

Amenemhet snorted in reply. "No, you will not. You will remind me of this with those Horus eyes of yours every time I think to question something you do. I was a complete fool to ever award you the office. You have but one redeeming feature," he growled.

"Yes, my lord?"

"You can save Egypt. For the second time, I tell you to do so."

"That which you command is that which shall be done, my lord."

Pharaoh regarded the two of us for some time in silence. "I have just been manipulated," he said at last. "You two must know each other well; you work too smoothly together. Explain."

I started to protest, but Amenemhet raised his hand. "I will not ask you to explain how it is you send my greatest rival packing in just two days, but when you punish my most loyal subject, *and he agrees,* I will demand to know why," he said flatly.

I turned away slightly. "You know I came to Egypt as a slave."

"Yes."

"Lord Potiphar purchased me."

"I see," Amenemhet said slowly, looking from my former master to me and back again. "And did he serve you well?" He turned to Lord Potiphar.

"He did, my lord."

"And what did he do to be put in prison?" he asked.

"He did nothing, my lord. He committed no crime."

"Then why was he there?" Amenemhet asked quietly.

"Because he very deliberately did not deny the accusation against him," Potiphar replied grimly.

"Which was?"

I stood rigid, held by the emotions of that time, three years ago.

"My wife accused him of attempted rape," Potiphar said softly.

It took Amenemhet just about 10 seconds to get the entire picture in his mind. "And what did you do?" he asked Potiphar.

"In my first anger, I very nearly killed him. And he did not lift a finger to stop me."

The silence grew heavy. At last Pharaoh said, "You have given me that same loyalty."

I raised my head. "Yes, my lord," I replied simply.

"In that case, you may write out the order for my own execution, and I will approve it," he sighed. "Truly the gods gave me a rare gift when they sent you."

"I think he will prove to be very profitable for you," Lord Potiphar said, and I blushed to the roots of my red hair.

"What do you mean?" Pharaoh demanded.

Chuckling, Potiphar answered. "Every master he has had has become rich. Very rich. His god honors him above everyone else, and honors the house he lives in as well. The wish of my life was to complete my tomb. Joseph did it for me."

"Then maybe as Lord Paanekh, he will give me the wish of my life too," the king said with a smile. "But why do you punish Lord Potiphar? Lady Tanefret falsely accused you."

"Lady Tanefret has been banished to a country estate for three years," Lord Potiphar replied.

Amenemhet considered that. "And you were in prison three years," he chuckled. "It is fitting. By that time, no one in court will remember her, and she hates the country. Now, how does stripping Lord Potiphar of his office fit in?"

"Lord Potiphar was not stripped of his office. I only removed the proprietary estates that accompany the office. I based my decision on your wish to break the power of the nobles, my lord," I explained.

"You truly agreed to this?" Amenemhet asked Potiphar.

Lord Potiphar smiled. "Certainly, my lord. The action will create confusion and allow us to introduce my replacement. I will be training him carefully, and during this time you can determine for yourself whether you trust his loyalty or not. At the same time, the uncertainty in the court will create opportunities for learning what we need to know. Lord Paanekh has uncovered evidence of another plot for the throne. A report from Scribe Nekhty was waiting for me when I returned."

Amenemhet shook his head. "It is a pity my father did not know you, Lord Paanekh. He would have enjoyed this so much."

Khay arrived the next morning and flashed his usual impudent grin. After bowing to me quite correctly, he then scandalized Nekhty by giving me a bear hug as he used to when a boy.

"I knew it," he exalted. "I knew you would be great some day." He stood back, looking as proud as if he were my father.

I had to laugh.

"But you are still wearing my best linen," Khay went on in disapproval. "I would have thought that you had acquired some better ones by now."

I looked down in surprise. "This is yours? You gave me the linen you were wearing?"

"Where else would I find a decent one in that prison?" he demanded reasonably.

"But what did you wear?"

"Your old one, what else?" he replied cheerfully.

"But it was ratty and stained," I protested.

Khay grinned ruefully. "And didn't Hetepi point that out to me when I got home that day," he said with a sigh. "But when I explained to her that the new Tate was currently wearing my best linen, she forgave me."

"I will get you a replacement at once," I said. "You should have told me before."

"I don't want a replacement. I want that one back, and no other. Do you think I am going to miss the chance to wear the very same linen that Lord Paanekh wore before Pharaoh, and during his ride around Memphis? Not by your Ka, I won't."

"You are just what I need, Khay," I said, laughing.

"Perhaps he is just what we need as well," Amenemhet's rich voice spoke from behind me. I turned around, startled, and Khay, with one amazed glance, landed flat on his face.

"I would see your face, young man."

Khay looked up.

Amenemhet studied him. "He has a good face," he said to me. "I believe he can be trusted. Let us see how he works out. Rise, Lord Khay."

I had to help Khay stand. "I—I am not a lord, Great One," he stammered.

"No?" Amenemhet asked. "I thought those who owned estates were lords."

"I do not own an estate, I manage for Lord Potiphar, Great One," he said, blushing.

"Well, since you have now acquired the proprietary estate belonging to the Captain of the Guard to Pharaoh, you are a lord," he said.

Amenemhet walked out, followed by Lord Potiphar, who had his head bowed as befitted one who was being punished. Khay couldn't move.

Back in my rooms, I found Mahesa waiting for me. He bowed when I entered, his eyes pausing when he saw what I wore. I knew he had just gauged the grade of linen under the royal one and found it wanting.

"Mahesa, I am glad you are here."

"Tell me how I can serve you, Lord Paanekh," he replied in his quiet way.

"I need someone to supervise my staff and take over the details of my appointments and rooms. I want you to do this for me."

Mahesa didn't flicker an eyelid. "As you wish, Lord Paanekh."

I called Chaf and instructed him to show Mahesa anything he needed. As I watched Mahesa's straight back disappear out the door, I felt much better. With Khay supplying information and Mahesa instructing me in court manners and etiquette and organizing the rest of my life, I knew I would have little to worry about.

That evening, I called Mahesa to my private room.

"I need to reward a serving woman," I told him. "What would be appropriate?"

He glanced at me in surprise. "Is it permitted to inquire what service she did for my lord?" he asked tactfully.

I smiled. "She saved my life."

His eyes widened, but he didn't hesitate. "A simple piece of fine jewelry would be acceptable."

"See what you can find in that box," I said.

He brought me a finely made gold necklace with small links and a tiny piece of silver in the center.

"Perfect," I said. "Send for Abana."

She came, looking a bit frightened as she entered and knelt. "What does my lord wish?" she asked, squeezing her hands tightly to keep them from trembling.

"Do not be afraid, Abana," I said, puzzled by her reaction. "I asked you to come so that I could say thank you for saving my life."

She looked up quickly. "It is true then?" she asked. "You are Lord Paanekh, and yet you are Joseph?"

I smiled. "Quite true," I said, taking off my wig to reveal my red hair.

"But Reret ordered no service staff for these rooms, or for you," she protested. "We did not know what to believe in the kitchens."

I pressed my lips together. This was the second time I'd heard of Reret. I needed to meet him. "Between you and Chaf, I have not needed a staff. I want you to have this, Abana," I continued, holding out the necklace to her. "You have served me very well indeed."

"Oh!" she gasped, reaching for the necklace with hesitant fingers. "It is so beautiful. And it has the White! Thank you, my lord. Thank you! But—but should my lord give me so much? My lord does not have to thank me. I would serve my lord anyway."

"But I do have to thank you," I said. "In my country, it is very important to express gratitude. Even the gods do it." While she listened with wide eyes, I told her of El Shaddai's visit to Great Grandfather Abraham, and how He honored Abraham for the meal provided Him by sending Isaac.

"I know this story is true," I finished, "because the little boy named Laughter grew up to be my grandfather. So you see, it is important to me that I say thank you."

"As you wish, my lord," Abana said, eagerly clutching the necklace.

When she and Mahesa had gone, I sat, trying to quiet the pounding of my heart. I was free—*free*—and my mind finally began to assimilate everything that meant. The story I told had reminded me that nothing stood in the way of sending a message to Abi. I could tell him I was alive, not dead. He would come; I knew he would come if I asked him to. I could see Abi again!

Shivering with excitement, I paced the room. As I undressed for bed, I kept brushing my eyes, trying to see what I was doing. Abi would be so happy. He would see how El Shaddai had honored me, and he would be proud. I lay there for a long time, planning just the right wording for my message. Abi was coming! I would see him *soon*. The first thing in the morning, I would have Mahesa send my message.

The moonlight shone in the tiny garden. I walked out into it.

"Joseph," the Voice called.

I looked around. "Yes?" I answered.

"Joseph," the Voice repeated.

I knelt by the tiny swirl of water in the corner. "What does my Lord God wish to say to His servant?"

"I am El Shaddai, the God of your father Jacob. See now, I have given you a father, a wife, and sons to comfort you until the time when I shall deliver your people into your hand, for the time is not yet."

My chest tightened, and I couldn't breathe. "That which You command is that which shall be done," I whispered, and the moonlight faded around me as I woke to find myself kneeling beside my bed. Silently, I wept until dawn.

CHAPTER 18

G reetings, Takamenet."
     She looked up from her table and slowly paled.

"Greetings," she choked out. "It has been a long time since you came to On, my lord," she added, trying to regain her composure. Takamenet glanced around, not wishing to look at the man in front of her. "What does my lord want?" she finally asked.

"I want your son, Saf."

"My lord!" she said desperately. "What possible use can he be to you? You have other sons."

"But none that look as much like me as Saf. You will call him now. He will remain with me."

"My lord, please, he is all I have," she pleaded. "He is trained as a steward. He knows nothing of courts and lords."

"It is time he learned," Lord Amony replied smoothly. "Do not fear. I will not leave you alone. One of my trusted retainers will stay with you at all times. You will not even have to leave your job."

Takamenet glanced at the hard face of the soldier standing by her table, then looked back into Amony's flinty eyes.

"Yes, my lord," she whispered.

▲ ▲ ▲ ▲

Jetur sat comfortably on the thick wool of the carpet and sipped the wine. He could afford now to drink only the best. Mishma came through the hanging and sat down across from him.

"There is much news," he said. "Pharaoh appointed a new Tate."

His father raised his eyebrows. "This may affect our trade with the Great House. What did our contact say?"

Mishma snorted in contempt. "He is too old to be useful, as I have told you before. The man had some child's story about how Pharaoh appointed a condemned prisoner as Tate. The new official is supposed to be very tall, with flames in his eyes and heavy taxes on his mind. They say he came from some foreign country."

Jetur looked up alertly. "Go at once to our contact from the Great House," he ordered. "Find out everything you can about this new Tate."

"Why?"

"He is a foreigner from a prison," Jetur said. "Does that not sound familiar?"

Mishma shouted with laughter. "You are obsessed with Isaac's

God," he said at last. "Do you really think your investment is now ruling Egypt?"

Gently the older man smiled. "You must learn, Mishma, not to let your feelings get in the way of your thoughts. Taking a man from prison and placing him on a throne is just the sort of thing Prince Isaac's God would do."

▲ ▲ ▲ ▲

Light flashed off the gold gleaming everywhere. The Pharaoh's palace here in Itej-Tawy differed greatly from the small, cramped Tate's palace in Memphis. The large, spacious rooms glowed with bright, new paintings. I studied them while I waited for the formal presentation confirming my appointment as Tate.

The wall opposite me portrayed Pharaoh offering food to Ra. He stood before the god's throne, surrounded by gifts for the gods. To my right, Pharaoh and his wife relaxed beside a pool covered with lotus flowers. On the left, he brought war captives to the temples as gifts for the gods, and behind the throne the gold-covered rays of Ra spread out with the gods on either side, watching over their son, the Pharaoh.

I wore the finest linen, the golden collar, the signet ring, and golden armbands on my upper arms. Now that Mahesa dressed me, I truly looked the part of Tate. My wig was heavy and full, and I wished I could do without it. I stood one step down from Pharaoh's throne, with Mahesa behind me and another step down.

The herald announced name after name, beginning with the southernmost nome represented and running through to the northernmost.

Lord Mose, of the Land in Front, the first nome, turned out to be an older courtier with sharp eyes. He was probably impatient with the eternal plottings of someone like Lord Amony, who was conspicuously absent. Lord Meritifi from the twelfth nome minced forward to be presented. I saw a good-looking young man with a tall form and a pleasant face. A strange depth to his eyes, however, bothered me. He was meticulously dressed, with rings on every finger, bracelets, and armbands. As he returned to his place, I noticed his personal scribe, a pale young woman who looked weary and withdrawn.

After the nomarchs came the priests from the principal temples. None of the southern temples were represented since they had not had time to travel north, but I would be going south soon anyway. I knew Pharaoh spent a large portion of his year in Thebes, and I resigned myself to another audience like this one sometime in the future.

I did, however, meet the Great Vision of Ra from the temple in On, and the Great Among Craftsman from the temple of Ptah in Memphis. Both of them had been in Memphis when Pharaoh appointed me. Then came one or two Brides of the God from various temples. After that were the principal lords with their ladies.

My head swam with the various titles attached to each person, and I wondered if I would ever learn them all. After the formal presentations, Pharaoh and I disappeared into a private audience room, and the courtiers mingled with each other and discussed their new Tate.

Lord Potiphar appeared, and soon others entered the room, old friends of Pharaoh, all of them. They spoke politely to me, studying me with hooded eyes, wondering what kind of Tate I would make and how Pharaoh could have possibly been persuaded to appoint a barbarian prisoner as his second-in-command.

That was not my problem, I reminded myself. I had enough to do storing grain for the next seven years and preparing for the famine that would follow.

Mahesa touched my arm to indicate that Pharaoh wanted to speak to me.

"Yes, my lord," I said, walking over to him.

"I want you to meet Poti-Phera, Great Vision of Ra, from On," Amenemhet said.

I nodded to the man again, having just met him in the presentations.

"I did not see your wife and daughters here," Pharaoh said. "Are they well?"

Poti-Phera looked a little uncomfortable. "My oldest daughter just got married," he said, "and my wife is recovering from the feast that we gave."

"I hope she is feeling better soon. You have pleased me, Poti-Phera, I wish to reward you," Pharaoh went on. "I shall honor you by giving your daughter to Lord Paanekh as wife. Lord Paanekh will be working from Memphis, so your daughter will not have to travel far from home."

A wife? *Me?* A daughter of Poti-Phera? But he was the most

powerful high-priest in Egypt. I managed to keep my mouth from dropping open, but my eyes must have been round as bowls. In the silence, I turned to the Great Ueb of Ra to thank him, as etiquette demanded I should, hoping I could make my voice work normally.

Then I sensed the hostility rising from the man beside me. Choking off the hurried words on the tip of my tongue, I tensed, watching him carefully, realizing Poti-Phera's anger was directed not at me, but at Amenemhet. A movement in the corner of my eye showed Lord Potiphar, watching closely from one side. Two husky Nubian guards eased closer to the three of us, and I realized I was seeing the final act in a drama of which I knew nothing.

When Poti-Phera did not speak, Amenemhet pounded his staff on the floor three times. All sound ceased in the room, which was quite full now.

The king raised his voice so all could hear.

"This is a joyous occasion," he said. "Poti-Phera, Great Vision of Ra, will give his daughter in marriage to Lord Paanekh, Tate of Upper and Lower Egypt."

The courtiers applauded and spoke their congratulations. Poti-Phera endured it for several minutes, then with barely controlled rage, took his leave. The expression on his face as he walked out burned into my mind. If ever I saw murder, it was then.

The next morning Mahesa announced that Lord Hernofret waited in the anteroom. When I went to the small reception room, the young man came forward. Almost falling when he bowed, he threw me one terrified glance, then kept his eyes on the floor.

"Yes?" I asked.

"I am Lord Amony's s-son," he said, his voice cracking.

"And your name?"

He choked once over his words, then tried again. "My name is L-Lord Hernofret," he stammered, flushing a deep red.

"Lord Amony sends you with commendable speed," I stated, looking him over. "Please attend me at the noon meal, and we can get acquainted."

"Yes, my lord," he said, bowing.

As I left the room I paused to look back through the door in time to see his legs give way, and he grabbed the nearest pillar to remain standing.

I waited until Mahesa had shut the door, and then started pacing the room. "What is it, Mahesa?" I asked. "What is it about me? Do I look like a monster, or have horns growing from my head? Are the clothes wrong? Tell me what is going on!"

He stared at me in bewilderment. "I do not understand, my lord."

"Mahesa, just about every single person I have dealt with since becoming Tate is frightened stiff. That young man out there was so terrified, he could hardly stand. Chaf thought I would take his head from his shoulders because he had been friendly to me. Abana saved my life, and she still—even Lord Potiphar—" I stopped.

"What did you expect?"

I shrugged. "Aloofness, dislike maybe. Respect for the office, curiosity—I don't know. Anything but terror." Halting my pacing, I turned to face him. "Mahesa, why is everyone afraid of me?"

He looked down. "It is not about you, really," he said, searching for words. "It is about power, I guess. Pharaoh gave you permission to execute or elevate whomever you wished."

"But there are laws, Mahesa," I interrupted. "They—"

"You are the law," he said calmly.

I stared at him.

He nodded. "In the end, all cases in law come to you, and whatever you decide, that is what happens. Pharaoh may review a sentence, but will he overturn one? Probably not, especially if it is a commoner or minor official. A high noble might have a chance, but not much of one."

"But the gods," I protested. "Your gods have a set determination of behavior. There is a judgment for every soul that passes to the West."

Mahesa watched me from cynical eyes. "The gods, Lord Paanekh, are concerned with how you have treated them, not how you have treated anyone else. If you have offered sacrifices and given gifts to their temples, why should they care about anything else? You have honored them, and they will judge you worthy to live with Osiris.

"When people come before you, their lives are hanging on you, and you alone. Of course they are afraid. How is it that you were a slave and did not understand this? Did you not fear when your master became angry?"

"Well, I suppose. But—"

"But?" Mahesa repeated, looking at me intently.

I couldn't answer.

"But what, Joseph?" he pushed, so intent that he did not notice his change of address. "What is it about you? I noticed it from the first time I met you. You were a slave. Your life was held in another's hand, *but you were not afraid.* I saw you anxious. I saw you worried. I saw you angry with yourself when you did not please your master, but I never observed that hopeless, helpless terror that every slave lives with. Why not, Joseph?"

I looked down. He was wrong, I told myself. I had felt that monster of terror. It nearly destroyed my mind after my brothers sold me. I had only escaped by giving my life to El Shaddai and—

Slowly, I sat down. El Shaddai. After giving my life to Him, I had never experienced that terror again. I had been very afraid when Lord Potiphar had me thrown into prison, but I had been protected from the clawing, insane fear that had nearly destroyed my mind those first days of my captivity.

"Why didn't you fear, Joseph?" Mahesa asked softly.

"Because I knew that El Shaddai held my life," I replied, only now beginning to understand what this had done for me. I glanced at him. "I know, deep down, that El Shaddai controls my life, and no one else. I gave myself to Him, and no one can take me away. He will hold me, even if I die."

Hunger glowed in Mahesa's eyes, a hunger I did not understand. Then he looked away from me and resumed his usual calm demeanor.

"Whenever someone comes to you, Lord Paanekh, that terror walks with them."

"But why, Mahesa?" I demanded again. "I have seen commoners and servants approach other lords, and they are not afraid. Why me?"

He looked down uncomfortably. "May I speak freely to my lord?" he finally asked.

"I wish someone would," I said in exasperation.

"Do not be angry with me, my lord," he said, looking away.

"Not you, too, Mahesa," I said despairingly.

He flushed. "I am sorry, my lord, but it is hard."

I waited.

"It is because my lord is not an Egyptian," he finally stated. "You are outside of maat. You are from Deshret, from the realm of Seth, the destroyer."

"But I have always been that," I said, puzzled.

"You were a slave before. You were controlled, with an appropriate place for those who would bring chaos. But now you have broken out of control. You have more power than anyone but the Pharaoh in Egypt, and no one knows how you will use this power. What if you gave it over to Seth? All of us could be destroyed." I heard real fear in his voice.

How could anyone think that I would wish to destroy this land? I wanted to shout that El Shaddai had sent me here to keep it alive, not to cause its death.

I stared at Mahesa's rigid form standing in front of me.

"You wonder, too, don't you?" I asked flatly.

"I—I cannot help it, my lord," he whispered.

For a long time I sat in silence. This was not something I had anticipated.

"Saying that I will keep maat will not help much, will it?" I asked at last.

"No, lord."

"I will have to show it, then."

▲ ▲ ▲ ▲

The chariot drew to a stop, and I wearily climbed down. Onami, the driver, looked around. "Where is the porter?" he asked.

I shrugged, staring at the imposing gateway to my residence here in Memphis. Having just returned from Itej-Tawy, I was dead-tired and hungry in the bargain. "It's probably been empty since the old Tate died."

My driver shook his head. "The estate would revert to Pharaoh until a new Tate was appointed." He looked around. "I do not like to leave you here, Lord Paanekh."

"Take care of the horses," I directed. "I'll be all right."

As I walked toward the gate, the stallion on the left shoved me with his nose, and I laughed softly. I thought it very fitting that the stallion I had tended when I first came to Egypt should have been one of the pair that pulled me through the streets of Memphis and the capital to the acclaim of the people.

I rubbed his nose. "Go on, boy. Get some food."

Reluctantly Onami drove away, looking for a place to put the animals. When he had gone, I unobtrusively slipped the signet ring off my finger and tucked it into my linen. I had not worn the golden collar for traveling, and without the collar and ring, I looked like a rather high official, but nothing more. Heading down the street, I searched for a side gate that might be open.

"No one there," a voice said.

I whirled around, startled.

"That's the new Tate's house," the voice continued. "When they heard the news, they all left. Afraid of their new lord."

A dirty, ragged-looking man gazed at me from the dust of a corner in the wall of the house opposite mine. His face was lined from the sun, and his hair uncombed and turning gray.

"What do they know of their new lord?" I asked.

The man shrugged. "What the steward told them. And he told them plenty." The man indicated the house. "Smart fellow, Reret. He told them the new Tate was a barbarian, and had flames sprouting from his eyes and black hair all over his face. He said they'd all be beaten the first thing and that barbarians demanded human blood to drink every new moon. By the time he finished with them, they were running for their lives."

I bit down my anger. It seemed Reret was determined to annoy me at every possible turn. I studied my informant, and his bright black eyes looked back sardonically.

"You didn't run," I said. "Aren't you afraid of what the new Tate might do to you?"

The man snorted. "What would he want with me? Only half of me works, and that half isn't as young as it might be. Besides, I know that steward for the biggest liar outside of Deshret."

"And how do you know that?" I asked, beginning to enjoy this conversation.

"Been to the barbarian lands. Campaigns under two Pharaohs, and I've fought and killed enough barbarians to know they're no different from us," he added bluntly. "They live different, but they live in a different place than we do. No better, no worse. Just different."

"What is your name?"

"Inti." He squinted up at me. "You a lord?" he asked, noting my clothes.

"I guess so. Pharaoh told me I was, so that must make it so."

He chuckled dryly. "Canny man, our Pharaoh. Young yet, and not quite on his feet in spite of his father's training him. But he did more than he knew when he appointed that new Tate. We'll see what we'll see," he said, nodding.

"Do you have a job?"

"Now, young man, don't you go lowering my estimate of you," Inti said plaintively. "Do I look like I got a job? I'm a worn-out old soldier with most of me cut up and none of me moving too fast. What kind of job could I do? About all I'm good for is to sit and spit at the beetles. Occasionally, I hit one."

"Live off your mouth?" I asked, raising my eyebrows.

He laughed. "Knew you were canny. I'm a regular here. The steward to the house lets me use this corner. Lots of people pass by, and they get to know me, and like to hear me spout off. I get enough to stay alive."

"How do you get yourself here?"

"Curious sort, aren't you? Well, I don't mind showing you. I got a few tricks left yet." He assembled his limbs and stood up somehow, bringing out a crutch from behind him to help walk.

My eyes widened at the scars all over his body. One leg was twisted, and his right arm was gouged in three spots and the elbow frozen straight.

"Takes a bit getting used to looking at me," he said candidly. "But people do."

Then he stumped down the street beside me with surprising speed. "Where we going?" he asked.

"Why did you come?" I countered.

He chuckled. "Figured you were good for a meal. Been slow today. Don't have much for me."

"What's all that bread in the sack for then?"

"That's for the pot," he said. "We all go together for breakfast. Noon and evening it is up to yourself."

"How many go together?" I inquired, fascinated by this man and his dry humor.

"It varies. Usually seven to 10. Most of us are soldiers, hurt too bad to fight anymore and forgotten by everybody. But we got a couple young men, thrown out from their home for one reason or another. Usually some lord that doesn't know when he has something good staring him in the face."

We reached the main gate again, and I looked it over. It rose high over my head, both the gate and porter's door tightly locked.

"Want in?" he asked.

"I'm supposed to get in," I said carefully. "I had not counted on everyone being gone."

The old soldier looked at me sideways. "I might know someone who could help."

"I dare say you do," I said dryly. "What will it cost me?"

Inti chuckled again. "I'm liking you more and more. There must be enough food in there for our group for two, three days. What say you feed us a little?"

"As you have already been eating that same food ever since the steward left, I don't see the harm," I said blandly.

He shouted with laughter. "You do be canny."

"You get me inside," I bargained, "and I will see if the market doesn't have some bread fresher than what is in that sack."

"For all of us?"

"It is all of you or none of you, right?"

"Yes, my lord, it is!" Inti exclaimed, and he went stumping off down the street on his crutch.

Onami returned, leading the horses. "There is no place near here for them, my lord," he apologized, "except the stables in the house. Is there someone we can find to let us in?"

"I think help is on the way," I replied. "I discovered that everyone ran after being frightened by Reret, the steward, with his stories of the horrors of barbarians."

The charioteer looked at me, shocked. "But why would he do that, my lord?"

"Probably for profit," I said sourly. "Once the new Tate showed up, he could offer to find new retainers, at a higher rate of pay, naturally, and then go bring the old ones back without telling them they should be getting more wages. He would take the difference for himself. It's been done before."

"Stay back, my lord," he said suddenly. "It looks like ruffians have found us."

I glanced over his shoulder. "That's Inti and his friends. I promised them fresh bread for supper if they would get us in."

Onami looked at me in disbelief. "You know them?"

"Sort of," I hedged. I understood his concern. The men approaching were far from respectable in Egyptian eyes. None were shaven, their hair was uncut, and their clothing was dirty and torn and barely enough to cover them. All bore scars somewhere. One had lost an eye, another was missing half an arm. They all carried crutches or sticks or canes. All the same, they had a spirit that had survived the ragged poverty in which they lived.

Onami stayed between me and the ragged group. Inti noticed and grinned. "Don't you worry, young man. I won't hurt your lord. Aside from you, there's that stallion you got. I seen war horses before, and I know what they can do. That one likes your lord, and I'm not about to argue with him over it."

I looked at the stallion with surprise. He had his ears half flattened and was watching the men with white eyes. His haunches were bunched, and he fidgeted his hind legs. "So, boy, so," I said soothingly in Canaanite. "You are very brave, I know, but take it easy now." The stallion lifted his ears and settled slightly.

Inti looked at me sharply, then motioned to his friends. Using the corner by the gate, his friends, and various sticks, Esse, the man with half an arm, climbed to the top of the wall. A second man, Defatsen, followed him, and in five more seconds the bar on the gate rattled, and the gate creaked open.

Onami watched in amazement. But he led the horses in and took them back to the stables.

I looked toward the house, much larger than anything Lord Potiphar had owned. The pillars of the porch stood on expensive stone pedestals, forming a large, deep portico. Inti and I walked into the empty, eerie building. After the porch we entered a large waiting room, then an equally large reception room, which had a raised dais and a chair overlaid with gold. Beyond that the dining room opened up. It still had food on the tables, flies buzzing around it.

"Sloppy man, Reret," I said.

"Don't let Reret hear you say that," Inti advised. "He fancies himself."

Off the dining room was a small waiting room, with a covered walkway down the side of the house to a garden with three pools. Beyond the dining room was a small reception room for more private audiences, and adjoining that was a large bedchamber with a separate dressing room. A door led to an enclosed courtyard that also had a pool, walled off from the side garden.

On the other side of the small reception room a hallway led to the women's quarters, and another to the courtyard with the kitchens for the great house, several storerooms, and quarters for the house staff. Beyond that was the large open court with various workshops and workers' huts around it.

The house was in good condition, but filthy. This steward did not do his job at all well. I became more and more eager to meet this Reret.

Between the order for supplies from the state storehouse that I wrote, the few copper deben that Onami had, and the ingenuity of Inti and his friends, we managed a passable meal. When we had finished, I thanked Inti again. "At least, tonight I will sleep within walls."

"I'd be thankful if we could sleep inside walls too," he commented. "The porter's room at the gate would be welcome."

I flicked a glance at him. He didn't look at me, and shifted his feet uncomfortably. "All right, Inti," I said. "But you must do something for me."

"What would that be, my lord?" he asked warily.

"Since you are going to be in the porter's rooms, I want you to act as porter and keep the gate."

His head jerked up in surprise. "Us?" he asked.

"Will you?"

He straightened up a bit. "Yes, my lord. But what about the back gate?"

"If you think it is necessary, man that one also, and anything else that you find."

Inti looked at me oddly. "Yes, my lord," he said, then stumped away.

The next morning I rose early. I had slept in the scribe's room, since the master bedchamber was unfit to occupy. After eating, I sent Onami to the state storehouse for supplies and checked the storerooms for anything we could trade at the market.

Esse found me there, bringing the news that two families waited at the gate, having heard that the new Tate needed house staff. The men of the families came slowly into the courtyard, glancing around nervously. They bowed to me, and I asked their names and what they did, and warned them that I would accept only the very best work. By the time I finished with them, Inti said another family had come. He told me this family belonged to the estate already.

I let them in with the same warning. Then I turned to Inti. "You heard what I require?" He nodded. "All right, you decide who shall come in and who shall not. Esse can show them where to stay and let you know which skills we still need."

Inti raised his chin. "Yes, my lord," he said crisply.

In the house, Benret, the wife of my new basket-weaver, took charge of the cleaning, and by the end of the day I had to send Onami to the storehouse again for more rations, as the workers' huts filled fast. I turned my attention to the records for the house.

▲ ▲ ▲ ▲

"It is a disgrace! Does he expect me to obey? I am the Great Ueb, the high priest, Great Vision of Ra. Send your daughter, he tells me. Bah! It is not to be borne."

"Have patience and caution, Poti-Phera," Lord Amony advised, taking another sip of the wine in the goblet. It tasted old and strong. He smiled to himself, making a mental note that he would have to reward the man who told him that Poti-Phera could not hold old wine. The priest was now nicely drunk.

"Patience! Caution! I need an army," Poti-Phera almost shouted. "Send your daughter, he tells me. Sopdu is already marked out for another. You must help me, Amony. If you want my so lovely step-daughter to marry that recalcitrant nomarch from the twentieth nome, you will have to help me."

"I shall, I shall," Lord Amony said, smiling. "But we must obey Pharaoh."

Poti-Phera snorted. "Pharaoh. The Great Amenemhet III, Ruler of all Egypt. May his Ka rot in the Nile."

"Softly, my friend," Amony admonished. "Let us not be hasty. Pharaoh ordered you to send your daughter, and Sopdu is your step-daughter, so we cannot send her."

Poti-Phera looked up in bleary surprise. "So he did," he exclaimed. "You are a messenger from the gods, Amony. Sopdu cannot be sent. She will go to the twentieth nome as we planned. But who will go to that hairy baboon of a barbarian?"

"Your daughter, Great Ueb."

"What? Asenath?" he exclaimed. "Ha! She is not fit to be the wife of any man. The girl has not come out of her rooms in years, and when she does haunt the house, I have never seen such an unfit disaster in my life. She trips over her sandals even when she has none on!"

"But, Great Ueb, the new Tate is not a man," Amony said slyly. "He is a barbarian."

"That's so," Poti-Phera said, looking into his goblet. "That's so."

Amony filled the empty goblet. "See how simple it is? Sopdu marries the one for her, and you obey Pharaoh by sending your daughter to the barbarian."

Poti-Phera looked over his drink suspiciously. "There is something wrong about this," he said. "Will Pharaoh be angry with me?"

"How can he be? He demanded your daughter, and you sent her."

The priest smiled and almost dropped the goblet. "That's so," he said again, nodding his head violently. "You are a good man, Amony. I shall mention you to Ra the next time I speak with him."

"How thoughtful of you," Amony replied sarcastically.

"Now, what do I do to send the minx?" Poti-Phera wondered, looking around blankly.

"Let me arrange it for you. Your captain of the guard can take her, and she will need an attendant. How about Iutem?"

"Iutem? Her husband was sent to the mines last year. Bad lot, Iutem."

"Then let the Tate handle her," Amony said. "He will be good at it, I am sure."

Poti-Phera laughed uproariously. "Good idea, Amony," he shouted. "Let the Tate have her." He hiccuped and looked back at his goblet. "It's empty," he said mournfully.

"Let me fill it," Amony said, pouring more wine. He set the jug on the table and signaled.

Iutem came forward from the shadows.

"You heard?" Amony said curtly, leading her across the room and into the hall.

"Yes, my lord."

"Good. Then accompany Asenath to the house of the Tate. After a suitable time, put some of this into her wine. Then you may go anywhere you wish."

"Yes, my lord," the woman said, accepting the small vial. She took it clumsily, and it dropped. They both dived for it, and Lord Amony caught it.

"Take care of it," he said savagely. "It is expensive, clumsy woman."

"Many pardons, my lord," she said meekly, tucking the scarab-beetle amulet she had jerked from Amony's wrist into the folds of her dress. "I beg your leave to go."

Amony waved his hand absently, and Iutem vanished. No one saw the small shadow that vanished from the hall after her.

▲ ▲ ▲ ▲

"Where is she?" Great Ueb Poti-Phera shouted at his steward.

"She will be here soon, my lord," Sosamen, the steward, replied in a trembling voice.

Lady Asenath bit her lip, standing outside the door of the dining room. She checked herself over. Hair properly disarrayed, wrinkled linen dress clumsily pleated in the fashion of two years ago, and her belt tied sloppily in the wrong place. Her eyes were unevenly kohled and she would not have to pretend to stumble over the hem of the dress since it was definitely too long.

"I am here, father," she said, walking in, tripping over the dress and nearly falling. Her father had been raging since returning from the audience for the new Tate, but she did not know why. The house staff refused to talk, which was most unusual.

She wondered if it had anything to do with Lord Amony's surprising visit two days ago. The new Tate had ordered him to his estate in the south. But little Hesy, the orphan girl that had wormed her way into her heart, had insisted that she saw Lord Amony. Asenath sighed. Hesy was never wrong. What brought Amony to On? Renseneb might know, but he would not return from Beni Hassan for another two weeks.

Her father stared at her in distaste. His look took her in for the first time in years, and she shifted nervously. Maybe some flattery would help.

"What does the Great Ueb, the High Priest of Ra at On, need from me?" she asked meekly.

Her father didn't answer, and that was a bad sign. He studied her minutely, then relaxed back against his chair with a cruel smile of amusement playing about his mouth.

"So, this is my daughter, the Lady Asenath," he said meditatively. "You will do very well, very well indeed." He started to laugh loudly and she flushed, uncomfortable with the sound of his voice.

"Why did you wish to see me?" she asked, fighting down the panic that rose in her throat. Her father had been drinking old wine for days. He might do anything at all.

"Pharaoh is pleased with me," Poti-Phera said. "I have served him well. He wishes to reward me, and he has done so."

Asenath looked down, her mind whirling. This made no sense whatever. Her father had followed Lord Amony ever since he had arranged her father's appointment as Great Vision of Ra. And Lord Amony wanted the throne. The court intrigues had pointed to that for years.

Her father had his eyes on the office of Tate, but she knew that Lord Amony would never allow that. Poti-Phera was useful now, but would be a liability later, and as ruthless as her father was, she knew he would lose in a battle with Lord Amony, for he could not think as far ahead as Lord Amony did.

"This is glad news," she said, watching Poti-Phera. "What reward did my father receive?"

"Amenemhet, may his Ka rot, has decided to connect our house with that of the new Tate," he replied.

The steward turned pale at Poti-Phera's words, and Asenath bit her lip again. Her father had to be quite drunk to make such a blasphemous statement against the Pharaoh in public.

"This could be a political advantage, could it not?" Asenath said hesitantly. If she could remind her father of the advantage to himself, maybe he would stop his dangerous talk.

"Advantageous?" Poti-Phera shouted. "To be connected with that barbarian, with his smooth talk and sanctimonious ways? He is not even of the race of men, but one of the species that sprang from the waste of Ra. And Pharaoh would force me to an alliance with him?

"Does Pharaoh think that I, Great Ueb of Ra, must bow to that donkey? Pharaoh is possessed by Seth! To give the land to a barbarian! To give our lives into that madman's power just because he explained a dream! Famine, pah! Nothing will happen. That scheming brother to vultures can no more interpret dreams than the dogs who fathered him!

"I know his barbarian kind. I have dealt with them before. They have come to my house and eaten my food, and brought their gold and White to my table, and fingered their knives while they did. But, when Amony is on the throne, things will be different."

Poti-Phera lifted the cup to his lips with shaking hands. Sosamen silently fled the room, leaving Asenath to face her father alone.

Once again her father's eyes wandered over her messy figure. He started to smile again and then laughed as before.

"He thought he would get Lady Sopdu," he said, naming her youngest stepsister. "That's what he thought. As if I would give her pretty face to anyone not useful to me. No, you shall go. You will do just fine. You are just what that barbarian son of a pig deserves. But I shall have obeyed Pharaoh!"

"Go?" Asenath asked, her breath catching. "The new Tate is truly a barbarian?"

"Yes, daughter," Poti-Phera mocked. "And a fine, big, handsome one he is, too. I have not seen his like since that very useful Syrian so many years ago. Too bad he was so attached to women." Her father laughed. "Ah well, I could afford to lose one now and again.

"Go now. Pharaoh demands that I send my daughter to the new Tate as wife. And so I shall. You are a fit mate for that black-haired baboon. Rempe!" he shouted.

Asenath stood frozen, her memories spilling into her mind.

Her father's chief guardsman came into the room and bowed. "Yes, Great Ueb?"

"My daughter is being honored to be the wife of the new Tate. I am commanded to send her to him. Take her there now."

Her throat closed in terror. Wife? Mate to a barbarian? The room whirled around her, and she almost fell.

"She is so happy, she swoons!" her father smirked harshly. "Get her out of here."

Desperately Asenath fought the fear. She had to think and plan. Time—she needed time. "If I am to be wife, I must pack appropriately," she started to say, fighting to stay erect.

"Pack?" her father mocked. "There is nothing here for you to take. You will go as you stand. If that barbarian wishes you to have clothing, or food, or a place to sleep when you are not tending to him, he will have to provide it. You are his, not mine! Take her, Rempe!" he commanded again, waving the cup in the direction of the door.

Grimly, the chief guard took her arm and led her from the room. Asenath couldn't even swallow. She was going outside, leaving the house. She hadn't left the gates for 15 years! Panic closed about her.

Rempe led her down the steps. A donkey stood waiting, and Iutem helped her onto it. They started away.

"Rempe! I must have something!" Asenath whispered desperately. All her records were in that house, her lists of properties and sources, her signet ring! Without them, she could do nothing. And what about Hesy? She had nowhere to go, and no one but Asenath herself to protect her.

"Rempe! Please!"

"Lady, I dare not," he said roughly. "He would kill us all. Later, when the wine is gone, you can send for some things."

She settled on the donkey, knowing he spoke the truth. Her mind screamed at her to do something, but she could not think of what. Although she desperately needed time, she had none. Feeling alone, she started to tremble. Rempe would not go against her father's direct orders.

Renseneb—she shook more. What would he think when he returned? That he would look for her she took for granted, but even if he found where she had been taken, he would be too late. She would be in Memphis in a matter of hours and dead shortly after that. Sumet hadn't even lived for one day.

Cold terror froze her heart.

CHAPTER 19

Early the next morning, Khay came strolling in, looking around in amusement and interrupting my breakfast.

"Where did you find that gatekeeper?" he asked.

"How did he happen to let you in?" I countered.

"I had to confess that I was a lord, and prove it," he said, trying to sound aggrieved and not succeeding.

I chuckled. "I found him sitting in the street against the neighbor's house."

Khay shook his head in wonder. "You would not believe what he is doing. He has a bunch of helpers who look like beggars keeping order in the street. There must be 100 people out there, all demanding to get in, and those beggars are keeping them strictly in line."

"Um," I said, eyes twinkling. "I need to get some decent clothes for them, don't I?"

"You are hopeless, Joseph," he said with a grin. "What would Mahesa say?"

I closed my eyes in mock despair. "He would be scandalized," I confessed. "But he will like Inti. Inti has a very fine sense of what is fitting."

"Now will you tell me who they are?" Khay asked plaintively.

"They are a band of old soldiers who have been scraping along in an attempt to stay alive. Inti helped me get into this place. The former steward terrified the staff into running with stories of how horrible barbarians were. When I got here, the place was shut up like a crocodile's mouth."

"How long did it take to get the gate open?"

"About 30 seconds."

Khay gaped.

"Inti is a very resourceful man," I said with a straight face.

"He must be," Khay said looking thoughtful. "Maybe I should make his acquaintance."

"That would be a very good idea. Why are you here?"

"To report. And Mahesa sent along some stuff for you. It is in the courtyard. Where should I put it?"

"I don't know," I confessed. "Find Benret and ask her if the master's suite is clean yet. I slept the last two nights in the scribe's room."

He departed, and I finished eating.

News of the boxes and bundles in the courtyard spread fast, and tension built high as the staff anticipated meeting the terrible barbarian Tate. I wandered around among them, without the cursed wig, most of the morning before anyone figured out who I was. By afternoon, everyone watched me, nudging each other and teasing about how afraid they had been for nothing. I smiled. One hurdle overcome.

When I walked out to the gate, Inti stood to attention as I approached. He and his friends all had decent linens now and had bathed. Sabestet, the barber, came that morning and shaved Inti and cut his hair. I hardly recognized him as the same beggar from the street of two days ago.

"You are looking well," I said to him. "I expect you to be the best gatekeeper in all of Egypt."

"Yes, my lord," he said, his eyes glittering and his back very straight.

Khay and Benret had just decided where all the stuff Mahesa sent would go until the rest of the house was properly prepared, when a disturbance at the gate brought me to the porch. The shouts stopped, and a loud hammering began. I waited. Inti limped toward me, blood flowing from a cut on his head.

"Who is it?" I asked, eyeing his wound.

"It is the steward, my lord," the porter said stoically.

"Steward?" I questioned. "I do not have a steward that I recall. Would you be speaking of Reret, the former steward?"

Inti straightened up and wiped the smile off his face with his hand. "May my lord pardon me. I will not make such a mistake again. It is the former steward, my lord."

"What does he want?"

"He comes with a guard from the state storehouse, my lord, accusing my lord of stealing from the storehouses with forged documents requesting rations."

"Does he accuse me directly?" I asked, surprised.

"No, lord," Inti corrected himself. "He accuses those within the house."

The pounding on the gate continued.

"See to your wound. When you are presentable again, let them in."

"I shall let them in immediately, my lord."

"I said *after* your wound was clean, Inti."

A gleam of appreciation lit his eyes. "As my lord wishes," he said, and limped back to the gate house.

Khay appeared at my side. "Did Mahesa send my collar?" I asked.

"I cannot imagine he would not," he said with a grin. "I will find it."

After dressing, I watched the gate creak open from my vantage point in the shadows of the porch pillars. Reret strode in first, throwing accusations right and left as he came. Behind him marched a dozen of the storehouse guards with an officer.

"I insist you arrest them," he said to the leader. "That man is not a porter, he is a beggar. You have seen him yourself in the streets and those others with him. How dare he bar the gate and refuse entrance to the proper official of the Tate? He shall pay."

A northern Egyptian of medium height and decidedly plump, Reret wore rings on every finger, at least three bracelets on each arm, and a gold necklace that had two pieces of the White in it.

I now knew where all the profits from this estate had gone. His rations did not allow the purchase of such jewelry. My new house staff all gathered in the courtyard, and the steward noticed them as he strode toward the house as if he owned it.

"What are these commoners doing here?" he demanded of no one in particular. "Throw them out! All of them. They do not belong here."

"We live here," Benret answered him fiercely. "You cannot throw us out. The lord of the house placed us here."

"I am the lord of the house," the steward said with a malicious grin, "and I know you, Benret, wife of Userkaf. I shall remember what you have said."

"You are not lord of the house," Benret answered him back. "The new Tate is the lord of this house."

"The new Tate is far away," Reret smirked. "He will come eventually, and I will be here to receive him. I will deal with whoever has decided to usurp my place and fill this house with riffraff like you and that cursed gatekeeper. He will rot in the Nile for his impudence. You, I shall have to think about."

By the time he finished talking, I reached the bottom of the steps and strode across the empty courtyard toward him. Here was the man who had insulted me at the palace by withholding a proper staff. He had lied to the people about me in order to profit from the situation.

I was angry—angry as I had never been before.

The steward caught sight of me, and for a moment stared in astonishment. By the time I reached him, he and everyone else was kneeling.

"I beg my lord's pardon," he said, looking at me. "I was called away for a few hours on my lord's business. I do not know how these people came to be here, but I shall send them away immediately and see that this house is properly staffed.

"The previous Tate left everything in my hand, and I served him well. I shall do the same for you, Great One."

His unctuous assumption that I would believe his lies galled my anger even more. "You were called away?" I asked tightly.

"Yes, lord, on my lord's business. My lord is very rich, and much time is required to tend to his wealth."

"You have kept the house and seen to its management without leaving since the old Tate died?" I asked.

"Of course, my lord," he said smoothly, without a flicker of an eye.

"Then, will you please explain why I found this house empty and locked when I arrived *three days ago?*" I asked icily.

"Three days?" Reret asked, sudden sweat forming on his plump torso.

"And how is it that you presume to arrest my gatekeeper?" I asked next, trying to control the rage I felt building in my chest. "I set him over the gates to watch them, and you would arrest him?"

"My lord," the steward gasped. "He is a beggar. Surely my lord would not—"

"Inti!" I shouted.

"Yes, my lord," the porter replied instantly, getting to his feet.

"Did I not say to you that if you stayed in the porter's room you were to perform the duties of porter and gatekeeper?"

"Yes, my lord."

"Do you still stay in the porter's room?"

"I do, my lord," Inti said, drawing himself up proudly.

"In that case," I said to Reret, "I have a gatekeeper. What I do *not* have is a steward."

"Oh, but I am your steward, my lord," the man said, smiling assuringly at me. "I have been steward here for many years, and I can continue to serve my lord—"

"How many jars of wine are there in the cellars?" I asked.

The steward blinked.

"How much grain is in the granary? Is there flour for bread baking? Do we have leather for belts? How many jars of raisins are there in the storerooms? What profit did you realize from the date palms last year? How much wine was pressed from the north vineyard? How long has it been since the pottery was left vacant?"

The steward was flustered and red.

"Can you answer even one of those questions?" I shouted at him.

"Let not my lord be angry," the man said, finally seeing my rage. "I will attend to the records immediately, and I will be able to answer my lord on the morrow—"

Some more people came into the courtyard from the gate.

I reached down and gripped the steward's arm, hauling him to his feet.

"And lastly, Reret," I ground out between clenched teeth, "where did you get the means to purchase so much gold?"

He could not answer me.

"You are a thief," I said harshly. "You have stolen wages from the workers on this estate. You have stolen profits from this estate; you might even have taken the jewelry that belonged to the master of this estate!"

When he went pale, I knew I had hit the mark. Not only had he embezzled, he had taken actual items belonging to his employer.

I wanted to shake the man. He could not meet my eyes, and he twisted in my hand. When I let him go, he landed in the dust, cringing away from me.

Turning to the officer of the guard, I demanded, "What are you here for?"

He swallowed. "My lord, the steward came and said that the requests for supplies to this house were unauthorized. He demanded that we come and arrest the culprits," he managed to say.

As I looked at the steward on the ground in front of me, suddenly I lusted for his life. I had never felt such rage as took possession of me. I wanted to see this man die, and I wanted to draw his life from him with my own hands. Swallowing the bile in my throat, I clenched and unclenched my hands to control myself.

Something was wrong with me. One part of my mind sounded an alarm, and I did my best to listen. Such rage was too much for what had happened. Where had it come from?

When I took a step toward Reret, he twisted on the ground, babbling pleas for mercy. I could barely keep my hands off him as I longed to bury my fingers in the soft flesh of his throat.

My rage grew still more, filling my entire being with boiling wrath that made a red mist in front of my eyes. In another moment, I would throw myself on that steward and tear him to pieces with my bare hands.

"El Shaddai! Keep me from this!" I cried with all my might. Instantly, the pressure inside eased, and I found I could breathe. Gulping great breaths of air and relaxing my arms, I looked around. Every person in the courtyard lay flat on their face. Even

Khay, the palace guard, and whomever they had escorted into the court. The only person not in the dust was a young woman sitting on a donkey right next to the gate, and she sat frozen in place, her eyes staring at me as if I was the soul-devourer himself come to feast on her Ka.

The place was deathly silent as the anger continued to rage in my mind.

"Lord Khay," I snapped.

"Yes, Great One," he said in a small voice.

"Take this steward and strip him. He's to be beaten and sent away, never to come to Memphis again as long as he shall live. And do it *now!*" I thundered, turning abruptly and stalking to the house.

Inside I headed to the small reception room. Though as large as Lord Potiphar's dining room, it now felt small to me. Restlessly I paced back and forth, the anger blazing in my mind. Where had it come from? What was it? I didn't know and didn't care. I ached to destroy something, anything, and my eye caught a bowl for fruit.

Reaching for it, I threw it with all my might into the corner of the room. It smashed into a thousand pieces on the gypsum floor. The pressure soon built again, and I cried to El Shaddai to help me understand what was happening to me.

Unable to stay still, I had to keep moving. I was angry, so very angry. Angry as—as Potiphar had been when he first heard Lady Tanefret accuse me. Angry as Judah must have been when Tamar tricked him. Angry as Imenhet when he thought Lord Potiphar had taken his family. I wanted to roar like a lion challenged. Another plate rested on the low table beside me. I hurled it through the air. It struck against the stone bases of the wooden pillars and smashed with a satisfying sound.

More hot rage boiled out of me. "El Shaddai, El Shaddai," I cried. What could I do to release this tension? It grew greater and greater again, and I did not know what to do with it.

Abi. This was Abi's rage when Reuben had taken Bilhah. It was Simeon's rage against the Shechemites for Dinah. It was Esau's rage against Jacob for stealing the blessing from Isaac. And suddenly it was none of those. *It was my rage.*

My rage against my brothers for what they had done to me. How I ached to have them here. I wanted their lives in my hand, wanted to crush every one of them, but especially Simeon and

Judah. Those two had done this to me. They were the ones who had taken away my life and put me into Sheol itself.

The fury inside roared in my head like a lion in battle. I felt all the anger I had not been allowed to feel from the day my brothers sold me. I raged against them, against Jetur who had taken me from my home, against Imenhet for all the blows he inflicted on me, against Lord Potiphar for the apprehension I felt every time he was displeased.

I had been a slave, and I could not feel angry then. But I felt it now. As I thought of myself there on the table with Lord Potiphar's knife at my throat for something I had not done, I cried out, "El Shaddai, *My own brothers sold me!*"

My voice echoed in the room, and I took a metal cup from the floor, hurling it against the nearest door. It would not break, and I seized it again, throwing it over and over until my arms were tired.

Finally, I picked it up, held it in my hands, and started to squeeze. I imagined that cup was my brothers. I pictured it as Simeon with his cruel amusement as I begged him for mercy. It became Judah who had turned from my frantic pleas with disgust as he played with my life. Then it was Issachar and Zebulun shoving me to the ground to be sold, and Dan and Gad and the others staring through me when I cried out my fear.

The cup became Jetur, who looked so like my Grandfather, Mishma with his contempt, Lord Potiphar who let me nearly die in prison. And it was Lady Tanefret, my mistress who had deliberately lied, hoping to see me butchered.

Harder and harder I squeezed, channeling all of my suppressed emotions into one physical expression. I was not my father's son for nothing. Both Jacob and Esau had been extraordinarily strong, and I inherited that strength. I squeezed harder, dragging in great gasping breaths of air. I heard something snap, then another. The gold armbands fell to the floor, and blood surged through the muscles of my arms.

Slowly, the cup began to narrow as the metal in my hands bent and gave. Success gave me more strength, and I squeezed harder still. The opening narrowed more and finally closed upon itself as the metal broke and crackled in my hands.

I dropped the crushed cup, then with one last surge of rage, I picked up the heavy table with its stone top and overturned it.

Gasping, I stopped and closed my eyes, thankful there was no living thing in this room with me. Tears wet my face, and I sat for a long time, letting their steady flow drain the anger from my heart, releasing the remnants of the suddenly broken dam. I must be careful never to let my anger build up to such a point again. With the power I held over other people's lives, I could not dare to lose control even for a moment. Finally, I pleaded with El Shaddai to show me a way to dispel any anger and frustration I might feel as I performed my daily tasks as Tate.

Exhausted, I sat in the now dark room, thinking back over my life and looking again at what had happened to me. I could not believe the magnitude of my rage. This was what had fueled Esau's hatred against his twin, Jacob, for 20 years. That I possessed this same kind of fury startled me.

"El Shaddai," I said hesitantly, "You have given me eyes to see what is hidden. Show me now what hides within myself." My hands hurt, and I sat with my elbows on my knees. What else was down there, buried in my mind?

Cruelty. I shuddered, but admitted that the lust I had felt for that steward's life was the same cruelty that I had seen in Simeon on more than one occasion.

Guile. A good portion of my success in the market was due to this. I could deceive others easily. One expected it in the market, but outside of the game of buying and selling, I must be very careful of this. Part of my heritage, guile was instinctive to me.

My father had deceived his father, and my mother her father. Then Abi was in turn tricked by his father-in-law and then his own sons. My brothers deceived an entire town, and Judah had lied to Tamar, only to be in turn deceived by her. I had only just begun to play the game of cunning and counter-cunning when I was sold, but living the life of a slave demanded a high art of dissimulation just to stay alive. And, as Pharaoh stated, This One Lives.

I was very good at lying. In fact, I had lied to myself to such an extent that I had not known how I really felt until I almost murdered another human being.

"El Shaddai, guard me from this," I whispered as I looked inside myself again.

Arrogance. I blushed at that. It took 13 years of slavery for El Shaddai to curb that in my life. I prayed He would preserve me from it in the future. I would need lots of help, for my new power would inevitably bring flatterers with it.

Most of all, self-will. I wanted my own will to govern my life, and the lives of those around me. Thinking of how I had treated Dan over the herds, how I had reveled in the coat Abi gave me, how I had turned against my God in the prison made me bow my head in shame.

But there were other things as well. I possessed a great deal of administrative ability, and I could work with people easily. I had learned, also, Isaac's submission to God's will, even though I could not understand it. And from somewhere in the darkness of my struggles, I had found faith—like Abraham's—that El Shaddai would finally bring things out right, that His promises would be true.

I shook my head in wonder at my pathetic family. Abraham deceiving Pharaoh in his time, fathering Ishmael of an Egyptian woman; Isaac lying to Abimelech of Gerer; Jacob stealing the birthright from his brother; Judah and Tamar—all the pettiness and machinations and lies that made up my family's history.

Looking back, I saw that my father could have stopped the slaughter of the Shechemites had he wished. Why did he wait until my brothers came home in order to handle the situation with Dinah? He had to have known that they would be very angry, and that they would plan revenge. If he had settled with Hamor, as was his duty as Dinah's father, none of it would have happened.

He even bore some of the blame for my slavery, I realized. His favoritism for me had been marked, as had his favoritism for Rachel. Only a blind man could have missed the trouble it caused. And Abi was not blind. He simply hadn't wanted to face it. So he ignored it, continuing to goad his sons until they finally exploded.

Again I paced the floor. What must it have been like not being Rachel's son? My brothers were far from perfect, but they worked hard, and they loved our father more than anyone else. How frustrating and galling to see him pour out all his love on me. What would it have been like to work and hope for praise from Abi, only to receive reproof because of a complaint I made? What had it felt like to always be considered second rate?

And yet, El Shaddai had honored my family. He tested and proved Abraham until he rang true. My God saved and protected Isaac through famine and hostility, then took my father Jacob and made him Israel, a prince of God. And now, with my talents and weaknesses, He had shepherded me through the shadow of slavery and prison in order to make me the most powerful man in my world.

Pharaoh held the throne, but because he did, he was limited in what he could do, constrained by the expectations and requirements of his office. No such limitations restricted me. Absent-mindedly I fingered the signet ring. I carried Pharaoh's authority without any of the boundaries placed on him. All my world knew and came to Egypt. They traded in Egypt, their ambassadors flocked to Egypt, and many times Egypt dictated to the nations whether there would be war or peace, trade or tribute, life or death. And I was Egypt.

Now I looked down from the dizzying height to which my God had raised me, and it was too much. Dropping to my knees, I put my face to the floor. Who was I, that He should do so much with me? Or my family, that His greatness should single us out?

"My Lord," I cried, "I am only a man who will return to dust after a few short years. Why should Your hand find me to do Your will?"

"I am El Shaddai, the God of Abraham, Isaac, and Jacob. You have not chosen Me, but I have chosen you. See now, I have raised you up and sent you to Pharaoh lest this land perish."

As the resounding voice died away in my ears, I hugged the ground as the glory of my God filled the room. It flowed into me as He chose me, and not I Him. I could not bear it, and cried out with the exultation that wrapped me in itself and then ebbed away softly, gently, laying me back to rest as tenderly as a mother does her child.

I shook uncontrollably; truly His strength and presence were overpowering. "My Lord and my God," I whispered humbly, "I will serve You with all of my life." And then, in awe, I worshiped.

Morning inevitably came. I woke to find myself on the floor and feeling like leftovers from a crocodile's lunch. Aching and my hands hurting, I crawled to my feet, swaying a little at first, and surveyed the room. I winced. The place looked as if someone had fought a battle. Broken crockery littered the floor, as well as the remnants of a large vase that I had no memory whatsoever of smashing.

The floor was littered with broken dishes, and the stone table lay on its side with a cracked top. Two stools were smashed beyond repair, the precious wood splintered and cracked. A third had one leg broken off, but could be repaired. The stone table had fallen on a wooden table and smashed it flat.

Nothing like a mess to bring one crashing back to earth. I wondered what my face looked like and wandered around looking for a rag. Not finding one, I looked down and discovered I wore rags. The royal linen had not stood up well to the activities of last night. Ripping off a piece that barely hung on to the rest of the garment, I used it to wipe my face.

The far door opened slowly, and Khay's voice said, "Master Joseph?"

"Come in, Khay," I croaked hoarsely.

He literally crawled in.

"Don't, Khay," I said, trying to clear my throat.

"Are you all right, my lord?" Mahesa's voice asked from the door.

"I seem to be, Mahesa," I replied, my voice hardly above a whisper. "Come in."

He came through the door bowing and crouched beside Khay.

"Please, don't," I repeated, but neither one of them moved. I walked over to the door and closed it, then offered my hand to Khay.

"Master!" he cried horrified, grabbing my hand. "Master, who attacked you? You are covered with blood!"

Mahesa grabbed my other hand and gasped. "Someone was in here?" he asked. "Master, we didn't know! Are you all right? What happened?" He looked around, searching for a dead body.

"The only man here was me," I said. "And that may not even be true. I don't—" I gasped as Mahesa pulled my hand open.

"Sit down," Khay commanded, looking around for a chair. "Where else are you hurt? What happened?"

"I am not hurt," I said, still not able to talk comfortably.

Khay snorted. "Go get some wine and oil, Mahesa. As usual, Joseph is blind as a bat."

I relaxed. My friend was back to his usual self. Glancing down, I saw that I was splattered with dried blood. Spots of it were around the stone table, and several objects on the floor had smears on them.

"What happened?" Khay asked for the third time.

"I am not sure," I said. "But I think I lost my temper."

He looked around at the destruction in amazement. "You just think? Don't you know?"

"I—This has never happened to me before," I confessed, looking sheepish.

"May it never happen again," he declared with unusual fervor, shuddering.

Mahesa returned just then and kept me fully occupied holding still while they bathed my hands with wine. My palms were sliced in several places, and the blood had gotten all over me.

"How did you cut yourself?" Khay prodded me again.

"Probably when I crushed the cup," I said, trying to think back to what had happened.

"Crushed a cup?" Mahesa said, puzzled. "My lord, are you feeling all right?"

"I am quite tired," I said. "But except for my hands, I feel fine. I will need to do something, however," I said to both of them. "I do not dare let anger like this build up again."

They stared at each other.

"Who was my lord angry with?" Khay asked in a faint voice, looking down.

"That contemptible steward opened it up, somehow," I said thoughtfully, "but I was actually angry at my brothers."

Mahesa raised his eyes to me. "Brothers?" he asked.

"Eleven of them," I said with a sigh.

Both men froze for a moment.

"Are you done wrapping me in linen?" I asked, looking at the bandages on my hands.

"Did my lord say *11* brothers?" Mahesa queried.

"Unless they managed to get rid of Benjamin also, yes, I have 11 brothers."

"Who is Benjamin?"

"He is my little brother, also a son of my mother. Four are sons of maid servants, and six are sons of my father's other wife."

"More than one wife?" Mahesa asked, surprised.

"It didn't start out that way," I said with a sigh. "Father agreed to work seven years for the hand of my mother Rachel, but at the wedding, her father Laban got my father good and drunk and then married him to Rachel's older sister Leah instead. When father woke up enough to realize what had happened, it was too late. He married Rachel soon after, but Laban demanded another seven years' labor from him."

Khay grinned. "Laban sounds like a real operator," he said.

"He is," I nodded. "But Jacob, my father, got rich off him. He worked for Laban for wages for six years after that, and by that time he was richer than Laban. His cattle always increased more than Laban's did."

"That's a good start on the story," Khay laughed, "but why were you angry with your brothers?"

I sobered. "My father always loved Rachel more than Leah, and he made no secret of it. Leah and the maid servants gave Father 10 sons before I was born to Rachel. Since I was her son, he loved me more than the others. I was 12 years old before Rachel had another child, my full brother Benjamin. She died giving birth."

I turned away, wanting to clench my hands, but the bandages prevented me.

"My father turned to me in his grief," I continued. "He favored me more than all the others—unwisely, as it turned out. In fact, he all but named me his heir, which would give me rulership over the family. My brothers were very jealous, and not without cause," I admitted. "I was pretty much of a brat by the time I turned 17."

"What then?" Khay asked in the silence.

"Neither Abi nor I realized how deeply my brothers hated me," I said softly. "When I naively put myself in their power, they turned on me." I stopped and swallowed, sick with the memory of that terrible day.

"And?" Khay urged.

"They threw me into an empty cistern to starve."

Mahesa sucked in his breath sharply.

"Then they had a better idea," I continued, unable to keep the bitterness from my voice. "They pulled me out of the cistern and sold me as a slave to some Ishmaelite traders traveling to Egypt."

"Let me get this straight," Mahesa began. "Your brothers, the sons of your father, sold you into slavery?"

I nodded, unable to speak.

"I thought I had it bad," Khay said grimly. "How did you react to that?"

"I was the pampered son of a very rich man," I said steadily. "What do you think I went through?"

Mahesa started to swear. Khay didn't say anything, but when I turned around to face them again, his face was dead white.

"I was a slave for 13 years," I said. "The one emotion I dared not feel was anger. I could be sad, or afraid, or worried, but never, ever angry. Last night I think 13 years of anger burst out all at once."

They sat there in silence for a while. Khay looked around at the mess. "At least all you did was smash things," he commented. "I think I would have torn the whole house down."

Exhausted, I sat down on the floor. For once Mahesa didn't say a word about etiquette. "What are you going to do to them?" he asked. "Does your father know?"

I shrugged. "Abi must think I am dead. That would be the only possible thing they could tell him."

Khay swore this time.

"You are Tate, now," Mahesa reminded me. "You can reach into Canaan. What will you do?"

"Wait," I said. "El Shaddai told me that the time to deal with this is not yet. So I will wait until it is time. But I do worry about Benjamin, and what they might have done to him."

I looked down. "Please do not speak of this to anyone," I requested. "It is something that my God has promised to resolve, and I do not want my family name to be publically shamed by this deed."

"As you wish, Lord Paanekh," Mahesa responded.

"Not even if Pharaoh should ask," Khay added grimly.

"Thank you. In any case, El Shaddai has given me a father, a wife, and sons to comfort me here, and that is enough for the present."

"A father?" Khay said, then grinned. "Lord Potiphar," he guessed.

I nodded. "He was very kind to me when he did not have to be."

"He put you in prison," Mahesa said bluntly.

"What else could he do? With his position, he could just as easily have tortured me to death, and no one would have asked questions."

"But what about the wife and sons?" Khay asked puzzled.

"The wife, yes, if you can call her that," Mahesa said sourly.

I looked at him in amazement. "She has come? When?"

"She arrived yesterday," he replied.

"What does Lady Sopdu look like?" I asked eagerly. "Pharaoh told me she was very nice."

"Lady Sopdu?" Mahesa asked. "Lady Sopdu is not your wife, although I am sure that is who Pharaoh thought you would get. He apparently forgot that Great Ueb Poti-Phera has two daughters by a previous marriage, and the youngest one from that marriage is the one he sent. It is Lady Asenath."

"What is wrong with that?"

"It is an insult," Mahesa said savagely. "Lady Asenath is the joke of the court. A recluse, she is never seen in public. Her own father hardly claims her. She is supposed to be gauche, clumsy, and half-witted in the bargain. Given your position, you will need an intelligent, able wife, and Lady Asenath is incapable of being either. Poti-Phera may have obeyed Pharaoh's order, but he has limited you immensely by saddling you with an unsuitable wife."

I thought of Aunt Leah, sitting so many times unwanted in her tent. "We shall see," I said. No matter what things turned out to be, I was determined that Lady Asenath would not feel the rejection I knew had blighted Leah's life.

"You must tell Pharaoh of this," Mahesa said. "It should not be forgotten."

I shrugged again. "Let it lie."

He looked at me in astonishment.

"Mahesa," I said, "when one has lived through what I have, do you think that being given an unsuitable wife will hurt very much?"

"Put like that, no," Khay answered, grinning. "May I help you to your room for the night? The master's bedchamber has been thoroughly cleaned by Benret herself."

"I slept some, I think," I said. "We need to get working today, Khay."

"Today?" Mahesa asked. "The day is almost over, Lord Paanekh. You were in here for more than 24 hours."

I looked around. "Well, that explains why I am so tired."

CHAPTER 20

The next morning, I woke early as usual. Khay and Mahesa met me in the small reception room.

"You are up, Lord Paanekh," Mahesa said needlessly.

"And thoroughly ashamed of myself," I said ruefully, looking around. "This is the worst mess I have ever seen."

Khay wandered to the overturned table where he bent down and picked up something. His mouth dropped open and he gasped, drawing Mahesa's attention.

"What is it?" Mahesa asked.

"I think it used to be a cup," Khay said in awe.

I looked up and blushed fiery red.

Khay passed the crushed cup to Mahesa, and they both stared at me.

"Well, that *does* explain your hands," Khay said, taking a deep breath.

I looked at the cup. The metal had broken as well as bent, and its jagged edges had sliced my palms.

Mahesa took the mangled remains back. "I will see that it is melted down and restored, my lord."

"Why?"

"It is of the White, my lord," he replied.

"Oh."

Benret gathered some of her women, and they tackled the small reception room. She shook her head and clucked in annoyance at the mess I'd made. I looked appropriately chastened and Mahesa and I went into the private garden off my rooms. "Now," I said, "tell me about Lady Asenath."

He told me in detail what the court gossip said, what the house staff said, and what people who had managed a glimpse of her said.

"It is a terrible insult," he added between his teeth. "Poti-Phera is very rich and yet he sent her with no gifts."

"What did he send along with her?"

"Nothing. She came with an attendant. The man who brought her on a donkey left—with the donkey."

"A donkey?" I said, jerking my head up. "She was sitting on it, by the gate?"

Mahesa nodded. "They entered just after I did with the palace guard. You were in the middle of chastising that cursed steward."

Suddenly I remembered the look in her eyes. My heart sank. "I saw her. She was very frightened. Have her things come yet?"

Mahesa went rigid. "She came with nothing," he repeated.

"Surely she had some baggage, with clothes or cosmetics," I protested.

"She came with nothing except what she wore. The attendant had a bag for herself, but the lady has nothing."

"You mean Poti-Phera sent her over here like a goat or some other animal?"

"Yes."

"Has anyone tended to her?" I asked aghast.

"No one can get in," Mahesa explained. "She went to a room and has not come out. Her attendant takes in food, but no one knows if she eats it."

She had gone to ground. I knew the feeling. If she was anywhere near as frightened as she looked, she would find a hole and stay there. I did not understand how Poti-Phera could do this to his own daughter, but if what Mahesa said was true, he had washed his hands of her and made her totally dependent on me for even kohl to put around her eyes.

And after the display I had put on over that steward I could just imagine what she must think of me.

"See to it that the best rooms are prepared for her," I said. "When they are done, I want to see her. Bring her to the small reception room."

"Yes, my lord. The next item is Lord Hernofret who is not Lord Hernofret."

"What did you say, Mahesa?" I asked, surprised.

"The young man sent to you by Lord Amony is not Lord Hernofret. He is a son of Lord Amony, but illegitimate. His mother was the daughter of a minor official in Thebes, and Lord Amony took a fancy to her. Amony seems to have taken a fancy to several women all over Egypt."

"Sounds like him," I commented with a sigh.

"The young man's name is actually Saf. His mother makes a living by managing houses for noble ladies who do not want to bother doing it themselves. She currently has a position in On. Rather than let her child run in the streets, she kept him by her all the time. He is very knowledgeable in the area."

"Could he handle this house?"

"In all likelihood, yes."

"How is it that the young man agreed to this deception?"

"His mother now has a personal bodyguard supplied by Lord Amony," Mahesa said in a wooden tone.

"Lord Amony is beginning to bother me greatly. Did Khay also find out where Lord Hernofret really is?"

"Not yet, my lord."

"I want to know just as soon as possible. Then we will keep an eye on him."

With a nod Mahesa left the garden.

I paced its length, hands behind my back, as I had seen Lord Potiphar do so many times. Lord Amony proved to be more trouble than I expected. I should not have underestimated him. In order for him to substitute Saf for Lord Hernofret so quickly, he must have gone immediately to On in blatant disregard of my orders when I sent him away.

Some minutes later Mahesa reappeared. "The rooms are ready, my lord. Shall I bring Lady Asenath?"

"Yes."

I went to the small reception room and resumed pacing, but for a different reason this time. I was nervous. El Shaddai had given me this woman for a wife, and I wanted to make a good impression if I could, especially considering the one I had already made by howling like a madman in the courtyard. I flushed just thinking about it.

My curiosity about my new wife was thoroughly aroused. If what Mahesa had told me was correct, she had stayed in the rooms of her father's house for many years. Why had she hidden herself away?

Mahesa came in. "Lady Asenath," he said, and stood aside.

The young woman I had seen on the donkey shuffled in, keeping her head down. Stumbling twice on an overly long dress of rumpled and worn linen, she wore no jewelry, and her uncombed hair fell sloppily over her face. The tension in her body was palpable across the room.

I wondered if she was fully conscious, even though on her feet.

"Lady Asenath, let me offer you my deepest apologies," I said gently. "There should have been a proper welcome prepared for you. The house has had a difficult time settling in, but rooms are now ready for you.

"Mahesa, the scribe who brought you to this room, will see that you have whatever you need for yourself and your rooms. Please consider anything in the house your own.

"I am sorry that I cannot open the door for you," I continued. "But my hands were cut, and the bandages make me clumsy."

Her eyes flickered toward me for the briefest moment, so at least she heard what I said. Then she sidled out of the room like a rabbit escaping from a fox, and her footsteps indicated that she ran as soon as she left my sight. I sighed in discouragement. But El Shaddai had said sons, so sooner or later it would come out right. I hadn't seen her face yet, but her hands looked small and finely shaped, and she had a very nice figure beneath the rumpled linen.

When Mahesa returned, I had a message for him to send. "Let Poti-Phera know that his daughter arrived safely, although it appears that her party was set upon by robbers, who stole all her belongings. Assure him that Lady Asenath is fine, however, and let him know that he need send nothing more, since I am more than happy to provide for such a beautiful and intelligent woman as his daughter."

"But—but—my lord, none of that is true!" he sputtered.

"She did arrive safely," I said. "And it truly does look as if she were set upon by robbers, does it not?"

"Well, I suppose so."

"And he does not need to send anything else because I am rich enough to provide for her, correct?"

"Well, yes. But beautiful? Intelligent?"

"Do we know for certain that she is not?" I asked.

He just stared at me.

"Right now, Mahesa, that woman thinks I am the personification of all the demons of the underworld. Until she loses that fear, we will not know what she is really like."

"I see what you mean, my lord, but she is known in the court as a disaster."

"No one has seen her for years, so no one else knows what she is really like either," I said meditatively. "I just get a feeling that even under her fear, she is playing a part. I very much want to know why."

With Khay off on business, I spent the next three days with Mahesa and the false Lord Hernofret at the old palace, getting ready to begin my official duties as Tate. But under the surface of my mind the problem of Lady Asenath nagged at me. Her attendant Iutem said that she had taken to her bed and was ill. I didn't like the sound of that. Something was wrong, but I couldn't put my finger on what. It bothered my mind, and I played with the thought at odd moments.

Mahesa played with the so-called Lord Hernofret. Again and again, the scribe took the man to the brink of discovery, only to back off before he made the deception obvious. By the time the morning was half over, the young man would be exhausted and covered with sweat. His eyes were haunted and afraid, and he could hardly look at me.

Grimly, I controlled the savage anger than ran through me. Lord

Amony had done nothing to prepare the young man for his part in this deception. He had not even informed him of the rudiments of Lord Hernofret's life or of how a lord lived.

The afternoon of the third day, I saw him look down at the ring with Lord Hernofret's seal with such loathing that I thought he would rip it off his finger and hurl it into the Nile. I silenced Mahesa, who was about to say something, with a look and slight shake of my head.

That evening, after eating, I took off my wig and the new gold armbands that Mahesa insisted I wear and picked up the pile of court cases waiting for attention. I would formally open my court with a judgment day. I made swift notations on each case as I reviewed it. Some of them were routine, and I never should have seen them. Others quickly caught my interest. I must find someone to sort through the appeals, since many could be handled without the parties appearing before me. Soon I was lost in the records.

A sound at the door made me look up.

"If I may have a moment of my lord's time?" Saf said from the doorway.

"You may," I said. "Come in."

He walked up to the table. With shaking hands he placed the signet ring in front of me. "I beg my lord's indulgence," he said. "I wish him to listen to what I have to say."

"I will listen."

"I am not Lord Hernofret," he managed to say. "Lord Amony is my father, but I am not a son of his wife. When Lord Amony came to On from the Great House, he demanded that I impersonate Lord Hernofret to you. I was afraid of what Lord Amony would do to my mother, and so I agreed to deceive you.

"But I—I can no longer do this. I cannot believe you have not noticed my ignorance of so many things." He looked at his clenched hands and took a deep breath. "I know that I have done what is hateful to Pharaoh in this matter, and I know that I must bear the punishment for it, but I would beg from my lord one favor."

He stopped.

"Go on."

"My lord is very powerful. If my lord would send for my mother from Lord Amony before he punishes me? She has done nothing, and if Lord Amony hears I have failed, he will harm her. Please, my lord, hear me on this matter! I could be held in prison if my lord wishes until my mother is away from Lord Amony, and then I—well, my lord can—if—w-whatever my lord decides shall be done. Only do not let my mother die because I have done this thing."

"What makes you think I care about your mother?" I asked.

Sweat dripped from his face. "I do not know that you do, my lord. It is lawful to punish the family for what one has done, and I would throw myself and my mother upon your mercy rather than Lord Amony's. But I would plead with my lord to let his anger fall on me, and not on her."

"You are very eloquent, Saf," I said. "I will not harm your mother."

"Thank you, my lord." Then he paused and stared at me. "You called me by name," he added slowly. "How long have you known I was not Lord Hernofret?"

I shrugged. "It is part of my job to know things. As soon as Lord Khay returns, the guard supplied by Lord Amony will be conscripted to spend time in the Sinai mines as a guard there, and Khay will bring your mother here."

Saf remained silent until he could control his voice. "Thank you, my lord. And what does my lord wish done with me?"

"I rather think I will condemn you to be my steward until you get old and gray."

"As my lord wishes," he replied. "I will be a faithful servant to my lord."

"Servant?" I said, looking up, picking up from his tone that he used the word in its meaning of an Egyptian slave. "You will receive wages fit for your duties."

The young man grew very still. "I do not understand my lord. I deceived you and lied to you."

"In order to save your mother's life," I added. "In my country, Saf, the duty of a son to his mother is very important."

"You are going to *reward* me with the job of steward?" he said, still dazed.

"Do you demand that I have you beaten first?" I asked testily.

"N-no, my lord," he stuttered. "But I deserve it."

"I do not agree."

He stared at me helplessly. "As you wish, my lord," he finally said in total bewilderment.

▲ ▲ ▲ ▲

Asenath shuddered. The last three days had been a nightmare of dread waiting for the next summons from the barbarian. How she had survived the first one she still didn't know. She couldn't remember anything about it. But she did remember the scene in the courtyard, however, and the sound of his voice filling the compound with wild foreign words, and the steward groveling in the dust, pleading for his life. Then she shivered as she thought of that same raging voice shouting from the house, and the crash of breaking things. That had been her husband, the barbarian. He came of Deshret and was obviously a true son of Seth.

In spite of herself, she thought of the things Iutem had told her. Her attendant had been outside of Egypt so she would know, but some of the things she said were unbelievable. People lived inside dwellings of skins, and everyone had hair on their faces. But more than that, the high-born ladies never cut their hair!

Iutem said that people ate from wooden bowls with wooden utensils, which was ridiculous since no one would waste wood like that. She said they even burned it for fuel! Asenath frowned. How could she possibly believe that?

Also Iutem declared that outside of Egypt all women were slaves, that they had to do anything they were told, and that no one cared if they lived or died. Asenath swallowed. She knew that much was true, having seen that herself. And Iutem explained that sometimes children were actually killed and sacrificed to foreign gods, and that their worshipers drank blood at the new moon, and—

"Here you are, Lady."

Asenath jumped, falling off the stool, crying out. She saw Iutem, and suddenly began to cry. She couldn't stop. "I want to leave. I want to go back to On," she sobbed. "I cannot stay here. I will die, I know I will."

"Don't cry so, Lady," Iutem said soothingly. "You just listen to me, and I will tell you what to do. Why, if you please this barbarian, he won't hurt you. I know of one wife that lived for more than five years. You just listen to me, Lady, and I will make sure you are fine."

Asenath clung to her, unable to see the malicious smile on the woman's face.

After a bit, Iutem went beyond the curtain for another lamp, and Asenath sat down again by the dressing table. On it were the basics of cosmetics, a comb, and a mirror. Beside it sat a linen chest and a jewelry box. Carefully Asenath looked around. It was a larger room than any she had had. The furnishings were very nice, if a bit old. And it didn't look foreign at all. It looked completely Egyptian.

Iutem brought the lamp and set it on a low table behind Asenath by the bed. "There, Lady. You do what I say and you'll have nothing to worry about."

Asenath clutched the mirror in her hands. "What should I do?" she asked without turning around.

"You must get used to this heavy wine, Lady," the woman said, pouring out a cup. "It is a favorite with your master, and you must know how to drink it. They take it in great gulps, the entire cup at once. Don't worry if it spills on you, that just means you like it."

The younger woman stiffened. Since her father had started drinking old wine, she had left it alone. She didn't like the way it made her head feel. But she could spill most of it and hopefully save herself the headache. As she fingered the mirror, she felt the urge to look into it. But then she hated her face, so why should she look in the mirror?

"Look in the mirror."

The urge wouldn't go away. Iutem talked on.

"Look in the mirror."

Asenath raised it and saw the woman pour several drops from a small vial into the wine. Then she slipped the vial into a fold of her belt, never once breaking the flow of her chatter about how to please the barbarian.

As she lowered the mirror, Asenath felt her chest tighten. Her mind fought against what she had seen, but she could not deny it.

"Is my lady listening?" Iutem demanded.

Her tone acted like an slap in the face. Asenath looked down. How was it that Iutem felt free to speak to her in such a manner?

"I am too tired to listen, Iutem," she said. "I must rest. Leave me now."

"All right, Lady. I know it will be hard for you to adjust to the tastes of this barbarian. I don't envy you at all, I will say. But I will help you all I can, don't you ever doubt that. Now, this would be a good time to practice drinking your wine, so take what I gave you in one gulp. I only put in half a cup, so it will be easier for you."

Somehow Asenath stifled her trembling. "Yes, Iutem. You are right. I must learn." From the corner of her eye as she turned around, she caught the satisfied smile on her attendant's face, and Iutem went behind the curtain again to bring linens for tomorrow.

Asenath tipped the cup to see the surface of the wine in the lamp light. A slight oily residue gleamed on the surface. Very carefully, she set the cup down and backed away from it, hands clutched to her chest.

Her attendant returned. "There, lady, you look half dead. Lie down now. Remember, I'm here. Your father gave me specific instructions to see that you settled in well before I left you, so don't you worry about that. With what I can find out, you will please your new master, and you may even outlive that wife who survived for so long. Such a wonder in the land! Five years! No one could believe it."

Through sheer willpower Asenath forced herself to stand still. "Yes, Iutem. Go now. I will drink the wine like the barbarian will expect."

The woman headed toward the door, and Asenath picked up the cup. She stared at it, and as Iutem glanced back, she opened her mouth, tossed back her head and tipped the wine toward her face.

"That's a good lady," Iutem said. "May you have a long rest."

Asenath shuddered at the sound of the woman's voice. She set the cup with most of the wine still in it on the table and pulled some bed coverings over the wine that had spilled over her shoulder. Rising from the bed, she automatically picked up the mirror, holding it to her chest as she used to hold her mother's mirror so long ago.

Then she sat down at the dressing table, feeling completely alone. And until Renseneb found her, she was helpless. All her records, the lists and sources, her signet ring and business necessities were in On. As she had 13 years before, Asenath fought down her fear and forced herself to think. With the same realistic courage, she faced what she knew now as she had done then.

Her father had ordered her killed. As she closed her eyes, tears squeezed from them, but the stark truth would not go away. Bitterly, she assessed the political damage her death would cause the new Tate. She was daughter to the Great Ueb, the high Priest of Ra at On, the most powerful political priestly position in the land. Tying his new Tate to her father's family was a very shrewd political move on Pharaoh's part. The Tate controlled the position of Great Vision of Ra, so her father would be subordinate to Lord Paanekh, who owed his office entirely to Pharaoh, thus placing her father under Pharaoh's control.

As a foreigner, he might not understand the position that priests and temples held in the land, but married to a Great Ueb's daughter, he would learn quickly to work smoothly with the religious segment of the government. Pharaoh indeed planned far ahead. How could he know Poti-Phera cared so little for her that he would sacrifice her for political advantage? Then she remembered that the king expected Sopdu to be the new Tate's wife, not her. She had been a recluse so long that no one counted her for anything.

Gritting her teeth, she accepted the facts. If she died in the new Tate's house, so soon after arriving, the political ramifications would be massive and possibly irreparable. If she was found poisoned, her father could accuse the barbarian of the murder of an Egyptian noble lady, proving his attachment to Seth and his inability to preserve maat even in his own house, let alone the entire country of Egypt.

Lord Amony would support her father with the weight of every nomarch in his control, and would rally the south as a whole to his side. Unless Pharaoh wanted an armed rebellion on his hands, he must depose the Tate and appoint another. With the entire south behind him, Lord Amony would undoubtedly get the office. Once there, nothing could stop him from taking the throne.

It made the perfect solution for her father and Lord Amony. It just required that she die. She bent her shoulders with silent tears of bitterness. Yes, her father had indeed instructed Iutem as to her care, for she had previously seen that vial Iutem had had. It had sat on her father's desk years ago when a guest had mysteriously died in their home.

She hung onto the mirror, finding the worn spot on the handle ornament that she always rubbed. The familiar feel comforted her, and she could almost believe her mother's arms hugged her.

Suddenly, with a choking gasp, Asenath wiped her eyes and studied the mirror in her hands. Again wiping them, she looked closely at the object in the lamplight. It was! It was her own mother's mirror! The one she had sold so many years ago to begin her path to independence. How had it gotten here?

What did that matter? She hugged it to her chest, crying now with joy. This mirror had always brought her luck. It would again.

Lovingly she smoothed its battered surface with her fingers, touching the old-fashioned ornamentation.

Then she sat very still. She would have to start from the beginning again since she could not trust Iutem for a moment. Perhaps it would be wise to discount anything the woman said until she had confirmed it for herself. That would mean leaving her room. She bit her lip, then reminded herself that she was in an Egyptian house in the middle of Memphis, and nothing was going to happen to her. Nothing had happened to Iutem, and she heard the staff in the house all the time. She couldn't really believe that they were replaced every day after being slaughtered.

Restlessly, Asenath paced the room. If she came out of her rooms, she needed to know what Lord Paanekh looked like so she could avoid him. He probably wouldn't be in the house, but she would keep her eye out for anyone covered with black hair just the same. Even so, she should ask Iutem what he looked like and where he normally stayed in the house.

After going through the door to the attendant's room, she called, "Iutem." But the room was empty. Asenath stood very still. Where could the woman have gone? She noticed that the table was bare. Quickly, she opened the box for linens. Empty. Numbly Asenath leaned against the wall. All of Iutem's things were gone.

Then she waited for the fear to come. She was truly alone now. But surprisingly, all she felt was relief. Iutem was not here to hover over her and feed her fears.

Returning to her dressing table, Asenath picked up the mirror, staring into it. "I think I have been played for a fool," she said to her reflection.

CHAPTER 21

Having badly overslept and needing to get to the palace as soon as I could, I hurried down the hallway carrying my wig and armbands. Much to Mahesa's disgust, I refused to wear them in the house unless absolutely necessary. By the time I reached the palace, I would have them on properly. But they were the bane of my life during the day.

"Where is the scribe?" a woman asked.

I turned, then stopped and looked again, closing my mouth, as I stared into two eyes the same deep, warm brown as my mother's. I felt myself flushing, and that made me flush more.

The lady didn't notice. She looked rigidly past me, her arms stiffly at her sides. Her hair was uncombed and the hem of her dress was soiled and torn where she had stepped on it.

"I am sorry, lady," I apologized. "What did you say?"

"Where is the scribe?" she repeated.

"He is in another part of the house. May I do something for my lady?"

She took a deep breath. "My attendant is not here. I am hungry."

Suddenly I felt as if no one else existed in the world but this awkward, raggedly dressed woman with enormous frightened eyes who stood alone in front of me. Not only was she small and delicate, but she was pretty under the stiffness of her face.

I stood silent so long that she finally dragged her eyes away from my left shoulder and looked at me. Those rich brown eyes went round as she stared at my hair. I hastily dropped my gaze from her face, easily slipping into the role of slave once again.

"You are not Egyptian," she said, her voice trembling a little.

"No, lady. I am of Canaan."

She drew into herself like a turtle into its shell. I thought she would run back to her room, but she didn't.

Her hands made small fists. "Is that where Syrians are from?"

"No, lady. Syria is a neighboring country to the north of my home. The peoples of my country often fight with them," I added wryly.

"Does everyone in Canaan have hair like yours?"

"No, lady. Only a few. Most people have brown or black hair."

"You are a barbarian, then," she said, raising her chin and finally managing to look me over.

"Yes, lady, I am."

"I heard that barbarians had hair all over them, but you don't," she commented, a faint hint of curiosity entering her voice.

"I do not, lady, but some in my family have much more hair than I do. It is something that is different from person to person.

Shall I bring my lady something to eat?"

She looked up, forgetting for a moment to be afraid, and I glimpsed a keen intelligence in her eyes. Then they clouded with apprehension again, and she backed up a step.

"Yes."

"Shall I bring it to my lady's room, or will you wait here?"

"I will wait here," she decided.

After bowing respectfully, I headed for the kitchens.

Saf caught up to me. "Was that Lady Asenath?"

"I don't see who else it could be."

We were almost to the kitchens, and he looked at me amazed. "Surely you do not mean to take the lady her food?"

"Why not?"

"But—but you are Lord Paanekh, Tate of Upper and Lower Egypt! Why should you run errands like a serving boy?"

"Because my wife asked me to," I said with a twinkle in my eye.

"I do not understand you, my lord," he said with a sigh.

"Commiserate with Mahesa. He doesn't either," I said unsympathetically, then entered the kitchen.

"Yes, Master Joseph, what do you wish?" Minemhet asked me as soon as I appeared.

I stopped in amazement. "Minemhet? What are you doing here?"

"Cooking," he said dryly. "What did you wish?"

"But, Lord Potiphar—"

"Lord Potiphar said you needed me more than he did. I agreed. Now, what did you wish? I do not have all day."

I laughed, delighted to see him. "Neither do I. I need breakfast for Lady Asenath. Her attendant seems to have vanished."

In seconds, he handed me a basket with bread, figs, and some sweetmeats for Lady Asenath. I hurried back to the house.

"Not one word, Saf," I said. "Let me tell her who I am in my own good time."

"But—"

"Saf!"

"Yes, my lord."

"And tell the staff that no one is to mention to Lady Asenath what color hair Lord Paanekh has."

"Yes, my lord."

I doubted she had moved more than two inches since I left.

"Here is some food, lady. I hope it will be sufficient."

"Thank you," she said, making no move to take it from me.

"Shall I take the food to your rooms, lady?" I asked, realizing she was too frightened to let me hand it to her.

When she backed to the side into the wall, I carefully passed her and walked to her rooms at the end of the hall. There I put the food on a small table near the bed while Asenath watched me warily from the doorway.

I went down on one knee. "Will there be anything else, my lady?"

"No," she replied, edging to the other side of the room.

"Shall I ask Saf to find your attendant?" I asked next, wondering where the woman was.

"No!" Asenath exclaimed.

I looked up briefly. My wife hugged herself, her face pale. "I—I sent her away. She will not be back."

"Shall I have one of the house women attend you?" I ventured.

"No, I am fine," she said, looking anything but that.

"As you wish, my lady. I must go now. If you need anything, ask for Saf."

"Thank you," she said faintly, and I left.

I stopped at the gate on my way to the palace. "Inti?" I called.

He appeared. "Yes, my lord?"

"Lady Asenath told me her attendant is missing this morning. Not long after, she told me that she had sent the woman away and that the woman would not be back. Do you know anything of this?"

"A moment, my lord," Inti said. He came back shortly. "Esse had the gate last evening, my lord. He said that Iutem left late with her bundle. She told him something about an errand for her mistress. She has not returned."

I considered. "Find her, Inti. Lady Asenath was afraid, and I wish to know why. If you locate Iutem, bring her to me before you let Lady Asenath know she is back."

"Yes, my lord. Would there be a reward for her?" he asked, looking straight at me.

I grinned. "Spend whatever you need to, Inti," I told him. "But find her."

"Yes, my lord."

At the palace, I plunged into work. Mahesa had the day completely scheduled. I formally opened my court with my first judgment day, personally handling more than 20 of the most serious cases. After the long day—and I understood why the former Tate avoided this duty—I felt completely drained.

Onami walked the stallions back to the residence, giving me time to relax a little. I wondered how things had gone at the house and if Asenath had come out of her rooms again.

We turned in at the gate to find Inti, Esse, and Defatsen confronting someone who held what looked like a rag pile. It squirmed suddenly, slipped to the ground, and resolved itself into a child who streaked toward me. She didn't look where she was going and bounced off me, landing in the dust, staring up at my face. Then she promptly wrapped herself around one of my legs and refused to let go.

The stranger strode toward me. "Come here, you little daughter of pigs! I will teach you to run from your master!"

The little daughter of pigs tightened her hold on my leg and stayed still.

"What seems to be the problem?" I asked coldly, stopping the man in his tracks.

He bowed. "My apologies, noble lord. I traced this runaway to the house here, and have come to take her back where she belongs. I ask many pardons for the inconvenience. I shall remove her at once."

I looked down at the child and back into the angry eyes of the man. "She does not seem to want to go," I commented.

The man flushed. "It is like her," he said between his teeth. "She is a bad child and requires a heavy hand. You know children only have ears on their backs." I frowned at his allusion to the beating he would give her.

"You are a lying son of a baboon, Sosamen," the child said in a surprisingly collected voice. "I belong here with Lady Asenath."

"You stole from the Great Ueb's house!" he said furiously. "You took what did not belong to you."

"It is not yours either," the girl flashed back. "It is the Lady's, and I will give it to her."

For the first time, I noticed the sack the girl wore around her neck.

"Stand up, child," I said quietly.

She let go and stood, a tiny thing with sparkling black eyes and an impudent nose.

"What is your name?"

"Hesy. I serve the Lady Asenath. She is a good lady and takes care of me. Then the Great Ueb sent her away. He did not allow her to take anything with her. I found the things she uses most, and I brought them to her. She is wife of the new Tate, and this is his house and I have come to be with her."

"What is in that bag does not belong to the Lady Asenath. It belongs to the Great Ueb," the man said furiously. "I am Chief Steward to Great Ueb Poti-Phera, Great Vision of Ra. It is my duty to return the items to my lord."

"What is in the bag?" I asked.

Sosamen blinked. "Items for my lord," he answered.

"What items?"

Sosamen stammered a bit and got red in the face.

"Inti, send a messenger to Poti-Phera at On and ask him what items are missing—"

"That will not be necessary, my lord," Sosamen said hastily. "The items are only small things that my lord the Great Ueb will not miss, and—"

"Then you will have no objections to my purchasing them, along with Hesy, will you?"

He choked slightly. "Purchasing them?" he asked, his voice cracking.

"Certainly. If Hesy ran all the way from On to be with her mistress, I think she should stay here. It would be best, then, if I purchased her to prevent any possible misunderstandings. You will accept three gold pieces for your trouble, no doubt."

A greedy gleam appeared in the man's eyes. "Three? My lord, the girl is a favorite of Lady Asenath and is very resourceful as you have seen. Surely—"

"Inti, about that messenger," I interrupted. "See that he is sent at once."

"Three gold pieces is more than generous, my lord," Sosamen said hastily. "The bargain is fine. There is no need to send messages."

I obtained a signed receipt for Hesy and everything she carried on her before letting the man out of my gate.

"Well, Hesy," I said, looking down into her sparkling eyes. "It appears as though you can stay. Let me send you to Benret, and she will get you cleaned up and presentable. Then you may deliver your sack to Lady Asenath."

"So she *is* still alive!" the child said triumphantly.

"Of course she is," I said, puzzled. "Where did you get the idea that she had died?"

"In the markets," she answered casually. "They are whispering that Lady Asenath is dead and that the new Tate killed her. But I did not believe that. If anyone killed her, it was that daughter of snakes, Iutem."

"Oh?" I asked, trying to quell my alarm. "Why would Iutem do something like that?"

"She was supposed to. Is Benret the lady who cleans in the house?"

"Yes, she is," I replied, slightly dazed. "Why would Iutem think she was to kill her mistress?"

"Because he told her to," Hesy replied. "I see her, now. I will go and get clean!" She ran off.

"Inti? Is she right?" I asked.

"Yes, lord," he said, his face wrathful. "The rumors are in the markets. Those of us here have been saying they are lies, but they persist."

"Inti, I want Iutem."

"Yes, my lord."

▲　▲　▲　▲

Asenath sat on the bed, clutching her midsection, gasping for breath from her terrified run to her room from the shadows of the porch. Her one glimpse of the gold armbands and the sound of that hard voice assured her that Lord Paanekh stood in the middle of the group in the courtyard. And he had Hesy! What would he do to her? What was Hesy doing here? The girl must have run away, followed her to this house. It would be like her to do that.

Desperately Asenath tried to contain her panic. Lord Paanekh had found Hesy, and who knew what horrible things he would do to her before he killed her. She could not let that happen. Hesy was—was—Hesy was just Hesy, and—

She must save her. Asenath found herself facing the door. She must go out there to the barbarian, and take the girl away from him.

Hesy was just an innocent child. The barbarian had killed Sumet. *He must not kill Hesy,* she thought incoherently.

Turning her head, Asenath could hear that slave, the one with the red hair.

"Well, you look much better," he said.

Hesy's voice answered. "That is what Benret said. Shall I get to see the Tate? Someone told me he had black hair all over him like a jackal and that he had flames in his eyes and that he drank blood at the new moon."

"What do you think about all that?" the man asked soberly.

"Well, I wonder about the flames," Hesy said judiciously. "That sounds like a child's story to me."

He chuckled. "I have to confess that I have never seen flames. And I believe that the Tate does not drink blood at the new moon, either."

"Not even a little?" she asked, disappointed.

"Sorry. And he has as much hair on him as I do."

"You don't have hardly any," Hesy said. "Does it grow on your face? There were barbarians in the markets, and they had hair on their faces."

"It does. I have to shave it every day, otherwise it grows long and prickly and hot, and I don't like that."

"You do not wear a wig," she observed.

"I don't like them, so I take it off whenever I can," he finished mischievously.

Hesy giggled. "Lady Asenath does not like wigs either, but she pretends she does. That is one reason she would not come out of her rooms at On."

"Lady Asenath sounds like a very nice lady," the slave said. "Run to the kitchens now, and tell Minemhet to fill you to bursting with whatever you like best. Then Lord Paanekh will have to decide what to do with you."

Asenath's throat closed up, and she couldn't breathe. Her memories crashed into her mind, only this time Hesy came into the room and not Sumet. *No!* Asenath screamed silently. *No! No! No!*

The child meant more to her than anyone else in the world. She would not allow her to be killed like that. Not even if she herself died for it.

▲ ▲ ▲ ▲

I turned around and saw Lady Asenath swaying in the hall doorway. She stared unseeingly at me.

"My lady, is something wrong?" I asked anxiously. Had she been hurt after all?

Asenath gulped. "Is it true?" she managed to whisper. "I thought I heard Hesy here."

"She is here," I answered. "She ran away from On, and followed you here."

A nod. "And—and L-Lord Paanekh? He saw her?"

"Yes. He came to the courtyard when Sosamen tried to take Hesy back to On. Lord Paanekh purchased her so that she could stay."

"You—you must not let him have Hesy. She must not be hurt. She is just a child, and doesn't deserve to be treated like that."

"Treated like what?" I asked, bewildered and alarmed. "Lady Asenath, why do you think Lord Paanekh will harm Hesy?"

"He is a barbarian," she said wildly. "He hurts people. That is what barbarians do. They hit and they scratch, and they make people cry, and he killed Sumet. I saw him. She came to his rooms, and—and—"

And words and tears tumbled out of her, incoherent at first, making no sense as she shook in my arms while I held her to keep her from falling. Easing myself down to the floor, I pulled her onto my lap, rocking slightly to soothe her, stroking her hair, asking questions, holding her tight against the horrifying memories that spilled out of her mind.

It took hours before I had pieced together the correct picture of what Asenath remembered and gleaned how young she had been when it happened. She alternately clung to me and fought me as she struggled to come to terms with her terrible memories, her fears for Hesy, and her own fears for herself.

Somehow I clamped down on the quiet rage burning in my belly. How Poti-Phera could have sent her to me the way he had with the fears she carried was more than I could fathom. The man must be a complete brute who would stoop to anything, even ordering his own daughter killed. I would deal with him, but later.

Sometime after midnight, Asenath fell asleep in my arms. I eased her into a more comfortable position and stared at the darkness of the hall.

"El Shaddai, what a terrible thing to carry inside," I whispered. "I do not know what to do to help her. Guide me in this matter."

I had almost dozed off, when the whisper of movement reached my ears.

"Will she be all right?" Hesy asked softly from the darkness of the main hall.

"I think so. What are you doing here so late, Hesy?"

"I could not sleep. My lady is afraid a lot."

"It might get better now," I said. "She finally talked about what happened. Go to sleep, Hesy."

"Will Lord Paanekh be angry that you are holding Lady Asenath?" she asked curiously.

I chuckled softly. "No, Hesy. I am Lord Paanekh."

After being startled a moment, the girl began to giggle. Then she ran off, her bare feet soft on the gypsum of the floor.

Not long after, Asenath herself stirred. She raised her head, and I felt her pulse quicken.

"Easy, lady," I said gently. "Take a moment while you wake."

"Oh," she gasped. "I remember—where is Hesy?"

"I just sent her off to bed. She came creeping down the hall to find out how you were."

"She is all right? Lord Paanekh has not hurt her?"

"I would not hurt Hesy for the world," I said quietly. "Nor will I hurt you, either."

"I know *you* would not. Did I cry?"

"Yes. You cried, and talked, and fought, and struggled, and hung on, until you finally got all those memories out of yourself. You saw a very terrible thing."

Asenath shuddered, leaning against me. "I was so small. And when I heard my father say I might marry, I was so afraid that I hid. For years I cowered in my rooms, and made myself ugly and worthless."

"You cannot make yourself ugly. You are a very beautiful woman."

"That is the problem," she said, shivering. "What if someone like that Syrian saw me?"

"Most people are not like the Syrian. Nor are most Syrians like him, either. I have known of men put to horrible deaths because they did just what you saw. It is not something accepted anywhere."

"Not even with barbarians?" Asenath asked slowly.

"Not even there," I replied. "Do you think I would do something like that?"

"No. You feel safe and welcoming, even though you are angry."

"I had hoped I was hiding that," I said ruefully. "I am angry about what happened to you, and about the way it has affected your life. I am angry about how frightened you are of people, and about the way your father sent you here. None of it is good."

"What is your name?" Asenath asked, sitting up. "Here I am crying on your shoulder, and I do not even know your name."

"Call me Joseph," I said.

"Joseph." She tried the Canaanite name on her tongue. "I cannot say it right."

"You say it fine. Are you feeling better?"

"Yes," she said, surprised. "I feel better than I have for years. Do you think it is all gone?"

"I doubt it," I said with a sigh. "I still have nightmares about some things that happened to me. They get better with time, but it does take time."

"I should go to my rooms. Lord Paanekh will be angry if he finds me with you like this."

"Lord Paanekh will not mind. He is very happy about it."

"He knows?" she gasped.

"Yes."

"How do you know he is not raging?"

"Because I am Lord Paanekh," I replied. "And I am very happy that I could serve you this way."

She didn't move—just froze in amazement.

"You are tired, my lady," I said, standing and helping her to her feet. I led her down the hall toward her rooms. She followed me, still dazed, not exactly afraid, but very uncertain. I seated her on the bed.

"Sleep as long as you need, my lady. Hesy will be here when you wake up. She brought some things for you that she is anxious to deliver. Good night, my lady," I finished. I knelt, kissed her hand, and then very firmly took myself out of the room.

I walked into the reception room the next morning to find my chief intelligence agent grinning at me.

"You are back, Lord Khay," I teased him.

"As always, Lord Paanekh. Right on time, too. You have got it badly, don't you?"

"What do you mean?" I pretended innocence.

"Head over heels for your new lady, are you?"

"Well, maybe sort of," I hedged.

He burst out laughing. "Sort of? You look like a wet-eared calf wandering after its mother."

I threw the nearest item I could lay my hands on at him. It was a fig, and he promptly started eating it.

"I assume you have news for me," I said. "What about Jetur?"

Khay frowned. "He vanished, Joseph. One day he was here and gone the next. No one knows where or how. His caravan is still here, resting the camels, they say. But those camels are so rested, they sleepwalk. I have ears and eyes open, but so far, no news."

"That is odd. There is something I want to ask him. Let me know the minute you find out anything."

With a nod he started on the grapes.

"Lord Hernofret?"

"Ah, yes, the darling brat of Lord Amony."

"Well?"

"Well, I found him, and he is ours."

"Out with it, Khay!"

His glance was pure mischief. "Our darling Lord Hernofret likes to travel. He visits friends along the way with regular frequency."

"He is Lord Amony's courier," I said triumphantly.

"He is. But, remember, he is a lord and cannot be bothered carrying things, no matter how important. Regrettably, his former personal attendant became ill. He had to hire a new one."

"And this new one does what?"

"He copies things," Khay said with an angelic smile. "Bad manners, I know, but what can one do?"

"Let me see them," I said, holding out my hands.

With impudent slowness, Khay took some tablets out of the sack he had with him and handed them to me. I read them swiftly.

"Just what we need." The letters were addressed to various nobles and nomarchs around Egypt. They documented Lord Amony's connection to these men and whether the relationship was business, personal, or both. There also contained several hints about an inner circle of friends who met periodically to discuss Egypt's welfare.

"Good work, Khay," I said. "Enough of this type of correspondence will tell us everything we need to know."

"I thought you would be pleased. I have arranged for our man to contact Hetepi if I am unavailable."

"Excellent. Now, here are the next things I need you to work on. In On you will find a woman named Takamenet, who works as a supervisor for a noble house, probably a smaller one. She has a bodyguard in the pay of Lord Amony. Here is the order conscripting the guard into the military service and sending him to Sinai for three years. Serve this order on the man. Do not give him time to do anything. Hand him the order, grab his arm, and send him to Sinai immediately."

"Yes, my lord."

"Then bring Takamenet here. She is Saf's mother."

"Yes, my lord. We seem to be involved with Lord Amony at every turn."

"I noticed that," I said dryly. "He takes up entirely too much of my time. Now dig into this inner-circle thing. I want to know who and what and when. It may be nothing important, then again it may be treason. I need to know which. Don't overlook the priestly angle, either," I added. "Lord Amony seems to be a fanatic for the purity of Egypt."

Khay grinned. "So long as Lord Amony is in it, Egypt will be far from pure," he said.

ChAPTER 22

Lord Potiphar walked into the personal audience room and bowed.

"What is it, old friend?" Amenemhet asked curiously.

"I received a rather curious message from Scribe Mahesa, Lord Paanekh's Chief of Staff," his Captain of the Guard replied. "He felt it his duty to send this to you, so that you would be prepared to guard the land from Seth if it became necessary."

The Pharaoh looked his astonishment. "What is it?" he repeated.

Without replying, Potiphar unwrapped the bundle he carried.

Slowly, the king picked up the object, handling it very carefully lest the jagged edges cut his hands. "What happened to it?" he asked in awe.

"According to Mahesa, Lord Paanekh's personal scribe, Lord Paanekh crushed it with his bare hands. Sliced his palms open in the process."

Pharaoh looked up in disbelief. "Why? What happened?"

"I do not know, my lord, but Lord Khay might. He brought the cup."

"Ah yes, your future replacement. How is he doing?"

"He will make a better Captain of the Guard than I, my lord," Potiphar confessed freely. "He has an amazing talent for uncovering information. The unsettled state of things has already brought some unexpected results. More danger threatens my lord than we thought."

"There is always danger for me, my friend," Amenemhet said with a drawn face. "It is part of the throne. Bring the man in. I wish to ask about this cup that my Tate has treated so badly."

Khay entered, kneeling immediately. "You sent for me, Great One?"

"Rise, Lord Khay," Amenemhet said. "Lord Potiphar has said that you brought a most unusual object."

He glanced at the table and nodded reluctantly. "Yes, my lord."

"Lord Paanekh crushed this cup with his own hands?" Pharaoh asked skeptically.

"Yes, my lord. He was angry," Khay replied, shifting uncomfortably.

"He must have been very angry," the king said, noting the young nobleman's unease.

"He was, my lord," Khay said fervently.

"What happened?" Amenemhet asked, gingerly picking up the cup again.

"He found the Memphis residence deserted because its steward told so many horrible lies about barbarians that the staff fled. When the steward returned, accusing Lord Paanekh of forging requests for supplies, Lord Paanekh became angry with him. He found the steward had stolen from the estate as well as from the former Tate.

"Lord Paanekh was so angry he spoke in Canaanite when he sentenced the steward and—"

"He pronounced sentence in Canaanite, you say?" Pharaoh asked.

"It must have been, my lord. No one could understand what he said."

"What was the sentence?"

"A beating, and banishment from Memphis."

"So he held back his rage enough to be fair about the crime," Amenemhet said to himself, again studying the mangled cup.

"Lord Paanekh went into the house," Khay continued. "He stayed alone in the small reception room. When he came out, the cup was crushed."

"How long was he in the room alone?"

"Over a day, my lord," Khay reluctantly confessed.

Amenemhet turned his back. "You still have not said why this cup is crushed, Lord Khay."

The young lord remained silent for a long time. "I find myself in a hard position, Great One," he said at last. "I am an orphan, and I lived with a great bitterness in my heart against those who had forced this upon me. I would probably be dead for some crime today if I had not met Joseph.

"He was a slave, and I annoyed him more often than not, but he always made time for me. He became my father. I owe him everything I have and am.

"Now, Great One, you ask that I reveal to you something which he trusted me with, which he spoke of in confidence lest it bring dishonor to that which is very close to him. I gave him my promise that I would not speak of it.

"Great One, do not ask me to do this thing."

"You are to be my Captain of the Guard, Lord Khay," Amenemhet said in a hard voice. "I took you from a mere steward and elevated you to a lordship with an estate and riches. Lord Potiphar reports that you are an excellent match for this position and that you will go far in it. I am your Pharaoh, Lord Khay. Do you dare to refuse me?"

"Great One, you are as the gods," Khay replied, his voice shaking slightly. "Let my lord ask of Lord Paanekh, and not of me."

"Again, you refuse me," the king shouted, whirling around. "I can have you beaten, stripped of your estate, executed!"

"Yes, my lord," Khay replied, dropping to his knees, his voice shaking badly.

When he said nothing further, Amenemhet snapped, "Well?"

The man bowed to the ground and waited.

"Lord Khay," Amenemhet said in a deadly tone.

"Great One, you must ask Lord Paanekh," he answered, his voice steady once again.

"Khay, one word from me and you will die today!" Amenemhet almost hissed. "I will give your body to the crocodiles of the Nile, and your Ka will never see Osiris. Where will you find yourself then?"

The future Captain of the Guard trembled on his knees, but when he raised his eyes to look at Pharaoh, his voice did not waver in the slightest. "I will be in the hand of Joseph's God," he replied.

"Joseph's God? Joseph's *God?"* Amenemhet thundered. "By all the gods in Egypt, how dare you say such a thing to me?"

Khay didn't speak immediately. "Because it is true," he said at last.

"Lord Khay, how is it that you have given loyalty to Lord Paanekh above what you give to me?" Pharaoh asked in a deadly tone.

"I have not done so," Khay replied calmly. "I would not knowingly bring harm to you, Great One, no matter who required it of me. But this matter of which we speak does not touch Pharaoh in any way. Should I betray my father's confidence for anything less than danger to Pharaoh? That is something which Pharaoh hates."

"And you would risk your career, your livelihood, your *life,* for this?"

"Great One, if I cannot be trusted in a matter that does not touch Pharaoh, how can I be trusted with matters that do?"

Amenemhet turned on Lord Potiphar. "Do you realize this is the second man you have harnessed to me who insists on giving me the highest loyalty no matter what I say?" he shouted.

"Yes, my lord," Lord Potiphar said, trying to look chastened.

"Get him out of here! But be assured, Lord Potiphar, *some day I will demand a full accounting!"* Amenemhet thundered again.

"Of course, Great One," Lord Potiphar said.

Pharaoh snorted. "When you start calling me 'Great One' I know you are up to something.

"Leave my presence," he snapped at Khay. "And on your way out, send me my jewelsmith!"

"Yes, Great One," he gulped, and fled.

Lord Potiphar waited while Amenemhet paced for several minutes.

"Where do you find these men?" the king finally asked. "They drive my Ka right out of my mind, but I would trust them with it just the same."

"Lord Paanekh suggested Lord Khay," Potiphar reminded him.

"Lord Paanekh, Lord Paanekh," Amenemhet repeated in annoyance. "Does the entire world come back to him?"

"It truly might, if your dreams are correct, my lord," he said seriously.

Pharaoh sighed. "You are right, old friend, as you normally are," he admitted. "Did Lord Paanekh affect you the same way when he was your slave?"

"At first, yes," Potiphar admitted with a smile. "But I will tell you what my old scribe, Snefru, told me. He said that Joseph served his God so faithfully that anything he undertook would succeed. Remember, my lord, Joseph's God is so powerful, it did not matter that Joseph was only a slave. I sat back and let Joseph make me a very rich man. His loyalty is unquestionable. He has given that loyalty to you, my lord. I suggest you sit back and let Lord Paanekh handle Egypt. He will give you your heart's desire."

Amenemhet chuckled. "Do you know, I think I will do that very thing. Now, bring in that jewelsmith. I want this cup recast, with jewels added. Mixed with Lord Paanekh's blood which I see on the edges, it will become a divination cup, a fitting gift from me. I will have to find a suitable occasion to present it to him."

▲ ▲ ▲ ▲

Lady Asenath was not in evidence the next evening though Hesy was very much so.

"She was so surprised," the child said, her eyes sparkling. "She could not say a word. She had thought you were a great bear of a man with black hair, and you turn out to be nothing of the kind. Now she is afraid she offended you."

"Not at all, Hesy," I said as the girl accompanied me through the gardens at the side of the house. "You can tell her that."

"Oh, I did," she replied. "I told her about all the house staff, too, how you came and the house was empty, and how you filled it with all these people who needed a place."

"How do you know all about that?"

"They talk about it all the time. I just listen."

"My lord," Inti interrupted.

I swung around.

"If you will come?" He glanced significantly at Hesy.

"Run along," I told her. "I must go with Inti."

With a nod she trotted away.

"At the gate, my lord," the porter said, leading the way.

In the gatehouse, two Nubians guarded Iutem. She stared at me defiantly.

"They found this in her things," Inti said, holding out a small vial.

Cautiously I opened it. It was half empty. Stoppering it again, I looked it over. On the bottom I found a tiny sign of the Great Ueb of Ra. I looked at Iutem coldly.

She spat in contempt.

"Take her to the prison," I said. "She is to be kept bound. Be certain she is available when I want her again."

"Yes, my lord Tate," the Nubian said, and he and his companion took Iutem away.

Later that night, I fell into bed, trying to quiet my mind so that I could rest. But thoughts of Asenath, Iutem, and Hesy filled it. Then, just as I fell over the edge to sleep, the reason for Iutem to murder Asenath sprang into my mind. It was simple and indirect, but it would have meant the death of Egypt. I wondered how long it would be before Poti-Phera appeared at my gate. As I relaxed, my mind finally quiet, it occurred to me that this was more Lord Amony's style.

▲ ▲ ▲ ▲

Asenath stole out of the room and down the hall past the empty women's rooms. She walked through the house to the small waiting room and slipped out the door into the garden. The gate creaked when she opened it, and she paused, but nothing around her moved. Leaving the gate open, she tiptoed down the path into the large garden.

Often she had visited her father's garden during the night. She loved the night, with its stillness and coolness.

"Lady?" a voice whispered from off to her right.

She froze, glancing around in alarm.

"Lady Asenath, it is Renseneb." He stepped from the shadows by the wall.

"Renseneb," she gasped, running toward him. "Oh, I have been so scared." She threw herself at him, and he caught her, hugging her tight.

"There, Lady, it is all right. I am here. But you must not deal so with me. You are married now and must remember that."

After a few more moments, he held her away from him. "Are you all right? You are not hurt? Does the new Tate treat you well?"

"I guess so," Asenath said, wiping her eyes with her hands. "He spoke gently, and he does not want me to be afraid."

Renseneb chuckled. "There, lady, you will get along fine. The worst is over now. I found you. But I must tell you that I could not find your seal, or signet, or the lists you have of sources and such."

"Do not worry, Renseneb," she said with a quiet laugh. "Hesy brought them to me."

"Hesy?" he asked. "That little child who runs about so much?"

Asenath nodded. "She took the things and ran here from On to bring them to me. Sosamen caught up with her in this very courtyard, and he would have taken her away, but Lord Paanekh made Sosamen sell him Hesy and everything she carried. So now Hesy is safe."

"Well, that is good news," he said with a sigh. "I wish my news was better."

"What has happened?"

"Sosamen nearly caught me in your rooms. Hesy was there before us both, and I wasted much time looking for what she had already taken. You know Sosamen has suspected you for years, and he found what he wanted. He took over all of your assets, Lady Asenath. You have nothing left."

"That is all right," she said with a shrug. "I have done it once, and I can do it again, only faster this time, since I already know all the mistakes to avoid!"

"True, my lady. I am glad you take it so easily. You are well-cared for here?"

"I can have whatever I want from Saf, the steward. Lord Paanekh gave him orders to get me anything I asked for."

"I may even like Lord Paanekh," Renseneb said, only half joking. "Do you still wish to keep your trade in the markets secret? To start again, we must be able to plan."

Asenath considered. "It might be best. I do not know what Lord Paanekh would think of it. Do barbarian woman trade?"

"Not usually," Renseneb said wryly. "We had better meet in the market somewhere. Can you come?"

"I will try," she answered slowly. "I have never been to the market, however, and I would have no idea what to do."

He paused. Lady Asenath had never seemed like a recluse because her information sources kept her up-to-date on the world around her. But on a practical level, her home was all she knew. "Just take one of the women here with you, and let them show you around," he advised. "I will be watching, and I will decide where it would be best to meet."

"All right," she nodded. "Oh Renseneb, I have to tell you what happened. F-Father wanted me to be killed!"

"I know," he replied grimly. "I figured that out eventually. I was afraid you had been killed already, since the rumors are rife in the market that you died."

"That will be Iutem. She disappeared one night. You must go, Renseneb. Thank you, thank you so much."

She kissed him quickly on the cheek and ran lightly back toward the house, leaving Renseneb kneeling in a daze on the path in the dark garden.

▲ ▲ ▲ ▲

A week passed. I went to the palace every day, and each day was busier than the last. Messages went back and forth from the capital, from Thebes in Upper Egypt, from Abydos, from On and Tanis and every other place in the whole land. Scribes from the treasury houses reported on Pharaoh's trade, who held what concessions, which lands supplied what commodities, and how much was supposed to come to Pharaoh. Quickly I noted that several nomarchs and high lords were overdue on their concession payments. That would need attention soon.

Pharaoh's architects reported on the building projects currently in progress with estimated costs, completion dates and corvee needs. The temples reported treasury estimates, land holdings, and numbers of craftsmen of various kinds attached to them and not available for corvee. Legal appeals from the Sasat court arrived, involving anyone from a simple potter to two nomarchs fighting over land surveys.

The overwhelming flow was never-ending. I knew it would eventually subside into manageable form as soon as I learned enough, but now I left each day with my head ringing with details. I could not have survived without Mahesa.

Khay reported in with Takamenet and a gleam in his eye that said he'd had a great deal of fun. But not a word could I get from either about what had happened. I sent him south with instructions to discover all he could about this inner circle thing, and not a word did I hear from him after that.

At my residence, I caught glimpses of Lady Asenath about the house, always in some place where she was not easily seen, but where she could watch me.

I asked Hesy about it, and the child giggled. "She is very curious about you, my lord," she confided. "She asks me questions all the time."

"What does she ask about me?" I prodded.

"Oh, everything. What you like to eat, how much wine you drink, if you have musicians play for you, if your eyes are truly blue, do they change color or always stay blue, does it hurt to have you look at me or other people, does—"

"Does it hurt to have me look at you?" I said in amazement. "Why would she ask that?"

"You have Horus eyes. Anyone can see that. And the eyes of Ra can see inside, and that might hurt."

"I guess it might," I said. I had never thought about it.

That evening I decided to take matters into my own hands. I took off my wig, armbands, and collar, everything that marked me as a lord. The signet ring I tucked into my linen. I never let that off my person. Then I waylaid Asenath.

"Would my lady care to see the garden?" I asked when she came around the corner of the hall.

Looking up in alarm, she glanced back down the hall to the women's quarters.

"Do you permit that?" she asked cautiously.

"Of course," I said, puzzled.

Lady Asenath blushed at my tone. "I had heard that people of your land do not wish others to see their wives. Is this true?"

"No, lady. Women in my country go out and about all the time. They do much outdoors."

"I can go about the house, then, and outside?"

"Yes, lady. I have worried that you were ill because you never leave the house," I added, studying her from the corners of my eyes. "I do not want you to be afraid of me, Lady Asenath," I said quietly. "Hesy tells me you are curious about me and how my people live. I would prefer you to ask me about it, instead of trying to get information through her. So, will you come to the garden? We can sit, and you can ask me whatever you would like."

When she looked at me out of those enormous eyes, I almost went dizzy with the emotion raging inside myself.

Slowly she nodded.

I took her to a little bench just inside the gate under a vine against the wall of the house where she would be half-hidden, yet able to see much of the garden. She took a seat on the bench, and I sat on the ground with my back to her and a little in front of her.

With a sigh she relaxed behind me. "It is a very beautiful garden. It is much bigger than the garden in my father's house in On."

"What is he like?"

"My father is very ambitious," she said tightly, and I dropped the subject.

Gradually she began to ask questions, and I told her about my home, and how I had lived. She found many things amusing to her, and I dug up funny incidents I remembered just to hear her soft laugh.

The next afternoon, I received word that the Great Vision of Ra, Great Ueb Poti-Phera from On, would call upon me that afternoon.

Mahesa was furious that the message was a notice, not a request.

"Let it rest, Mahesa," I said. "It is not worth bothering about." I sent a message of my own to the prison, directing that Iutem should be brought to my house.

Great Ueb Poti-Phera arrived at my gates with a full entourage. I had planned to receive him in the small reception room, but that was now impossible. Mahesa hurriedly retrieved the gold collar and armbands, and had me formally dressed by the time Poti-Phera walked up the steps to the porch.

Esse, the reception-room porter, entered and announced my visitor. I stood on the dais to meet him. Sitting on the throne would have been a bit much for him to swallow. He deigned to lower his head to me, and we exchanged the usual formal phrases of greeting and divine blessing.

"What brings the Great Ueb of Ra to my house?" I asked finally.

"A desire to see my daughter," he said. "She has been gone for some little time, and I have a wish to see her face again."

I smiled to myself. I had been right.

"It is a pity I did not know this," I said. "I would have had her with me when you arrived. Saf," I directed, "please go to Lady Asenath's rooms and tell her that her father is here and wishes to see her."

My steward bowed and went out, returning shortly.

"My lord, the Lady Asenath says that she has no desire to see her father. She refuses to come."

That startled me. I noticed the quick gleam in Poti-Phera's eye and the glances exchanged between several of his party.

"Ask her if she is certain," I said. "Her father says he is eager to see her."

The silence was strained until Saf returned.

"She refuses, my lord."

I turned to Poti-Phera. "Lady Asenath refuses to see you. It is unfortunate you have made the trip for nothing."

"It is unfortunate for you that I have come," Poti-Phera said, his voice hard. "I did not believe what I heard in the markets—until now. They say that Lady Asenath died in your house soon after arriving, but I did not credit such talk. It continued, however, and spread even to On and Tanis.

"I decided I would see for myself how false these whispers are. But now you tell me that my daughter will not see me. You say that she refuses. This is not like Lady Asenath, who has never in her life refused to come when I requested her presence. In light of what I have heard, I demand to see my daughter, the Lady Asenath of On!"

I did not reply but simply looked at him for some time. "I do not wish to be precipitous in this matter," I said softly. "Am I to understand, Great Ueb Poti-Phera, that you are accusing me of murdering the Lady Asenath?"

"I wish to know if my daughter is alive and well," he answered, staring straight at me. "If she is, I will say no more. But if she is not, if you cannot show her to me at this time, I shall certainly demand that the matter be looked into immediately."

If he insisted on forcing a showdown, he must be very certain of his ground.

"Great Ueb, shall we discuss this in private?" I asked. "I will be happy to speak with you in the small reception room and ease your mind on the matter of your daughter's health."

"I do not see that that is necessary," the priest replied. "I wish to see her now, and here."

"As you wish," I said. "I will speak with Lady Asenath myself."

Mahesa followed me out the door, and I handed him my gold collar and wig as soon as we were in the women's quarters. I did not want Asenath to respond to Lord Paanekh, but to me, Joseph.

"My lady," I said softly at her door, "I would speak with you."

"I do not wish to see my father," she answered through the door.

"May I come in, my lady?"

After several moments of silence, I opened the door and stepped in, closing it behind me.

Asenath stood next to the curtain across the back of the room, her arms wrapped around herself, her face stiff with anger and fear.

I sat down by the door. "Your father wishes to see you. He says he is anxious for your health."

"My father has never been anxious for my health," she said bitterly.

"Yes, my lady. But he has heard the whispers in the markets that you are dead."

"That must have been good news for him! Why should that bring him here?"

"He wishes to accuse me of your death. If he does so, and you refuse to see him, that would mean—"

"Oh, I know exactly what it will mean," she interrupted, her voice shaking with rage. "It will mean Lord Amony gets the throne!"

I carefully held myself still. The throne? I knew Amony would take the Tate's office if anything happened to me, but the throne? What leap of logic had brought about that comment? What did she know that I didn't?

"How would that be true?" I asked carefully.

"Such an accusation could rouse the south against you," she said curtly. "Unless Pharaoh wished war with his nomarchs, he would have to appoint another Tate. With the south already united, Lord Amony would be appointed. If he takes over the Tate's office, it is only a matter of time before Amenemhet loses the throne."

For a recluse, she certainly had an unusual grasp of court intrigue. Now that she pointed it out, I saw the obviousness of it all. Bits and pieces of reports and messages suddenly coalesced into a coherent whole. The power the southern nomarchs held with their trade contracts, standing armies, and wealth stacked up in my mind.

With a sinking feeling, I calculated that Pharaoh did not have enough resources to win a war with the south, barring some miracle. This threw an entirely different light on a lot of things. At all costs I must remain Tate, for the land faced famine. Answering Poti-Phera's veiled accusation was essential.

"If you know the consequences, why will you not come?" I asked, hoping she did not know what I did.

"Because *my father is the one who ordered my death,*" she choked out, tears falling from her eyes. "Do you hear? He sold my life for his political ambitions when he sent Iutem with instructions to murder me. I never wish to see the man again in my life!"

She knew. But how? "I do not blame you, Asenath. I understand that feeling, for there are two members of my family about whom I feel the same. But I am learning that it does no good to hang on to the anger and hurt. It only causes more pain.

"There have been terrible things in your life, and I know them. So if you refuse what I ask, I will understand. Asenath, I ask you to come and face your father. I will be there for you. I can answer this charge if you do not come, but it will take up much time and energy that should be devoted to building storehouses for grain. The decision is yours, however, and I will honor whichever choice you make."

Bowing, I left. For a moment I lingered in the hallway, but she did not come. Mahesa put the gold collar on me, and I settled the wig on my head again, then went back into the reception room.

"Where is my daughter?" Poti-Phera demanded.

"In her rooms," I replied. "I have spoken to her. She told me plainly that she did not wish to see you, and I told her that she may do so—or not—according to her wishes. We will have to wait and see what she decides. In the meantime, I have arranged for refreshments to be served."

As I spoke, Saf directed the attendants to bring in the fruit and bread that Minemhet had prepared. The house retainers helped themselves, watched closely by the visitors, who eventually decided nothing was poisoned and also ate. Subdued talk rose sporadically in the room, the tension stunting all conversation.

I ate a roll and some fruit and said nothing. Poti-Phera ate nothing and paced restlessly.

"Enough of this charade," he finally said. "Lord Paanekh, where is my daughter?"

"I am right here, father," she answered from the door.

Poti-Phera swung around, genuine surprise on his face. "Asenath?" he gasped.

She looked atrocious, as usual, but she carried her head up, and her eyes were direct, clear, and angry.

"Why so surprised, father? Didn't your little plot succeed?"

"What plot?" he asked, bewildered.

"The one where you told Iutem to poison me," she said plainly and loudly enough for the entire room to hear. Everything grew very still. "It would have been perfect for you, of course. Lord Paanekh would no longer be Tate, and that would suit you just fine."

"Why do you speak so to me? I would never do such a thing. What is the meaning of this?" he demanded.

"The meaning of this, Great Ueb, is that I also heard the rumors in the markets," I said. "They were not something I wished to ignore, and I took pains to track them down. They led me to one Iutem, the attendant you sent with Lady Asenath. Iutem disappeared from my house the night she tried to poison her mistress."

Poti-Phera's mouth opened, shock appearing in his eyes. "This is impossible," he sputtered. "How can you say such things!"

"I did not say them, Iutem did," I replied, signaling to Mahesa, who opened the door, and two Nubians led Iutem into the room. "When we found her, she had this," I said, holding out the vial.

Poti-Phera turned as white as royal linen when he saw it, a fact noticed by his entire entourage. They murmured among themselves, edging away from their master.

"It is not mine, my lord," Poti-Phera said. "I did not order its use."

"Mahesa, show this to the Great Ueb's people," I said, holding out the vial.

The scribe took it and circulated around the room. Everyone could plainly see the mark on its bottom. By the time Mahesa had finished, Poti-Phera stood alone.

"Once again, Great Ueb, shall we discuss this in private?"

"Yes, my lord," he answered as one in a trance.

Saf, Mahesa, Asenath, and I adjourned to the small reception room. The Nubians brought Iutem along, and two retainers for Poti-Phera also entered.

"You have much to explain, Great Ueb," I said sternly. "Lady Asenath arrived at my house with nothing except the clothes on her back. The only attendant she had confessed to trying to poison her and said that the orders to do so came from you. After putting poison in Lady Asenath's wine, Iutem left and began the rumors in the markets about Lady Asenath's death.

"I am aware, Great Ueb, of the political advantage such an event would bring you."

By the time I finished, Poti-Phera stared around desperately.

"I have not done so, my lord," he said. "I would not sell my daughter's life. I do not know anything about this, except that word reached me of my daughter's death in your house. Iutem must be lying, for I gave her no such orders."

"Would you remember, father?" Asenath said coldly, standing beside me. "You were drunk. Very drunk. How do you know what you said? Do you remember cursing Pharaoh? Do you remember the words you used to describe Lord Paanekh? Do you remember anything at all?"

Slowly Poti-Phera collapsed. "How can you say this?" he moaned from his knees on the floor. "She lies. Iutem lies—she must be lying."

I watched Poti-Phera closely. His surprise and bewilderment seemed quite genuine. What if they were?

Iutem looked at him with hatred in her eyes. "I tell no lies," she said.

"You do, all the time," a small voice piped up from the pillar by the door. "The Great Ueb did not tell you to poison Lady Asenath. Lord Amony did. I heard him."

"Hesy!" Asenath gasped. "What are you doing here?"

"I came because you were here," she said. "And Iutem lies."

"Why would she tell such a lie?" Asenath said.

"Because the Great Ueb sent her husband to the mines last year. She has hated him since then."

"I did not do it, I did not do it," Poti-Phera insisted. "Asenath is my daughter, I would not order her death."

"Hesy, how do you know this?" I asked.

"Because I heard it. I heard the Great Ueb and Lord Amony talking of Lady Asenath, and I went to listen. The Great Ueb was drinking old wine, and Lord Amony had Iutem there to suggest that she go with Lady Asenath. He gave her the vial. I remember because they almost dropped it. At least, Iutem pretended to almost drop it. She took something from Lord Amony and hid it in her dress."

"Search her," I ordered immediately.

Iutem made no move until the Nubians began to examine her dress carefully. Then she tried to run, hitting at them to drive them away.

One Nubian ripped something and brought an object to me. I stared at the scarab-beetle amulet of the White that Huy had given to Lord Amony at Lord Potiphar's feast. Turning it over in my hands, I examined it closely. I could not be mistaken. It was the same amulet.

"It would seem that Hesy is telling the truth," I concluded.

"Lord Amony?" Poti-Phera said in amazement. "Lord Amony ordered my daughter killed?"

"It very much looks that way," I commented.

"Why, that slime from the Nile mud, that thrice cursed son of a crocodile, that hairy-backed traitor—"

While Poti-Phera expressed his feelings, I dismissed the Nubians and their charge as well as the Great Ueb's retainers. Saf took Hesy out, with instructions to make certain that she did not get in again. Asenath looked at me, her eyes wide.

"You may go or stay, my lady," I said, "whatever is your wish."

"I think I will go," she said unsteadily. "I am sick of this." She followed Saf from the room.

Mahesa set up a scribe's table and readied materials to take a statement.

Poti-Phera ran out of words to curse Lord Amony with, and I leaned one hip against the cracked top of the stone table, tossing the scarab amulet up and down in my hand.

"Now that we have the murder charge taken care of, Great Ueb," I said, looking down at him, "let us discuss treason."

His face turned a sickly gray, and he flattened himself on the floor.

CHAPTER 23

I began my first inspection tour in the Delta. Storing grain would be much more of a challenge in the damp, misty Delta than anywhere else in Egypt, and I wanted to get things started there first.

I had with me a young engineer named Shenbu. Mahesa sent him with me because he had difficulty in the schools. He stuttered and constantly wished to do things differently than he was supposed to. Considering the challenges I had in front of me, he was perfect for what I needed.

Chaf came along as captain of my guard, and Sheshon, the public scribe Mahesa had hired to help Hutor with Lord Potiphar's tomb, served as my personal scribe.

I stopped first at the twenty-fourth nome, ruled by Lord Sety.

"My Lord Paanekh," Sety said as he knelt on the deck of the transport.

I wondered at his humble greeting, but said nothing. Lord Sety did me honor. The question was why.

"Rise, Lord Sety," I said. "I have come to speak with you about the granaries that must be built in your nome."

"Yes, my lord," he said, standing up.

"You do me honor by greeting me on board," I added, with a slight ironic twist that reddened his face.

"I wish my lord to know that I have tried to do what he suggested in the palace," Sety muttered, unable to look at me.

"I am glad to hear it," I answered, dropping the irony. "I shall be staying for some time in your nome, Lord Sety. Are there rooms in your house for me and my staff?"

"If my lord wishes."

"Good. I will come tomorrow. Good day, Lord Sety."

"Good day, my lord," he replied, and left.

The next day I arrived at the nomarch's palace. Sety had prepared his father's rooms for me, and they would do nicely.

I spent mornings with Lord Sety, explaining what I wanted in regard to the state storehouses. He listened with such intentness that I began to study him. Soon I realized that he knew nothing at all about administration and governance and watched me in order to learn. I began to plan out loud whenever he was around, and before long I noticed him trying out several things I had discussed. More than once, I delayed entering a room when I heard him questioning Sheshon. As the days went by, Sety's steward did not look so frazzled, and Sety himself gained much in confidence. He dropped some of the vain mannerisms that, as I suspected, he used to hide his feelings of total incompetence.

After Sheshon and Shenbu had settled into their jobs, I left for Memphis, looking forward to seeing Lady Asenath again and spending a few days in my own house.

▲ ▲ ▲ ▲

"I don't know what to do about it, Lord Paanekh," Mahesa said in a worried voice. "There is nothing that I can get hold of. It just takes three or four times as long to do anything as it should. If I complain, everyone is most polite and most attentive, but nothing changes. At this rate, we will have one storehouse built at the end of seven years."

"Whom did you say was Lord Treasurer?" I asked.

"Lord Hordef."

"What have you found out about him? Is there someone there who might be able to expedite things for us?"

The scribe looked at me in frustration. "I am not Khay. I do not know how to walk through a room and discover who had a father that gardened at midnight during the full moon!"

"I am not asking you to do that," I said with a chuckle, "although I would be curious to know if someone does. Let me see what I can come up with."

Two hours later, Hetepi burst into my room in response to my summons.

"My lord, is it Khay? Is he all right? Has something happened?" she panted, her eyes wide with alarm.

"I am sorry, Hetepi," I apologized immediately. "It is nothing like that. As far as I know Lord Khay is fine. I did not mean to frighten you with my summons," I added, truly upset at how disturbed she was. "Sit down. Chaf, get some wine for the Lady Hetepi."

"I am sorry, my lord, for my interruption," she apologized after calming down. "But the only reason I could find for you to send for me was something to do with Khay."

"The mistake is mine, Lady Hetepi. I should have made clear what the summons was about. I need someone to get some information for me, and I hoped you would know an associate of Khay's who could do this."

Recovering her usual composure, Hetepi straightened. "I might, my lord. Where would this person need to go?"

"I need to know who on the Lord Treasurer's staff would be inclined to work with me to build storehouses."

She thought for a while. "I believe I know whom to send. I should be able to report to you in a week. Will that suffice?"

"That will do nicely, Hetepi."

She bowed and left.

I thought for some time after she had gone. The interview had taken four times as long as it should have because of the state she had arrived in—and that was my fault. With me, people feared the worst, and when summoned, they believed the worst. I needed to take that into consideration from the moment I decided to see a person.

The problem still bothered my mind when I arrived home that evening.

I stepped down from the chariot, patting the stallion as I went by, and Onami led the horses away. Carrying my wig and armbands, I entered the house, thankful for the coolness of the reception room after the heat of the sun outside.

The place looked old and faded. It needed attention, and I had no time. Saf was a good organizer, but I hesitated to ask him to redecorate. I would end up with a very formal and very correct interior decor if I did, and I wanted something different, at least in the private part of the house.

"You are back, my lord," Hesy squealed, running down the hallway.

"How are you, Hesy?" I asked, smiling. "What secrets do you have today?"

Her eyes grew big. "My lord, there is so much to tell you. My lady went to the market."

"She did?"

"Yes," the child said proudly. "She did not know what to do at first, so she just sat and watched. We went twice. We met Huy, and he gave her a pretty gold ornament for a necklace."

"That is wonderful," I said.

"Oh, you have returned from the Delta," Lady Asenath said from behind me. I swung around, then stared. She had cut her hair and put kohl around her eyes. Her linen was old, but hung neatly on her.

She blushed under my gaze and glanced down.

"Yes, I am back," I said a bit unsteadily. She made me dizzy with those accented eyes.

"Will you be in the garden later?" my wife asked in a low voice.

"If you wish it, my lady."

She nodded, and Hesy went happily off with her to the women's quarters.

I ate faster than I usually do and had to laugh at myself. I was so eager to get to the garden that I all but bolted my food.

I found her on the usual bench and sat down on the ground beside her. "Hesy says you like the market," I commented.

Lady Asenath laughed. "Hesy is forever talking. I do like the market. I never dreamed it was so busy and noisy and alive. There are so many things."

"You will have to buy some. I cannot imagine you want to keep all those old worn things in your room. Would you like to get something different?"

"I might," she said tentatively. "Would you mind?"

"Not at all."

"How much may I spend?" she asked a bit hesitantly.

"I am very rich, Asenath," I reminded her. "Spend whatever you want."

The very next day she had attendants carrying out items from the rooms. Hesy met me in the hallway as I left for the palace, all excited about the changes that her mistress planned. The child insisted that I come see.

"Doesn't it look better?" Hesy demanded, dragging me to the doorway of Asenath's room. "Doesn't it look better? And we have not even gone to the market yet."

I glanced around. The room seemed restful and pleasant. Asenath came through the dividing curtain and looked up at me, a small smile on her face. I thought I would never start to breathe again. My pulse pounded in my chest, and I wanted to take her to me that instant. And scare her to death, I reminded myself. Instead, I stood still and just looked.

"Do you like it?" she asked shyly.

I nodded. "I will be eager to see it when you are done." Somehow I managed to make it out of the house, but I didn't really wake up until Onami dropped me off at the palace and reminded me to put on my wig.

Khay waited for me inside.

"You look terrible," I greeted him.

"Don't remind me," he replied with a yawn. "Quick report. Jetur is not back yet. He went to Canaan."

"If you are that tired, why are you here?" I asked.

"Because of this." He handed me a bunch of tablets, copies of Lord Amony's correspondence. I scanned them quickly, then threw them down in disgust.

"Is every single nomarch in the south part of this?" I fumed.

"Not quite. Lord Hisemi from the eighth nome is never mentioned, and strangely enough, neither is Lord Mose from the first nome."

"This gets bigger and bigger, Khay. Three of the high priests are part of it, and several temples in the Delta favor Lord Amony because of the gifts he has brought to the gods. Lord Amony has the southern nomarchs, and the northern temples. The only thing he still needs to complete his plans is the office of Tate."

Khay whistled. "I wonder if Pharaoh knew what he was doing when he appointed you. Amony must have been furious when he heard. Your appointment would affect everything."

I nodded. "I am learning that. Anything more about this Inner Circle?"

"It seems to be a religious thing," Khay replied. "Something about the afterlife and living as a god, or with the gods, or being like Pharaoh. I cannot get good information since only the nomarchs are allowed to attend. No retainers, no wives, no priests even. It is strange."

"Keep digging. Anything else?"

He was silent for a bit. "You are not going to like it," he stated finally.

I raised my eyebrows.

Khay handed me a sealed courier pouch with the side seam carefully opened. When I pulled out the tablet, I didn't even have to read it. The royal cartouche, pressed from a signet ring, at the bottom jumped to my eye. I read the tablet, an undated order for the execution of Lord Amony.

I set the tablet down. "Someone is thinking way ahead, Khay," I said grimly. "Lord Amony must be only a cat's-paw. We must find out who is using him."

After Khay left, I sat in frustration for some time. I didn't have time to deal with court intrigues like this—I had storehouses to build. First the Lord Treasurer dragged his feet, and now this! Yet, clearly, I must solve this problem before I could build anything. And if Egypt was to live, I must be erecting those granaries now, so that there would be places to store the crop. Inundation began soon, then Planting, then Harvest. By Harvest, I must have storehouses ready. Next year, I would need even more.

"Help me with this, El Shaddai," I whispered. "I need to build."

In the garden that evening Lady Asenath noticed my preoccupation.

"What is wrong?" she asked.

"A problem at the palace," I said absently. "There must be storehouses built to hold the grain during the years of plenty, and the Treasury is dragging its heels. It worries me."

"It should," Asenath agreed. "Lord Amony will not let anything stand in his way."

I paused. What did Lord Amony have to do with the Treasury?

"He certainly was not happy about my appointment," I said neutrally.

"He would not be," she said with a laugh. "That would be a twist in the Nile he had not counted on. It must have made him furious. Now he will try to sabotage you any way he can."

I threw a quick glance over my shoulder at her. She stared into the distance, her mind busy with what I had said. And the shrewd, intelligent look on her face made my heart leap. Perhaps the Great Ueb Poti-Phera had done me a very great favor.

"Surely Lord Amony could not block the building of storehouses," I said doubtfully, testing her. "How would he be able to do that?"

"Well, you must work through the Lord Treasurer. And Lord

Hordef is a firm believer in Lord Amony. Half the officials in the treasury are."

"Half of them?" I asked skeptically.

"At least," Asenath laughed again. "I discovered that nearly—" she broke off abruptly. "It is late," she said hurriedly. "I must retire."

Quickly she left.

I meditated on what she said for some time. How had she discovered the connection between the Treasury and Lord Amony, something even Khay hadn't picked up yet? Who was this woman who was my wife? What did she hide?

I put that aside. At least I knew what Mahesa's problem was. How was I to solve it?

"My lord?" Saf said from the gate.

"Yes?" I answered.

"I have found some palace records here in the house records. They pertain to a trip the Lord Treasurer took to the porphyry mines for Pharaoh several years ago. What shall I do with them?"

Instantly I sat up. "Let me see them!" I demanded.

▲ ▲ ▲ ▲

"He is doing *what?*" Amenemhet asked in amazement.

Nekhty read the message again.

"Send for Lord Potiphar," the king said.

Lord Potiphar came immediately. "Yes, my lord?"

"Nekhty received a message from Lord Hordef," Pharaoh said. "Lord Paanekh is sending half of the officials in the Department of the Treasury to the Sinai to inspect all of my copper mines."

The Captain of the Guard looked his amazement. Then he checked himself. "May I see the list of who has been ordered to go."

Nekhty handed him it, and Potiphar scanned it, then began to laugh. "My lord, it is rumored that Lord Paanekh is having difficulty getting prompt service from the Department of the Treasury in regard to building storehouses. This must be his solution."

Amenemhet smiled in appreciation. "It is galling to me that my father is not alive," he mused. "He would have so loved this. Now, a wager, Lord Potiphar. I will have Lord Hordef begging for an interview within three days."

"Four," Potiphar countered. "He is incapable of moving faster than that."

▲ ▲ ▲ ▲

I received Overseer of the Treasury Scribes Khafra in one of the audience rooms of the old palace.

"Thank you for coming from the capital so promptly," I greeted him.

"It was my pleasure, Lord Paanekh. I was present when my lord was made Tate. I will never forget that day."

"Neither will I," I said wryly, and a smile passed across his face. "The Lord Treasurer and several of your fellow officials will be going to the Sinai. While they are gone, you will be in charge of the Department of the Treasury."

"Yes, my lord."

"You will have full authority to remove any scribe or official who does not perform to expectations while Lord Hordef is away."

Khafra looked a bit surprised, but nodded.

"I want you to meet with Mahesa, my personal scribe, tomorrow. He will give you work orders regarding building granaries throughout Egypt. I start south soon on an inspection tour, and I will expect these orders to be in the hands of the officials when I arrive to assess progress."

"That which you command is that which shall be done, my lord," Khafra said, the smile on his face telling me he fully appreciated the situation.

"Now, how much is available in Pharaoh's treasury to begin building?" I asked.

He looked down. "Not much, my lord."

I glanced up in surprise. "Oh? Why not?"

"There have been some difficulties collecting royal taxes of late, to say nothing of trade concession payments. The treasury is, therefore, less full than it should be."

"Why is this, Khafra?"

He left two hours later, and my understanding of why Amenemhet wished to control the nomarchs had taken a giant leap forward. Pharaoh had not been exaggerating. If the famine did not destroy Egypt, the nomarchs would.

▲ ▲ ▲ ▲

"We both lost," Amenemhet said as Lord Potiphar accompanied him to the audience room. "It took six days."

Lord Hordef bowed when Pharaoh entered the room.

"Lord Hordef, I am surprised to see you here," Amenemhet said. "I would have thought you were busy getting ready for your trip."

"Yes, my lord. It is about the trip that I have come to see you."

"Do you find it too much for you? I shall be sorry to lose you, Lord Hordef."

"Lose me?" the noble repeated, bewildered. "My lord, why would you say such a thing?"

"If you find the trip too much of an ordeal, Lord Hordef, I am afraid I shall have to find another Lord Treasurer," Amenemhet said sorrowfully. "Is this the case?"

"No, decidedly no," Lord Hordef said, gulping. "It is no trouble at all."

"I am glad to hear it. But now I am truly puzzled. I cannot think of anything else to discuss about this trip that would bring you to me. Any questions you may have should be directed to Lord Paanekh, naturally."

"Lord Paanekh?" Lord Hordef echoed. "But my lord, why would—I mean—is it truly necessary—that is, can it be attended— My lord, it is necessary that I stay in the capital," he finally said. "The press of work is great, and to leave now would be a—a—" he stammered to a halt at the frown appearing on his ruler's face.

"Lord Hordef, what can possibly be more important than carrying out my commands?" Amenemhet asked sternly.

"Well, that is, uh—nothing, my lord."

"I am glad you agree. I shall expect your first report from the border in two weeks."

"Two weeks?" Hordef gasped. "But that will mean I must leave—"

"Immediately if not sooner," Pharaoh interrupted. "Had you begun to prepare as soon as you got the order instead of dithering about and running to me, you could have left tomorrow. Stop in Memphis for final orders from the Tate. Will there be anything else, Lord Hordef?"

"No, my lord. That which you command is that which shall be

done. May Pharaoh live forever, may his Ka prosper," he said, bowing out of the room.

Amenemhet glared at the door after he went out of it. "Miserable traitor," he fumed. "Watch him, Potiphar."

"I will, my lord. But I have a feeling Lord Paanekh has everything well in hand."

▲　▲　▲　▲

Lady Asenath waited in the little room Renseneb had hired not far from the main Memphis market. She had sent Hesy about her business some time ago and now enjoyed the few moments alone before Renseneb entered.

"Greetings, Lady," he said. "You have had a message?"

"Yes. Lord Hordef leaves for the Sinai within the week. What do we have that he will need?"

Her agent thought. "Nothing here, I'm afraid. You lost everything to Sosamen. But in Tanis there are several items. Salt for one, and packs and harness for the animals. You also control some sandals, for the desert sands get very hot. That is all I can think of now, but I believe there are several more items I could get for you."

"Good. Make certain Lord Hordef's buyers know supplies are to be had closer to the border, then go to Tanis and sell to him."

"Yes, my lady," Renseneb said with a smile, glad to see that she had regained her assurance and was not looking over her shoulder every second in fear. He studied her a moment. Getting away from her father had made a difference in her. She looked presentable in public for the first time, having neatly combed her hair, put kohl on, and was wearing a dress of good linen, belted nicely. Her eyes sparkled too. Maybe it was more than just leaving her father's house. Perhaps Lord Paanekh had a hand in this.

"Now, what do we have here in Memphis?" Lady Asenath asked, interrupting his meditations.

"Leather," he replied and plunged into the details.

▲　▲　▲　▲

"My lord, it is an outrage," Saf sputtered to me. "I had to purchase that leather at twice the market price. I could find it no where else, and only this Renseneb had some."

"Renseneb?" I said. "Is he at it again?"

"You know him, my lord?"

"I have run into him a time or two," I said with a chuckle. "He is agent for someone, a very smart someone. I must connect you with Huy."

"Huy, the entertainer?"

"The same. He has worked for me for many years and can tell you anything going on in the city. Often he has advance warning of ships arriving at the docks. Don't forget Inti. He has a network of beggars that will ferret out anything at all sooner or later."

"But we must pay for that," Saf protested.

"How much did you lose to Renseneb?" I countered.

"Enough to pay Inti several times over," he admitted.

"How is Takamenet doing?"

"My mother is happy dealing with your Memphis estate," he said. "I often see her at the markets."

"Good. If you can work in tandem with her, you may have another advantage against Renseneb."

"I had not thought of that. I will do that, my lord."

▲ ▲ ▲ ▲

I went south, always meeting with politeness, consideration, and assurances of cooperation. But I mistrusted every assurance. Each nomarch expressed delight at aiding the staff I stationed in each nome. After carefully giving the nomarchs a full understanding of what I expected from them, I urged them to build storehouses on their own in addition to the ones already used by the nome.

Mahesa grew grim and tense. "They will do nothing, my lord," he said to me. "I have seen this before. Everyone is very friendly and cooperative, but nothing will happen."

"Perhaps," I replied. "But we cannot do anything about it now. Later we can do more, but we shall have to wait."

"Do we have time to wait?"

"No," I admitted.

At the twelfth nome, Lord Meritifi greeted me at the docks, the first nomarch since Lord Sety to do so.

"I have eagerly awaited your coming, Lord Paanekh," he said, mincing forward, his arms covered with gold bracelets.

"You honor me," I replied, biting my tongue at his insincerity. He was the worst offender in the matter of royal trade concessions.

"I have prepared a feast for you tomorrow," he said. "Would you condescend to come?"

"I will."

"Then I will leave my lord and make final preparations," he said, sidling away. His personal scribe, the young woman I had noticed at the presentations, followed him from the docks, moving as if every muscle ached.

"He reminds me of a snake," Mahesa muttered afterward. "I would be careful at that feast, Lord Paanekh."

I arrived after several other guests had already come, and Lord Meritifi was effusive in his greetings. He led me to the place of honor and personally supplied me with food. I immediately determined I would not eat any of it. Through constant conversation, I managed to avoid eating until the entertainment began, and then I pretended such absorption in it, that I forgot the food by my elbow and took from passing bowls and trays instead.

Halfway through the party I quietly rose to go, and Meritifi appeared immediately at my elbow. "Surely my lord will not go so soon," he protested. "We have not yet brought out the best wine or the special entertainment."

"You do me honor," I said, "but unfortunately the press of Pharaoh's business will not allow me to remain much longer." Then I sat down again. Glancing up, I suddenly noticed Lord Khay two tables away, dressed in the most amazing gold jewelry and sitting with a woman. He met my eyes and his slid away casually.

Lord Meritifi ordered the best wine brought out, and along with it came a mummy carried on a bed. Toasts were drunk and exhortations made to enjoy the pleasures of life, and this party, while we could as we would soon all be as desiccated as the mummy. I moved impatiently. Such entertainment commonly appeared at feasts, and could hardly be called special.

Then Lord Meritifi stood up and waited for silence. "Friends, fellow nomarchs and honored guests, I thank you for attending my humble feast. You have tasted the best wine and seen the end to which we all come. But that is not the only reason to enjoy yourselves each day. There are other fates than death, and other pleasures than feasts to liven our days. I bid you welcome to my auction," he said, drawing aside.

Involuntarily, Khay and I exchanged a glance.

Two of Lord Meritifi's retainers led into the room a young Kushite fettered to a yoke across his shoulders. Already large for his age, he would be a giant of a man when he had grown.

"We will honor fate first," Meritifi said. "Fate provides destinies worse than death sometimes. Now, who would like this handsome reminder of captivity? He is strong and will grow stronger. Notice the promise in his size. He will be a wonder to show your friends in days to come. All yours, friends, for a reasonable price.

"I will not sell him to just anyone, for as you can see, he will take a bit of handling before he bows to fate, as we all must."

I stopped listening, struggling to master the flood of memories of my own sale by my brothers. The Kushite also reminded me vividly of my friend Kush. He was the same size and age, and had the same proud carriage despite the bonds. I looked into his face, half fearful this was some sort of nightmare and that young man really was Kush. But the features were different and no merriment twinkled in his eyes. Only a burning sense of waiting.

The retainers led him among the tables so all could inspect him, and when they returned to the front, sweat beaded the Kushite's face.

Raising my goblet, I tilted it without letting the wine touch my lips and put my fingers in the buy position. Khay scratched his head and listened to the woman beside him. She watched the Kushite with admiring eyes.

Someone started the bidding at one golden deben. Meritifi scoffed and asked for more, quickly getting it. Khay bid, looking slightly tipsy. I raised his bid with a flick of my finger, which Meritifi immediately acknowledged. When the price reach 15 golden deben, I shrugged and dropped out.

When I scanned the room I saw that most guests watched with eager interest.

Khay looked my way, and I signaled him to buy. It had been a long time since we worked this particular method in the markets. He met every bid, his lady squealing in delight. Although he raised his cup to his lips again and again, and appeared to get more and more tipsy, I noticed that cup never did get refilled.

As the price went higher, Khay checked, but I kept my hand in the buy position on the goblet.

"Twenty deben," Khay finally said loudly, hiccuping, "in the White," he finished.

After a moment of completely stunned silence, applause broke out, and Lord Meritifi looked at me. "You bid previously, my lord. Last chance."

I shook my head, then raised my cup to Khay, sending him the sale.

"Sold," Lord Meritifi announced. "Sold to the lord with the loveliest lady in the room."

Khay's companion blushed furiously, and the retainers shoved the Kushite to Lord Khay's table. He stood up, steadying himself on the yoke across the slave's shoulders. "Come 'long, my boy," he said, swaying slightly. "I must get your price from my steward." He stared around. "How much did I pay?"

The guests laughed. "Twenty deben of the White," I replied, raising my goblet to him again.

Khay peered at me. "You are the new Tate," he said, carefully pronouncing his words. "Yes, you are. And if you say I paid 20 deben of the White, then I must have because that which you command is—is—" he paused, thinking deeply. "Is something or other. I will think of it later. Now, where is that fellow?"

He looked around vacantly until he spotted the Kushite right behind him. "Ha! Tried to run already, have you? Well, no more of that. I could find you anywhere, I could." Hooking his arm around the Kushite's, he started for the door. "Come 'long, come 'long. Must find the steward. Have to pay for you. You best be good, you were expensive, you were. Even the Tate said I paid 10 pieces of—"

"Twenty!" several guests said at once.

Khay stopped, swaying backward dangerously and blinking. "Twenty? Ten? What's the difference?"

"Ten deben," I said dryly.

"Is that which shall be done!" Khay roared triumphantly. "Told you I'd 'member."

He disappeared out the door. One of Meritifi's stewards followed him.

"Having honored fate, we will honor pleasure now," Meritifi announced when the laughter at Khay's exit subsided. His retainers led out a pair of twins with white skin and hair like gold. The crowd gasped, and bidding began immediately. I quietly left, taking Mahesa with me. Meritifi's entertainment did not appeal to me. But by the time he finished, he would undoubtedly take in much more than he had paid to give his feast. As I walked out the door, I caught a glimpse of Meritifi's personal scribe watching me with despair in her eyes.

Outside in the courtyard, Khay and Meritifi's steward were having an argument. The steward wanted payment immediately. Finally Khay lay down on the rope dangling from the Kushite's neck and started to snore. I watched in amusement while my party assembled and prepared to go. Mahesa returned from the river with enough gold to equal the purchase price Khay had bid, and one of my own retainers took it to Khay.

Grabbing the bag, he flung one arm around Meritifi's steward and started back into the house, shouting that he had the payment. Then he stopped halfway there, turned, and told my retainer in a most dignified voice to take the Kushite away. Then he started back into the house.

Not once had the steward tried to get away, and I laughed to myself. Khay knew more uncomfortable holds on a man than anyone else I'd ever met. People were so busy watching him that no one noticed as the Kushite left with my retainers.

Once aboard my barge, I ordered debarkation at once though I waited until nearly dark to send for the Kushite.

Mahesa brought him, then removed his bonds and threw the yoke over the side into the Nile. The young man's eyes widened in surprise.

I looked him over. Highborn, if I was not mistaken. He had that carriage and air that said royalty.

"The food on the table is for you," I said impulsively in Canaanite. "Sit down and eat."

He didn't move for a long time, but he couldn't take his eyes from the food either. Finally he sat and ate.

When he had finished, I asked, "What is your name?"

"I have no name. I am a slave," he replied, also in Canaanite, with a voice just beginning to deepen.

I smiled, pleased my guess was correct. "You have one," I said. "But you do not want to tell it to me."

He looked at me curiously. "Why did you not buy me yourself?"

"I did not wish to pay too high a price," I replied, "and I would have paid any price asked for you."

"Why?"

"I am repaying a debt. When I was young, a Kushite just about your age saved my life. I have not forgotten. So I bought you. I give you now a choice. If you wish, you may continue south with me to the first nome. You can travel back to your home from there. Or you can remain and work for me."

When he hesitated, I regarded him with renewed interest. Was it possible he did not want to return home?

"What sort of work?" he asked casually.

"My house steward needs an interpreter in the markets," I improvised. "He does not speak Canaanite. You do."

He thought about it, and the longer he did, the more he revealed. Chances were that he dared not go home. Why not?

"Where is your house?" he asked next.

"Memphis."

His head jerked up, and a pleased light sprang into his eyes.

Definitely he did not want to go to Kush. I remained silent.

"When do you go there?" he asked next, rubbing the side of the little table with his thumb.

"I am on an extensive tour of the southern nomes. You can either come with me, or I shall arrange for you to be taken to Memphis immediately. Saf will be very glad to have you."

For a time he said not a word, undecided about which course to take. "I will go to Memphis," he said finally in a low voice. Then he took a deep breath. "What does my lord wish to call me?"

The only reason I could think of for him to choose slavery was that death waited as the alternative. Who was this young man? Tears glittered unshed in his eyes, and he still rubbed the side of the table.

"I would call you 'Benabi,'" I said. "In my language, that means son of Father. You have a beloved father somewhere, that is plain."

His lips trembled, but he quickly steadied them. Touching the floor with his forehead, he said, "My name is Benabi."

CHAPTER 24

At last I reached the first nome, the Land in Front. But Lord Mose did not meet me at the docks. His staff had to call him in from the fields when I arrived at his residence. Lord Mose walked in looking annoyed and still dusty from his inspection tour.

I liked him at once.

He bowed grudgingly and studied me from beneath his eyebrows. "Lord Paanekh?" he barked.

"Yes, Lord Mose. I will be brief, if I may, since you are busy."

The nomarch snorted. "Never known a courtier yet who could do that. Come into the audience room, and we will talk there."

I followed him into the chamber, noting the high quality of the sparse furnishings.

"Well, speak your piece," he said, sitting down with a sigh in his chair and leaving me standing. Mahesa opened his mouth, and I stopped him with a slight gesture.

"Storehouses must be built to store grain for the coming famine," I said. "A series of them will spread across Egypt. They will be built near the cities and towns for easier distribution of food. I need your cooperation in raising these granaries. You know the best places to put them for easy access to the river and central locations for your people."

He grunted, eyeing me.

"I also need a place to work from, a permanent building to house my staff. Until one is built, I would like to work from your estate, if you permit."

"If I permit? You are Tate; you can order and I must obey."

I shrugged. "Why order and get half-hearted obedience? You know as well as I that when danger threatens, the response must be quick and decisive. Half-hearted obedience is neither quick nor decisive."

Lord Mose waited, and I remained silent. I had said what I came to say.

"I am loyal to Pharaoh," he said shortly. "Understand that. I will do nothing to betray that trust. We take it seriously here in the Land in Front."

I liked this man more and more. He was rough, honest, and knew how to speak his mind. And he reminded me a lot of my uncle Esau.

"We are alike in that," I said, looking him in the eye. "Egypt faces certain death unless action is taken, and there will be nothing to guard unless all work together."

Mose glanced at the steward who had walked in. "Bring Lord Paanekh a chair," he ordered. "Sit down, young man, and we will discuss this," he added, turning to me. I smiled in satisfaction. I'd have him calling me "my lord" yet.

▲ ▲ ▲ ▲

"What is it, Lady Asenath?" Renseneb asked as they sat in the little room off the market. "You seem very far away."

She blushed. "I feel so silly," she said with a sigh. "I cannot stop thinking about Lord Paanekh. I have never seen red hair before. Do you think it feels hot?"

"I doubt it," he chuckled. "Do you see much of him?"

"Yes, we talk in the garden in the evenings. He tells me all about barbarians and where they live and what they do. Lord Paanekh does not want me to be afraid. I try not to be, now."

"You like this man?"

"Yes, I do," Asenath replied simply. "He is gentle and amusing, and I can relax when he is around. Lord Paanekh makes me feel as if I am the most special woman in the world." She laughed. "I know he makes other people feel the same way, but it is nice just the same. And he is the most handsome man I have ever seen." A smile on her face, she stared into space.

Renseneb read there what Asenath had not yet discovered. He sighed, knowing he could never give her the happiness between a husband and wife.

"At first I hoped he would get tired of my looks and manners as father did," Asenath went on. "Then I could go on just like before. But he has not lost interest, and I am not certain I want him to anymore. I have to be careful what I say, though," she said with a smile. "Last time we discussed a problem, I almost let slip how I knew so much. He is so puzzled!" She laughed softly.

Renseneb kept his anxiety to himself. Asenath had little experience with gentleness, and he prayed that Lord Paanekh was truly interested in her, and not just playing with her. And that comment she made about Lord Paanekh's looks stirred a memory dangling just out of reach.

▲　▲　▲　▲

I chuckled as I entered the room in the Memphis palace where Mahesa worked.

He looked up. "What is it, my lord?"

"Renseneb," I said. "Saf got taken again, over a matter of linen this time. He is fuming, and he and his mother are plotting revenge. What is there for me today?"

"Nothing good," the scribe said. "Reports from all the nomes south of Thebes are very discouraging. Nothing has been done. It is the same sort of thing we ran into in the Treasury. Lots of words, but no actions."

I thought for a minute. "All of the nomes south of Thebes, or just most of them?"

"Lord Mose is moving forward rapidly," Mahesa admitted, "and the eighth nome is also doing well."

I studied the map Mahesa had on his wall. "We seem to have two centers of trouble," I said. "Thebes, where Lord Amony lives, and Lord Meritifi in the twelfth nome. Lord Mose doesn't care, and the eighth nome is between Amony and Meritifi and on the western bank.

"Push things along as much as you can, Mahesa," I decided. "I must accompany Amenemhet to Thebes in about a month for the formal audience there and will have to deal with the nomarchs of the south then. I just wish I knew what to do."

Later, I sat in the garden waiting for Lady Asenath. She had been to the markets again, and I wondered what treasure she had found. The house was beginning to fill with them. Once assured that I would not mind if she redecorated, she started immediately. She had the large waiting room and reception room repainted with the usual formal scenes, but in the small waiting room and reception room where I worked, she had found someone to do less common themes.

When Asenath arrived, I listened while she told me all about her trip to the market, and then she listened while I talked about things at court. Asenath opened up to me more and more during these quiet evening talks. She surprised me with her awareness of currents and trends in politics and the court, and had a way of summarizing a person in just a few words. Some of her comments reminded me of the pithy comments Abana made. I wondered more and more often how Asenath knew what she did.

With great reluctance, I prepared for my second inspection tour. I left final instructions with Saf about some wood I expected to be delivered and listened to his plans to best Renseneb. When I suggested a couple things, he seized on them immediately. He and his mother were as involved as I in this quiet little war. I still wished I knew who Renseneb acted for. Whoever it was had a very acute and shrewd understanding of business and politics. Saf told me how much Lord Hordef paid in Tanis for supplies. I did not know whether I should laugh or weep. Pharaoh's Treasury could not stand any more victories by Renseneb. He seemed even better informed now than I remembered.

Also I must be extremely careful handling essential purchases for the Great House and not just because of Renseneb. The nomarchs who held concessions did not hesitate to charge heavily when they had the chance. I needed desperately to talk to Jetur. If I could convince him to work the markets for me, I could save a lot. And I had to start immediately, for I did not have enough in the storehouses to support the corvee this year, and I needed it to build granaries.

▲　▲　▲　▲

After stepping out of the sedan chair at the bustling work site on the delta, I just watched for several minutes. Shenbu consulted with someone over some drawings and he looked discouraged. I wandered over and he glanced at me, bowing absently.

"B-b-but h-h-how can we make it work?" he asked his companion.

"There must be a way," the other replied. "Surely we can do something." I started in surprise. I hadn't seen Siamon since Lord Potiphar had put me in prison.

"What has happened?" I asked.

"It doesn't w-w-work," Shenbu said despondently. "S-S-Siamon built a granary that kept all the g-g-grain dry at his pasture, but my adaptation doesn't w-w-work. I cannot figure out w-w-why."

"Explain the drawings to me," I requested.

Siamon went over his drawing, and then Shenbu explained his. We went to the square platform that the small model granary rested on, and they pointed out to me just how the reality fit the drawing. The gravel on the slope up to the granary rolled under my feet, and I glimpsed something on the ground.

"Shenbu," I asked, "did you just tell me that you must avoid clay at all costs?"

"Yes, m-m-my lord," he said. "C-C-Clay will hold the water and—"

"That looks like clay."

Shenbu looked down, then he and Siamon began to dig in the mound under the platform.

"That lazy supervisor!" Siamon exclaimed. "He put down clay!"

"B-b-but we specifically t-t-told him not to," Shenbu protested.

"Well, he did it anyway," Siamon said. "Now we have to redo the entire platform. But that may be our problem. The clay would hold the wet, not drain it away."

"That c-c-could account for it," Shenbu said to himself. "W-W-Well, let's g-g-get started." He walked away without giving me a second glance. Siamon took the time to give me a hurried bow and followed after him, without recognizing me. I went back to my sedan chair. Things were going fine in the Delta.

Leaving the barge at the docks of Memphis I spotted Huy working the riverfront. I stopped to watch briefly on my way to the palace. He gave me a grave double nod, letting me know that Jetur had returned.

I sent a messenger for the old trader as soon as I could. While I waited for him to arrive, I dug into the work that had piled up during my time in the Delta. But the messenger returned with a message, not Jetur. Puzzled, I opened it.

"To Lord Paanekh, Tate unto Pharaoh, from his servant Jetur of Canaan. I beg pardon from my lord. It is not fitting for me to come to my lord as the days of my mourning are not complete. I have but recently attended the burial rites for my father's brother, Prince Isaac of Canaan. He was buried with his father by his sons, Prince Jacob and Lord Esau. I shall notify my lord when the period of mourning is ended."

Suddenly I couldn't move or breathe. Grandfather Isaac was

dead. A terrible icy cold settled over me. Although I shivered violently, I could not get warm.

"Joseph! Joseph!" Mahesa's hands gripped my shoulders and he shook me.

"Mahesa," I gasped, trying to focus on him.

"Joseph, what is it? What is in that message?" His voice was urgent and insistent.

I shook my head, trying to clear it, trying to think of what to say. "Grandfather's dead," I said with great effort. "He's buried and—"

"Joseph, answer me in Egyptian!" Mahesa commanded, his fingers digging painfully into my shoulders.

"I—my—he said my grandfather is dead," I finally managed to say. "I will never get to see him again. He loved me and he told stories to Benjamin and me, and now—now—I wasn't there. I wasn't there for Abi!"

"Chaf!" Mahesa roared.

My bodyguard stepped into the room, saw me, and gasped.

"Get Onami with the chariot," Mahesa said. "We must take him home."

"What happened?" Chaf asked on his way out.

"He just got news that his grandfather died, I think. Half the time he is speaking Canaanite."

Between Chaf and Mahesa, I made it to the chariot. The charioteer looked frightened, and the horses wouldn't stand still. The scribe lifted me into the chariot and stayed with me the entire drive home. The stallion acted as he never had before, snorting and screaming and snapping to clear the way in front of him during the short ride. Mahesa got me out at the gate.

Inti began shouting orders to somebody. The stallion rebelled against Onami and shoved his way heedlessly to my shoulder. He followed me all the way to the stairs and would have gone up them, but the chariot driver finally got him under control again.

Saf came running from the house, holding onto his wig, asking questions. Mahesa took me to the bedchamber and finally let me sit down.

"What is it? What is it?" Saf kept asking.

"A close family member apparently died," the scribe snapped. "His Ka wants to leave and go to his home."

And that is exactly how I felt. I wanted to go home, to be with

Abi, to mourn with my family over the death of my grandfather. And I could not. Mahesa placed a goblet in my hands. It felt warm and I cupped it gratefully.

"Drink it," Mahesa commanded.

I took a sip of the warm, spiced wine. It made me feel better. By the time I finished the goblet, the cold numbness had left. I simply ached with grief, and tears spilled from my eyes.

"He will be all right now," Mahesa said, speaking to Saf. "We had best leave him alone."

I was grateful. That was what I wanted now. To be alone.

▲ ▲ ▲ ▲

Asenath sat on the garden bench wondering what she could do. The entire household was upset. Saf told her that Lord Paanekh had lost a close family member, leaving him prostrate with grief. She had been dubious at first. He was a barbarian after all, and not supposed to be really human. What sort of attachment could he form for a family? On the other hand, he seemed human enough when she talked to him.

"Quit lying," she whispered to herself sternly. All that about barbarians not being human was just so much state rhetoric, and everyone knew it. To be truthful, she couldn't stand Lord Paanekh's grief, and yet didn't know what to do about it.

Finally she decided that she had to do something about the situation. While she wasn't family for him or wasn't from Canaan, maybe that wouldn't matter. Who else in the house dared approach him? He was their lord, and while they would grieve with him, they could not comfort him as he needed. Only she could. Maybe. She got up and went back into the house, pausing at the door to the small reception room.

If she did go to him, where might that lead? She hesitated. Well, she would just have to face whatever happened, she decided. Anyway, she did not need to think about that now. When she stopped at the door of his bedchamber she saw, in the light of the single lamp lit, papers scattered on the low table.

Hugging herself, she stepped into the room. In sharp contrast to the rest of the refurbished house, the room contained only an old chair, a battered scribe's table, a mended stool, and the bed. In a corner the gold collar and armbands gleamed in the lamplight, partially covered by the wig. An open wooden chest held linens. The walls had once been brightly painted, but the pictures had faded and the plaster was peeling.

It was a servant's room, not that of a lord. It held nothing personal, nothing that spoke of the man who rested here, except the open box of myrrh on the table and the kohl beside it.

He was lonely.

The realization broke on her quietly, as she looked around the bare room he lived in. He could order other people's lives as he wished. Lord Paanekh was cheered by all in the streets, hated by some in the palace, and ignored and slighted by the nomarchs while he struggled to save them from famine.

There would be a famine. Asenath had looked into Lord Paanekh's Horus eyes and knew that what he said would happen. She understood how much he would have to overcome in order to store the grain for the future. The intrigues went deep and Lord Amony would risk much to acquire his goal.

Asenath looked around the room again. The most powerful man in the world came home to this lonely, bare room. Then she saw the small shelf on the wall above the bed. On it rested a single stem of dried wheat with seven ears on it. Beside it sat a little husk doll that Hesy had made and given to Lord Paanekh when he admired her work.

Some emotion inside her broke open and flooded her soul. "I am the luckiest woman in all of Egypt," she whispered. Then she walked into the garden.

▲ ▲ ▲ ▲

I stared blankly at the still pool. The moon would soon rise over the wall and be reflected in the pool, and I would stare at it and wish that the pain inside would go away. I had shed tears and torn my body with sobs until my stomach was too sore to touch, but the pain did not lessen. I didn't even know why I mourned any longer. Grandfather Isaac was dead, and I couldn't change that. He had been dead for some time, if Jetur had the time to go to Canaan and get back and observe a period of isolation.

Why did I ache so? What was it that my heart needed? I heard something and looked up. Lady Asenath stood a few feet away, watching me. I should stand up, or something, but what did it matter? Had she come to ease her curiosity about how barbarians acted when someone died?

I looked down. It didn't matter. I hurt too much to care. She would go away eventually, and I could try to make it through another night alone. Something warm was near me, and the faint perfume of myrrh reached my nose. I opened my eyes. Lady Asenath sat beside me.

Tensing, I started to edge away. What was she doing here?

"Please let me sit with you," she said softly.

What for? I wondered, but it wasn't worth a struggle, so I stayed still. Silently she sat beside me until the moon's reflection traveled halfway across the pool. Then she reached out and stroked my hair. I didn't know what to do about it.

"Do you know when I first saw your hair I wondered if it felt hot?" she asked softly.

I looked at her in surprise.

"It doesn't," she said. "It feels just like your hair should feel."

"Do you like it?" I asked, just to say something.

She considered. "I don't know. I see you when you come back from the palace, and you have your wig off and your hair is all ruffled up because you have been running your fingers through it and I think you are the handsomest man I have ever seen. But then I see you with your wig on, and the gold collar from Pharaoh, and the signet ring and armbands, wearing the royal linen and a gold belt, and you look just magnificent. I haven't decided yet which is best."

I closed my mouth and gulped. "Oh."

"And then this happens," she went on. "You grieve so much. You must have loved your grandfather a great deal."

"I did," I said, clearing my throat. "Next to Abi and Benjamin, I loved him most after Mother died."

"Your mother is dead? So is mine. I loved her more than anyone in the whole world."

It was the wrong thing to say, or maybe it was the right thing. I reached for Asenath, stretching on the ground and burying my face in her lap. I hung on for dear life while the dam of pain that had been inside since my brothers tore Abi's gift from my body burst open. I wept until I was too exhausted to move.

Asenath awakened me the next day. She had a tray of food, and

I ate it, the first I had really eaten since learning of Grandfather's death. Then she took me into the garden and asked questions. I didn't answer much at first, but she persisted until I let the memories of my grandfather come and poured them out to her.

The moon rose again before I finished, and then we sat silently, watching the reflection in the pool until very late. I knew I should send her away.

"You had better go," I finally made myself say.

Asenath looked at me. "I do not want to go."

I gripped her hand tightly. "You know what will happen if you stay?"

"Yes."

That night, out in the garden, Asenath became truly my wife.

I observed a full 30 days of mourning for Grandfather Isaac. Then I shaved and had my hair cut. Mahesa had informed Pharaoh of my loss, and he replied that I was not to come to Thebes until the middle of Planting.

Asenath drew me away from my grief faster than I imagined anyone could. I talked to her every night and found her better than Mahesa at noticing political and diplomatic ripples in the court. When I tried to learn how she knew things, she just shrugged and said she had been following the court all her life.

That told me nothing at all.

Saf and Takamenet between them now held their own against Renseneb here in Memphis. I followed the war carefully, for it distracted me from my grief.

At last I could put off the visit to Jetur no longer. After much personal debate, I decided to go to him, much to Mahesa's annoyance. We dressed plainly and went to the market. There I spotted Mishma and waited for more than an hour before he ducked into an alley. We made our way there and knocked on the door after the guard had scrutinized my face and then smiled briefly.

When we entered Jetur's private reception room he glanced up to see me, then bowed where he sat.

"You do me a great honor, Lord Paanekh. My humble house has never sheltered one so great before."

Mishma gave me one startled look before bowing as well.

"I do believe this is the softest carpet yet," I said.

The old man smiled. "It should be. It was made especially for me. Please sit down, my lord."

I sat on the floor and dug my fingers into the rug. "I think I will want some of your rugs. But I will have to discuss it with my wife."

"My lord is married?" Jetur asked politely.

"Yes, to Lady Asenath, daughter of the Great Ueb Poti-Phera of On."

"I have heard of the lady," he said neutrally.

"Lady Asenath has been a very wonderful surprise," I said. After a silence, I looked at Jetur. "How long have you known who I was?"

Mishma tensed, exchanging a glance with his father.

"I come in peace, Jetur," I added. "There is no anger in my heart."

"Since the moment Mishma pointed out the prince's coat on the ground when I bought you," he replied.

"Yet you still bought me."

"You would have died had I refused."

I thought back to that day. "You are right," I admitted, remembering the hatred swirling around me from my brothers. "And you chose very carefully where you placed me, did you not?"

"Yes," he said simply.

"Thank you. And now I will tell you why El Shaddai took me from my home and made me Tate in Egypt. There will be a famine after seven harvests. But the harvests will be like no harvests before. The grain will run like the Nile throughout the land. I will be storing the grain, for the seven years that follow will bring neither sowing nor harvest.

"I must build storehouses to hold the grain, and Pharaoh's treasury is all but empty, for it is hard to collect the royal taxes."

"Why do you come to me?"

"I want you to work the markets for me. I wish to give you a portion of what is left in Pharaoh's treasury, and I want you to buy and sell for Pharaoh."

It took his breath away. He didn't move for several seconds.

"Tell me more," Jetur said, recovering. "I am interested, very interested. Where would I work from?"

"It makes no difference to me. Memphis, On, Tanis, take your choice. You, and any merchants you recruit, can keep a tenth of what you make. But Pharaoh's treasury will supply the means to begin, and Pharaoh's treasury must reap the profits."

We discussed it for some time, and he agreed to act for me in the Delta region, Canaan, and beyond.

As I rose to go I said, "Thank you for telling me that Grandfather Isaac had died. And thank you for letting me know that my father still lives."

The trader bowed his head. "I knew Prince Isaac. All I could do for him was keep his grandson alive, even if I could never tell him that."

"Thank you, Jetur."

▲ ▲ ▲ ▲

"Well, Mishma?"

"You were right, Abi," the son admitted. "And yes, it's a good thing we were kind all those many years ago. I feel Isaac's God in him. It's unsettling."

"It need not be. Remember to respect Isaac's God, and he will respect you." He looked at the door. "Who would have guessed what my 20 pieces of silver would turn into!"

CHAPTER 25

I sent Mahesa to assess progress in the lower nomes and the Delta while I started south to Thebes for the formal audience with the southern nomarchs. To my delight, Asenath decided to accompany me. She rarely left the barge, but she watched everything, and her eyes sparkled more and more often. Hesy was both a great help and the bane of our existence all at the same time.

Even with Asenath to distract me, the days of travel gave me much time to think. As Mahesa warned me, nothing had been done. I grew more and more discouraged. Reports from every supervisor made it clear that the nomarchs did not intend to cooperate, with the exception of the first and eighth nomes. Every night I turned to El Shaddai in desperation, pleading with him to show me the way to save Egypt, as I pleaded now.

I knelt in the darkness at the edge of a field. I needed to be away from everyone, alone with my God. The barge was below me, moored to the bank only a day's journey from Thebes. Pharaoh would ask me what I had done and I could tell him nothing. I bowed to the ground empty of words, left only with a feeling of total inadequacy and failure. I had nowhere else to turn but to El Shaddai, the One who in His strength provided and nourished those who called in their need.

As my heart poured out my desperation, I heard footsteps. Two people approached, one staggering.

"My lord, you must rest," a voice said very softly.

"No time," a second voice answered thickly. "Get to Thebes."

"My lord, you are not going to make it without rest," the first insisted.

"Can rest in Thebes."

Listening with all my being, I rose from my knees.

"Come this way," the first spoke again, and the footsteps approached me.

"Get to Thebes," the second spoke again, half out of his head. "Lord Potiphar, or Joseph."

Out of the gloom two men appeared, one supporting the other. The second man started to fall and I stepped forward, catching him.

"Chaf!" I shouted.

Chaf and two other guards appeared instantly, quickly surrounding the men.

"Get them to the barge," I snapped. "It is Lord Khay!"

Once on board, we cast off immediately and made for the middle of the river. I wanted distance, and I had Chaf set guards to watch all sides of the barge as we traveled. I put the man with Khay inside the barge under heavy guard. Khay would hardly let go of him, so he must be of great importance.

The young lord had a bad wound, days old, in his thigh. I sent for oil and wine and personally cleaned it, thankful that he was unconscious. As I poured the soothing oil in the wound, the pain lines in his face relaxed. Impatiently I waited for my best intelligence agent to awaken.

About dawn he opened his eyes and looked around, puzzled. When he saw me he stared. "Joseph?" he asked in disbelief.

"You know anyone else with red hair?"

He lay back and sighed with relief. Then started up again. "Where is he?"

"Below, under heavy guard," I said. "Lie down."

"Bring him up here—and Mahesa. I want this recorded as soon as possible," he ordered.

"Rest a bit first," I admonished.

"No," Khay insisted. "Now."

I called my scribe. He brought writing materials, and Chaf brought our guest.

"This is Irtisen," Khay said, beginning his statement in a tired voice. "He is a jewel smith, and he made a seal and a signet ring . . ."

Amenemhet sent for me as soon as I arrived in Thebes. The palace at Thebes resembled the one in Memphis, being small and cramped. I entered the personal audience chamber and bowed.

"You are here, Lord Paanekh," Pharaoh greeted me. "How goes the building?"

"I am afraid it doesn't, my lord," I said. "In the Delta the first attempts at keeping granaries dry have failed. But we think we found the problem and are trying again.

"The northern nomes are building if the nomarch was present in Memphis when you made me Tate. The others wait to see what the south is doing. And the south is doing nothing at all."

Amenemhet frowned. "What do you mean, nothing?"

"They are not building, and they do not intend to. Only Lord Mose and Lord Hisemi of the eighth nome are cooperating. Lord Amony controls the nomes from the Land in Front to Thebes, and Lord Meritifi has influenced the nomes around him near Abydos."

"Lord Meritifi?" the king exclaimed. "That puppet?" He slapped the table in frustration. "And I can do nothing," he fumed. The old frustration and worry descended on his face again. "Must Egypt starve because I have nomarchs who cannot see beyond their own houses?"

"That will change soon, my lord. When is the formal presentation?"

"Day after tomorrow. I am worried, Lord Paanekh. You must build. I have had the dreams again. You must save Egypt."

"It shall be done, my lord. El Shaddai is not one to let stubborn nomarchs stand in His way. I have just learned that last night."

"You give me hope," Amenemhet sighed. "Although I do not know why."

As soon as I returned to the barge, I opened the sack of correspondence Khay had carried. Copies of the usual letters from Lord Amony to his cohorts told me nothing more than what I already knew until I picked up the last one. Summoning Mahesa, I took him with me to see Khay. He had awakened when the attendant cleaned the wound once more.

Khay looked up as we entered. "What did you find?" he asked, reading me instantly.

"This," I said, holding it out to him.

He scanned it, Mahesa looking over his shoulder.

"This is it," Khay said. "It must be. The Inner Circle is holding a meeting tomorrow night."

"It looks like that to me, also," I said. "The timing is interesting. The formal audience for me is the next day."

"What do you think?"

"I suspect Amony plans to tip his hand then," I said grimly. "We must attend that meeting. Who is to come?"

"From the signs at the bottom, all the southern nomarchs in nomes one through 16," Mahesa said.

"That was a mistake," I replied. "Lord Mose will have nothing to do with what they plan."

"Provided Lord Mose is alive to protest," Khay grunted. "This is the crisis, Joseph. As I well know, they will not allow interference."

"They will get it anyway," I said, narrowing my eyes. "I have had enough of this nonsense, and I must put a stop to it. Egypt must build storehouses, not play games with the office of Tate. Now that you are awake, what happened to you?"

"Lord Hernofret resisted when we took him. I forgot to tell you that he will be arriving in Thebes tomorrow, under arrest. When I found Irtisen I ordered Hernofret taken. We managed to do it without letting anyone know. Irtisen should have the sealed pouch we found along with the other correspondence."

I went immediately to Irtisen. He gave me the pouch, and I took it back to Khay's bedside. Breaking the seal, I took out the papyri. The first was a proclamation announcing the unfortunate death of Amenemhet III and signed with the strange signet cartouche. There were four other death orders as well.

"He is a fool to have written this!" Khay gasped.

"That is what worries me," I said. "He is not a fool."

Leaving Mahesa with Khay, I went back to the high stern deck to think. Asenath sat there alone, and on an impulse I briefly outlined the situation, leaving out the strange cartouche. Her face went white long before I was done, and I knew she had grasped the situation in its entirety.

"I must end this at the meeting," I said. "But I am not certain just how to do it."

"It would depend on what was said," she replied. "Is there anyone you can depend on?"

"Lord Mose is loyal to Pharaoh," I said. "Lord Hisemi knows intrigue means trouble and will gladly see it end."

"It will probably come under the guise of religious rhetoric," Asenath mused. "That would be the safest way. Chances are the attack will be directed against you, not Pharaoh. If you could be there and listen until their plans are revealed, you could arrest them all and execute them for rebellion."

"It is an attractive thought, but I want to have Egypt build storehouses, not thrown into chaos," I sighed.

My wife glanced at me. "There is always blackmail."

I stood up and started to pace. "I know," I said softly. "I have enough to send every one of them to the ax, but I had hoped to find another way."

"You do not know them as I do," she said. "If you do not force them, they will not build. But if Lord Mose is truly loyal, place him over them. They will accept that. What about the temples?"

"Your father and I have already discussed that aspect," I said. "If the temples object, Pharaoh will get to appoint several new Great Ueb's. That being the case, I doubt they will object too strenuously."

Asenath smiled. "So, my father was good for something, at least. I wondered why he is being so quiescent lately."

"I took a page from Lord Amony's book and honored him with a personal guard from my house."

She laughed.

I waited in a small reception room in the Thebes palace soon after my talk with Asenath. Lord Mose should be here any minute. Her suggestion made a great deal of sense, and I wanted to be certain of him before that meeting tomorrow night.

When he entered the room, he looked around in surprise.

"My apologies for the subterfuge," I said, drawing his attention to me. "I want to be certain you live."

His eyes turned cold as he looked at me. "I do not appreciate being deceived with Pharaoh's name," he said. "If you wish to see me, send for me in your own name." He turned his back and started out the door.

"*Lord Mose!*" I said, my voice cracking like a whip.

Involuntarily he stopped.

"Had I sent for you in my own name, you would have taken your own good time in coming. Time is something I do not have a lot of just now, and neither do you, whether you know it or not. I am surprised you would try to leave without knowing what you are here for."

He turned around. "As you wish, Lord Paanekh," he said between tight lips. "What am I here for?"

I handed him a papyrus.

He took it roughly from my hands and barely glanced at it. "You need not consult me on an execution order," he almost sneered.

"Whose name is on it?" I asked calmly.

This time he read it and stood in frozen shock. "But I have done nothing!" he said in disbelief. "I have never been disloyal to Pharaoh! Why would Amenemhet condemn me?"

"Did Amenemhet condemn you?"

He looked again at the cartouche at the bottom and stiffened, then raised his eyes to me. "Where did you get this?" he asked hoarsely.

"The same place I found the announcement of Amenemhet's demise," I replied. "Now, Lord Mose, will you condescend to listen to me?"

He had the grace to turn red. "I will listen, Lord Paanekh. I am not a fool if I can help it."

Later I stood in the dimness of a room not far from Lord Amony's house in Thebes fingering the tablet of instructions given me by Amenemhet. After consulting with Lord Mose yesterday I had contacted Lord Potiphar. He approached Pharaoh, and the tablet I held was the result.

The 50 guardsmen with me lounged on the floor, waiting. Lord Amony's feast was almost over and the Inner Circle would meet. When they did, we would move in.

Lord Mose's retainer came to the door. "It is time, my lord."

Lord Potiphar led the way to the gate. His men quietly removed the gatekeeper, tucking him away in the gatehouse. One of the guardsmen took his place, and 20 more spread out in the estate compound. Another 20 entered the house and with polite firmness escorted the guests not in the Inner Circle meeting out of the house. The rest surrounded the room where the meeting was and waited.

The house steward emerged, also to be quickly seized by the guardsmen. Mahesa checked the room, then nodded to Lord Potiphar and I. We slipped inside the dimly lit chamber. Lord Amony stood at the front in the light of only three lamps. As long as we remained still, Lord Potiphar and I could not be seen in the shadows of the first row of pillars.

"My friends," Amony declared, "you all know of my concern with Egypt's welfare. It is the only true land of the gods and must be preserved for them. It is our duty, our place in maat, to see to this task.

"As you know, much has been unsettled lately. Senusert, that great Pharaoh, has gone to join his father Osiris. Amenemhet, may his Ka prosper, now rules our land. But the Tate, the wise, understanding Tate, whom Senusert trusted, has also died.

"And as a result, Seth has gained a toehold in the land. Whom do we have ruling over us? Amenemhet, our great Pharaoh? No, we have a barbarian, a former slave, a foreigner from Deshret. This is an insult to the gods, my friends. Shall a barbarian rule over the land of the gods of Egypt?

"We of the south know how important is maat. And maat cannot survive with a slave from Deshret interfering with our Pharaoh. There is a spot upon the land, a spot of offense, a spot of abomination to the gods." Amony paused, looking each nomarch in the eye.

"It is our duty, friends, our sacred duty, to cleanse this defilement from among us. How can Pharaoh preserve the land of the gods with this son of Seth blocking his way? Will the gods be pleased if Seth invades their land? It should not be so.

"We must cleanse the land. We must make atonement for our negligence, for allowing such a situation to develop. We must free Amenemhet from the bonds, the influence of this foreign slave of chaos.

"The gods will be pleased, my friends. They will be grateful that we serve them so well. Know you not that all those who truly follow them will be richly rewarded? Do you think they will forget the great service we will perform?" Amony raised his hands.

"They will remember, and they will repay you in the afterlife.

All who perform this task of cleansing will be taken to the bosom of the gods. They will be given milk from Mother Isis, and in drinking it they shall become gods even as Pharaoh is a god.

"In the afterlife, all those who protect Egypt for the gods will be elevated to like stature, and will attain the graces and power of the mightiest divines in the world. Is this not a reward worth seeking?

"Come, friends, let us rise to this task. Let us aid our beleaguered Pharaoh. Let us defend Kemet from the invasion of Deshret. Let the Red Land learn that the Black Land will not tolerate destruction of maat, that the Black Land will fight, will rise to the defense of the land of the gods!"

My hair stood on end on the back of my neck. Lord Amony had taken the nomarchs and turned them to his will. They leaned forward, eyes riveted on him, and drank in his words. A spell held them, and their eyes shone with the desire for gain. Beside me, Lord Potiphar's eyes glittered dangerously, and I felt the anger in him.

"Piffle! Amenemhet himself appointed the Tate," Lord Mose said into the charged silence, and his matter-of-fact derision shattered Lord Amony's hold on the nomarchs. "Furthermore, if there really is a famine coming—and Amenemhet had those dreams, not the Tate—then we had best be preparing. My people do not deserve to starve."

A flash of rage crossed Lord Amony's face, but he had the wit to see that he had lost the advantage. The room broke out into tense conversations as the nomarchs turned to each other and discussed the situation. Lord Meritifi went from group to group, putting in a word here and a thought there, gradually pushing the group toward a final decision.

In the gloom behind us Potiphar's guards, having emptied the house, slipped into the room and quietly took up positions next to the walls, standing like statues.

"What do we decide?" Lord Amony asked at last. "Who will fight for the gods and for Pharaoh? Who will dare to cleanse the land of Pharaoh of this abomination? Let us rid the land of this foreign Tate and present Egypt without blemish to the gods!"

"Yes, let us preserve maat!" Meritifi cried, and other voices joined in until the room rang with the din.

Lord Mose stood to one side, watching with sardonic eyes. I

moved unnoticed to the front of the room and when the shouting subsided, I stepped forward into the light.

"Open the doors!" I commanded. The guards threw open the three doors to the room, and several scribes entered, bringing lamps.

Lord Amony whirled around, his face white with rage at the sight of me. "You!" he choked out. "How dare you enter my house uninvited!"

"As Tate to Pharaoh I am convening special court for a trial," I replied.

"You cannot!" he shouted. "You have no right to move against the lawful nomarchs of Egypt!"

"Lord Mose, will you read this?" I asked, holding out the tablet from Pharaoh to him.

Mose took his time getting to me, then accepted the tablet.

"From Amenemhet III, Pharaoh of Upper and Lower Egypt, Lord of the Two Lands, Son of Ra, to Lord Paanekh, Second to Pharaoh, Tate of Upper and Lower Egypt, and Great Judge of Sasat. You, alone, shall call a special court of inquiry into the matter of the so-called Inner Circle. You, alone, are to investigate with all speed the accusations against this abomination of the land. You shall go and question any who know of this abomination and shall punish these conspirators according to their crimes. Those who must die, you will cause to die without my knowing anything of it. Those who deserve punishment, you will punish without my knowing anything of it. You shall settle this matter to the good of Egypt and Pharaoh. It is in your hands entirely."

Lord Mose's hands trembled by the time he finished reading. "It is stamped with my lord Pharaoh's signet," he finished.

"This is an outrage," Lord Amony shouted, his voice joined by others. The guards at the walls stepped forward in unison and pounded their spears once on the floor, leaning the points toward those in the center of the room. The sound startled the nomarchs into silence, and Lord Potiphar stepped up beside me.

"My lord Paanekh, as Captain of Pharaoh's Guard I place myself and my men under your hand to do your bidding in regard to this court of inquiry as commanded by Pharaoh Amenemhet III, Ruler of the Two Lands."

In the silence the nomarchs eased themselves away from me, glancing around in apprehensive disbelief. I watched the knowledge that Pharaoh had given me complete and entire discretionary power over them sift through their stunned minds. Even Lord Mose looked subdued by the completeness of their dependence on me.

Lord Hisemi of the eighth nome recovered his voice. "I will submit myself to Pharaoh's wishes," he said, bowing to me.

"I am well aware that you know little of what this is about, Lord Hisemi," I said. "Go stand with Lord Mose."

Bowing again, Lord Hisemi made his way to the side of the room and stood very straight beside Mose.

I turned to the group in the center of the room. "Lord Amony, you stand accused of conspiracy against the life of the Tate, the Second to Pharaoh, Beloved of Pharaoh, and appointed personally by Pharaoh to serve him. You also stand accused of conspiracy against the life of Lady Asenath, daughter of the Great Vision of Ra in On."

The nomarchs stood frozen, held by the sudden, horrible nightmare conjured up by my words.

"Bring in Lord Hernofret," I commanded.

A guard brought Amony's son and forced him to kneel in the middle of the room.

"Lord Hernofret, you are accused of conspiracy against the Tate, the Second to Pharaoh, Beloved of Pharaoh, and appointed personally by Pharaoh to serve him. You also stand accused of treason against Pharaoh himself, serving as a courier to carry treasonous messages to the members of the conspiracy."

"This is outrageous," Lord Amony shouted. "My son would never countenance treason against Pharaoh, the son of the gods!"

"Do you deny that he carried messages?" I asked, turning on Lord Amony and holding up the message pouch Lord Hernofret used.

"He carried personal messages from me to my friends," Lord Amony protested. "You cannot accuse him of anything more."

"Lord Hernofret, what else did you carry?" I asked.

"If it please my lord," he said in a trembling voice, "I carried messages for other lords as well."

"Other lords?" Amony gasped. "Why would you do this?" he asked his son in disbelief.

"I thought that is what you wanted," Hernofret said, his voice strained. "You consulted with him all the time. He advised you. You said I should listen to him. He told me your true goal—"

"Hernofret!" Amony snapped, and his son bit back his words.

"As a consequence, you carried pouches like this one?" I asked, showing him the sealed pouch I had opened.

"Yes, my lord," he said, his face white.

The sight of the pouch brought a gasp from behind me.

"Lord Meritifi!" I snapped. "Do not think to leave for you are the next accused. You stand accused of conspiracy to murder Pharaoh himself!" At my signal guards took position on each side of him.

"I, my lord?" he asked unsteadily. "I am but a poor nomarch, my lord. I have no dreams to the throne. I would not be able to plan such a thing in any case."

"Lord Mose!" I called.

He stepped forward.

"Go to Lord Meritifi and inspect the large ring on his left hand."

The nomarch did as I said.

"Press the two jewels at the top of the ring."

Meritifi froze at my words, then began to struggle wildly. The guards subdued him and dragged him to the center of the room beside Lord Hernofret and Lord Amony.

Grasping Meritifi's hand, Lord Mose opened the ring.

"What do you see?" I asked.

"A cartouche, Lord Paanekh. It is a signet ring."

"Stamp it on this tablet."

He took it from Meritifi and pressed it against the tablet.

I took the seal from my linen and handed it to Lord Mose as well. "Roll this out."

"The cartouches are the same," Lord Mose said.

Mahesa handed me the papyri I had taken from the pouch earlier. "I hold in my hands execution orders, stamped with the cartouche you just saw taken from Lord Meritifi. They are made out for Lord Mose of the Land in Front, Lord Peun of the sixteenth nome, Lord Hisemi of the eighth nome, and Lord Sety of the twenty-fourth nome. I also hold the execution order for Lord Amony of Thebes.

"And this is the proclamation, stamped with the signet taken from Lord Meritifi, which announces the death of Amenemhet III, Pharaoh of Egypt."

Lord Meritifi looked at me wildly. "I did not write them, I did not write them," he screamed.

Lord Amony stared at his own execution order, and then at Lord Meritifi, a growing hatred in his eyes. Lord Hernofret huddled on the floor and prayed to the gods that he might live.

I looked into the horrified faces of the nomarchs in the room. "My lords," I said, "shall we discuss Pharaoh's will regarding traitors such as yourselves?"

The next morning Khay called to me when I passed his room. Asenath had moved us into my residence in Thebes.

"Did you hear?" he asked.

"I doubt it, I just got up," I confessed.

Khay's lips pressed together. "Lord Meritifi is missing this morning."

"I sent him to Pharaoh's prison!" I exclaimed. "How can he be missing?"

"He escaped," my agent said, lying down with a soft groan. "Someone helped him, of course. Two guards and the keeper are dead."

I frowned. "Well, there is nothing we can do about it now. Does Lord Potiphar know?"

"He brought the news. I worry about this, Joseph. That man gives me the shivers. He will stop at nothing. When he looks at me I go all cold inside."

"I know the feeling," I said. "I met a beggar once in Shechem that did the same to me. I felt the evil in him."

Khay leaned back in relief. "Nice to know someone else has had this feeling. I thought I was crazy for a while."

"I doubt it. And I will attend to this just as soon as the audience is over."

"Wish I could go," Khay said wistfully as I walked out.

"Asenath," I called, "are you ready to go? The audience is to start soon." I turned around and froze in amazement.

She stood in the doorway, but a stunning Asenath I had never seen. Rather than come elaborately dressed as most court ladies did, she had chosen to remain very simple. Her linen was spotless and pleated to fall gracefully to the floor. The gold belt holding it flashed in the light. Her simple sandals had a single jewel in the center of her foot and most surprising of all, she wore no wig. Instead her own hair was perfectly coiffed, and she had put in a single blue lotus. Her face was perfectly made up with nothing more than eye paint and lip color.

I gulped.

"Shall we go?" Asenath asked demurely. "We don't want to be late."

Unfortunately, I seemed rooted to the floor.

My wife smiled faintly with satisfaction and walked past me trailing a light scent of myrrh. I followed her as if pulled by a string.

"Do I really look well?" she asked in a low voice as we bumped along in the chariot to the palace in Thebes.

"I never thought I would see anyone as beautiful as my mother, until now," I said softly.

With a sigh she leaned against me in contentment.

As we walked onto the porch of the palace, an attendant discreetly told me that Pharaoh had requested both Asenath and me to come to his rooms. I smiled in anticipation.

"Yes, my lord?" I bowed as I entered the room where Amenemhet waited.

"Did Lady Asenath come with you?" he asked tersely.

"Yes, my lord."

"Perhaps it would be best if she did not come to the formal reception," he suggested. "It is not a venue in which she seems comfortable."

"That would be very disappointing for her," I said. "She dressed very carefully for this event. I know she looked forward to it. Would you like to see her?"

The king turned slightly red. "Well, I suppose," he said, looking uncomfortable.

I went to the door and ushered her in. She bowed gracefully and murmured her greeting in a perfectly modulated voice.

Pharaoh didn't even bother to try to respond. He just stared at her with all the power of his being.

Then he looked at me as I put my arm around my wife and just smiled.

Amenemhet swallowed, then swallowed again. His face grew extremely red. "Get out," he whispered.

Very quickly I turned Asenath, and we hurried from the room. Once in the hall, she turned worried eyes to mine. "Was he angry?" she asked.

I shook my head. "No, he was about to laugh harder than he ever has in his life. I wager the audience will begin a bit late. It will take him a while to control himself."

"Do I look funny?" my wife asked in alarm.

"Oh, no," I assured her. "You look absolutely stunning. And Amenemhet is anticipating the reaction of every courtier and lady to seeing you. You see, the entire court has been snickering behind my back since your father sent you to my house. Pharaoh must preserve his dignity, however, so he has to laugh in private."

"They have been laughing at you because of me?" Then she paused. "Yes, I suppose they would. I hadn't considered that." Then her chin came up, and a gleam appeared in her eye.

The old palace in Thebes sparkled that afternoon. It was the most important audience of the year, and everyone with any status came to renew their allegiance to Pharaoh, look at what the nomarchs wore, and disparage every other person in court except themselves.

Asenath and I stood quietly in the small anteroom waiting for Pharaoh, and I listened to the whispers and conversations in the hall. Everyone wondered what would happen today, for all knew of the nomarchs' opposition to me.

I smiled grimly. They would have several surprises today. Then I looked at the woman at my side and my smile softened. Not the least of which would be my wife.

Amenemhet arrived with his Great Royal Wife, who looked for the longest time at Asenath with a twinkle in her eyes. Asenath blushed, and the lady leaned toward her. "You outshine them all," she said.

Then Amenemhet signaled Nekhty, and the door opened to begin the audience.

When Pharaoh and his wife were seated on the thrones on the dais, Nekhty faced the door and announced, "Lord Paanekh and Lady Asenath."

We walked into the room, and I kept the pace a little slow, unable to resist the temptation to show off who I had beside me. I was not disappointed. The more gasps and whispers that swirled around us, the higher Asenath carried her head and the more desirable she looked. After bowing to Pharaoh, I took her hand and ushered her to the side, then assumed my place by the throne.

We went through the formalities of announcing my appointment, and then the nomarchs came forward to pledge their loyalty.

Lord Mose appeared first. He bowed correctly to Pharaoh.

"That which you command is that which shall be done, sovereign and lord."

Amenemhet nodded his head graciously, and Lord Mose turned to me. I caught the glint of humor in his eyes when he touched one knee to the floor and said, "I am yours to command, my lord."

Pharaoh sat extremely still, his eyes wide.

"Thank you, Lord Mose," I said. "I shall depend on you."

"You may, my lord."

When he stepped to the side, I composed my face for the next nomarch. He approached the throne and bowed to Pharaoh, repeating the same words as Mose. Then he turned to me, his face white. He dared not do less than Lord Mose and he fully realized the peril in which he still stood.

Amenemhet sat and watched in amazement as the southern nomarchs, one and all, trembled as they made their obeisance to him and to me, some of them hardly able to speak.

The Great Ueb's of the principal temples brought greetings to Pharaoh from his brother gods, and the principal lords and ladies were presented next. Long before the end, I knew my ankles would exact payment for this, and I did not look forward to paying up.

After the formal audience Pharaoh withdrew to the private reception room, and the court moved to the state dining room where tables piled with food awaited them.

By the time Lord Potiphar signaled to me to attend to Pharaoh, Asenath had enjoyed herself thoroughly. She gave me the wickedest smile as I left.

"By my Ka, you are the most impossible man in my kingdom," Amenemhet greeted me the moment I walked into the personal audience room with Lord Potiphar.

I bowed. "Have I displeased you, my lord?"

The king put his head in his hands. "You are lucky I do not order your immediate execution," he said, exasperated. "Two days ago, the southern nomarchs would not build storehouses for grain. Now, if I mistake not, those same nomarchs are begging for orders so they can obey them."

"My lord, El Shaddai wishes your land to live," I replied. "The instructions you provided proved very effective."

"Instructions?" Amenemhet echoed, frowning. "I don't remember ordering instructions written."

"In regard to the Inner Circle, my lord," Potiphar spoke up.

"All I said was to let Lord Paanekh handle it and not to bother me about it."

"Yes, my lord. That is what Nekhty wrote up," Lord Potiphar replied.

Pharaoh looked hard at me. "And I suppose you stamped them with my signet," he growled.

"I understood they represented your will, my lord," I said, glancing at Lord Potiphar. He had said nothing to me of how he got the orders.

"Well?" Amenemhet said.

"I convened a special court of inquiry under those orders my lord."

"And the change I saw today resulted from that, I suppose. Now, if you will explain how squashing a religious charlatan frightened my nomarchs so much that they tremble when you look at them, I will go to my death satisfied."

I glanced again at Lord Potiphar who avoided my gaze. "Well, my lord, one thing sort of led to another," I explained, unsure how much I should reveal.

Amenemhet folded his arms and looked murderous.

"Lord Paanekh is correct, my lord," Potiphar said, coming to my rescue. "The investigation moved quickly beyond religious charlatanry, taking some very surprising twists. I believe Lord Paanekh handled it wisely and well. At the end, we arrested Lord Meritifi for treason."

"Against whom?" Amenemhet asked sharply.

"Against you, my lord. We placed him in Pharaoh's prison last night, but he escaped by this morning. Two guards and the keeper were killed."

"It seems we underestimated him," Pharaoh remarked.

"To my shame, my lord," Potiphar confessed. "I have not served Pharaoh well in this matter."

"No one could have done better, friend. What else?"

"Lord Meritifi's nome was taken from him and his family. He was sentenced to death, his family to exile from Egypt," I answered. "Lord Amony and his son, Lord Hernofret, were found guilty of conspiracy against my life and against Lady Asenath's life. They have been stripped of lands and estates, sentenced to severe beating, and exiled from Egypt along with their families. All properties and estates are now the possession of Pharaoh, to be handled as you wish."

"So the investigation turned into a trial for treason, did it?" Amenemhet smiled grimly. "I wager those haughty nomarchs found a treason charge very uncomfortable. I am surprised they submitted to questioning."

"As you gave me complete and entire discretionary powers in the matter, they didn't have much choice," I told him.

"Complete and entire—" Pharaoh sputtered, jerking around to stare. "Potiphar, what is the meaning of this?"

Lord Potiphar slipped to his knees. "I could think of no other way, my lord," he said. "I suspected more to this than heresy. Lord Paanekh needed the nomarchs entirely at his mercy, and you would have hesitated to abandon them. Lord Paanekh's loyalty is unquestionable, my lord, so I exercised my own judgment in the matter. I beg your indulgence, Lord Nimaatre, I did not know how else to protect Pharaoh's life."

Amenemhet turned his back, in spite of Lord Potiphar's use of his personal name. "And you?" he snapped at me.

"Lord Paanekh knew nothing of this, my lord," Potiphar answered. "He accepted the orders as coming directly from your hand."

"You have seriously displeased me, Lord Potiphar," the king said in a hard voice. "And it galls me exceedingly to admit your wisdom," he added, softening. "But entire discretionary powers? Without my review?" He turned back to Lord Potiphar, shaking his head in wonder. "What they must have thought!"

Then a smile crept onto his face, and he looked at me. "No wonder they shook in their sandals this afternoon. They would have no idea what a barbarian Tate might take it into his head to do! By the gods, I wish my father was alive. If he could have seen this day, watching those haughty nomarchs lick the dust like the snakes they are—especially that pestilential Peun from Beni Hassan." He chuckled at the thought.

"I will overlook your action, Lord Potiphar," Amenemhet decided, "since you were correct, and all turned out well. However, see that nothing like this happens again. I expect to be kept fully informed from now on."

"That which you command is that which shall be done, Great One," the Captain of the Guard replied as he rose from his knees.

"Now that you have tamed my nomarchs, what happens next?" Pharaoh asked, turning to me.

"The nomarchs will leave tomorrow for their respective nomes and will begin building storehouses for grain," I answered. "Lord Mose will oversee their progress. Be prepared to receive a great many back taxes and concession payments."

"And after that?"

"After that, we build more storehouses."

CHAPTER 26

I stayed in the south until the end of Harvest. Remembering Teti, the Inspector of the Works who had impressed me so much at Lord Potiphar's tomb, I made him Chief Superintendent for Building Pharaoh's Storehouses at Thebes.

Under his guidance, the storehouses rose rapidly. Many of the nomarchs concluded there would indeed be a tremendous harvest this year and saw the need for some place to put the grain. In the Delta Shenbu's third try produced a storehouse that kept grain dry, and Sheshon dizzily tried to get more storehouses ready. That first year he filled one section of a storehouse before the next was even finished. Somehow we managed to house all the grain.

Spending endless hours with Mahesa working out the details of administration and distribution of food, I divided Egypt into three departments. The Department of the Head of the South included the first 12 nomes and had its headquarters in Thebes. The Department of the South took in the next 12 nomes and currently had its headquarters in Memphis, but that would soon change. The Delta became the Department of the North.

I designed the administration buildings for the three Departments of Egypt myself. They consisted of a series of large open courts, one for each nome. Offices, reception rooms, and anterooms surrounded the courts. Storage rooms for documents and records attached to the courts as well.

On the trip back to Memphis, I debated where to put the headquarters for the Department of the South. I sat on the upper deck, the breeze ruffling my hair as we floated with the current northward. The wadis on the west bank caught my eye as they did every time I traveled the river. Some provided avenues for run-off from Inundation to flow back into the Nile, but others seemed to flow into the desert.

"Mahesa, where do the wadis going into the desert flow?" I asked suddenly.

"There is a long channel beyond the ridge where a second Nile sometimes flows," he answered. "It goes from south of Abydos to the great basin of the Fayyum beyond Itej-Tawy. During Inundation it always makes a second river."

"Does it, now," I muttered, staring at the west bank. "Mahesa, we will put the headquarters for the Department of the South west of Itej-Tawy, between it and the Fayyum," I decided.

"Yes, my lord, but why there?" he asked, puzzled.

"I think the Fayyum needs a lake," I replied absently. "Send Shenbu to me as soon as we get to Memphis."

"Yes, my lord," Mahesa said, making a note and privately thinking I was overstressed.

▲ ▲ ▲ ▲

"I don't like it," Khay said for the hundredth time as he limped around the room in the Memphis palace.

"I know," I said, "but there is nothing to be done about it now. Lord Meritifi has disappeared. We will just have to keep a sharp watch. He will show up again."

"That is exactly what worries me," he muttered, walking out.

I wanted to snap at him to keep his worries to himself, but I bit my tongue. I felt tired and drained, and I wanted to throw the whole of Egypt into the Nile and watch it wash away.

Mahesa had just returned from an inspection tour, I had numerous reports from the supervisors all over Egypt, and Lord Mose reported in as well. It didn't take a priest to interpret what I had before me.

The nomarchs did not believe there would be a famine. Only those who had actually been in the throne room that day were serious about building. The others did it because they must. I had counted on the nomarchs to build private storehouses for their nomes as well as helping with the state ones, but I had to accept the bitter truth that they would not.

This doubled the burden on the state and on me. The nomarchs were delighted with the crops growing in the fields, but Khay told me they planned on selling the grain, not storing it. But we needed that grain!

I looked at the report from Khafra in the treasury. Supplying the corvee to build the granaries to hold the first year's harvest had drained Pharaoh's resources, even after applying the back taxes from the nomes. And now I faced the building season for the second year with nothing.

I could have gone insane with frustration. The nomarchs had the means to build hundreds of private storehouses, but they refused. No matter how much I tried to convince them, no matter what I said or did, they would not believe. If they sold the grain, they couldn't get much for it. It would be a glut on the markets, more of a nuisance than a commodity . . .

I stopped right there. "El Shaddai," I whispered, "El Shaddai, make this plain to me." Picking up a reed pen, I pulled a sheet of papyrus toward me. By the end of the day, I had the entire answer drawn out. Everything fitted. I did not need to beat my head against the wall of the nomarchs' stubbornness. Nor did I need to worry about anything except building storehouses and filling them with grain. The rest would take care of itself.

"Thank you, El Shaddai," I said aloud. "You have provided for me once again. Now, I need the pieces to put together. Please send them."

"Talking to yourself already?" Khay inquired as he entered the room and saw that I was alone.

"You know how it goes," I said. "Sometimes only El Shaddai listens."

"He certainly listens to you, and sometimes I swear he listens to me."

I glanced at him. "Have you asked him to?" I asked casually, getting to my feet.

"Yes. More than once."

"That pleases Him," I said. "Ready to go?"

"Yes, Joseph," Khay replied. He did not look at me, but I knew that the conversation we had just had was very significant to him. I respected his privacy, however, and did not press the matter.

The next day, I told Khay what I needed him to do now. Then I contacted Jetur.

▲ ▲ ▲ ▲

"Well, I have done what I could," Khay said with a sigh as he and I lagged behind Amenemhet and Potiphar in the garden of the palace in Itej-Tawy. Almost six months had passed since I sent him out on his assignment, and we were here for a private dinner with Lord Potiphar and Amenemhet. We planned to discuss the final arrangements for Khay's training.

"Every part of the networks you wanted are in place except one, and you have to establish that one yourself," Khay went on. "You can now buy grain anywhere, and no one will know."

"Good," I said with a sigh. "That is a great burden off my mind."

"I still don't see what you will do with it all," he added, puzzled. "I did some figuring, and if the next five years are like these, you will have collected more grain that Egypt could possibly use for the next 20 years! And the famine is supposed to last for only seven."

"I cannot explain it myself, Khay," I said softly. "I just know that I must store all the grain I can get my hands on. Nothing else will give me peace."

"So you will buy."

"Yes, I will buy. I will purchase every bushel of grain in the country if I can, and for that I will need more of the White, gold, and goods than Pharaoh has. I am depending on the trade networks you just set up to make up the lack. When it is over Pharaoh will be a pauper, but there will be food for the famine. How did you do it so fast?"

Khay grinned. "Most of my information networks involve traders and merchants," he confessed. "Mahesa's father, Chety, is the central point in the south in Thebes. Jetur is the hub in the north, and he already has an astounding operation going for you."

I nodded. The old Ishmaelite trader had somehow managed to provide enough gold, White, and barter goods to stay current with the corvee. And that only because I insisted on paying most of the corvee in grain. But in the years to come I must store grain, not pay it out.

"I smell leeks!" Khay said, looking ahead to the attendant approaching. "And here comes our food. Oops, he nearly had our meal on the ground," he grinned. We walked to the bench where

Amenemhet waited. "You are looking well, Lord Khay," the king said. "What is this I hear of another child?"

The young lord blushed. "To be born before next harvest, Great One," he said proudly. "Little Khay, our first, will have a close companion as he grows up." He glanced up as the attendant nearly lost the basket again, awkwardly correcting to ease it on the table. Then Khay frowned as the man stepped back slightly.

I looked into the basket and turned to Chaf.

"My lord Pharaoh!" Khay shouted, launching himself forward.

I whirled around, my heart suddenly in my throat. Khay's bad leg hindered him, but he managed to thrust his body between Amenemhet and the attendant. I saw a flash of light, and then Khay tumbled to the ground.

The attendant turned to flee, but Lord Potiphar had his sword out already, and a split second after he struck, Chaf thrust with his spear.

Scrambling forward, I dropped to my knees beside Khay, turning him over. The dagger was deep in his chest, and his blood stained my hands and linen. His eyes fluttered open, and he looked at me.

"Your God has very strong arms," he said. "He is holding me."

And then he was gone.

"Khay?" I said. "Khay?"

He did not answer, nor would he ever again.

Above my head, Amenemhet asked in a hard voice, "Who is it?"

"Lord Meritifi," Potiphar replied. "He will not trouble my lord again."

"Throw his body into the desert," Amenemhet ordered. "Let the vultures and jackals take their own."

"Yes, my lord," Potiphar replied. "Chaf, will you bring two more guards? You did well," he added. "Either of us would have killed him."

The guard nodded. "But neither of us saved Lord Khay," he said bitterly.

I heard the voices above me, but I could not make myself feel they were important. What was important was the body in my arms, the boy who had teased me, the young man who had stood by my side and found out things in the markets, the steward who risked his life to save me from Lord Potiphar's anger, and then the builder of the trade system that would provide the means to save Egypt. What was I to do without him? He had never failed me.

"You must let him go, Lord Paanekh," Chaf said beside me, loosening my hands.

"No," I said. "He means too much to me."

"Please, Lord Paanekh."

"No," I cried. "He is my brother!" Tears streamed down my face.

The next thing I knew Asenath had her arms around me, holding me tight. "Joseph, Joseph," she whispered. "You must let him go. Pharaoh has ordered that he be embalmed. There is a chamber near Pharaoh's own tomb for him. You must come home. You must let go."

I did, and they took his now cold body away from me. "El Shaddai," I cried out. "Why? I don't understand."

Once again, Asenath held me while I wept.

We mourned Lord Khay for 30 days. Ten days after that, we placed him in a chamber near Amenemhet's pyramid near Itej-Tawy. The ceremonies and rites did nothing to comfort me. Only the last words Khay said to me brought a measure of ease.

After the funeral I continued on south while Asenath returned to Memphis with Hetepi. Khay's wife stayed at our residence while she considered what to do. With another baby coming, she needed some way to support herself. Asenath forbade me to offer her a job of any kind, and I bowed to her superior knowledge of the young widow's mind.

The problem solved itself when her husband's information network simply switched to her. By the time she was halfway along to the birth, she fed me information as efficiently as Khay himself. Quietly I put her on the state payroll, and just as quietly she accepted.

Only then did I allow my mind to turn away from my friend's death. Now I must think of the living, for famine waited for no human being.

I finished my inspection tour. We had enough storehouses to hold the royal fifth of grain this second year as well as to hold what I would purchase. Now I turned my attention to the missing piece of the trade networks that Khay had left for me.

I had set up the networks on the premise that the nomarchs had plenty of income to build storehouses, but refused to do so on their own. I would insert a middle man between the nomarchs and their vendors and buyers. By heavily taxing those vendors or buyers who did not go through the middleman or his agents, I could control the majority of trade. As trade concessions became available I would place them with my agents, gradually gaining even more control. The nomarchs would make payment in goods and precious metals when they bought and sold from my middleman who would then use those same metals and goods to purchase grain that would be selling for an extremely low price because of the surplus. The rest of the profits would go to Pharaoh's treasury to support the corvee.

Jetur had quickly obtained a good hold on the markets in the north. Several important trade concessions had come up for renewal, and I placed them with his agents. Others had been revoked or ignored because they were too small to bother with.

Lord Meritifi had held several concessions in the south, and I placed them in Chety's hands. But the principal luxury trade in the south was with Kush. The feathers, skins, and wood from south of the great desert of Deshret in Nubia were in much demand, and the lords and nomarchs would pay well for them. To control this trade, I needed a treaty with Kush that would restrict the importation of such luxuries through Chety and his agents.

As I sat in the darkness on the high deck of the barge I listed in my mind the possible assets available to me to negotiate a treaty. Not least, I would need a reliable translator, preferably one who understood what I needed to do.

Benabi. Time and again he had proved his trustworthiness to Saf, faithfully carrying out his duties. Jetur tried to purchase him from me, but I flatly refused, much to Saf's relief.

Again I marveled at how El Shaddai arranged events so that I would have what I needed when I required it, although I should have been used to that now. I sent immediately to Memphis for the young Kushite.

"Thank you for coming," I said when Benabi bowed before me.

"I was happy to, my lord."

"I understand Saf was reluctant to let you come," I commented.

The Kushite showed his white teeth in a grin. "He came close to cursing you, my lord. I have never seen him in such a state. Inti finally confessed that he spoke Canaanite and promised to take my place. Only then did we get any peace!"

I looked the young man over. He was growing into a giant of a man and had learned much in the time he had spent in Memphis. Then I stared out on the Nile as it glided past the sides of the transport.

"If I were to offer you a trip home now, would you accept?" I asked without warning.

Benabi glanced at me, and then blushed as much as he could beneath his dark skin.

"I thought so," I said with a smile. "It is hard to be away from home."

"Yes, my lord, it is," he agreed softly.

As I usually did, I attended on Pharaoh as soon as I arrived in Thebes.

"I am glad you are here," Amenemhet told me. "I just got word that a deputation from Kush is coming. It is time to renew our trade treaties, and the Kushite king is on his way."

Bowing my head, I silently gave thanks to El Shaddai whose timing is always perfect.

"Do you wish me to conduct the trade sessions, my lord?" I asked.

"That is exactly what I want. You know these trade treaties are the bane of my life. But you seem to revel in them. At least you have lately. I wish you all luck with this one, however. The Kushite king seems bent on opening up trade as much as possible. He has come to the throne since the last treaty, so I know nothing of him or his mind.

"The nomarchs favor open trade, naturally. I cannot afford to lose control, for I will get even less profit from it than I do now. At the same time, I dare not limit it more than currently. If I did I would have armed revolt on my hands. I shall, therefore, leave it up to you to find a way to control trade when both sides want it open."

"As you wish, my lord," I said. "I will do my best."

Amenemhet chuckled. "I will wait to see what you pull from the air this time, Lord Paanekh," he challenged.

"Yes, my lord," I said with a smile.

My smile faded as soon as he left. This was very bad news, considering what I needed to do. Would the trade networks Khay had established fail because I could not put in place the last piece? What would happen to Egypt? I turned to El Shaddai again, begging him to provide for my need.

The state audience took place in the formal throne room and was mercifully short. My ankles had bothered me a lot lately, and I stayed off them as much as possible. Standing in the throne room made them ache unmercifully.

The Kushite king was a giant, at least seven feet tall, with an imposing dignity and presence that matched Amenemhet's own. They greeted each other and then arranged for the negotiations to take place without either of them present. Amenemhet introduced me as deputizing for him, and another large Kushite stepped forward in his turn. I worried even more, since I must try and understand the Kushite king from second-hand knowledge as I worked on a treaty, putting me at a double disadvantage.

In spite of my own worry, I noticed Benabi's nervousness as we headed for the negotiation room the next morning.

"What is it, Benabi?"

He hesitated, then said, "My lord, I do not know what my reception will be by the delegation. There were events in my country that forced me to leave. The people who have come will either be very glad to see me—or very unhappy."

"How unhappy?"

"They may try to kill me, my lord," he confessed.

"Thank you for telling me this, Benabi. We will just have to take what comes."

"Yes, my lord."

I was prepared then, when we walked into the room. No one noticed Benabi until he spoke, and then every head in the Kushite delegation jerked up to see him.

The next instant, pandemonium broke loose. The Kushites jumped up, shouting and gesturing in their own language. One Kushite rushed from the room. The guardsmen in the room leaped forward to protect me, but I waved them away. The Kushites wanted Benabi, not me. Some of the delegation began to weep, and all of them reached out to touch the young man, crowding around with hands outstretched.

Benabi let them approach and touched each one.

I smiled to myself, having judged him rightly. He was royalty to them.

The door to the room burst open, and the Kushite king entered. The delegation quickly sorted itself out and drew away to leave the young man facing the king. Benabi bowed formally and spoke.

The Kushite king drew himself up and responded, then could hold back no longer and held out trembling arms. Benabi took two steps and threw himself into the king's arms, clinging to him tightly. It could only be his father.

A dagger of pain struck my heart. I had to get away. The longing for Abi overwhelmed me, and I entered the first empty room I found. Leaning against the wall, I bowed my head and wept for my lostness.

When I finally composed myself, I returned to the negotiations room.

The Kushite king waited for me there. "My son says he is a slave," he said in Canaanite.

"He is," I replied in the same language.

"I'm grateful to have found him. I wish to buy him back."

"He's not for sale."

The king's eyes darkened with anger, and he moved in his chair. Benabi spoke to him, and he eased back, studying me.

"Why?" the king asked.

"I'm repaying a debt," I replied. "Your son brought to mind a Kushite who saved me from a lion when I was young and lived in Canaan. I purchased him to keep him from masters who would have been cruel. Allow me now to repay the debt I owe your land. Take him with you. There is no purchase price for your son."

The king's eyes widened, and he stared at me, looking keenly at my eyes.

"You are not Egyptian?" he asked.

"No."

Again the king studied me, puzzlement in his expression.

"Where was this lioness?" he asked.

I paused. I had said lion, not lioness. "Near Shechem."

The king cocked his head and stared at my face and wig for the longest time.

"Habiru, would you by chance have red hair?" he asked, his eyes full of merriment and a huge smile on his lips.

My mouth dropped open. That smile, those eyes! "Kush?" I nearly shouted.

He threw back his head and laughed. Getting up, he removed the ceremonial cape covered with feathers and turned his left shoulder to me. There were the thin scars that matched my own.

Tearing off the gold collar I wore, I showed him my right shoulder.

"Habiru, Habiru," Kush said, putting his great hands on my shoulders. "How often I have wondered what happened to you."

"And I you," I said, gripping his arms. "I see you are king now."

"Yes. When my uncle died, my father became king, and when he died, I became king. There were those who didn't want me to rule, and they raised a rebellion. My son was threatened, and I sent him to Egypt to remain until the situation settled one way or the other. But he ran into trouble and ended up enslaved.

"Thank you, Habiru, for treating him with kindness. You have amply repaid your debt, and I now owe you." He smiled that huge smile. "I never dreamed when I threw us both off the ledge that I was saving my own son!"

"And I didn't guess when I purchased him how critical he would be to the salvation of Egypt," I replied.

I returned to Memphis after successfully settling the trade with Kush in Chety's hands. As the second harvest ended, grain came onto the market, and the trade network Khay had organized began to operate. Soon grain flowed constantly into my hands. I required only one thing of the trade merchants—a strict accounting of every bushel of grain they sent to the storehouses—and I demanded that the storehouses keep an equally strict account of every bushel they received. Mahesa maintained the records and sent me a daily summary.

Potiphar had remained as Captain of the Guard and I lent him Chaf, who had become adept at organizing a personal guard. Pharaoh approved of him, and I reluctantly gave Chaf up to Amenemhet.

I left the palace early the afternoon Lord Potiphar presented me with the records of the investigation into Khay's death. Taking them into my private garden, I began to read. Lord Meritifi had gained admission to the palace by bribing an attendant named Tais to smuggle him in and let him take his place serving Pharaoh. His name seemed familiar, and I searched my mind until I remembered Abana had talked of him when I first became Tate. She had overheard him telling Sekhmet where my rooms were.

A cold chill ran up my spine. In all the excitement of finding Lord Sety and sending Lord Amony away, I had never dealt with Tais. My hands shook. At the very least he should have been banished from the palace, barred from working there again. I read on. The other kitchen staff reported that Tais had been no more sullen and bitter than usual, so no one suspected anything out of the ordinary.

Abana reported that two days before the attempt on

Amenemhet's life, Tais had bragged to her that soon he would leave his job, that he would not have to work anymore. He had seemed highly pleased with something.

I skipped over the report of what happened in the garden. What I had not known was the discovery of Tais' body in a little-used storage room. Lord Meritifi had apparently murdered him after taking his place as Pharaoh's attendant for the meal. The body was formally identified as Tais, son of Manakh, the baker.

The name hit me like a body blow. Manakh, the Chief Baker executed by Pharaoh when I was in prison. The words Abana had heard ran through my mind. "Feels good to get paid for revenge, doesn't it?" Sekhmet had not meant his own revenge, as I had thought, but Tais' revenge against me and Pharaoh. I had missed it! Everything about Tais cried out for investigation, and I had done nothing! And because of that, Pharaoh had been endangered and Khay had died. My carelessness had cost Khay his life.

Sorrow and guilt flooded through me. I had failed my brother here in Egypt.

Asenath found me late that night still in the garden. She sat beside me in silence, her warmth comforting me.

"What is it?" she asked. "Khay's death?"

How did she know these things? I let the question slip my mind and nodded in the darkness. "I should have known," I said bitterly. "Tais was the son of Manakh, the baker condemned to death by Pharaoh years ago. The man never should have been in the palace. I should have investigated. I should have seen. Then Khay would still be alive."

"You are not a god, Joseph," Asenath reminded me gently. "You cannot see and do everything perfectly all the time. Lord Potiphar is responsible for Pharaoh's safety, and he, too, missed recognizing Tais as a danger. You cannot blame yourself."

"But I still do," I confessed. "I miss Khay so much, Asenath. It hurts all the time."

"We all miss him. But what of El Shaddai? Does He not direct your affairs? Surely He had a hand in this as well."

I did not know what to answer her, so I said nothing.

My depression followed me for days. I struggled to understand why my God had not interfered. Why had He not directed me to investigate Tais? Why did Khay die at the beginning of his career with a family that loved him growing around him? It seemed so senseless and wrong. Night after night, I stayed in the garden after Asenath had retired and looked at the stars and argued in my heart with El Shaddai. One night as the moon shone into the garden, I noticed that the branches of a tree created a rough square of light and shadow. It took me back to the days of my imprisonment when I would go into the anteroom at night and stare up through the grill to the outside.

Then I remembered what El Shaddai had said to me then. He did not ask me to understand, only to obey. I played with the thought, realizing that in obeying I eventually came to understand. I could not see any reason for my sale into slavery, yet now I knew it for an essential part of my life. I had to come to Egypt. I had to learn to govern, and to serve, and to understand the markets of the world. I had to go to prison to know dependence on El Shaddai, so that I would be ready and close to Pharaoh's hand when this great land faced death. El Shaddai had chosen me, not I Him.

The God of my fathers had chosen Khay as well. My life had been under El Shaddai's direct control, and from what Khay had said, he too had placed himself in El Shaddai's hands. I had to learn this lesson again and again. While El Shaddai knew what He was doing, I did not. It was not necessary for me to understand what He did or why. My part was to obey, to do as best I could what He placed before me to do. The rest was in His hands.

"Forgive me, El Shaddai," I whispered in the night. "In my grief, I forget."

In my heart, that small pinpoint of warmth appeared again, growing slowly until it filled my whole being with peace and rest.

▲ ▲ ▲ ▲

I listened in puzzlement as Mahesa verbally chewed up a second scribe this morning. Although he had been unusually silent for the past several days, this was the third time he had exploded over a trifle. When the scribe scuttled away, white-faced and certain his job would be taken from him, I summoned Mahesa into my room and had him shut the door.

"Sit down," I said.

He took his usual spot at the other scribe's table and picked up the pen expectantly. His face was composed, but the pen shook in his hand.

"What is troubling you, Mahesa?"

"Nothing is troubling me, my lord."

"Mahesa, I am not a fool."

When he glanced up involuntarily, I held his gaze. He endured it for several seconds, then had to look away.

"It is not fitting for me to tell my lord," he hedged.

"I am not concerned with what is fitting. You are an old friend, Mahesa. What is troubling you?"

With a sound like a sob, he put his elbows on the table and his head in his hands. "I cannot forget Khay," he said, clearing his throat. "He would have gone far and been great, and he was cut down by that—" Mahesa stopped and swallowed a few times. "It is all so useless.

"But you," he burst out, "you mourn for Khay and are troubled for a while, yet now you are at peace. I cannot find peace. Khay should not have died. He had a wife and child, and—"

He looked up at me. "It is the same as before," he said, almost savagely. "You were not afraid when you were a slave. You grieve and mourn deeply for Khay and your grandfather, but you have peace. What is it? Khay found it. Why not I?"

By now Mahesa was practically shouting. In his eyes I saw that strange consuming hunger I had seen once before and had not understood. "What do you have? Please, please tell me!" he pleaded.

"I will tell you, Mahesa. But first, tell me what you meant when you said Khay had it, too."

The scribe sighed, rubbing his eyes with his palms. "How much do you know of Khay's background?"

"Only that his family came from the south somewhere and that a great wrong was done them. Lord Potiphar took them in after they nearly starved to death."

"They were neighbors of my family in Thebes. Khay's father was a very rich man who supervised the construction of royal tombs. He offended a nomarch, however, one of Lord Amony's friends. The nomarch decided to ruin him and hired Hutor to do it."

"Hutor?" I asked quickly. "The same Hutor?"

"The very same. As you know, Hutor was very efficient and absolutely loyal to his employer, whoever that might be. He did his work well and drove Khay's family from Thebes penniless. The nomarch rewarded him well, and that is how he got started as a Supervisor of Works. He lived the rest of his life in peace, living comfortably on his income and standing on the ruined lives of Khay's family.

"Khay hated him bitterly. And then he met you on Lord Potiphar's estate. He grew up and became a lord and set up an information network for the Tate of Egypt. Do you know what he found during its very beginning? Proof that Hutor had destroyed his father.

"He brought it to me one night. Showed me the records. He had the power to crush Hutor, but when I asked him what he would do, he just flashed that grin of his and said he thought some man that you knew would take care of Hutor and that he had other things to attend to. He never said another word about it.

"Who is this man?" Mahesa demanded. "You mentioned him before, when I asked about your not being afraid. Who is this man that you sent Khay to? How does this person do what he does? How does he help you?"

The scribe's voice broke, and he lowered his head again, squeezing his eyes shut.

I had to steady my own voice before I spoke. I had no idea that Khay had watched me so closely or come to understand so much from just the few times I had talked to him of my God.

"El Shaddai is not a man, Mahesa," I said. "He is my God."

"Your god?" Mahesa echoed, jerking his head up. "Your god cares? How do you get him to pay attention to you? What offerings do you bring?"

I raised my hands to stop his questions. "El Shaddai needs no encouragement to care about you, Mahesa. He loves you already just because you are alive. You see, El Shaddai says that He made the entire world and everything in it. That includes you, Mahesa. When I first was sold, I gave myself entirely to El Shaddai and vowed that I would serve Him with all that I had. He put me where I could learn what I needed to know and then honored my efforts to please Him."

"Where is His temple?" Mahesa asked. "Where can I go and see Him?"

"He has no temple. The Creator, He cannot be found within walls or in a stone statue. Nor does He need priests to tend Him or people to protect Him or feed Him or remind Him to retain maat.

He is above and beyond and separate from all that. He is everywhere, all the time, and as close as His name.

"If you would speak with Him, Mahesa, just say His name wherever you are, and He will hear. He will come and listen, and you can tell Him whatever is on your heart. If you give Him your life, He will accept it and direct it and bring to you all the good things that you need. But you must trust Him, for He will not do things in the way you think He should or would like Him to.

"I did not think I should be sold as a slave, but you see where El Shaddai placed me in the end. It is this which gives such peace. I cannot direct my life as well as He can, so I give it to Him and He takes care of everything. He is as strong as a mountain and as tender as a mother nursing her child. El Shaddai will provide, he will comfort, he will even give you understanding if you obey and wait and trust."

"How do you know these things?" Mahesa asked urgently. "Who told you? Will He accept me? I am not of your land."

The door to my room remained shut long into the night, and no one dared to interrupt as I recited for Mahesa the stories of El Shaddai's dealings with my family and talked to him of the ways and wishes of the Creator God. His hunger for my words was almost frightening, and his sharp mind and incisive thought tested and tried my knowledge and understanding of the things I told him. I do not know if I always said the right things or gave him the right answers. But I simply told him what had happened in my own life. It was all I had to tell.

CHAPTER 27

I rubbed my eyes and reread the message from Jetur, not knowing what to reply. Renseneb had cut deeply into Pharaoh's profits again over a matter of wood that we desperately needed for building. As always the treasury was all but empty, and I could not afford to lose so much as a single deben.

Nor did I have the time to investigate. Hetepi had sent out word to her networks, but nothing had come back. I was incredibly tired, torn between the necessity to build storehouses and to juggle grain, goods, and gold in payments from one place to another to try to keep up with the demands of the building supervisors and the corvee.

Onami took me home through the dark streets and I fell into bed again, too tired even to talk to Asenath who was probably long asleep anyway. But I lay there on the bed unable to rest. I could build, or I could buy and sell, but I could not do both. In wild moments of despair, I thought of sending for Renseneb and ordering him to stop, but that would not halt the merchant he worked for. I needed to find that person.

At last I got up and went into my private garden. There I knelt in the moonlight. "You must show me what you want me to do," I told El Shaddai. "I do not know if I should turn my mind to trade or to building. Guide me, for I am too weary to go on."

Returning to my bed I at last fell asleep.

Two months later I sat at the stone table in the small reception room too tired to move. Mahesa had just left with Khafra, now Lord Treasurer to Pharaoh. Renseneb had beaten us again. Embalming spices this time. I could not let Pharaoh's household, which included every temple in the land, be without the essentials for burial. Khafra brought his records, which Mahesa had already checked, and I went over them a third time. The Treasury could not pay for the order.

I rested my head in my hands. Tomorrow I would send payment from my personal treasury for the spices. It was the third time I had done this in the past few months.

"El Shaddai," I groaned, "why have You not answered me? Must Egypt die because I cannot buy sufficient grain? Because I cannot support the corvee? Who is this merchant who always knows just where to strike? I have done all I know to find him. I beg of you, El Shaddai, reveal him to me for I must deal with him in order for Egypt to live. Show me the way for I do not know where to turn."

I wanted to go to Asenath to hear her soft voice and feel the comfort of her arms, but I hesitated. I didn't know what to make of her lately. She seemed happy enough since she had finished redecorating the house. I loved the way she had done my bedchamber and now that she had finished I expected her to be home more. But she spent more time at the market instead, even though she rarely came home with anything. I wondered what she did. One or two probing questions brought me no information, and I didn't know what to do.

I smiled bitterly. That seemed a chronic state of affairs for me lately. I didn't know what to do about Asenath, about the markets, about the corvee, about the constant, scheming intrigues of the palace—about anything.

I told myself that she just enjoyed the goods offered for sale, but I didn't believe it. The thought entered my mind that she met there with someone, and after it surfaced I couldn't get rid of it. She came to me just as readily as ever, and her eyes always lit up when she saw me, but sometimes she seemed preoccupied, and I could never find out why.

I stared at the cracked table top. Inti stumped down the hall from Saf's room. Saf was working late too.

"Inti?" I called.

"Yes, my lord?" he said, stopping at the door.

"Inti, what does Lady Asenath do at the markets?"

The porter looked down. "Do not ask me that, my lord."

"But I am asking, Inti."

He remained silent for a long time. "I think she meets someone, my lord," he said finally.

"Who?"

"I do not know, my lord. If they do meet, they are very careful."

I ran my finger down the crack in the table top and back again. "Regularly?"

"Yes, my lord."

"When will she go to the market again?"

"Tomorrow."

"I think we will go to the market also, Inti."

"Yes, my lord." He stumped away.

I sat at the table until long after moon rise, tracing the crack with my finger and trying to understand. I had avoided asking Inti that question for weeks. What made me bring it up now? One part of me wanted to explode with rage and storm into Asenath's room and demand an explanation from her. Another part of me accepted the situation as inevitable. I was a barbarian after all, and she came from a family with roots in the South. Another part of me wanted to crawl into a hole and hide for the rest of my life. All of me hurt. Finally I went to bed. Tomorrow would come soon enough.

I waited in the shadow of an awning. The vender beside me had pomegranates, but for once I didn't want one. My stomach was upset. After I found out what there was to know, then what? I could have them both severely and publicly punished if I wished, but that would not heal the wound in my heart. I could send Asenath out of my house and leave her to the mercy of the streets, but no matter what she had done, I wouldn't do that. I loved her too much. As Potiphar had loved Tanefret.

And as for whom she met, I just didn't know. I could banish him, or send him to the mines, or some other such vengeful act, but what good would that do? My wife still preferred him to me, and the ache in my soul would still be there.

I saw Abi with new eyes, thinking back to what Reuben had done. At least I wasn't dealing with my son in this situation. I understood his anger now, for my own soul raged.

Asenath hurried into the square. She sent Hesy off and then crossed to the doorway I watched. But she didn't look guilty or furtive. In fact, she looked quite pleased about something. My wife went in with a smile on her face.

Almost I turned and walked away. But I knew that I must know the truth, so I grimly went to face the man Asenath wanted. I stepped through the doorway and looked around, but the room was empty. The curtain still stirred, however, so they were behind it. Inti, Esse, and Defatsen followed me in.

"You are here, Lady," a man's voice said. "Are you ready?"

"Yes," Asenath replied. "I found out—"

I couldn't wait any longer, and I stepped forward and swept aside the curtain, confronting the man who stared at me from across the small room.

"Renseneb!" I gasped.

"Lord Paanekh!" he said at the same time. His face turned whiter than linen as he dropped to his knees and froze.

I sat down on the first stool I saw, just staring at him. His pulse throbbed in his neck, and I counted the beats. Automatically I took off my wig and ran my hands through my hair. Now I really didn't know what to do. To think that my wife met with a stranger was bad enough, but to find that it was Renseneb was more than I could handle.

"What are you doing here, Joseph?" Asenath asked in bewilderment.

Renseneb jerked his head up in amazement, then his eyes widened. "Joseph?" he gasped. "Lord Potiphar's steward?" He looked around as if searching for someone and then brought his eyes back to me. Then he saw the wig on the table beside me. *"You* are Lord Paanekh?"

"Yes."

"Lord Potiphar's steward?" Asenath echoed, her eyes widening. "The one who attacked Lady Tanefret?"

My own shock melted before the growing apprehension in her eyes. Suddenly I realized that she could become afraid of me all over again.

"Asenath, you know what Lady Tanefret was like," I said wearily. "You also know that if Lord Potiphar thought I had really attacked her, he would have fed me alive to the crocodiles. I believe he mentioned it then. I would not have attacked her, and I did not."

"Then why did she— Oh!" Asenath said in a subdued tone. "But why did Lord Potiphar put you in prison?"

"What other choice did he have?"

"Why, that terrible woman!" she blazed. "How dared she? You were in that terrible prison and you had not done anything? That's—that's—" she stopped, too angry to find words.

Her rise to my defense soothed my pain a little. At least she cared some for me.

"Asenath, will you go outside with Inti?" I asked. "I wish to talk to Renseneb."

My wife looked from me to Renseneb and back, suddenly feeling the tension between us.

"Joseph, I should—"

"Now, Asenath," I said, barely controlling the sudden rage that exploded in my body.

Inti did not wait. He took her arm and drew her out of the house.

I stared at the wall over Renseneb's head, struggling to maintain my self-control.

"Will my lord listen?" he whispered.

Like a splash of cold water, I remembered how it felt to tremble before Lord Potiphar's rage for something I had not done.

"I have nothing better to do," I finally answered roughly.

He flushed and sweat broke out on his forehead.

"My lord, I have not acted dishonorably with your wife," he

said. "My lord must believe me in this. Lady Asenath is innocent. We have done nothing."

"Then what is your relationship?" I asked stiffly, holding onto my temper with all my might.

Renseneb remained silent.

"Answer me, Renseneb!" I thundered, sending the dish by my hand crashing against the wall.

He jumped, and the sweat dripped off him as he crouched lower on the floor. "My lord, I—that is, we—well—if it please my lord, I act for her in the markets."

Struck dumb, I couldn't look away from him. Had I heard correctly?

As my silence stretched longer and longer he gasped for breath.

"You are agent for *Lady Asenath?*" I finally managed to get out. He nodded.

"Lady Asenath has directed you all these years in the market?"

"Yes, my lord, and that is all," he said, looking up.

"Is it?" I asked, catching his eye and holding it. He loved her. I read it there in his soul.

"My lord, please!" he begged, and I broke the gaze.

"Perhaps you had better tell me the whole story," I said slowly, wondering about the broken sadness in the back of his eyes. "When did you begin working for her?"

"When she was 11. She gave me a mirror to sell."

"Eleven? A mirror?"

"It belonged to her mother, I believe," he went on. "It was of the White and very valuable. I sold it, and she told me what do to with the proceeds. At first she bought small things, but as she grew older, she went to larger and larger deals. At the time she came to you, she owned a house in On, two caravans, and two estates in the south."

I shook my head. "And now?"

"She had to start over. Her father sent her to you with no warning whatsoever and with nothing but what she wore."

"I noticed that."

"She did not have time to go to her room and get anything. My lady had her records there, her lists of sources and goods and her signet. I came back from a trip to Beni Hassan, and she had vanished. Gossip told me what had happened, and I managed to get into her room, but Hesy had already taken the most important lists and her signet."

"That is what she brought!" I exclaimed. "No wonder Asenath was pleased."

Renseneb took a deep breath. "I heard the rumors in the markets that she had died. I had to find out for myself, and not knowing whom to trust, I thought it best not to trust anyone."

"Wise of you," I said. "It turned out that Iutem, the attendant sent with her, was ordered to poison her."

"That is something Iutem would do," he said bitterly. "I hid myself in your garden one night, my lord," he said, his voice strained. "I saw Lady Asenath then, and we arranged to meet in the markets. She did not know how you would feel about her involvement in trade. After all, she had hid her activities from her father, and with you being a barbarian . . ." His voice trailed off. A pause. "It has always been of paramount importance to her to be independent and able to support herself," he finished finally.

"I am aware of why," I said quietly. "She told me."

"That is more than she has done for me. I have never known what happened." He waited.

"Go on," I directed.

"Before I could return to On and get the rest of her documents, Sosamen, the Great Ueb's steward, found them. He helped himself to all her properties. She had nothing left, and no way to recover her property without revealing what she had been doing.

"So, with her signet and contact with me, she began again. She is not quite back to where she was before, but she will be by next year. My lady owns property in Memphis, On, and Thebes. It has been slower this past year. We have been unable to acquire caravans, and someone has taken control of several concessions that . . ." his voice trailed away, and he looked at me, sudden understanding dawning in his eyes.

"I should have known," he groaned. "I should have known when I started having trouble in the south. I kept thinking the pattern was familiar, but the last I knew you were in prison, and I never dreamed—" He stopped speaking.

Surprisingly, I believed him. Now that I thought back, I should have guessed Renseneb acted for a woman long ago. She probably had attendants from the palace and noble houses feeding her information. She would know what court ladies planned, and could get to the market before them. It fitted perfectly.

"You love her," I stated.

"Yes, my lord," Renseneb admitted, looking down. "But I cannot love her as a man," he added. He drew his arms against his midsection and swayed slightly.

"Why not?" I asked, ignoring his obvious pain.

"I was born son of a slave in Mesopotamia," he said, his voice barely above a whisper. "They waited until I had grown, and then—" he stopped. "I am a eunuch, my lord. She is a daughter to me, the only one I can ever have. I beg my lord, do not take her away from me."

I stood, turned my back, and stared into space. Once again, El Shaddai reminded me that what had happened to me was much better than what could have been. Truly I had been sheltered under His wings. How would I have lived with the wistful sadness Renseneb carried in his heart? I had been born a prince, and he the son of a slave. How had he gotten here, to Egypt, and become a scribe? What of his mother, a Babylonian slave? Who was his father?

"Get up, Renseneb," I said at last.

Slowly he climbed to his feet.

"Inti!" I called.

"Yes, my lord?"

"Bring Lady Asenath."

My wife rushed in immediately, looking quickly from me to Renseneb.

"Tell me about the wood from Byblos."

She did. When I asked her about other deals, those she had won and those she had lost, she told me about every one of them. I just stood there and shook my head. I had ransacked Egypt, unable to see what was in my own house.

"Are you angry, my lord?" Asenath asked in a small voice, her shoulders hunched the way they used to be when she had first come to my house.

"I am disgusted with my own blindness," I said with a sigh. "I am in too much trouble to be angry. Asenath, I need your help."

Her eyes opened wide, those deep brown pools that could drown me in an instant. "I will do whatever I can, Joseph."

"Asenath, will you trade in the markets for Pharaoh? I must have someone to oversee the networks for buying grain that I have set up from Kush to Canaan. If you do, you will finally find out how I bested you in Tanis and Memphis."

After several seconds of unbelieving astonishment, a little smile drew up the corners of her mouth. Then she walked over to me and put her arms around my neck.

"Put like that, my lord, how can I refuse?"

▲ ▲ ▲ ▲

The years of plenty passed peacefully. Hetepi helped when Asenath bore my first child, a son I named Manasseh. A couple of years later, she assisted again when Ephraim was born. I looked up at the stars and bowed my head in gratitude. "Surely Your promises are true," I whispered. "You promised a father, a wife, and sons. I have had a brother as well, and lost him. But I would not have chosen to live without Khay."

I smiled at myself in the darkness. Just before Ephraim had been born, Renseneb and Hetepi married. They were well-matched, for with Khay's two rambunctious boys, Hetepi did not want more children. The boys, Little Khay and Geb, benefited more from Renseneb's quiet steadiness than they ever would have from Khay's impulsive unpredictability. Renseneb loved those boys as if they were his own, and they in turn adored him.

And while all this went on, I built storehouses all over Egypt until the land was dotted with them. As fast as they appeared, we filled them. Truly, "the earth brought forth by handfuls." I took grain in taxes, I accepted it in payment for government services, I bought it in the markets and on the streets. The records showed that during the first five years very little grain made it out of Egypt. I bought it all. Time after time, I emptied the treasure houses of Pharaoh, and time after time, Asenath, Renseneb, and Jetur brought me just enough to buy more grain or to supply the corvee.

As for the nomarchs, they soon recovered from the fright I gave them over Lord Meritifi and Lord Amony, and began making demands of Pharaoh. Pharaoh came to me, and I advised him to give them what they wanted as long as it did not harm the rest of Egypt. Pharaoh sold them a few trade concessions (for grain); gave them larger consignments of Royal Servants (for more grain); let them build magnificent tombs with the royal workmen (paid for with grain); and allowed them to grow secure and complacent in their power.

Only Lord Mose had the wit to look about him and notice the incessant rise of state storehouses in the land, all ridiculously and heavily guarded—for who would steal grain when it flooded the land like the Nile during inundation? He silently laughed at his fellow nomarchs. "I am loyal to Pharaoh," he repeated to me again. "What do I care what happens to these others? Only let me and my house serve Pharaoh forever."

"You shall, as long as it is in my power," I replied, touching his shoulder affectionately. "You have sidetracked more than one intrigue, and I am grateful. And yes, I do know about them," I added, noting his discomfort. "You have raised your sons to follow you, and Pharaoh has no concerns for the Land in Front."

"Thank you, my lord," he replied, straightening his shoulders. "I am honored to have served well."

Mahesa entered the room as the sixth harvest of plenty began. He looked at his wit's end and dropped to his knees in front of me, something he had not done in years.

"My lord," he pleaded, "it is too much. Please do not send more."

"Do not send more of what, Mahesa?" I asked.

"Reports, records, transactions about grain," he said in exasperation. "My lord, you must stop."

"I dare not stop collecting grain, Mahesa. There must be enough for the famine."

"Not grain, my lord, records. Please come and see," the scribe said, nearly in tears.

Concerned, I followed him to some rooms he used on the far side of the palace. When I walked in I stopped in amazement. The tables and floors were piled with tablets and papyri. They were everywhere. The scribes just sat, staring at them.

"What are these?" I asked.

"Records," Mahesa said in a small voice. "Records about the grain. I directed they be put here until we could get to them since our other rooms were already overflowing. Look at them. We have no place to put them. They are pouring in like a flood. We cannot keep up with them."

Knowing Mahesa and his concern with strict accounting, I could see how this mess would upset him. I thought, however, that something could be worked out. But after spending two hours seeing all that he had done to try to keep abreast of the information, I had to admit defeat.

"Stop counting," I said finally.

He stared at me in a daze. "Stop, my lord?" he asked, stunned.

"Yes, stop counting," I repeated. "We must continue to build storehouses, and you can keep track of the storehouses that are built and keep record of when they are finished and filled. But do not try to keep track of how much grain there is."

The scribe looked bewildered. "But, my lord, how will we know how much we have?"

"We won't," I said. "We will just know that we have enough."

"Not know how much we have?" he repeated, trying to comprehend such a situation.

"We have too much to count," I said.

"But, my lord, there is this harvest, and then still another year to go," he protested, unable to grasp what I had suggested.

"Yes, and we will build storehouses and fill them, but we will not bother to count how much grain is in them."

The other scribes looked glassy-eyed at such heresy.

I waited while Mahesa sat and stared at the stacks and piles of reports spilling all over everything. "But what will we do with the records?" he asked plaintively.

"Dig a hole and bury them," I suggested.

"My lord!" Mahesa gasped, utterly scandalized. "We could not possibly do such a thing!"

"Then leave them here in the offices, shut the doors, and build more offices for yourselves," I said, walking out.

"Yes, my lord," Mahesa said automatically as I left.

And then came the eighth year.

▲ ▲ ▲ ▲

"What is this that I see?" Amenemhet asked testily. "This report from Lord Khafra in the Treasury says that the treasury is empty!"

"It is correct, my lord," I replied, looking at Pharaoh steadily. "All of the storehouses of Pharaoh are empty."

"In the midst of plenty, I am a beggar?" he asked tightly.

"Yes, my lord."

For a moment, it appeared as though I would lose my head, then the king sat down, a frown on his face. "Why?" he demanded.

"They are empty so that they can be filled again. And this time, they will stay filled. I recommend that you begin building a place to put all your wealth."

"I have no wealth," Amenemhet growled. "From this report, I have not even enough to feed the palace. And I have little way of getting wealth, since I have given most of what I have to the nomarchs!"

"That is true, my lord. But you have grain."

"Everyone has grain," he roared. "All of Egypt is packed full to choking with grain."

"Yes, my lord, and almost all of it belongs to you."

"What good does it do me?" he asked bitterly. "It sits there for the rats to eat. Inundation is upon us, and the Nile is rising as in the past."

"Not as in the past, my lord," I corrected. "This is the eighth year."

"You know what you are doing?" Pharaoh asked soberly.

"I have saved Egypt. That was the order you gave to me, and I have done as you ordered. But I also remember that you had a wish, and I will fulfill that wish, if my lord will be patient just a little longer."

Amenemhet sighed. "I am always patient with you, although I have no idea why," he complained.

Nekhty entered. "My lord, a message has come from Semna."

Pharaoh looked up sharply. "What has happened at the fort? Is there trouble in the Land in Front?"

"No, my lord, it is the report of the rising of the Nile. The report is confirmed by the measurements at Kumma on the other side of the river. The Nile has reached maximum flood for planting and is still rising."

Amenemhet looked at me. I shrugged. "It is the eighth year," I said. "There will be no planting or harvest."

Nekhty left, and Pharaoh studied me. "You have all the time you want. Your God is very punctual."

The Nile rose—and continued to rise. Water rolled down from Upper Egypt, flooding the docks and markets, the villages and towns until it peaked at last, almost 12 feet higher than ever before recorded. For weeks every village, every city, every nome strained to accommodate the disaster left behind when the Nile finally loosed its grip on the land. It had washed away homes, villas, and estates. Irrigation systems were gone, temples flooded, and livestock lost.

By the time the nomes pulled themselves out of the Nile mud and began to rebuild on what the river had left behind, planting season was irretrievably lost. A few of the upper fields were surveyed and planted, but without irrigation few hoped for any harvest. The people began to make bricks, and houses and cities rose again from the mud. No one worried for the nomarchs had plenty of grain to distribute.

Inundation was nerve-wracking for me. I waited anxiously for every daily report from the Delta. Sety sent them punctually, and I read with growing relief that the flatness of the land absorbed most of the water that cascaded upon it. The storehouses remained above the waterline, and the drainage built into the platforms on which they stood successfully preserved their contents. Siamon's design and Shenbu's engineering had proven successful. Nevertheless, I determined to empty those storehouses first!

As the months passed and what would have been harvest drew near, I paid careful attention to the reports Hetepi supplied. The nomarchs opened their stores and distributed to the people. They still dismissed the flood as a coincidence and not the herald of the seven years of famine.

I sent instructions to Teti, now Director of the Department of the Head of the South, to double-check his security and guard carefully all the state-owned storehouses of grain. He worked closely with Lord Mose and reassured me that the grain was secure.

On the second morning of Harvest, I went out to the barren fields of my Memphis residence. As Ra rose in the east, I knelt on the hard ground and remembered all the ways El Shaddai had honored me. All the things He promised me had come true—all but one. I had become great, I ruled Egypt, I had been justified in my interpretation of Pharaoh's dreams, I had my glorious Asenath and two strong, active boys. Lord Potiphar still lived, and we visited often as father and son should. His title went to one of the lords from the Palace School, but Chaf, who was now trusted by Pharaoh as much as Lord Potiphar was, did the work. I had everything El Shaddai promised, except that I had not yet seen Abi's face. I was 38 years old, and I had to wipe the tears from my cheeks as I stood after my worship was complete.

My heart ached for Abi.

Mahesa ushered Jetur into my work room.

When he bowed respectfully, I gestured him to a seat.

"What do you wish to tell me?" I asked.

"I bring word from the caravans. Famine reigns everywhere."

I looked up. "Everywhere?"

He nodded. "Yes. Each caravan reports the same. Wherever they trade, there is no food. The caravans have spread the word that you have grain. The world will come to buy."

I looked blankly at him and saw the twinkle in his eyes. Once again, he had seen what I should have. In an instant, I understood why El Shaddai had pushed me to store every kernel of grain I could get my hands on. Not just Egypt suffered from famine, but the rest of the world as well. Did I have enough to feed the world for seven years?

For a moment, panic rose in my stomach. Then I calmed myself. El Shaddai had known it would be a world famine, even if I had not. He would not have given me less that what I needed. I would have enough.

"Let them come and buy," I said. "I will sell."

Jetur rose. "Thank you, my lord. That is what I needed to know." He paused in the doorway. "My lord, the famine is especially bad in Canaan."

I sat in silence after he had gone. Why would he emphasize that to me? Then I jumped up. My family! My family was without food, and I sat on millions of bushels of grain. What could I do? How could I save them?

"El Shaddai, what shall I do?" I asked. "Is the time now for me to see my father? Am I to send food to him? What do you want of me in this matter?"

"The world will come to buy." Jetur's words echoed in my mind. "The caravans have spread the word that you have grain." Slowly I sat down again. The old merchant knew my family. They would learn of the grain in Egypt, and they would come to purchase it. I did not have to do anything. When El Shaddai was ready, He would deliver my family to me as He had said. I must be ready.

CHAPTER 28

M ahesa!" I called.

He appeared in the room.

"Jetur brought word that peoples from other lands suffer from famine as we do. They are coming to Egypt to buy grain. I want you to send the word out that any strangers who seek grain must be interviewed by me before anyone can sell it to them to take out of the country."

"Yes, my lord. But that will take up a great deal of my lord's time."

"It will," I said. "But it is necessary for the security of Egypt. We cannot take the chance that spies will enter the land to plan an attack while we are dealing with this famine. I do not trust anyone else to do this properly. It is crucial for Pharaoh."

The scribe raised his eyebrows. "I had not thought of that. But with the amount of trade during the last few years, the barbarians have come to like the luxuries of Egypt. My lord is wise to think of such a thing. I will send out the orders at once."

He disappeared just as quickly as he had come, and I grinned to myself. Mahesa still had not appreciated the situation. The barbarians would not come to get gold and goods, although that was part of it. They would want Egypt's grain. If this famine was as severe as Pharaoh's dreams indicated, whoever controlled the food controlled the world. Right now, Pharaoh had the food. And I meant to keep it that way. My ruler had asked for the nobility on its knees. El Shaddai would give him the world.

Later that afternoon, I looked up to see Amenemhet himself entering my room. Hastily, I scrambled to get up from where I sat working. "My lord!" I exclaimed, finally making it to my feet and bowing.

"What is this I hear about selling grain?"

"The famine is also in other lands, my lord. They will come here to buy. If the famine lasts for seven years and we do not sell, there will be no stopping them, and they will overrun the land in spite of all we can do. But if we sell, however, we will save ourselves and replenish your treasure houses. The nomarchs, of course, do not have grain to sell. They must hold their grain for their nomes. Only you have grain to sell. All the state storehouses are filled with your grain."

Surprise crossed his face. "You mean to tell me that all those storehouses, those huge storehouses, the ones that cover Egypt from Front to Delta are filled with *my* grain?"

"Yes, my lord. That is why your treasury is empty. I used all of it to purchase grain."

"But if this famine continues, that grain will be worth twice its weight in the White, or anything else I might ask for."

"Yes, my lord."

A little grin appeared on his face, and it grew and grew until he burst out laughing. "Oh, Lord Paanekh, how the gods have favored me with you! I shudder to think what might have happened had you belonged to Babylon, for instance. I have no doubt that I would be crawling to you on my knees, as the world will be coming to me."

Then he sobered. "I am fortunate that you believed my dreams more than I did. All along, you have been counting on the famine, as well as the plenty."

"It was decreed by El Shaddai," I said. "It was, therefore, something to be counted on."

"If your God is powerful enough to cause famine in any land in the world, then what I have to give you will not mean much," Amenemhet said. "But it is a beautiful thing, and I wish to give it to you. I bring this gift to say thank you, and to say that you were right about this eighth year."

Chaf stepped forward, and handed something to Amenemhet, who gave it to me. I gazed in awe at a cup made wholly of the White, studded with jewels.

"It is magnificent, my lord. I do not know what to say."

"I give back your own," Amenemhet said. "Your blood is mixed with that metal. It has been blessed by each of the gods in Egypt, and will protect you from poisons and sickness. Because it has blood, it is also a divination cup. But I doubt very much that you will use it as such. You do not need it for that. Your God talks to you directly, does He not?"

I looked down. "When my need is great, He speaks to me, although I am not worthy."

Pharaoh looked at me in disgust. "That is a matter of opinion," he said testily. "I must go. I will soon leave for Thebes. Are you coming also?"

"No, my lord. I must stay in Memphis. I wish to personally interview all foreigners who seek to buy grain in Egypt. There is danger of spies and attack while we face this famine."

"Quite correct," Amenemhet said after a moment of thought. "I am certain, however, that your God will point out any spies to you." He turned to the door.

"Thank you, my lord. I will treasure this cup."

"You should," he said tartly. "It is possibly the only thing of the White I have at this moment!"

▲ ▲ ▲ ▲

"Who is it?" Benjamin asked, approaching Judah and Dan.

"A merchant to see father," Judah said, looking away.

"It appears quite a big caravan," Benjamin said. "What are they carrying?"

"Jewelry, gems, cloth, and papyri," Dan replied. "But look at the grain sacks. They're bulging, and there are so many of them."

"Also look at the guards," Judah said, frowning as he gazed at the parched fields. "Don't even try to get near those sacks. Why don't you go to Abi, Benjamin," he suggested. "You know how he likes to have you there when he buys things."

"All right," Benjamin said. He walked toward their father's tent, swinging his youngest son into his arms as he went. "Let's go see what Abi has," he said to the boy.

As soon as they were out of earshot, Dan turned to Judah. "What's wrong?"

Judah's face tightened. "I don't know," he said. "I wish I knew what that merchant was telling Father. He's just come from Egypt."

"And?"

"I swear, Dan, it's the same caravan that we saw more than 20 years ago. Its owner hasn't changed a bit."

Dan looked startled. "How can that be? We've never seen him since then."

"Until now. What can it mean?"

"What's worrying you? Judah, it can't possibly be the same one. We've observed every caravan through here for years, and we've never seen that one since that day."

Levi walked by Abi's tent, glanced in, and stiffened. He stared for a moment, then hurried to Judah.

"Did you see that trader?" he asked. "Is this his caravan?"

Judah nodded.

"It looks just like the same one who—" he left the sentence hanging.

"I know," Judah said softly.

"What are we going to do?" Levi asked. "Do you think he knows who we are?"

"I don't know," Judah said, turning to leave.

"Where are you going?" Levi demanded.

"To my tent. Father will send for me if he has anything to say."

Levi looked at Dan. "It really bothers him, doesn't it?"

Dan nodded. "He can't get away from the grief his idea caused Father. He could live with it until he lost his two sons. Then I think it really came home to him what we did. He broods sometimes."

"Who broods?" Reuben asked, walking up to them.

"Judah."

"Oh." Reuben looked over the camels. "Well-fed," he remarked. "I don't remember them coming around before, but they sure look familiar."

"You too?" Levi said. "Think back far enough, and you'll realize why."

Reuben's face went white. "It can't be!"

"I think it is," Levi replied. "You know, he changed a lot after Tamar," he added, returning to the subject of Judah.

"We all have," Dan replied. "We all know now what fools we were."

Someone came around the tent and called, "Uncle Reuben, have you seen Abi?"

Reuben turned to look and nearly fell, a clammy sweat breaking out on his face.

"Are you all right?" Shelah asked anxiously, running up. "Uncle Reuben, you look terrible. What's wrong?"

"Nothing, just a bad meal," his uncle mumbled. "I'll be fine. Your Abi is in his tent."

Shelah left the little group and headed for Judah's tent.

"It's uncanny, sometimes, how he looks so much like *him*," Levi said to Reuben. "His voice is the same, too."

"How long is this going to haunt us?" Reuben demanded, trying to stop shaking.

"For the rest of our lives," Dan said softly. "His blood is on our hands, and El Shaddai will require it of us as long as we live." He looked down at his hands as he spoke, and then turned blindly away.

"They were from Egypt, Abi," Shelah said later that afternoon. "They stopped by to give us word about grain."

"Grain?" Judah said, looking up.

"Yes, Egypt has grain. He said Egypt has been storing grain for seven years, and that there's enough to sell to those who must buy."

"Why would anyone store grain for seven years?" Judah asked. "Are you certain that's what they said?"

"Yes, Abi. And Grandfather wants you to come to his tent. He wants to talk to you. All of you."

Judah swallowed. "Thank you, Shelah," he said, carefully steadying his voice. "I'll go."

Shelah left, and Judah slowly got up. What did Jacob have to say? Something about grain—or something more?

"We are all here, Father," Judah said when everyone had gathered.

"Sit down, sit down," their father said.

The brothers seated themselves, Benjamin on Jacob's right as always, and Judah closest in the front.

"Jetur says there is grain to be had in Egypt," Jacob began. "I think we should buy some. We must decide how much we will need, and whether we must buy for seed for next year as well."

Judah looked up as Jacob ceased speaking. "Jetur? Did you know this man, Father?"

"Certainly. He's Ishmael's son, my cousin. I haven't seen him in years, since we buried Isaac. He's a good man, the best of his family. Looks a great deal like Isaac, don't you think?"

Judah looked down in confusion. "I don't know," he said, trying to keep his hands from shaking. "I'm afraid I didn't notice."

"You should notice these things," his father replied. "Jetur noticed you. He mentioned that he had not seen you all for more than 20 years. Only he said he was on his way to Egypt then, instead of coming back."

Unable to breathe, Judah felt as if the tent stifled him. He longed for the coolness of night. Somehow he made himself sit still. His eyes had not deceived him. The caravan owner remembered them. Had he known who they were back then? Had he known who Joseph was? Had he said anything to Jacob? Surely if he had, their father would have exploded in his anger by now.

"Judah!" Jacob's sharp voice cut into his thoughts.

"Sorry, Father," Judah said, looking up. "My mind wandered."

"Well, keep it here. We must come to a decision. Shall we buy grain from Egypt?"

No one spoke.

"I think it is a good plan," Shelah said hesitantly, knowing that someone older should speak first.

"I think so as well," Benjamin replied. "If we get enough for seed and to keep us through to harvest, we can sell, or spread out the herds, and keep the animals alive until next rainy season."

"That is what we will do," Jacob announced. "I'm grateful Jetur stopped to tell me about this. Now we can get there in time to buy enough to last until next harvest."

The brothers sat, looking at each other in silence.

"Well?" Jacob said.

"Are you certain it's necessary?" Judah muttered.

"Am I certain? Of course I'm certain. Do you see any food in this camp? Is there any in the fields? In the markets? Where else will we buy?" His voice rose in anger. "What is the matter with you all? Why do you just sit there staring at each other? Do you want your families to starve? Go down to Egypt and buy us food to live on!"

"Yes, Father," Judah said, closing his eyes momentarily. "How soon do you want us to go?"

"How soon?" their father roared, looking at his sons as if they were demented. "Tomorrow! Do you think we can survive without any grain?"

"Yes, of course, Father," Judah said hastily.

Jacob snorted. "Get ready immediately."

"Yes, Father," Judah replied, and followed the others from the tent.

"That's the most spirit Father has shown in a long time," Gad commented. "What are we going to do?" he added.

"Pack," Judah answered.

"You mean we are really going?" Issachar said. "How can we?"

"How can we not?" Judah replied. "You'd best get busy. Father said tomorrow."

"But if we go down there— What if, I mean, what if we see *him* or something?" Zebulun almost whispered.

"And what are the chances of that?" Judah asked harshly. "You've heard the stories of what Egypt is like. He's dead. He has to be."

But what if he's not? was the thought on all their minds.

▲ ▲ ▲ ▲

As I did every day I stood on the rooftop, surveying the crowd waiting to enter the palace this morning, noticing the mix of peoples. Cypriots, Syrians, Canaanites, Babylonians, a Kushite or two, Libyans, Egyptian officials off by themselves, Ishmaelites, Midianites, Amorites, and if I did not mistake that red hair, Edomites as well. The famine covered Canaan and points north and east for the most part.

Kush did not fare too badly, and neither did Libya, but the caravans brought word that Haran and even Ur were badly hit. With Mesopotamians coming, I could assume that region suffered as well.

Smiling, I picked out the ones who had never been to Egypt. They stared at everything. In spite of the hard worry on each face, they spent most of their time gazing around. And this was just Memphis, with its old palaces and buildings. Itej-Tawy would have dazzled them blind.

A Canaanite entered the crowd, pulling his coat close about himself, and I glanced beyond him to see an Egyptian noble woman on her way to market. I grinned, remembering my first reaction to the way people here dressed. I could imagine the embarrassment tormenting the man. He looked vaguely familiar, but I didn't have time to study him. The crowd was restive, and I must go down and open court. I would be interviewing all day again.

The interpreter led in a group of men who awkwardly "kissed the ground" before the throne where I sat wearing the royal linen and enough gold to buy half their cities. Mahesa absolutely insisted that I wear formal dress at all times, and I had to admit it made a deep impression on everyone. The interpreter began the usual spiel.

"Lord Paanekh, Second to Pharaoh, Tate of Upper and Lower Egypt, Second after the King in the Court of the Palace, Leader of the Great Men of the South and the North, Father to Pharaoh, Nearest Friend of Pharaoh, Friend of Pharaoh, Great Advisor unto

Pharaoh, Chief Judge of Sasat in Upper and Lower Egypt," and on and on until finally the interpreter came to the point.

"—come your servants to plead before you, who are as Pharaoh, a petition for purchase of grain."

I used the time spent naming my titles to study the men who entered. There was a technique to reading backs, and I amused myself sometimes wagering how closely the back would agree with the face when the group looked up.

Mahesa had worked out a set of questions that each independent buyer answered before entering the palace. Buyers were then divided into groups according to language, and interpreters brought in anywhere from 6 to 20 at a time. I reviewed the answers to the questions before the group entered, and usually asked one or two questions through the interpreter. Occasionally I detained separate buyers for further investigation, and I had already uncovered three that were too suspicious to ignore. One I sent back to his home with a stern warning; the other two were on their way south to Lord Mose, having become Royal Servants to Pharaoh.

Mahesa had his own ways of communicating what he thought of any group, so when he handed me the last question tablet for the day with the blankest of expressions, I knew he had extreme reservations about this group of Canaanites. I had seen several groups from Canaan during the past weeks, and it refreshed my Canaanite as I listened to them talk among themselves.

As usual, Mahesa was right. As the interpreter announced all my titles, I looked over the most tense backs I'd seen yet. All 10 of them. When the interpreter finished and the men glanced up, none of them really looked at me. They kept their eyes down, but they could not keep still and cast little furtive glances at each other. One kept wiping the sweat from his face, and another nervously rubbed his fingers together.

The one in the forefront finally raised his face enough for a good look. As he did, I froze, my fingers digging into the arm of the throne. My chest tightened up and my stomach twisted into a knot. I had the absurd urge to run. Every muscle tensed, ready to defend me. For a moment, the face swam before my eyes.

Finally I blinked and managed to suck in some air. Judah knelt before me, and to one side was Reuben. Levi was next, then Simeon, who had to wipe his forehead one more time. The interpreter had finished, but I did not notice the silence. Gad; Asher; Zebulun, still rubbing his fingers; Issachar next to him; Dan looking tired and apprehensive; and lastly Naphtali, wishing he was anywhere but here.

I had thought I was ready for them, but I wasn't. Their attack on me had occurred more than 20 years ago, but my body reacted as though it was yesterday. I had to shut my eyes to block out the cruelty on Simeon's face and the hatred in all their eyes. I couldn't decide whether to flee the room or start executing them. And then I went icy cold. There were only 10 of them. *Where was Benjamin?*

If they had hurt him, if they had done anything at all to him, I would kill them, every one! Rage boiled inside of me.

"Where are you from?" I grated out.

The interpreter repeated my question, and Judah answered.

"We are from Canaan, my lord. We have come to buy food." He bowed again as he spoke.

My fear evaporated. My dreams came forcibly to my mind. They had laughed at those dreams, then had laughed at me, and sold me and—more fury choked my throat. Suddenly I stood and advanced toward them, hurling the question tablet across the room, narrowly missing one of the guards.

"You are spies!" I shouted. "You have come to see if we are defenseless after the Nile flood!" I couldn't think of anything else to say to cover my now obvious emotions.

"No, my lord," Judah said, bewildered by my accusation. "We are not spies. We only want to buy food for our family. We are all the sons of one man. We are all honest men. Your servants are not spies."

Honest! *Honest?* They dared to call themselves that? After all the lying and murdering and thievery they had committed, they had the gall to tell me they are honest? After living a lie before Abi for more than 20 years, they say honest? I couldn't believe my ears! The interpreter finished speaking, and I laughed.

I looked into Judah's eyes, seeing the fear and guilt there that made him finally glance down. One after the other I stared at them, and not one could meet my gaze.

"No, you are not honest," I said, stepping closer still, my voice hard. "You are spies. You have come to see if the land is unprotected, if Egypt can be attacked and conquered during this famine."

"No, no, my lord," Reuben spoke up desperately. "We are 12

brothers, all sons of the same man, not spies. One of us is—is not, and the youngest is with his father in Canaan."

Somehow I calmed myself a little while the interpreter said what I had already heard. If I could trust them, Benjamin was still alive. But could I trust them? I doubted it as I glared at them. "Anyone can invent a brother," I said, suspicion in my voice. "I think I am right, and you are spies. But I will give you a chance to prove yourselves.

"By Pharaoh's life, you shall not leave until your youngest brother comes here. Choose one of you to fetch him. The rest shall remain in prison until he gets here. That way I will know you are telling the truth.

"But if he does not come, if you do not have a younger brother, as sure as Pharaoh lives, *you are all spies!*" I roared. "Take them to the prison," I snapped at the guards.

The guards surrounded them and hauled them to their feet. Shaking like a leaf in the hot desert air, I turned and strode from the throne room to my work room. I stalked past the scribes to the private room beyond, and Mahesa found me there a short while later.

"My lord?" he asked, entering.

Unable to keep still, I looked up and resumed pacing.

"Come," he said. I followed him. He led me to a side entrance where Onami waited and rode with me to my residence. Then he took me into the house and to the small reception room. There he sent for Asenath, and she arrived at once.

"What happened, Joseph?" she asked, seeing the state I was in.

"His family came to buy grain," Mahesa said.

She looked at me again, her eyes wide. "What did you do?"

"I put them in prison," I said.

Her mouth dropped open. "But why?"

"I did not know what else to do," I admitted a bit sheepishly. With Asenath to talk to, I began to calm down. Mahesa slipped out of the room.

My wife studied me, her eyes measuring and shrewd. "Let us go into the garden, shall we? I think you have quite a lot to tell me."

I looked at her, at those clear brown eyes, and suddenly all the energy drained from me. I reached my arm for her, and she slipped to my side. We walked into the private garden and sat by the small pool.

"Start at the beginning," she said.

"The beginning?" I repeated. "I am not certain where the beginning is. It is all connected to something else that happened before, but I guess for you, the beginning is the day you first came to this house, and I threw the biggest temper tantrum of my life."

Asenath smoothed my hair back, after removing my wig, and said, "Hmm."

"I had been a slave, Asenath, for 13 years, and I dared not get angry. So I bottled it up inside until the day you came, when that miserable steward brought it all out. I was not angry at him, not really. I was raging because of what happened 13 years before, when Abi asked me to go to Shechem and check up on my brothers."

"Brothers," Asenath echoed.

"Yes, 11 of them. Only Benjamin, my youngest brother, was just 5, so he stayed home, naturally. All my other brothers are older than I, but I was the older son of my father's favorite wife, so Abi decided that I could be his heir, and—"

"Abi?" she interrupted.

"My father," I said. "Anyway, my brothers thought that Reuben should be the heir, since he was oldest by Leah, father's first wife, but Abi did not count that since he thought he was marrying Rachel, my mother, and not Leah—"

Naturally, it took awhile to tell it all. The stars watched us by the time I finished, and I lay with my head in Asenath's lap while she still smoothed my hair.

"So these men who came to buy food are your 10 brothers, the sons of Leah and the two servants," she summarized.

I nodded.

"And these are the same brothers who hated you so much that they planned on killing you, but decided to sell you into slavery instead."

Again I nodded.

"And now they have come to you and bowed to you as your dreams said they would, and you put them into prison?"

"Yes."

"Why?"

"I do not know if I can trust them," I said slowly. "They said that Benjamin is home with Abi, but what if he is not? What if they sold Benjamin as they did me? Or did something worse to him? Since they have lied all their lives, why should it be any different now?"

"There is more," my wife said.

"You know me too well," I grumbled.

Asenath chuckled.

"I want to see Abi," I said, reaching up and taking her hands. "I love him as I love no one else in this world, and he loves me the same way. They took that away from us," I said bitterly. "They said he was alive, but how do I know that is true? And if he is, how does he live? Benjamin and I are all he had from Rachel, and he loved Rachel with his entire being. I know what happened when she died; I cannot stand to imagine how he reacted when I did not come back."

Trembling again, I paused. "If Benjamin is gone, I do not know how Abi can live. If they sold Benjamin, maybe I can find him and get him back—if he is alive. I want to bring Abi here to live. He will come—once he knows I am alive and here, he will come. I will send an army to fetch him if necessary."

My wife waited until my shaking stopped. "Twenty years is a long time," she commented.

"I know," I admitted. "Look at what happened to me during that time."

"Maybe your brothers have changed."

"I considered that. If they have, I want all of them in Egypt. I can care for them here better than there. But how can I know if they have or not? They are liars, Asenath. They murdered a whole town. Why should I dare trust them?"

"You have a point. But are they married? Do they have families? Have you had no indication at all that things have changed?"

"Well, the incident with Tamar suggested that Judah changed some," I said. "If he admitted, in public, that she was right and he was wrong, he has to be at least a bit different."

"Tell me about Tamar."

I did.

"So one brother at least has children."

"They probably all do. I wish I knew how bad things are there. I do not want them to starve."

"Well, why don't you keep just one here, and let the rest go home?" she suggested. "When they return for more food, they can bring Benjamin then, and you will know if they are telling the truth, and no one will go hungry."

"But I already said only one could go back," I protested.

"Joseph," she said, "they are not going to question what the Tate of Egypt decides to do. You could change your mind as many times as you wish, and they will say, 'Yes, my lord,' like everyone else."

"They will, won't they?" I said in wonder. "I guess I still think of them as my older brothers and that they have the power. But that is not true any longer. El Shaddai has given them to me."

"Just as your dreams said He would," my wife replied, her voice soft. "Now, Great Tate of all Egypt, are you going to get some sleep tonight, or are you going to stay up until Ra comes in the morning?"

"Does that mean I am being ordered to bed?"

"I believe so," Asenath replied wickedly.

I sighed. "When a mistress speaks, what can a slave do but obey?" I picked her up and carried her into the house despite her laughter.

CHAPTER 29

I left them in prison for three days after deciding that one day for each year I had myself spent there was a most generous gesture on my part.

"Be reasonable," I said to myself in amusement as I sent for them to come to court. "You don't dare leave them there any longer, and you know it."

Also, to be truthful, I needed those three days to calm down and make some rational decisions. Asenath pointing out to me that I truly held the power in this situation made a big difference in how I saw things. I spent two evenings in my private garden laying the problem before El Shaddai and asking for guidance. My wife's solution seemed the best one after that, so I implemented it.

The escort from the prison paraded them through the morning's crowd, and the story of what I had done spread rapidly. It would be told and retold, I knew, making every new buyer a bit more nervous than he already was. There were advantages to that, as well as problems, but I would have to deal with them later.

The guard left them in the throne room, and when I entered, they all dropped to their knees again. They all looked frightened, but Judah appeared haggard. I doubted he had slept much during the past three days. My brothers waited in silence to see what I would do with them.

"You say you have a father?" I asked.

"Yes, my lord, an old man," Judah replied.

"And a younger brother?"

"Yes, my lord. He is the only remaining son of his mother."

"I am a merciful man and have respect for the gods," I told them after some thought. "I have decided what you will do, so that your families—if you have them—will not starve. One of you will remain here. The rest can purchase grain and go back to Canaan. But you must bring your youngest brother back here to prove your innocence. If he does not come, I will execute all of you."

Fighting to control the rage that burned inside me—fueled by the fear of what they might have done to my little brother—I struggled to remain still on the throne.

"Yes, my lord," Judah whispered. After waiting to see if I had anything else to say, he got up, and the rest collected around him, talking to each other. I noticed Judah led them now, not Reuben. I wondered when that switch had come about, and I bet my life Father had decided on Judah for the birthright. He had very efficiently usurped my place.

"It's because of Joseph," I heard Dan say. "Didn't I tell you? We're being punished because of what we did to him."

"I told you not to," Reuben put in.

"El Shaddai is requiring his blood at our hands," Levi agreed heavily. "Remember how he pleaded with us to let him go? He begged us, and we didn't listen."

"I told you not to hurt him," Reuben repeated. "But none of you would listen. Now this is happening to us."

"He haunts me," Issachar said slowly. "I can't forget the look he gave me when I shoved him to the Ishmaelites."

"He haunts us all," Judah said, looking pale enough to faint.

"Well, now we have to pay," Dan said. "There will be nothing but trouble for the rest of our lives. We might as well accept it. We're guilty of his blood."

"Abi hasn't forgotten either," Gad said, looking down. "I hear him cry sometimes."

The remark about Father undid me. Hearing that Abi still mourned after 20 years went straight to my heart. I felt the prick of tears and knew I would be unable to stop them. Quickly I stepped into the personal audience room, which was fortunately empty.

Abi cried. I knew how he cried, for he had done the same for Rachel when she died. Now he cried for me. I let my own tears flow as silently as I could. Mahesa appeared mysteriously, and I let him repair the damages to the kohl around my eyes.

Giving myself a stern lecture on self-control, I went back into the room. They still hadn't decided who would stay, and I took the decision from them. Simeon had his mouth tightly closed, and the hard look around his eyes reminded me of his past behavior.

"Take him," I commanded, pointing to Simeon.

The guard strode toward him, and Simeon backed up, protesting. "I don't want to stay. I can't stay, please." He looked at the others.

I looked straight at him. "You are very willing to sacrifice someone else for your own wants," I said sarcastically through the interpreter. "How brotherly of you!"

I turned to the others. "Unless you return with that younger brother you keep talking about, this man will die."

"My lord, please," Judah gasped. "My lord would not do such a thing! Our father's life is wrapped up in our brother's life. He may not let him go."

"Then you have a problem," I said, eyeing them. "You surely don't wish to lose another brother, now do you?"

Every face went white.

I pointed to Simeon again. "Take him and bind him. Send him to prison immediately." The guards closed in, forcing Simeon to his knees and tying his hands while the rest looked on helplessly. "Go," I commanded them. "Take grain with you this once, but if you return, your youngest brother is the only thing that will keep you alive."

"Yes, my lord," they said, and Simeon watched as the guards herded them from the room.

Glancing at him, I bit back my rage. Then I jerked my head toward the door, and the guards took him away. I didn't dare keep him near me for fear of what I might do.

As soon as he left, I called Mahesa.

"Yes, my lord."

"Let them purchase from the nearest storehouse," I said. "They will pay in the White. Take the payment, but when you fill the sacks of grain, put it back in the top of each sack. Give them additional food for their journey as well."

Mahesa looked at me. "Yes, my lord."

That night, I told Asenath what I had done.

"Do you think they will come back?" she asked.

"I don't know. Simeon is not well liked, especially by Abi, since the massacre of the Shechemites. Abi will have to decide between his dislike of Simeon and the needs of the rest of the family. The rest of the family will win, unless they find another source for grain. Then he might just remain here."

"What will you do if that happens?"

"Put him to work," I said. "He is strong."

"There is bitterness in your voice," my wife said gently.

"When they sold me, they told the Ishmaelites I was strong."

"They were right," she said, coming to me and putting my arm around her.

Drawing her close I rested my head on her shoulder.

"You are the strongest person I know," she said. "I am glad you came to Egypt."

I looked into her eyes. "I am, too," I agreed.

▲ ▲ ▲ ▲

"You better check that sack, Gad, the binding is loose," Dan commented as he walked by the donkey.

"What? Oh, I see." He took the sack from the donkey and heaved it to the ground. His cry of alarm seconds later drew everyone to him.

"What is it?" Judah asked.

"It's my silver," Gad gasped, holding up the pouch. "It's the silver I used to pay for the grain. It's here in my sack, right on the top."

The brothers stared at the pouch in Gad's hand. Nobody moved.

"What is this that El Shaddai has done to us? What are we going to do?" Issachar asked.

"Go on home," Judah replied. "They can't last without this grain. We don't have time to turn back now. When we go again, we'll just have to make certain Gad takes twice the money."

"I don't like this," Zebulun said, rubbing his hands together.

"You don't have to like it," Dan replied. "You just have to live with it."

"What are we to do? Blame every trouble on what happened to Joseph?" Zebulun retorted.

"Exactly," Dan said savagely. "And we'd be right. Isn't it clear by now what happened?" he practically shouted. "We murdered our brother! Can we say it right out? Can we stop dancing around the truth, and stop hoping to avoid it, and stop talking about it by not saying a word? We murdered Joseph. We took our own brother, the son Abi loved more than anything else on earth, and we killed him."

"We sold him, Dan," Levi protested.

Dan whirled on him. "Yes, we sold him. We couldn't even murder him quickly and decently! No, we had to send him into a living death. You saw those slaves from the mines. How long do you think Joseph lived? A month? Maybe two? Or did he get lucky and last for a year? We're guilty! His blood drips from our fingers.

"He looked to me to speak for him that day. He crawled to you, Judah, begging for mercy. He even went to Simeon and pleaded for his life. Did we listen? Did we answer? Was there anything that we did that day that we aren't ashamed of?"

Dan looked at each of his brothers. "Yes, we hated Joseph, but did you ever wonder why? Oh, yes, he was an interfering pompous brat, but was that enough to kill him for? Do you know why he haunts us? Because he was good.

"We can make excuses that he was Rachel's son, that it wasn't fair that Abi loved Rachel more than anyone else. Well, who are we to tell Abi whom he should love? Abi can love anyone he wants to. Leah didn't have to go along with that farce of a wedding. But she did, knowing that Jacob loved Rachel and not her."

Reuben and Levi protested. "Now just a minute, Dan!"

"Oh, be silent!" he said, his voice raging. "For once in our lives, let's look the truth squarely in the face. Because Rachel had Joseph, Abi loved him more than us. Joseph was good, and Abi loved him even more. And so we hated him. He made us look bad. He made us face the fact that we were bad. So we murdered him, and in the process we tore the heart out of Abi's breast, and he bleeds to this day.

"What right do we have to protest any trouble that comes our way? *We are guilty of the murder of a blood brother. Every day that we lie to our father we are slowly killing him.* And we told that Egyptian we were honest men! I could have laughed as he did. I only hope that when El Shaddai is done with showing me the blackness of my crime, He'll have the mercy left to strike me dead." Dan turned and strode blindly away, leaving the rest staring after him.

▲ ▲ ▲ ▲

The cries of welcome when they arrived home quickly died at the sight of their lined, haggard faces.

"What's wrong?" Benjamin asked Judah as soon as he saw him.

"I must see Father," Judah said. "There is something we must tell him."

"Where's Simeon?" his wife asked, coming up and looking around eagerly.

Judah winced. "Simeon is still in Egypt," he said heavily. "Benjamin, I must talk to Father."

"Come," Benjamin said, taking Judah's arm. "Must it be now? You look half dead."

I am half dead, Judah wanted to say, *half of me died 20 years ago.* But he stopped himself. "It's been a hard trip," he said instead. "Bring Simeon's wife."

Benjamin glanced behind him. "She's coming," he said, leading the way to Jacob's tent.

"You have come back," Jacob greeted them with a smile. "You have grain?"

"Yes, Father," Judah said. "We have grain. The servants are unloading it now. There is enough to last for a while."

"Only a while?" Jacob asked concerned. "Will we need to buy more? Will there be grain left when we need it?"

"Yes, no fear of that. The land is literally dotted with storehouses, all full to bursting. Jetur was right, the Egyptians must have been storing grain for years."

"Well, perhaps if we are careful, we can make do with what we have until next harvest," Jacob suggested. "Then you will not need to go to Egypt again."

"We must," Judah said. "We had to leave Simeon there."

"What do you mean 'leave Simeon there'? He did not return with you?"

"No, Father."

"Why not?"

Judah looked down. "We had to see the lord of the land before we could buy grain. He was very harsh and suspicious and accused us of being spies. We told him we were honest men, sons of one man from Canaan, that one of us was dead, and the youngest with you. But he kept saying we were spies. And then he put us in prison for three days."

"In prison? But why? Surely you did not do anything to anger him?"

"No, Father. We did everything we were told to do, but the governor still accused us of being spies. After he brought us out of the prison, he announced that the only way he would believe our story was if Benjamin came to Egypt. He took Simeon and bound him right there at the audience. If Benjamin came the next time, that would prove our innocence, and we could have Simeon back, and could buy whatever we needed."

Before Jacob had time to reply, one of the servants came panting up. "Master Judah, Master Judah, please come quickly. We don't know what to do. There is silver in your sack."

"What do you mean silver?" Jacob said, looking at his sons suspiciously. "Do you mean to tell me you stole the grain?" he shouted angrily. "What did you do in Egypt?"

"Father, we didn't steal," Judah said. "We paid for the grain. We gave the silver—"

"Master Jacob, all the sacks have silver in them," Ebed shouted from outside the tent, pushing his way in. "I heard about Judah's, and I checked. All the silver we sent has been returned."

"Let me see," Jacob said, rising with Benjamin's help. He walked out of the tent and to the donkeys. In the top of each sack of grain sat a pouch of silver. "What have you done?" Jacob cried, turning to his sons. "How is it that you come home with your silver? Did you steal it? Or did you steal the grain? Or did you sell Simeon and come with a lie to me about the governor of Egypt?"

"Father, no!" Judah protested, "we did not sell Simeon." We sold Joseph, he almost added, but caught himself in time. He flushed, seeing Ebed's eyes on him, dark with suspicion. Was it possible he knew something? "Father, we paid for the grain," Judah forced himself to go on. "We gave them the silver. The Egyptians took it. We didn't steal. We took nothing from Egypt but what we purchased. Father, please, we don't know how the silver got here."

"You must know," Jacob said. "You must have done something in Egypt. Otherwise you wouldn't have been in prison. You've lied to me. I think you've always lied to me. You have taken my children. Joseph is gone. Simeon is gone. Now you want me to give you Benjamin so you can take him away? How much more must I suffer?"

"Father, we did nothing," Reuben protested. "The lord of Egypt took Simeon away from us. We must have Benjamin to get him back. I have two sons. Put my sons to death if I don't bring him back to you. Entrust him to me, and I will surely bring him back."

"You are all lying," Jacob retorted. "Benjamin's brother is dead already, and Benjamin is all I have left of Rachel. If anything happened to him on the trip, I will die from grief. *He shall not go to Egypt.*"

Jacob returned to his tent, and the brothers gathered around Judah. "What will we do?" Asher asked, his face tight.

"What can we do?" Judah asked. "If Benjamin doesn't go, we die." Turning away, he walked off by himself, shaken by Jacob's accusations. His father must have been suspicious of something for all these years. Judah stumbled, his vision blurry. He dared not answer his father, for the accusations were true. Truly he had robbed his father of his children, and he lied to him every day of his life. Now he couldn't even tell his father the truth about what happened before the governor of Egypt. The governor said he would kill them all, not that he would give Simeon back. Nor had he said anything about selling them more grain.

Climbing the hills just beyond the tents, Judah looked down on the encampment spread out below. His lies were finally bearing fruit. Must they all die as punishment for Joseph's life? Was this the final result of what he had done? Had they made Jacob so protective of Benjamin that he would refuse to let him go in the only chance to save them all? When he had pushed through the idea of selling Joseph to the Ishmaelites, had he signed the death order for his entire family?

He agreed with Dan. Although he, too, wished for death, he had no illusions about El Shaddai's mercy. With his luck, he would be the last of his family to survive the famine, and then be miraculously saved so he could be haunted by the horror of it for years to come.

▲ ▲ ▲ ▲

Since we had no harvest this year, I instituted the corvee early, and for a longer period. The headquarters for the Department of the South near the Fayyum were nearly completed, and I consulted with Shenbu and several other engineers about my idea concerning the second waterway of the Nile.

They told me that in theory my idea would work. I wanted to divert part of the Nile inundation each year down the secondary channel. The water would flow into the great basin of the Fayyum, creating a lake. It would lower a high flood and provide water for irrigation in a low flood. Thus we would store water the same as we stored food. However, the old channel did not quite reach the Basin, and part of it must be dug. We also needed water gates and such to direct the flow either toward or away from the Nile, depending on demand for water.

Shenbu worked long and hard over these concerns, building model after model, and now he thought he had solved the problem. The corvee brought thousands of workers to the Fayyum area, and they started to dig a channel connecting the basin with the old waterway.

I spent several weeks in Itej-Tawy overseeing the beginning of the work and then returned to Memphis, wondering how long it would be before my brothers arrived. In the meantime I took Simeon out of prison, but only in order to put him to work. But weeks and then months passed, and no one came. Inundation arrived, and once again the Nile rose and kept on rising. This year's flood crested even higher than last year's, and Jetur informed me, once he could get to me, that the famine continued on the caravan routes. I settled in for another year of selling grain.

"What bothers you, Joseph?" Asenath asked one evening during the middle of Planting.

"They have not come," I said.

"They will."

"But it is almost too late. The grain they took cannot last them much longer. The famine is worse this year than last. They will die."

"Perhaps they found grain somewhere else."

I nodded. "I thought of that, but that means that they will not return for Simeon, and that means Benjamin is gone."

"Or else your father will not let him come," she pointed out.

"Yes, there is that. I hate to think he would sacrifice Simeon, but I cannot rule it out. His love for Rachel and all who are her's is greater than anything else in his life, except his loyalty to El Shaddai."

"Be patient, Joseph, they will come yet."

"Yes, mistress," I said meekly.

She always laughed when I acted meek, and I loved to hear her laugh.

▲　▲　▲　▲

"The grain is almost gone."

"I know, Shelah."

"Abi, you must do something."

"What can I do, Shelah? We must have Benjamin, and Father won't let him go."

"He's weakening," Shelah said. "The caravans won't sell grain to him, and the only place to buy food is Egypt."

Judah sat in guilty thought after Shelah left. How many more lies about what the Egyptian governor said would he have to tell his father before he let Benjamin go to Egypt?

▲　▲　▲　▲

"Did you send for me, Father?" Judah asked, stepping into the tent.

"Yes, Judah. The grain you brought from Egypt is gone," he said heavily.

"I know, Father."

"Go down to Egypt, Judah, you and your brothers, and buy us a little food."

"What do you want from me, Father? A miracle? The lord of Egypt solemnly swore to us that we could not see him unless we had Benjamin. And without his permission, we can't buy. If you let Benjamin come, we'll go buy food. Otherwise it's useless, for the governor won't see us."

At least all of that was true, Judah thought to himself while Jacob restlessly shifted on the cushions, trying to decide what to do.

"Why did you bring this trouble upon me?" Jacob exploded. "Why did you tell him you had another brother in the first place?"

"He asked us, Father," Judah lied. "He questioned us specifically about our family, asking if you were alive, and if we had more brothers. We just answered his questions. How were we to know that he would demand we bring Benjamin to see him?" The words left bitterness on his tongue, but he dared not admit they had actually volunteered the information. If Jacob became angry again, he might refuse to let Benjamin go, and that meant death for the entire encampment.

Levi came in, followed by Dan and Asher. "There is nothing left, Father," Dan said. "Please let us go and buy more. I don't want to see my little ones die."

Judah knew the decision must be made today. Food supplies were so low that they dared not wait even another day. It was all his fault in the first place. How could he convince his father to allow Benjamin to accompany them?

Dead silence reigned in the tent for everyone knew that life or death rested on this decision. Judah looked at the faces around him. They were thin and drawn, the pinch of famine already noticeable. The children did not play as much. He glanced at Benjamin, who had nine sons and another one on the way. He wife needed food, and Judah saw the shadow of pain in Benjamin's eyes because he could not provide it.

There must be a way. There had to be a way. He would give his own life if it would make a difference. His own life?

Judah stepped forward, and Jacob raised his head, his old worn hand clutching Benjamin's. "Send him with me, Father," Judah said. "I swear my own life will be guarantee for him. If I do not bring him back to you unharmed, hold me personally responsible. I swear to bear the blame any way you wish for the rest of my days. Please, Father, send him with us. If we hadn't waited so long, we could have come and gone twice by now."

Benjamin turned to Jacob. "Please, Abi, I must go. Otherwise all of us will die. Simeon's wife cries for him. My children ask for more to eat. Abi, I must go."

Jacob sighed in defeat. "I see there is nothing else to do. Go, and take a present with you for the lord of the land, something special that he may not have in Egypt. Maybe he will look favorably on you if you do. Take spices, honey, and the last of the almonds and pistachios.

"And be certain to take twice the silver and to pay for the grain from before, then buy more. Maybe the silver in your sacks was a mistake of some kind."

Jacob stood, never letting go of Benjamin's hand. "Go to Egypt. I will pray that El Shaddai will journey before you, and grant you mercy with the lord of the land so he will send Benjamin and Simeon back with you when you return."

Then he motioned Judah forward. "Take Benjamin, Judah, and go at once. You all must live and your wives and little ones. For me, it doesn't matter. If I am bereaved of my children, then I am bereaved."

A sigh ran through the crowd, which quickly dispersed to get things ready for the trip. Benjamin stayed behind.

"Thank you, Abi," he said. "It will work out all right. I'll come back."

"You have been a good son to me, Benjamin," Jacob said. "Go now, to Egypt."

Benjamin ducked from the tent. Judah waited for him. "We'll be leaving within the hour," he said. "Shelah and Ebed confessed they have had things packed and ready for three weeks now."

Benjamin nodded. "I know. I helped. If Abi had refused to let me go, I would have left tonight with Ebed and Shelah."

"Don't be silly. Father would have been frantic. We would've caught you and brought you back."

He stared back. "No, you wouldn't have found us."

Judah looked at his youngest brother closely. The quiet certainty in that comment opened his eyes. Somehow he had still considered Benjamin a boy, but his brother had grown into a self-contained, forceful man while Judah hadn't been looking. He thought about Benjamin's comment. Shelah he could understand running off like that, but Ebed? How had Benjamin persuaded the herder to help?

Midmorning the next day, Benjamin caught up with Judah and walked beside him for a while. "Abi acted oddly," he said finally. "I don't think he expects me to return."

"He doesn't. Father thinks we're lying, and that we'll bring you harm."

"Are you lying?" Benjamin asked.

"No, not this time," Judah couldn't stop himself from saying.

"Would you?" Benjamin asked, looking directly at Judah.

"Would I what?"

"Harm me."

"No, Benjamin."

And if you buy that, I have a three-humped camel to sell, Judah thought in self-disgust. His father had actually entrusted Rachel's remaining son to him because he pledged his life as security for him. Once again, the irony of his success in deceiving his father rose up and gagged him. Would he let harm come to Benjamin? He didn't know. He had lied and deceived and cheated so much he couldn't even trust himself anymore.

"Why were all of you afraid to go to Egypt?" Benjamin asked.

Judah looked up in surprise. "We don't know what the lord will do," he said.

"Not this time," Benjamin said. "I know why you don't want to go now. But last time, all of you were afraid to visit there. Why?"

"We did something once, Benjamin, and it was wrong, and it involved Egypt."

"Oh," Benjamin said, casting an odd glance his way.

Judah suppressed a shudder of self-loathing. Dan was right about them all. So terribly, terribly right.

▲ ▲ ▲ ▲

"They have come, my lord," Mahesa said early one morning as I arrived at the palace.

"When?" I asked.

"Late last night. They are in the court now, waiting."

"How many of them?"

"Ten, my lord."

I shut my eyes in relief. Maybe Benjamin really was all right. I would have to see him for myself to be certain. Already I had decided that I did not want to interview them here, but at my home.

"Have them escorted to my residence, Mahesa. I will make a feast for them there at noon."

"Yes, my lord."

"You had better take them yourself, and make sure they get to Saf. I already told him what I want done."

"Yes, my lord."

▲ ▲ ▲ ▲

Several soldiers pushed their way through the crowd, with an interpreter.

"Judah of Canaan?" the interpreter called.

"I am here, honored one," Judah replied, stepping forward.

"You and your party are to come with us," the interpreter said.

"Yes, honored one." The brothers collected their things and followed the interpreter out of the court. The guards surrounded them, and they met with an Egyptian official outside the gate of the palace. Their interpreter bowed, then turned to them.

"This is Mahesa, Chief of the scribes to Pharaoh, Superintendent of the Building scribes, Superintendent of the Records, Personal Scribe to the Tate of Upper and Lower Egypt, and Director of the Works on the Nile under Pharaoh," the man said. "You will follow him."

Looking puzzled, the brothers fell into line, leading their donkeys. They left the palace complex and started through the streets and squares of Memphis.

"Where are we going?" Benjamin asked.

"I don't know," Judah answered. "Honored one, where are we bound?" he asked the interpreter.

"To the residence of the Tate of Upper and Lower Egypt."

The word spread quickly down the line.

"It's got to be about the silver," Gad said. "They mean to make us all slaves and take our animals. What can we do?"

"Maybe you should tell the official that we have double silver with us," Benjamin said hesitantly. "He couldn't harm us then, could he?"

"Maybe not," Dan said. "If we show them that we have money to pay for what we got before, then they can't accuse us of stealing."

"And we still don't know about Simeon," Levi said grimly. "Maybe we waited too long, and they killed him."

No one looked at Benjamin after that comment.

"It's not my fault Abi wouldn't let me come until now," he protested.

"We're not blaming you, Benjamin," Judah said heavily. "We blame ourselves."

Benjamin looked at him curiously, but remained silent.

"This must be the gate," Issachar commented when the guards paused before an estate. "Do we go in?"

"Let me speak to the official, first," Judah decided, walking a little faster. "Scribe Mahesa," he called.

Surprised, the Egyptian official turned around and looked at the interpreter.

"Please, honored one, if you would listen for a moment," Judah began. "The first time we came, we brought silver to buy grain. We paid and started on the way home. At the first stopping place, one of us opened his sack and found his silver in the sack. We had to hurry home, for our families badly needed the grain we bought. Then we found silver in all of our sacks, the exact weight that we paid to you. Now we have brought that silver back with us and have it to pay. Also we brought more silver, to buy more food. We don't know how our first silver got into the sacks. We want you to know, honored one, that we wouldn't steal. We are honest men, and have brought sufficient silver for both purchases as necessary."

"I remember you from your first trip," Mahesa replied through the interpreter. "You paid me, and I received your silver. Your God must have given you treasure in your sacks, for I have your accounts marked paid."

"Thank you, honored one," Judah said, thoroughly puzzled. El Shaddai put treasure in their sacks? Not likely.

The gate opened to the residence, and the brothers hesitantly walked in. Several men appeared and took the donkeys, leading them toward stables lining one wall of the courtyard. The official spoke briefly to someone, who hurried away. In minutes the man returned, leading a tired-looking slave with him, dressed in an Egyptian kilt, but with a full beard and dark hair.

"Simeon," Levi gasped.

The slave looked up, then stared. "Levi?" he asked incredulously, then glanced around guiltily and back down. But the official said some sharp words to him, and he raised his eyes. A slight shove sent him walking toward them, looking dazed.

Levi ran out to him and seized his shoulders. "Simeon, are you all right?"

"I guess so," he said, staring around. "You came back."

"Of course we did. What did you expect?"

The former hostage flushed. "It took so long that I didn't know what to think, and Father loves Benjamin so much, and hates me—" he broke off, staring at the group.

"I'm here, Simeon," Benjamin said, stepping forward. "Father finally had to let me come."

"How are my wife and the boys?" Simeon asked next.

"Doing as well as they can," Judah replied. "Everyone is pretty hungry back home."

"I see that," Simeon said softly. "All of you are thin."

"We'll manage somehow, we always do," Judah said. "Now that we have you back, things will go better again, I'm sure."

"Do you have me back?" Simeon asked uncertainly.

Judah turned to the interpreter. "Thank him for returning our brother to us. Ask if we may go buy grain now."

"He says your brother is your own again, but you may not buy grain. You have not yet feasted with Lord Paanekh."

"I don't understand," Judah said. "What feast, and with whom?"

"Lord Paanekh is the Tate unto Pharaoh," Simeon said. "This is one of his houses."

"Lord Paanekh commanded that you be brought here and he will eat with you today at noon," the interpreter explained. "All is being prepared. You are to follow Scribe Mahesa to the house."

Taking Simeon with them, they went up the steps to the porch, where another official waited.

"This is Saf, the Chief Steward," the interpreter said. "The other official will leave us now." The brothers bowed politely to Mahesa and turned to Chief Steward Saf.

"You must make yourselves ready," he said through the interpreter. "Lord Paanekh will arrive at noon, and you must be washed and dressed to eat with him. I will show you rooms you may use."

"Well," Benjamin suggested, "if he plans to eat with us, surely that is a good sign."

"It should be," Simeon said. "I have heard that Lord Paanekh does not often entertain."

"Let's get ready," Judah said.

▲ ▲ ▲ ▲

I paid strict attention to my duties that morning, but when noon came, I signaled that the interviews were over for the day. I had no idea what the afternoon would bring, but I did not intend to have to rush back to the palace. Having planned some experiments to see what my brothers were like, I wanted plenty of time to put them into operation.

Asenath waited for me in my bedchamber, and I gave her a quick hug. "Rather rough-looking lot, don't you think?" I commented apologetically.

She nodded. "They remind me of the men who used to do business with my father," she said. "But these are your brothers, so they cannot be all bad."

"Don't count on it," I warned.

"I know, they have done some terrible things, but their eyes look as if they have suffered."

"I will try to notice," I said, twitching my kilt.

My wife took my hands in hers. "Joseph, will you relax? That is your family out there. You know them well. You will get to see Benjamin, your own full brother. He will either stay here, or you will find it safe for him to return to Canaan and bring your father to you. El Shaddai has given them to you. All will be well."

With a sigh I forced my shoulders to relax. "What would I do without you?" I said. "Thank you, Asenath."

"Now, Great Tate of Upper and Lower Egypt, go out there and hold a feast for your brothers!"

"Yes, mistress," I said with a wicked grin.

She threw the nearest cushion at me as I ducked out the door.

CRAPTER 30

When I walked into the formal dining room I saw that Saf had done a magnificent job. Three tables were prepared, one for me, one for my brothers, and one for the officials from the house and palace who normally ate here due to my workload. My brothers' table was long enough to put them all on one side, so everyone faced me. The dishes on my table were silver, including the jeweled cup Pharaoh had given me. My brothers all had gold ones, and the others polished stone.

As soon as I entered, the officials bowed and my brothers kissed the ground. After I acknowledged their greeting, Judah, Dan, Gad, and Issachar came forward, carrying some dishes. When I sat down at my table, they put the gifts on it, bowing again and backed away.

I opened the dishes, knowing that myrrh was in one. I could smell it, along with the balm. Other dishes had spices, and in the last two were almonds and pistachios!

"You do me honor," I said. "Tell me," I asked, trying to conceal my anxiety, "is your father well? The old man that you spoke of, is he still alive?"

As the interpreter translated, I realized I had asked the dual question that assumed my father had a Ka. It brought home to me how long it had been and how much had changed since I had last seen Abi.

"Your servant our father is well," Judah answered, bowing again.

I fought to keep my composure as Saf conducted them to their assigned places. I had carefully described my brothers to him, and he did not make one mistake. First Reuben, then Simeon, Levi, Judah, Dan, Naphtali, Gad, Asher, Issachar, Zebulun, and Benjamin.

For the first time, I allowed myself to look at my younger brother. "Is that your youngest brother?" I asked, rising and stepping toward him involuntarily.

The interpreter translated briefly.

"Yes, my lord," Judah replied. "He is Benjamin."

I walked around the table and looked him over, searching his face intently. He had been 5 the last time I saw him, but this was undoubtedly Benjamin. Now he met my gaze squarely, the only one of my brothers who could. And he was thinner than I liked to see—they all were, except Simeon. The famine fell hard upon their land.

Unable to stop myself, I had to touch him. Approaching closer, I reached out and put my hands on his shoulders. They were hard with muscle and tense. I wanted to hug him, to fill my arms with him as I used to when he would run at me and throw himself into the air for me to catch. But I didn't dare. Not now. Later—I could do that later.

Instead I gripped his shoulders hard. I saw our mother in his face. Abi too, and he and Dinah must look very much alike. I remembered how he had waved at me the day I left for Shechem, running after me to remind me anxiously that I had promised to teach him to track a wolf when he turned 6. Now he was 26.

It was too much. "May El Shaddai be gracious to you, my son," I whispered, then abruptly turned and fled from the room.

Everywhere I looked people stood, waiting to serve the feast. I had to get away. I wanted Asenath, but the sounds from the women's rooms told me she was busy. A glance at the gardens revealed several officials waiting to meet with me. Finally I made it to my bedchamber, shut the door, and threw myself on the bed, weeping into the coverings so that no one would hear.

He stood so tall, almost as tall as I. And strong and handsome, with that clear open gaze that told me he had escaped the curse of guilt that followed our family. My blood brother, he resembled Rachel. And he was alive and safe. They had at least let Abi have Benjamin.

I don't know how long I lay there, but the door opened slowly and Asenath slipped in.

"Joseph, they are waiting," she said, gently pulling the coverings away from my hands. "What happened?"

"It is Benjamin," I replied. "He is alive and well and grown, and I missed it all. I never got to see him grow up."

"Hush, hush," she said. "That is for later. You have guests now and must go back out there. What a mess you have made of yourself! Everyone is worried."

Sitting up on the bed, I pulled her onto my lap.

"I don't care."

"I do," she said. "I see I must wash your face."

"Do I look that bad?"

In reply, she pulled her mirror out of its pouch and held it in front of my face.

One look made me shudder. "Wash my face," I agreed.

I had to dress for the feast a second time, but soon was ready again.

"Don't make me do this again, if you please," Asenath said as she straightened my gold collar. "I was supposed to be at the market right now, but if you insist on acting like—"

I stopped her with my finger on her lips. "I will be a good boy," I promised. "You go to the market, and I will go the feast, and I will promise to wait until the new moon comes before I go howling into the garden thirsting for someone's blood."

My wife looked at me suspiciously. "You are dangerous when you talk like that. Maybe I had better stay home after all."

"I am fine now. You will come back to find me the model of the perfect host."

"Somehow that is exactly what I am afraid of," she said, walking out the door. Then I walked back into the dining room acting as if I left guests hanging every day of the week.

"You may serve," I said to Saf, sitting down.

▲ ▲ ▲ ▲

Judah tried to contain his hunger as he watched the food coming into the room. The servers presented it first to Lord Paanekh, and then distributed it to the rest of them. As he looked down the line of his brothers, he noticed something odd.

"What is it?" Dan asked, glancing at him. "Don't frown, he might not like it."

"We're seated in exact birth order," Judah replied, puzzled.

"You're right," Dan said after a moment. "How could this happen? Do you think he could possibly know?"

The others heard them, and looked as well.

"It must be chance," Reuben said.

"It can't be," Levi protested. "How could any one know how old we are? Asher looks as old as I do, but he's down there where he should be."

"It's odd. I wonder what it means?" Gad commented.

Judah remained silent, but worry creased his forehead.

"What kind of person is this Lord Paanekh?" Zebulun asked in a low voice.

Benjamin shrugged. "I don't know. But I've heard stories about him just in the little while I've been here. Some Ishmaelites said that he knows the future, that he can see things. The Egyptians say he has the eyes of Ra, one of their gods."

Zebulun shivered. "I believe it," he said. "When he looks at me, it feels as if he can see right through me, as if he knows all about me."

Judah looked down the line of his brothers again. "From the looks of this table, I'd say he knows a lot more than we give him credit for. You notice no one has offered Asher any raisins."

"Asher doesn't like raisins," Zebulun replied. "What's odd about him not having any?"

"I didn't say he didn't take any, I said he wasn't offered any."

Zebulun stopped chewing. "That's impossible."

"You just watch," Judah replied. A serving woman placed yet more food by Benjamin's plate.

Gad glanced at Benjamin and grinned. "You made quite an impression. You have at least five times as much as the rest of us."

Judah looked again at the food surrounding Benjamin's place and glanced up at Lord Paanekh, and his heart stood still. Then he shook his head. For a moment there, the way the man held his head, it looked just like— It couldn't be, of course. But still—

▲ ▲ ▲ ▲

I looked at the table across from mine. All my brothers were pretty well drunk except Benjamin. I waved the interpreter away. While my brothers thoroughly enjoyed themselves at the table, I listened closely to every word.

They told themselves repeatedly that I wasn't such a bad fellow after all. That what had happened before was just a silly mistake. After commiserating with Simeon over his year in Egypt, they then rejoiced that he was with them again, assuring him again and again that his family was fine and eager to see him. Simeon complained of the prison and how hard he had had to work, but then said I was an honorable man, since I had released him as soon as they arrived with Benjamin.

My brothers said how wise Jacob had been to send a gift along and how nice that Benjamin made such a good impression on me. Not once did I hear anything at all that suggested they were jealous of him, or that they hated him or wished him harm. To the contrary, they all seemed very protective and concerned about him.

As he was the second son of Rachel, I found that very odd.

Asenath glanced into the room from the hallway, and I nodded, signaling the end of the feast. Staff appeared to help my brothers to rooms where they could sleep off the wine before leaving in the morning. I got up and went to my wife.

"Mahesa is here," she said. "He is done at the palace for today and wondered if you needed him for anything else."

I looked over my shoulder at my brothers, tottering out of the dining room, and then down at the silver cup in my hands. The final test for my brothers popped into my head.

"Yes, I do need him. I just had an idea and want him to help with it."

"What now?" she asked. "I recognize that look in your eye. What devilment are you going to lay on your brothers now?"

"I have to be certain they have changed. I don't dare trust Benjamin to them unless I am. I showed marked favoritism for him today, and—"

"And?"

"Asenath, they hated me because my mother was the one woman my father loved. Benjamin shares that with me. They sold me away from Abi, even though I had done nothing to deserve that. I was an annoying and idiotic brat, yes, but not deserving of the fate they expected me to meet. My brothers hated me because I did not break the laws El Shaddai gave to us as they had. Benjamin also shares that trait with me. They hid that hatred for years from both Abi and me. I must be absolutely certain it does not exist toward Benjamin.

"I want to know how they will react if they think Benjamin has done something against El Shaddai. They sold me when I was innocent. What will they do with Benjamin if they assume he is guilty?"

"You are very hard on them," my wife said.

"If they are to come and live in Egypt, I have to be. I cannot govern Egypt if I must worry about what they might or might not do behind my back. If I have to, I will take Benjamin and Abi from them and leave them to starve."

She looked at me. "And all the women and children as well?"

"Well, maybe I would bring them all here and just make my brothers royal servants," I admitted. "They can live on the Delta and herd kine for the rest of their days."

"That I will believe. But you could not leave them to die, could you? Even when they first came, and you were angry about what they did to you and frightened about what they might have done to Benjamin, you still would not have executed them, and you know it."

"No," I admitted, "I could not bring that pain to Abi. He loves them, and they are my brothers. But how am I supposed to be a fearsome ruler of Egypt when you keep reminding me how soft-hearted I am?"

Asenath pulled my head down and kissed the tip of my nose. "Oh, I don't know," she said. "It is just something we women do." She moved down the hallway walking as a woman does when she—

"Lord Paanekh," Mahesa said, breaking into my thoughts, "did you send for me?"

At times the scribe's punctuality was a real trial to me. "Yes, I did," I admitted reluctantly, pulling my mind back to the idea I had. "When my brothers wake up in the morning, sell them grain and put their payment back in the sacks as last time."

"Yes, my lord."

"Then, in Benjamin's sack—he is the youngest—I want you to bury this," I said, handing him the cup Pharaoh had given me.

Mahesa raised his eyebrows. "Yes, my lord."

▲　▲　▲　▲

"We're on our way," Simeon rejoiced, urging his donkey faster on the trail. "I can't wait to get back home."

"Don't kill the poor thing, Simeon," Levi protested. "We have a long way to go. That donkey has to last until Canaan."

"The way I feel, I'd carry that sack myself," he replied, but he slowed his pace a little.

"Why did I drink so much?" Asher groaned, holding his head.

"Good question," Benjamin said.

"You certainly look well," Asher replied grumpily. "I suppose you didn't drink at all."

"I had some," Benjamin replied reasonably. "I just didn't get drunk."

"Lucky you," Issachar moaned. "Stop talking, would you?"

Judah glanced along the line. Benjamin obviously hadn't had much to drink yesterday, and he had himself kept his own drinking down to a reasonable amount. As a result he had had to handle the financial transactions today.

He felt encouraged. They had Benjamin, Simeon, and enough grain to last for a long time. Maybe by then the famine would be over, although the Egyptians seemed to think it would last for seven years. Judah considered that. It might be true. After all, the Egyptians had stored grain for seven years because Lord Paanekh predicted a famine. And here the famine was. He would have to discuss that with Father.

Yells and shouts behind them made the brothers turn around. A troop of soldiers led by a chariot rushed down the road. Urging the animals off the trail, the brothers waited for it to pass. But it didn't. Instead, the soldiers surrounded them.

The official in the chariot stepped down. "What is this you have done?" he asked sternly through an interpreter. "After my lord Paanekh showed you such favor yesterday, how is it that you repay him by stealing his cup made of the White? It is the one he uses to see the future. This is an evil thing you have done."

Judah looked at the man in amazement. "Surely you are mistaken, Honored Scribe Mahesa," he protested. "We have done nothing. We wouldn't steal from your lord."

"I am not mistaken," Mahesa said. "The cup was gone this morning, and you have taken it. It is made entirely of the White and extremely valuable, as Lord Paanekh told you yesterday. It was a gift from Pharaoh. Lord Paanekh uses it to keep Egypt safe."

"We are innocent, honored scribe," Judah said with a sinking heart. "We are honest men. Remember, we brought back the silver we found in our sacks last time. We offered it to you again. And we brought more silver to buy grain for our families this time. Your lord was gracious to us. He returned our brother Simeon and honored us with a feast. Why would we steal from him? We didn't do this thing."

"You must have," Mahesa insisted, "for the cup is gone, and only one of you could have taken it. Although I am surprised, being barbarians, that you had the wit to take it and not the gold."

Numbly Judah looked at his brothers. They had all been drunk yesterday. What had happened? Surely, even drunk, no one would have touched that cup. "Did anyone take it?" he asked, looking at all of them.

They all shook their heads. For once in his life, Simeon looked frightened, Judah noticed. He'd already been here a year. Maybe he knew something they didn't.

"Simeon, did you?" Judah couldn't resist asking. "He made you a slave, after all."

"Judah, I swear I didn't. I know better than to try anything with Lord Paanekh. I've seen enough of him to know nothing gets past him. And I wouldn't want to face him angry for anything in the world."

"We were drunk. Try to remember anything that would give them the idea we stole it," Judah implored.

Gad held his head, Issachar squinted in the rising sun, and Reuben resembled a sick bear.

"We did not do this, honored scribe," Judah said, turning back to the scribe. "Search us and see. If you find the cup, the person on whom it is found will be put to death and the rest of us will become Lord Paanekh's slaves."

"All right," Mahesa said. "I will search as you say. But only the guilty person will become my slave. The rest of you will be free to go."

"Get the donkeys unloaded," Judah directed. "Let him search."

Mahesa performed the search himself, starting with Reuben and examining his clothes, then his pack, and lastly the sack of grain. A collective gasp rose when he opened the sack, for there on the top lay Reuben's silver. Mahesa looked sternly at him.

"I didn't put it there, my lord," Reuben almost sobbed. "I paid you, you know I paid you."

Mahesa said nothing. Removing the pouch, he thrust his hands and arms deep into the grain. Then he moved to Simeon, Levi, and Judah. Each grain sack had silver in the top. And each time he found it, the brothers looked more and more worried and ashamed. "We paid you," they kept repeating. "You know we paid you." At last the scribe came to Benjamin.

From the way his youngest brother stood, Judah knew he was uncertain and apprehensive. But the scribe quickly completed the body search, then went through the packs. Judah turned away, knowing that the scribe would never find the cup in Benjamin's things and started packing his stuff again. That should settle this. Now, maybe they could go home with this food.

"No!" Benjamin cried out. "I didn't take it. I didn't!"

Judah whirled around as the scribe slowly pulled the silver cup from deep in the grain in Benjamin's sack. Judah stared in dumbfounded horror. "Benjamin?" he said, unable to believe his eyes. "Benjamin?"

"I didn't," his brother exclaimed. "I swear, Judah, I never touched that cup! I wouldn't. I must go home to Abi!"

Judah reeled slightly, memories of Joseph calling for Abi filling his mind. He saw the same look of stunned terror on Benjamin's face, and the same dawning fear. With growing horror he remembered how Joseph had screamed when they dragged him away, and he shuddered again and again.

Grabbing the edge of his robe, Judah tore it. The ripping sound echoed as most of his brothers did the same. Now what were they to do? Benjamin kept insisting that he had not done it, but how else could that cup have gotten into that sack? He must have taken it.

Since he wasn't drunk yesterday, either, he would have been the only one sober enough to steal.

"Pack up," Judah said grimly. "We must go back."

The soldiers pushed Benjamin away from the others. He looked dazed and disbelieving, just as Joseph had been more than 20 years before. Judah felt like throwing up. With no way to prove they were innocent, they would be lucky if the Egyptian let them live. What would happen to their families?

"We have the guilty man," Mahesa said, the interpreter repeating his words. "Lord Paanekh is a merciful lord and will demand only him. He will not punish the entire family, as is allowed by law. The rest of you return to your homes. Take the grain to feed your families. You may have your brother's grain as well. Only he shall bear the punishment for his crime. He shall serve Lord Paanekh, and you are free to leave."

"We are coming back," Judah said, finishing loading his donkey.

"There is no need," the scribe insisted. "The rest of you go."

"No," Levi grunted, heaving the sack of grain onto the back of the donkey. "We all come."

"Lord Paanekh will not receive you," Mahesa warned. "He will take only the guilty brother."

"Well, he gets us all," Judah replied, his voice implacable.

As they trudged back along the trail, surrounded by soldiers, stared at by everyone, Judah fought with himself. He couldn't accept that Benjamin had taken that cup. But what else was there to believe? What had come over his brother? Stealing wasn't like him, but then, what were any of them like? Stealing a cup was child's play compared to what he'd done himself. It was a nasty thing for Benjamin to do, but that never stopped any of them before. Nastiness was their trademark.

Leaving his donkey with Levi, Judah increased his pace until he walked beside Benjamin.

"I didn't take it," his youngest brother said woodenly.

"Don't worry over it, Benjamin," Judah replied. "We'll get you back home somehow."

"But I didn't take it," he repeated, bewildered.

Judah stumbled. How could he get Benjamin and that food back to Canaan? He had to find a way out of this mess. Although he had pledged his life as surety for Benjamin he had never dreamed he'd have to fulfill the pledge. He glanced at Benjamin. Tears filled his brother's eyes, and he looked young and scared. His hands shook as he walked. Judah looked down. Father's favorite, a thief. Well, he didn't have room to complain. He was his father's heir—and a murderer.

In any case, what did it matter? Guilty or innocent, Abi would still die without Benjamin. The thought of Abi's reaction if he returned without Rachel's only surviving son turned Judah's stomach and nearly drove him to his knees there on the trail. Stumbling back to his donkey, he hung on to stay erect. He couldn't face it. Jacob's wails for Joseph still rang in his ears and haunted his nights. What could he do? He had gone surety for Benjamin. Judah pulled his head covering further down over his face.

His life for Benjamin's. He caught his breath. If he could convince Lord Paanekh to accept him instead of Benjamin, the others could go home with the food. Abi would have Benjamin. Everything would come out all right.

Judah steadied himself. He had to do it. Bathshua, Er, and Onan were all dead. Only Shelah—the thought of his son nearly broke his resolve. No, he must do this. Shelah would be taken care of. He had enjoyed more than 25 years of his son's life, while he had robbed his father of Joseph's life and love. Now El Shaddai demanded justice.

The irony of it burned itself into his mind. He had sold Rachel's innocent son as a slave, and now El Shaddai demanded he become a slave to keep Rachel's guilty son free. Judah bowed his shoulders in acceptance of El Shaddai's will. Let the punishment fall where it was deserved. If he did this, maybe in His mercy, El Shaddai would preserve the lives of his family. Perhaps Shelah would live, and Tamar and her twins, his father and brothers and their families. He had led the way into this abhorrent sin, and justice demanded that he pay its price.

▲ ▲ ▲ ▲

Mahesa entered the small reception room with an odd expression on his face.

"Did you bring Benjamin back?" I asked.

"Yes, my lord. He is here. And so, I might add, are the others."

"The others?"

"Yes, my lord. The others. They refused to go without him."

"They did what?" I gasped.

"They refused to leave. They came back. They are all waiting in the formal reception room right now. You have all 11 of them to deal with."

I had to sit down. "You did what I said? You made it clear Benjamin had taken the cup? You pressed it on them that they were expected to go back home?"

"I did. I even went so far as to say that you would not receive them if they did return. Judah's reply to that was that you got all of them anyway."

"Judah said that?" I asked in amazement. "Not Reuben?"

"Judah, my lord."

That didn't make any sense. He was obviously the heir now, and I was sure that he had wanted that birthright badly enough to murder me for it. That he would turn his back on it and voluntarily become a slave just because another of Rachel's sons had gotten caught in theft did not sound like the Judah I remembered. Well, as Asenath had pointed out, 20 years was a long time. Clearly something had changed.

I walked to the reception room. All of them dropped on their faces. The murmur from the staff and officials already waiting to see me died down to total silence. Benjamin stood off to one side, guarded by two soldiers. He seemed dazed, and scarcely knew what to do. The others appeared even more miserable, guilty, and ashamed than I'd ever seen anybody look.

Sitting on the raised throne, I studied them for several seconds. "Just what did you think you were doing?" I finally asked. "Did you really think you could steal from me when I can see into men's hearts and divine their thoughts?"

"How can we answer my lord?" Judah replied, looking up. "What can we say? El Shaddai has left us no way to prove our innocence. We are all slaves to my lord, all of us, as well as our brother who took the cup."

"Absolutely not," I replied impatiently before the interpreter had finished. "I would never do such an unjust thing. I am a merciful man. I shall not punish your family, only the guilty brother, and I will not even require his life. He shall not be executed but shall remain as my slave. The rest of you are free to go. Leave at once and take food to your families."

Nobody moved. Only Benjamin kept staring at me and wiping his eyes as if he saw something that he could not make himself believe.

Then Judah crawled forward, stopping at the edge of the dais, just three feet away. "Please, my lord, let your servant speak to my lord," he pleaded, "and do not be angry with your servant, for you are as powerful as Pharaoh."

"Continue," I replied, hardly crediting what my eyes had just seen.

"When we came, my lord asked if we had a father or a brother. We told my lord that we had an aged father and a youngest brother who was the only one left of his mother, and whom our father loved so much that he could not live without him.

"Then you commanded your servants to bring our youngest brother so that you might see him yourself. We protested that he could not leave our father. And you said to your servants that unless we brought our youngest brother, we would not see your face again.

"Then we returned home, and told your servant our father what had happened. Our father was very distressed and did not know what to do."

I looked down, squeezing my eyes against the tears. I could imagine Abi's feelings. Suddenly I signaled the interpreter to stop, for he distracted me, and I did not want the others in the room to understand what else Judah might say. My brother never noticed.

"Then, when we had no food, and hunger came to our little ones, your servant our father told us to go down to Egypt and buy food. But we told our father it would be of no use, that without our youngest brother you wouldn't let us come before you. Only if he came could we buy food.

"Your servant our father reminded us that his wife bore him only two sons, and one of them had left him and never come back because he had been torn in pieces by a wild beast."

I sucked in my breath, gripping the arms of the chair. They had told Abi that I had been killed by a wild animal? How could they? Abi must have gone nearly out of his mind imagining that had happened to me! Judah came closer to dying right then than he ever had in his life. It took all my willpower to hold my tongue. Only feeling Benjamin's eyes on me held me back. I glanced his way. He stared at me, clearly fighting the impossible hope that gleamed in the back of his eyes.

Judah had also paused, steadying his voice, then continued. "Our father said to us that if we took this son away, and some harm came to him, he would die of grief. He would go down to his grave in misery.

"But your servants had to buy food, and so at last our father told us to take our brother and go. And we obeyed. But now, my lord, if I go back to my father without his son, my father will die of the grief and sorrow. I will have caused my father's death."

Again Judah paused, and I remained still, commanding all my self-control. This man, down on his knees before me, had willingly told Abi that I had died a horrible death. In order to take the birthright, he had deliberately sold me into a terrible life to satisfy his hatred of a son of Rachel, and he even now knowingly allowed Abi to think that I had screamed out my life in the jaws of some predator. Knowing he had done all this, was I really supposed to believe he would feel remorse at causing Abi's death? Why was he even speaking to me? What did he want? Judah looked up into my face.

"My lord, I pledged to your servant my father that my life was guarantee for his son's life. I vowed that if I did not bring him back unharmed, I would bear the blame before my father forever."

His words fell on my anger like the Nile's inundation, washing it away on waves of amazement. *Judah* had become surety for *Benjamin?* I couldn't believe my ears. That Judah would put his life on the line for a son of Rachel went beyond my comprehension. And that he would actually follow through on that vow, knowing it meant losing everything he had murdered to gain, left me breathless with disbelief. But what other reason could there be for him to kneel before me?

"So now, my lord," he continued, holding out his hands to me, "I beg my lord to let your servant stay here as my lord's slave in place of the lad. Bestow your mercy upon my father, and let Benjamin return with his brothers. My lord, I—I cannot go back to my father without him and see the grief and misery that would crush out my father's life. Be merciful to me, my lord, and let me remain as your slave so that my father may have his son."

I couldn't look away from Judah's eyes. For once, he spoke the truth. I read it in the pain and the sorrow, the guilt and self-condemnation that oppressed his soul. He would not go back to Canaan without Benjamin. Judah was doing this—the one who had planned my murder, and then convinced the others to sell me instead. He who had haggled over my purchase price and took the money they paid for me, callously indifferent to my pleas and terror.

Finally I managed to look away, my stomach in knots. Judah pressed his advantage.

"Please, my lord, let the one my father loves return to him. Let the guilt and punishment fall on me."

And it should, I thought, staring at him again. But I couldn't hold onto my anger. I saw too much suffering in his eyes. He bore the torture of what he had done to Abi every day of his life, carrying a wound that could not heal because of the lies and deceit that surrounded it. Now, he utterly refused to bring more sorrow upon our father. He would submit to anything I commanded, strip himself of the birthright, leave Shelah behind, or sacrifice his blood rather than hurt Father again.

Feeling the wave of emotion rising in my stomach, I glanced up at my staff and the officials watching the Canaanite plead before me while they waited for my time. Why hadn't I thought to use the private reception room? I could not stop the tears, and I had no time to go anywhere else.

Abruptly I stood up and turned away, gripping myself and leaning against one of the pillars. "Go out from here!" I commanded harshly. "Mahesa, take everyone away but these men."

Instantly the scribe snapped the orders, and the guards jumped to clear the room.

The doors shut as tears started down my face. For a second my tongue would not work. I fought for breath. Then, "I am Joseph," I said, speaking in my native tongue for the first time. "Is Abi truly still alive?"

No one answered, but I heard the gasps of fear.

When I turned around to face them, they stared at me from white faces, not knowing what to do with my claim.

"I am Joseph, your brother, the one you sold into Egypt," I repeated. Still they stared, frightened, unsure.

With a slight smile, I reached up and pulled off the wig I wore, dropping it onto the throne beside me. "I really am Joseph," I insisted. "Please tell me, is Abi alive and well?" I asked, stepping forward.

At the sight of my hair, a moan of stark terror rose from their throats, and one and all they scrambled away from me, cowering on the floor, too terrified to speak.

Only Benjamin stood to one side, mouthing my name in a daze, tears streaming down his face.

"Joseph?" he asked. "Is it really you?"

With a nod I reached out my hand. He came up to me, and for the second time in two days, I touched my brother, putting my arm around his shoulder and gripping him hard.

"They said you were dead. How can you be alive?" he asked, still uncertain whether to believe what he'd been told or what his eyes saw.

"They didn't kill me, they sold me. They lied about what happened." I reached up and undid the gold collar, turning my shoulder to Benjamin. "See? Here are the lion scars."

His fingers traced the scars. "I remember them. Even though I was so young then, I have always remembered the scars."

Putting my arm around his shoulders again, I turned to the others. None of them had moved. Tears came to my eyes. I was so tired of seeing people afraid of me. I had finally overcome that with the Egyptians. Now to see my own brothers trembling on the floor, so terrorized they couldn't even look up, wrenched my stomach like a crocodile whipping its tail.

"Please, get up," I said. "Don't be afraid. Come closer to me." Nobody moved. "Judah, Dan, Gad, please come closer," I tried again. "Get up, all of you."

Dan moved first. Standing, he walked shakily forward a few feet before kneeling again. He hadn't looked at me yet, but at least he was off the floor. When nothing happened to him, Issachar rose to his feet, followed by Zebulun.

"All of you, come here," I coaxed. "Don't be afraid of me." The rest finally approached, Judah and Simeon last. I sighed. Simeon had to know that if I had wanted him dead, it would have happened already. And how Judah could imagine I would kill him after that plea he made to me was more than I could understand.

"Look at me," I said. "I am Joseph, your brother, the one you sold into Egypt. Don't be afraid or upset. I had to come to Egypt. El Shaddai chose me to save your lives by sending me here before you."

Dan looked up at me. Fear and despair spilled from his eyes with his tears.

"Please, Dan, don't be afraid," I said. "El Shaddai sent me here because of the famine. It has lasted for two years, and there are five more with no planting or harvest. That's why El Shaddai chose me to come to Egypt—to prepare for this, and to save people from death.

"You see, it really wasn't you that sent me here, but El Shaddai. He chose me and raised me up to become a father to Pharaoh, and lord of Pharaoh's house, and ruler over all of Egypt."

More of them looked at me now. I kept tight hold on Benjamin, and he hung onto me just as tightly.

"I'm not angry. Don't be afraid," I repeated. "Go back to Abi and tell him what El Shaddai has done for me. Tell him he must come without delay. Bring your wives and children and grandchildren, the flocks and animals—everything you have to Goshen. I will provide food for you. Tell Abi to come now, before you lose it all to the famine."

At last I had everyone's attention. They watched me, still afraid but no longer so terrified.

"All of you must urge Abi to come," I said. "You and Benjamin have seen for yourselves that I'm really Joseph, and that I'm still alive and speaking to you. Tell Abi about all my glory here in Egypt, about everything you've seen here. Urge him to come quickly, please."

The thought of seeing Abi again was more than I could handle, and I turned to Benjamin, wrapped my arms around him and sobbed so hard I thought I would split in two. Benjamin cried also, clinging to me as he used to do as a child.

When the storm of weeping eased somewhat, someone touched my shoulder, and I looked up. Dan stood there beside me.

"Joseph, can you forgive me?" he choked out. I turned to him and hugged him, starting to weep all over again. And then Gad was there, and Issachar, and Levi, and everyone. I went from one to the other, hearing their apologies, accepting them and trying to bridge 22 years of separation.

All but Judah. I looked around for him and saw him still on his knees, his head in his hands.

"Judah," I said, approaching him.

He shook his head. "How can you possibly forgive me after what I did? After what I told Abi? You can only hate me."

In spite of his words, he clung to me like a leech. I put my hands on his arms. "Yes, Judah, I hated you," I admitted. "At one time, I would have gladly killed you, as you wished to kill me. But I am done with hatred now. Hatred does nothing but destroy. El Shaddai chose me to come to Egypt and bring about a great deliverance for Him. Why should I hate you? I was a pompous, posturing brat, flaunting Abi's love for me in your face. I can hardly stand myself when I think of it.

"I'll forgive you if you'll forgive me."

Judah broke, tears streaming down his face.

Since he clearly could not stand up, I knelt down with him.

CHAPTER 31

A knock on a door interrupted the buzz of our conversation hours later.

"You may enter," I called.

Mahesa opened the door. "If my lord will come to the dining room, there is food ready." He looked at me for a bit. "I will tell the staff to serve as soon as you are properly prepared," he hinted.

"Of course, Mahesa. Is Lady Asenath here?"

"Yes, my lord. Will you require her?"

"Yes."

I left the reception room. Asenath met me in my bedchamber where she stared at my disheveled appearance in disgust. "I thought you said you were not going to make this a regular practice," she said finally.

"I had not planned on it, but you never know," I replied with a grin. Suddenly I scooped her up in my arms and whirled her around and around, landing us on the bed, too dizzy to stand.

"What was that all about?" she gasped when she could breathe.

"My brothers are here," I said. "And Benjamin is fine, and Abi is alive, and they are going to come to Egypt to live, and—"

"—and you are happier that I have ever seen you," she finished for me. "Well, happy or not, you have to eat, and that means you have to look presentable. What have you been doing?"

"Crying and embracing," I said.

"The crying we know about," she replied primly. "The entire house heard you."

"Well, now the entire house can know that my brothers are here," I replied, blatantly unrepentant. "And Benjamin is fine, and Abi is still alive, and they are all going to—"

"I know, I know, they are all going to come to Egypt to live," my wife said, getting out another linen for me to wear.

"Leave the dressing to me," I said, pulling her down and giving her a kiss. "You are going to be too busy."

"Doing what?"

"Dressing. You have to eat with us."

"Now?" she gasped. "But I look terrible."

"No, you don't. You look more beautiful now than you ever have in your life, but—"

"Do you really want me to eat with you this meal?" she asked, closing my mouth with her hand.

I nodded, since I couldn't speak. Asenath went flying out of the room, and I laughed as she left. I took my time getting ready, knowing she would want as much time as she could get. When I met her in the hallway, she looked as composed as if she'd had all day to get ready, not just a few minutes.

We went in to a very late noon meal, and I proudly introduced her to all of her brothers-in-law. Saf informed me while the meal was being served that Mahesa had already left to inform Pharaoh that my brothers had come to Egypt.

▲ ▲ ▲ ▲

"Well, what is it, Shelah?" Jacob asked.

"It must be a caravan, Grandfather," he replied. "There are lots of donkeys, some loaded with grain and several wagons with all sorts of bundles."

"So it is not your father," Jacob said heavily. "Will the caravan stop here? Is there anything we have to offer them?"

Shelah went to the door of the tent. "Yes, they're stopping. And someone is getting down." He gasped. "Grandfather, it's my father," he exclaimed, and ran from the tent.

"Abi, you're back," Shelah shouted, running up.

"Yes, Shelah, we are," Judah replied with a big smile. "Run now to my father and tell him that we are all here. All of us. Simeon and Benjamin too."

With a quick, curious look at the wagons and loaded animals, Shelah raced away. "They're back, Grandfather," he said, panting. "Benjamin is with them, and Simeon, too."

"You're certain?" Jacob asked, sitting up straighter. "Benjamin has returned?"

"I have, Abi," Benjamin said, hurrying into the tent.

"My son, you are well? You have come to no harm?" Jacob asked anxiously, looking him all over.

"I'm perfectly fine, Abi. And we have exciting news to tell. The others are coming now."

"Nothing could be more wonderful than that you are back," Jacob said. He looked up as the others trooped in, everyone smiling.

"You look well," Jacob said. "Simeon, you are here?"

"Yes, father, I am. Thank you for sending Benjamin. I'm grateful."

Jacob glanced at him in surprise. If spending a year in Egypt made this much difference in one son, maybe he should send them all.

"Benjamin tells me you have great news. What is it?"

"Didn't you tell him?" Judah asked.

"No, Judah, it's your news," Benjamin said, "but tell Abi quickly."

"What is it?" their father asked impatiently.

"It's about Joseph," Judah continued. "He's alive, Father, and is ruler over all of Egypt."

"Joseph?" Jacob said faintly. He looked at his sons in dismay.

"Yes, Abi, isn't it wonderful?" Benjamin put in excitedly. "We saw him and talked to him, and he says that you must come immediately and see him. He sent all sorts of things to you. We have them outside in the wagons."

"He lives in a big house with walls painted with odd pictures of people and boats and gardens," Gad said. "He told us that you must come—"

"And he really is ruler of all of Egypt," Reuben interrupted. "We were afraid at first. He looks just like an Egyptian except that he keeps his hair covered so the red doesn't show."

"They call him Lord of Upper and Lower Egypt, Father to Pharaoh, and a dozen other things," Zebulun put in. "And he has this strange Egyptian name that Pharaoh gave him."

"And he's married and has two of the busiest boys," Dan added. "Father, you must go to see him. He—"

"Stop, stop," Jacob cried. "What are you doing? Joseph is dead! He's dead, do you hear? A wild beast tore him into pieces! I have his coat with his blood. What are you saying? What happened to you in Egypt?"

The brothers stopped speaking, looking abashed as tears coursed down their father's cheeks. "He's dead, he's dead," he repeated. "Why do you bring him up?"

"I think I had better talk to you, Father," Judah said in the silence. "Preferably alone."

"Come, Benjamin," Dan said, gesturing the others to leave the tent.

The brothers went out and moved the crowd away from the tent.

Judah stood in silence for some time, then he approached his father and knelt down with his face between his knees. He waited.

"What is it, my son?" Jacob finally asked.

"Father, I have sinned a great sin against you," he said, raising his head.

"Tell me, my son," Jacob said, his eyes sad.

"I robbed you of your children and lied to you, Father."

"In what way, Judah?" he asked sternly.

"It's about Joseph," Judah went on, his mouth dry. "It's about what happened that day, more than 20 years ago."

Jacob stirred. "Must you bring him back for me?"

"Yes, Father. It is a terrible thing we have done." Judah paused.

"Go on."

"Father, you sent Joseph to see about us when we were at Shechem. We saw him coming on the road; he wore the coat you gave him."

Jacob nodded. "Yes, he did."

"We hated him, Father. We had always hated him."

"You hated him? But why? He was a good lad, a wonderful son."

"I know. He was good, and we weren't. You loved him more than you loved us. He could always please you, and we never could. He was Rachel's firstborn, and we just didn't count. Then he had those dreams, the dreams that said he would be great and rule over us. We were jealous. We hated him, Father."

"Go on." Jacob's voice hardened.

"We saw him coming to us alone. I hated the way he looked in the coat, and I decided to kill him and say that a beast had done it."

Judah paused to control his shaking, then continued. "We jumped on him and tore off the coat you gave him. Then we dragged him to an empty cistern and threw him into it."

A low moan came from Jacob, and he rocked back and forth. "You, his brothers? You did this?"

"Yes, Father," Judah whispered.

"Did he die there? Did he die in that cistern?"

"No, Father. He didn't die. Reuben kept telling us we shouldn't hurt Joseph, that we shouldn't kill him, because he was our brother. That's why we threw him in the cistern instead of killing him right away. We were eating the food he had brought when a caravan of Ishmaelites came by, bound for Egypt."

"Egypt?" Jacob said, stilling himself. "Ishmaelites? Jetur?"

"Yes, Father, although we didn't know it was him. To us it was just a caravan going to Egypt. I kept thinking about what Reuben said, and then I had the next idea."

"And what was that?" Jacob demanded.

"I decided that Reuben was right. We should not kill our own flesh and blood. So I suggested we get him out of the cistern and sell him to the Ishmaelites instead."

"You sold him?" Jacob said in a low, savage voice. *"You sold my son* as a slave?"

"Yes, Father."

Silence reigned while Jacob struggled to control himself. "And then what?" he finally grated out.

"They took him away, and we finished eating. Reuben came back, wanting to know what had happened to Joseph. He had planned on getting him out of the cistern and bringing him back to you. When he found Joseph gone, he got very upset. We told him what we had done and gave him his share of the money."

"How much? How much blood money did you get?"

"Twenty pieces of silver," Judah replied in a low voice.

"So little?" Jacob said scathingly.

Judah remained quiet. What could he say?

"What next?" his father hissed.

"We wondered what to tell you. Since we still had the coat, we killed a kid and put its blood on the garment. Then we ripped it up some and left it out in the open for several days before bringing it to you."

"All those years—all those years that I mourned him as dead, and you knew he had been sold? How could you? How could you do that?"

Judah swallowed and was unable to speak for several moments. "We didn't know, Father. We didn't know you would mourn so, and then we were afraid to tell you, and finally we figured Joseph was dead by now anyway, so why tell you at all? So we didn't."

His father could only stare at him. "You actually sold him, to be a slave, in Egypt? You did that to my son, Joseph, the first child Rachel gave me?" His voice rising, he stood up also. "Do you mean to tell me that all those years I mourned Joseph as dead, he was alive, and toiling in Egypt for some foreign master?" He shouted now at the top of his lungs. "You deceived me? You let me think he had been devoured by a lion or something? When I could have sent to Egypt and found him? And brought him back? Judah, *do you know what should be done to you?*"

"Yes, Father. El Shaddai's hand has been heavy upon me, and I do not expect anything less from you. Only let your hand fall only upon me, Father, for the rest only went where I led. Let me alone bear the blame before you, and do with me whatever you think best."

"Judah, can you give me even one reason you should live?" Jacob thundered, pacing the tent in his rage.

"No, Father," he replied steadily.

"I can, Abi," Benjamin interrupted.

"You have no business here, Benjamin. Leave," Jacob shouted.

"No, Abi, I will not go. You can't sentence Judah to die."

"Why not?" their father demanded, pausing to glare at his youngest son. "Do you know what he did?"

"Yes, I know. But Abi, you can't sentence Judah to die because Joseph didn't die. There is more to what happened."

"Did Judah ask you to do this?" Jacob stormed. "Did he tell you to come in here and ask for his life?"

"No, Father," Benjamin said sharply. "I'm here because in Egypt Judah pleaded to be taken in my stead when I was accused of a crime I could have been executed for."

"You accused of a crime?" Jacob asked in alarm. "What happened, Benjamin? Were you harmed?"

"Thanks to Judah, no. The lord of the land gave a feast for us, and the next morning his silver cup was missing. They found it in my sack of grain, and accused me of stealing it."

"Surely you didn't do such a thing!" Jacob gasped.

"Of course not, Abi. But with the cup in my sack, who would believe that? We found out later how it got there, but that is another story. Anyway, when they took me before the lord of the land, Judah got down on his knees and begged to remain in my place so that I could come home."

Jacob looked at Judah. "You did that?"

Judah nodded. "Yes, Father."

"But why?"

Judah raised tortured eyes to his father. "I had already taken one of Rachel's sons from you. After seeing what it did to you, do you really think I could stand to return without the other?"

Jacob slumped down into his cushions. "You would have stayed in Benjamin's place?" he asked incredulously.

"Yes, he would have, Abi," Benjamin said. "And that is why I came in here now. You must listen to the rest of what happened before you make any decisions about Judah."

"What happened? Tell me, Benjamin."

He related all that had happened to Joseph in Egypt. "And so you see, Abi," he finished, "El Shaddai set Joseph over the land of Egypt so that he could store grain for the famine. That is why Egypt has grain for us to buy."

"But how do you know all this, my son? Who told it to you?"

"Joseph, of course. He is the lord of the land my brothers went to see the first time they visited Egypt. When he saw that there were only 10 of them, he was afraid they had done something to me as they had to him. So he demanded to know more about their family.

"That's why he made them bring me to Egypt. He wanted to be certain I was alive and well. Wondering if my brothers hated me, as they had him, he tested them. Joseph had his steward put his cup in my sack, and then accuse me of stealing it.

"But Judah and the others would not leave me, and they all came back. And when Joseph tried to send them away and leave me there in Egypt, they wouldn't go. Judah pleaded for me, and after that, Joseph told us who he was. I had seen it already, but I couldn't believe it. Joseph was supposed to be dead. But then he took off his wig, and his hair is as red as ever!"

"Joseph is truly alive?" Jacob asked in wonder. "He is the ruler over all of Egypt?"

"Yes, Father. El Shaddai made him great, just as the dreams said he would be. And he showed me the lion scars on his shoulder. They are still there. I remembered them from before he went away.

"So you see, Abi, Joseph didn't die. He is alive, and you can't have Judah die, because he pleaded for me. And besides, you will need him to help move all our possessions to Goshen."

The old man sat in silence for a long while. "Come near me, Judah," he said at last.

Judah approached him, and Jacob put his hand on Judah's shoulder. "How can I blame you too much, my son? I deceived my own father and my twin brother. You learned to deceive from me, and El Shaddai's hand has been heavy on us both. Let us forget the past."

"Yes Father," Judah said, hesitantly taking his father's hand.

A movement at the tent door made Jacob look up. Dan stood there, with Asher behind him. They joined Judah as Levi, Issachar, and Zebulun followed.

"We have all sinned against you, Father," Simeon said as he and the rest joined those in the tent. "We are as guilty as Judah, and bear the blame as well."

Tears fell from Jacob's eyes, and he held out his arms as his sons knelt and confessed what they had done.

"Let there be forgiveness for us all," he said at last. "It is El Shaddai's will that will prevail." He turned back to Judah and gripped him hard. "But you are certain that it's Joseph you saw?"

"Come and see for yourself," Benjamin invited. "Joseph sent lots of things especially for you."

Their father stood and walked from the tent. The encampment trooped after them as Jacob went to inspect the wagons and loaded animals. His eyes widened as he saw everything sent for him. All the best of Egypt was there, carpets and clothing, gold and gems, beautiful inlaid tables, and cushions to sit on. He found pitchers for wine, packs of dates, dozens of things.

"Pharaoh himself ordered the wagons," Judah said. "When he found out we were Joseph's brothers, he sent a message that we were to move to Goshen, just as Joseph told us to. He said anything we wanted was ours. Joseph says there will be five more years of famine, so we must come now. The wagons are for you and the women and children.

"He gave each of us gifts, too, and then warned us not to argue about what we had done during the journey home," Judah finished ironically.

"See, Abi, here's more for you," Benjamin said.

But Jacob shook his head. "No. No more," he said, tears streaming down his face. "It's enough. He's still alive. I will go down to Egypt and see Joseph before I die."

▲ ▲ ▲ ▲

I waited. I reviewed court cases and passed judgments, and I waited. I went to the Fayyum again with the corvee to check up on the works there, and I waited. I attended receptions and audiences with Amenemhet, and I waited. Amenemhet sent me out of the capital, and Asenath kicked me out of the house, so Mahesa was stuck with me. He took base advantage of me, digging through the files for all sorts of things that were supposed to get done and never had been. Then he dragged me off to the Delta to inspect possible sites for building the headquarters for the Department of the North.

"What do you think of this place, Lord Paanekh?" he asked.

"It looks good, the best of any we have seen yet," I said. We were south of Tanis, on the edge of Goshen. "This would do very well," I repeated, looking around. It truly was the best of the sites we had seen, but the main attraction for me was its proximity to Goshen, where my family would be. Looking eastward longingly I sighed. I had waited more than 20 years already. What did a few more days matter?

They mattered a lot. I paced uncontrollably for the next few days. Although I did all my duties, I did them while pacing, even eating on my feet. I wandered through my residence in Bubastis driving the house staff wild, since they never knew when I would show up. After enduring their silent protests, I wandered out to the stable and went to see the stallion.

He pricked his ears and nickered, reaching his nose toward me as he always did. I patted him.

"So boy, we have come a long way," I said, feeling myself relax as I fiddled with his mane. "You're getting pretty old, and I'm not so young anymore either. But there's still fire in you yet, isn't there?"

As always, I talked to him in Canaanite. He nudged me, wanting to scratch his head on my shoulder.

"Oh no," I said. "Not now. You'll get me all mussed up, and that will upset Mahesa. He's upset enough with me as it is, so you'll just have to scratch on the stall post, and not on me."

The stallion stamped and bobbed his head.

"You know I'm waiting, don't you, boy?" I said with a grin. "Well, when the time comes, I'll tell you, and you can run to your heart's content."

Feeling much better, I left the stables and went back to the house, absently snatching a fresh-baked loaf of bread on my way through the kitchens, much to the baker's dismay.

In the formal reception room the next morning, I made myself listen to the empty phrases that this particular delegation insisted on spouting. I hoped they had something of substance to say by the time they finished, but the longer they went on, the less likely that seemed.

They were priests from the local temple to Bast, the cat goddess. Bast was the goddess of pleasure, and as the priests went on and on, the idea gradually sifted through the rhetoric that they wanted me to visit the temple.

I was saved from trying to find a tactful answer when a messenger entered the room.

"My lord," he said, interrupting the delegate. "They are here."

I shot off the chair and out the door like an arrow from a bow. Mahesa met me at the stairs of the porch.

"Your jewelry, my lord."

I stripped off the few rings I wore, except Pharaoh's signet, and handed them to him along with the gold arm bands. I wanted to meet Abi looking as much like myself as I could. Mahesa had convinced me to leave on the collar, however, to signal my rank to the travelers on the road. I fumed out loud, looking about for Onami and my chariot. My driver came from the stables at a gallop and pulled up at the bottom of the steps. As I started down them, Mahesa trailed behind, yelling something at me.

Finally I figured out what he had said as I stepped into the chariot. I yanked off my wig and threw it to him. "Go," I said to Onami.

The stallion fought the reins all the way through town, barely keeping behind the runners that cleared the way before the chariot. Once out of the town and past the huts that straggled from the gates, I took a good grip on the handholds and yelled, "Now, boy, go!"

That stallion took off like a bolt of lightening. He put his head down, bared his teeth, and ran like the wind, dragging his harness mate with him. It didn't take long for the other stallion to catch the feeling, and soon he matched my stallion stride for stride.

Onami gripped the reins, spread his feet and barely managed to keep us on the road while he bounced from side to side. Up ahead I could see some travelers on the road. The stallion screamed in fury, thundering down on them. Onami shouted, and the people scrambled off to the side just in time to avoid being knocked down. The other stallion decided we must be at war, and the next travelers we met were nearly trampled and bitten.

And then in the distance, I saw them. I don't know how I knew they were my family, but they were. I leaned into the wind, staring ahead. The stallion laid his ears back, reached down inside himself, and surged ahead faster than ever. His companion strained to keep up, the pounding of their hooves matching the pounding of my heart. Abi had come. Abi, whom I hadn't seen in 22 years. He waited for me just up the road.

The horses' hooves drummed on the road. I leaned forward again, straining to get there faster. The wind whipped tears from my eyes. "Abi, Abi, Abi," I kept saying. The stallion found one more burst of speed. Onami clung to the reins, shouting for the gods to preserve us and swearing at the horses in really shocking Egyptian.

But the stallion only listened to my voice, and his companion responded only to him.

Someone climbed down from a wagon, helped by two other men. His hair was gray, and he moved stiffly, but I knew instantly that it was Abi.

"Abi!" I shouted. "Abi, Abi!"

We thundered down the last stretch of road, and I thought my heart would burst. When I leaned to the right, the stallion veered. The people scattered, but Abi stood straight and still, waiting. Then we were there—finally there.

I leaned back and yelled, "Whoa!" while my driver tugged on the reins. That stallion sat down on his hind legs, pulling his companion with him, and skidded to a stop, the chariot halting just past

Father. I jumped off the chariot before it had even stopped, took two steps, and threw my arms around my beloved Abi.

I was shaking and trembling and crying, gasping "Abi, Abi, Abi," repeatedly.

And for the first time in 22 years when I called his name, he answered. His arms gripped me and he pulled me to him. "Joseph, Joseph, I'm here. I'm here. I have come. Joseph."

I could feel his hands and arms, his strength as he hugged me tighter and tighter. It was real this time—it wasn't a dream. I could feel the cloth under my arms and smell the dust and spice and oil that meant home. "Abi!" I sobbed. I buried my face in his shoulder, and I cried.

When I came to myself again, he sat on a stool in the middle of the road, and I knelt in front of him with my arms still wrapped around him.

"Joseph," he said. "So long. So very long."

Pulling back a little, I gazed up into Abi's face. Pain and grief had left lines of sorrow, but now his eyes glowed with joy. He kept touching me, and I didn't want him to stop. I buried my fists in his robe and hung on.

Proudly he stroked my hair and my face. "You shave," he said. "You have no beard."

"No, Abi. The Egyptians do not wear them, and it's cooler and easier to keep clean."

"And this around your eyes? You wear eye paint?"

I nodded. "I must. The glare from the sun is too much if I don't."

"This collar! Is it pure gold?"

"Yes, Abi. It's from Pharaoh. I received it when he made me Tate. It's a symbol of one of my ranks."

Letting go of him long enough to unfasten the collar, I took it off and dropped it in the dust. Then I took Abi's hand and put it on the scars on my right shoulder. "They're still there, Abi. That lioness marked me for life."

Jacob nodded, his fingers tracing the scars. "Yes, the scars, and the eyes and the hair. Rachel's face, and Esau's manliness. It is you, truly you, but bigger and a ruler greater than any of us dreamed."

CHAPTER 32

My brothers waited nervously beside me in the formal throne room of the palace in Itej-Tawy.

"Stop staring, Issachar," Levi admonished.

"It just looks so strange, and there is gold everywhere," he said in awe. "Have you ever seen anything like it?"

"No, and likely we never will again, either. But that doesn't mean you can stare all the time with your eyes round as moons."

"Quiet," Judah interrupted. "Here comes Pharaoh."

The entire court bowed as Amenemhet entered the room. He signaled me to follow him up to the throne, and I took my place beside him. It was a short audience, only three ambassadors here about trade treaties, and the usual greetings from the gods of two temples in the south to their brother the Pharaoh.

Then the porter announced, "The brothers of Lord Paanekh, Tate of Upper and Lower Egypt, Father to Pharaoh, Nearest Friend to Pharaoh, Friend to Pharaoh—"

When he finally finished speaking, I signaled my brothers and they came forward, kneeling before the king of Egypt.

"Which ones are these?" Amenemhet asked, turning to me.

"Judah, Levi, Dan, Gad, and Issachar, my lord," I replied indicating each brother as I spoke his name.

"They look well," Pharaoh commented. And they did. Their hair was cut and beards neatly trimmed. Each wore the new clothes I had given them.

"What is your occupation?" Pharaoh asked.

I translated.

"My lord, your servants are shepherds, as our fathers were before us," Judah replied formally. "We have come to live in my lord's land because the famine is severe in our land. There is no pasture there for our flocks and animals. Please allow your servants to live in Goshen, where there is grazing for the animals."

When I finished translating, Amenemhet raised his eyebrows at me. "How long did you coach them?" he asked in a low, amused voice.

Reddening slightly, I replied, "Apparently not long enough."

Amenemhet bit his lip to keep from laughing. Then he said,

"Choose whatever you want of the land of Egypt. The best part is Goshen. Let them live there if they wish. And if anyone is especially talented, set him over my flocks as well."

I interpreted, and my brothers bowed again, thanking Pharaoh for his kindness to them. They left, and Amenemhet ended the formal audience. We went back to the private audience chamber, and Pharaoh sat down with a sigh.

"These trade treaties will be the death of me yet," he said. "Is your father here also?"

"Yes, my lord," I said. "He is waiting to see you."

"Have him enter."

I went to the door and told the scribe to bring my father. I had stood with Pharaoh when my brothers were presented, but this time, I approached the throne with Abi, while he leaned on my arm. We knelt together, and then Abi stood up.

"You are Israel, Prince of Canaan?" Amenemhet asked.

"I am. Does my son Joseph serve you well?"

I translated the conversation exactly as they spoke, wondering what Pharaoh would think of my father's words and actions.

"Yes, Prince Israel, your son serves me well. We owe him a great debt, for he has saved Egypt from certain death. He himself has said that your God, El Shaddai, sent him to me to save my people alive. I believe this."

"It caused me great grief when he was missing," Jacob replied. "But the ways of El Shaddai are wiser than those of human beings. My grief has been a blessing to thousands of people in the lands of the world."

"Your God has honored your son," Pharaoh agreed. "Pray, tell me, Prince Israel, how old are you?"

"I have been a pilgrim in the land for 130 years," my father replied. "My years are few and they have been hard. I will not live to the age of my fathers." Then Abi handed me his staff and raised his hands upward.

Automatically I knelt, bowing for the blessing about to be given. And Pharaoh on his throne bowed also.

"May El Shaddai be gracious unto you and the land you rule," Abi said. "May you prosper above all your family, and may you be beloved by your people. Let your enemies be placed in the dust before you, and may El Shaddai grant you a long and gentle life."

When Abi finished and lowered his hands, Pharaoh looked up with awe. "Thank you, Prince Israel," he whispered.

My father took his staff and bowed again before Pharaoh, then we turned and left the room. At the door, Abi looked back. Amenemhet still watched us, frozen on the throne.

"He is a good man," Abi said. "He cares deeply for his people."

When I returned I stood with my head bowed before Pharaoh, wondering if I should apologize for the way my father had handled the interview.

"What did he say?" Amenemhet asked. "He spoke there at the door. What did he say?"

"He said you were a good man, and that you cared deeply for your people," I replied.

The king sighed. "I used to think I would never see anyone's eyes like yours," he said. "But your father is the same. Your God looks back at me from your faces. I have been greatly honored."

▲　▲　▲　▲

I stood on the edge of a wheat field belonging to my Memphis estate and watched Ra creep over the horizon. The dawn light blazed around me with golden glory, the sun's rays banishing the dawn's coolness as soon as they touched me. I knelt to worship El Shaddai on this day that might have been the second day of Harvest had there been anything to harvest.

The ground was hard to my knees, but I didn't care. My life overflowed with blessing, and I had to pour out my gratitude to the One who provided for me. I smiled as I thanked my God for the happiness that was mine. Last night at the feast Asenath gave, my father, Lord Potiphar, and Jetur sat together and laughed over stories about me until far into the night. All my brothers were there, Minemhet provided the best food of his career, and Huy walked among the tables amazing us afresh with his tricks and little gifts. My heart overflowed as I stood to face the day.

"I would speak with you, my lord," someone said, and I jerked around in surprise. A woman stood only a few feet away, her head carried proudly in spite of the strange garments she wore. They resembled Canaanite robes, only shortened and with the sleeves cut from them. A leather belt wrapped around her waist, and she wore sandals, but her face was pure southern Egyptian and of the monarchy if I was not mistaken.

"I did not hear you come," I said. "Not many know to find me here."

She smiled slightly, and the expression that crossed her face tugged at my memory. Her eyes burned into mine, deep and hauntingly familiar.

"I have ways of learning what I wish to know," she said. "I wish to speak with you in private."

"We are private here. No one will come to this field."

"I am aware of that. I have come to tell you of hatred and blood, and hope that my life will at last be rid of its torment."

"Speak to me then, my lady," I said courteously. "The light of Ra can stand dark secrets and El Shaddai will hear and bring peace to your heart."

We moved to the edge of the field and settled on the ground.

"He said you would be courteous and give a blessing, even to one so strange as I. I did not believe it. But he was right. My name is Nebtet and I am of Lord Meritifi's household." She paused and looked at me defiantly.

"Go on," I said, ignoring the challenge in her eyes.

She looked down and her hand trembled slightly. "I came to tell you how Lord Meritifi found his ruin."

I remained silent for a time. "It has puzzled me," I admitted. "When we took him at Lord Amony's house, he protested that he had not written the documents that condemned him, and I knew that he spoke truth. At the same time I knew he was guilty, that the documents simply said what he intended to do. That is why I reserved him for trial and did not have him executed there in the courtyard.

"I have often wondered if I did right. Perhaps Lord Khay would be alive if I had made a different decision."

"Had you tried to execute him there would have been much bloodshed," Nebtet replied. "His personal soldiers had orders to fight, and they would have. You did not know it, but they arrived just as the trial ended. By sending him to prison you turned their attention to getting him out."

"You know much," I said softly.

"It is bitter knowledge. Lord Meritifi was an evil man who had given himself fully to Seth. Even as a child, he lived to bring chaos. As he got older, he played for larger and larger stakes. Cruel to us all, he had many cravings, and all of us in the house feared the night time."

She shuddered where she sat, and I felt the horror of her memories.

"I trained as a scribe," she went on. "He knew he could control me, and I wrote all his personal letters so that no one else would know his secrets. When I realized that he planned to rule Egypt, I was desperate. Knowing what he did with his power every day of my life, I could not contemplate what would happen if he gained the throne.

"Then he ordered the seal and signet made. I warned Irtisen that he would be killed when he had finished the job, and the artisan fled in time. Meritifi never knew that Irtisen had made both seal and signet before he ran. I kept the seal back, thinking I could use it somehow to expose Meritifi. I was with him in Memphis when you were appointed Tate. He sent immediately for Sekhmet, the assassin and scribe, at On.

"He made me tell Sekhmet what he wanted done, thus keeping himself in the clear as much as possible. I tucked the seal in Sekhmet's linen and prayed to the gods that it would be found and would warn Pharaoh."

I stared at her in silence.

She wiped the tears from her face and continued. "When I heard nothing about the seal after Sekhmet was caught, I did not know what to think. Then I learned of Lord Khay's search for Hernofret and I realized that you were watching Lord Amony.

"Several months passed before I could do anything more. I managed to take the signet one night when Meritifi got drunk. I wrote the proclamation and death orders that he planned when he boasted to me of his greatness, and stamped them with the signet. Then I put them in the courier's pouch where Lord Khay's man would find them.

"Then you came."

As she fell silent I marveled at her story. I had never paid much attention to her. She was just another woman in the house. I had not thought to count Asenath either, or Hetepi. I frowned a little, realizing that I could not afford to have a blind spot like this. I was no longer in Canaan and I had best remember that from now on. In Egypt, women could and did do a great deal.

"I wish I had known this and how you acted," I said. "I would not have punished you or the household as I did."

"It was not a punishment—it was a relief," she said. "We did not want to stay and could not get away quickly enough. Meritifi had been especially harsh toward the end, and his wife and mother took the brunt of his cruelty. His wife died before we got to the border, and my mother became ill just two months ago in Jericho of Canaan. She did not ask to be buried in Egypt, but I knew it would comfort my oldest brother and I to have her here, so I brought her back. She died three days ago."

"His mother is your mother?" I asked.

She nodded. "I am Meritifi's sister. That is why he thought he could trust me not to betray him. But after what he did to our mother and his wife, he should have known better."

I saw her pain, understanding all too well the agony of families torn apart.

She rose and I stood up with her.

"Nebtet, I know it is expensive to have the proper funeral procedures done. Do you have sufficient to support you?"

The woman stared at me in amazement, then tears sprang to her eyes. "Knowing who I am, you care enough to think of that?" She laughed shortly, almost a sob. "He warned me you might ask, I should have believed him. He has been right about everything else about you. Even the color of your hair."

I blushed a little. I had not worn my wig since the day I threw it to Mahesa when I went to meet Abi. At first I would not put it back on because of a childish fear that my father would not recognize me if he saw me in it. After several months, no one expected me to have it on and I never touched it again. It pained Mahesa every time he saw me, but I refused to give in.

"Who is 'he'?" I asked.

"My brother, Lord Debaset. He should have been nomarch, but Meritifi tried to kill him when they were still children. Debaset was not perfect physically, and as I said, Meritifi has always been evil. He attacked Debaset, badly injured him, and left him for dead, then told our parents that a crocodile had seized him during a swim in the Nile.

"It shocked Mother to hear from Debaset after all those years, but it gave her strength to survive those last few months with Meritifi. Debaset is rich now and has supported us well since we left the nome for Canaan. We have you to thank for that as well." Nebtet turned and walked away.

"I know no one named Debaset," I said to her.

She glanced back over her shoulder. "He calls himself Huy now."

Soon after Nebtet's visit, I began a rotating corvee that shifted from nome to nome and provided the Fayyum with a year-round stream of workers. I also encouraged the commoners to move from the countryside into the villages and towns where it was easier for them to obtain the food stored for them.

For the third year, the Nile rose far too high for planting. During the flood, the corvee worked on the headquarters for the Department of the South, and as the flood died, they dug the channel between the old watercourse and the great basin.

I divided my time among my family, the Fayyum, and Memphis, where I still interviewed foreigners who came to buy grain. However, that became more and more routine, and I directed Jetur to organize the caravans and merchants to ship grain to Canaan for disbursal there. By the end of the year we had emptied the last of the storehouses in the Delta. I breathed a sigh of relief. Now the Nile could rise as high as it wanted to.

The Headquarters for the Department of the North were now almost completed. While it was not as elaborate as the ones for the South and the Head of the South, Sheshon was more than grateful to move into the facilities. We had placed the buildings on the site south of Tanis, and it came to be known as Hatwaret. I built a large Canaanite palace there for my father, and my brothers settled close by.

Mahesa looked up as I walked into my work suite in the Memphis palace one morning during the third year of famine. "Lord Sety is here to see you," he said.

"Anything else special for today?"

"No, my lord. Just the usual."

"I will see Lord Sety immediately," I decided. "Where is he waiting?"

"In the private audience room, my lord."

As I entered Lord Sety bowed deeply. He had changed much from the vain, frivolous young puppy I had first known. Since then he had worked hard to govern his nome properly, and he gained more and more respect from his peers.

"Greetings, Lord Sety. What did you wish of me?"

"Greetings, Lord Paanekh," he replied. "I have come with a problem I hope you can solve."

"I will be glad to do what I can. Tell me about it."

"It is very simple," Lord Sety replied. "My storehouses are empty of grain, and my people could not plant this year. They will starve if I cannot buy grain for them. I have come to request an order to purchase grain from Pharaoh."

"The storehouses would not sell to you?" I asked, fishing for more information.

"No, my lord. When I tried to buy, I was informed that no one would sell grain from the state storehouses without an order with your seal saying the buyer could purchase from Pharaoh."

Rapidly, I thought back. What had I said to Mahesa? I thought I had told him that no one could sell to anyone taking grain from the country without my permission, but it appeared that somewhere down the line that order had become shortened a bit. Now, no one could buy grain at all without my authorization.

I suppressed the chuckle that rose in my chest. What the other nomarchs would make of this, I dared not think.

"That will be easy to handle, Lord Sety. I will have the order sent to you today."

"Thank you, my lord. I was worried for my people."

"They are Pharaoh's people as well, and we stored the grain so no one would starve," I commented. "You may buy all that you need."

The next week, the nomarch from the fifth nome and Lord Mose arrived. I had Mahesa send Lord Mose in immediately. He strode in, dressed more formally than I'd seen yet, and he bowed respectfully.

"Lord Mose, how is the Land in Front?"

"Doing well, my lord. I am here about the expected problem."

"You need grain," I guessed.

He nodded.

"If you will wait for a bit, I will have the order delivered to you here and you can take it with you when you go."

"Thank you, my lord," he said simply. "I am not the first?"

"No, Lord Mose, but I know you have the best excuse. How many times did you have to drop your tools and take up weapons?"

"About three, during the plenty years," he admitted.

"I thought so. I will make the order open, so that you can use it as long as you need it."

"I appreciate it, my lord. The trip here is long. It gives a person a lot of time to think."

"It would," I said.

He went to the door, then turned back to me.

"Yes?" I asked.

"Don't you give in. You make them all come to you!"

"I had not quite decided if I should," I confessed. "But since you recommend it, I certainly will."

Lord Mose grinned. "Make them crawl a little too," he advised, leaving the room.

And come they did. The first nomarchs found me in Memphis. The rest chased me around the country as I moved from place to place, seeing to the building projects and catching time with my family.

Pharaoh's treasure houses filled rapidly. At the end of another two years, they practically burst with the White, gold, gems, jewelry, bronze and copper, skins, wood, feathers, exotic fabrics, and spices.

When the fifth harvest season passed without a crop, Mahesa met me with the news that Hetepi waited in my office.

"What has happened, Hetepi?" I asked as I entered.

She stood and bowed. "I wanted to tell you this myself, my lord. I have double-checked the information. All the nomarchs, every one, have gone to Itej-Tawy." Her face was strained with worry.

"Has Renseneb picked up anything about this?" I asked.

She shook her head.

I sat back and thought. Asenath had not mentioned anything either. Lord Mose would warn me of any trouble brewing, and possibly Lord Sety as well. The solution popped into my mind suddenly, and I started to chuckle.

"Hetepi, didn't you tell me after last harvest that the nomarchs were broke?"

"Yes, my lord."

"They have gone to Pharaoh," I said. "All of them want to plead their case to him, personally."

"What will Pharaoh do?"

"He will send them to me."

"They will not like it, my lord," she warned.

"I don't think that will mean much to Amenemhet. They have made ruling Egypt too hard for too long to expect any sympathy from him. Mahesa," I called.

"Yes, my lord?" he replied, entering.

"I must leave for Itej-Tawy first thing in the morning."

Two days later, I stood in the personal audience chamber with

Amenemhet. "They are furious," he said. "They wanted me to supply grain without your knowing. I told them you had my signet, so they would have to speak with you, then I had the guards drive them from the room." He chuckled. "I have wanted to do that for a long time."

"Do not be too harsh with them, my lord," I requested. "They do rule under you."

"And it is time they remembered that," he retorted. "But you are right. I will restrain myself next time."

That afternoon, I entered the formal audience chamber to face the assembled nomarchs of Egypt. To my surprise Lord Sety stepped forward as spokesman, bowing respectfully.

"We have come to you at Pharaoh's bidding, Lord Paanekh," he began. "The famine continues in all the nomes of Egypt, and as my lord knows, we have been buying food from Pharaoh for the people to eat."

He paused, and I nodded. "The first and second years, we supplied grain for our people, but when the third year came, our grain was gone and we turned to Pharaoh. He sent us to you, my lord, and you sold us grain.

"But now, my lord, we have nothing with which to buy. All the White, the gold, the precious metals and gems, the jewelry—everything has been spent to buy grain. We have nothing left. Now we have come before my lord to beg my lord to tell us what we must do. Do not let us and our people die before Pharaoh. Give us food that we may live."

I looked over the assembled nomarchs. Gold flashed everywhere in the room, except from them. They wore no rings, bracelets, necklaces, collars or belts. Just the gold armbands that signaled their nobility, and one or two did not have even that.

"What of your cattle?" I asked. "Do you still have them?"

"Yes, my lord," Sety replied.

"Then sell them. I will trade grain for kine, goats, sheep, horses, camels, whatever you have."

"Thank you, my lord."

"I shall send out scribes to value the herds," I continued. "Let each man in your nomes have his herds ready to be inspected. The value shall be taken by the scribes and sent to the storehouses, and the storehouses will pay out in grain. Each man will take his herds back with him to manage for Pharaoh. An accounting will be taken every year on how well they are handled for your lord Amenemhet III."

No one moved for a moment. "Yes, my lord. Thank you, my lord," Sety said, his eyes wide at this unexpectedly generous arrangement. "That which you command is that which shall be done, my lord."

After they left, Mahesa looked at me resignedly. "When am I to leave to inspect herds?"

"You don't. You know nothing of the value of animals. My brothers, however, do. And I have a lot of them."

I sent Judah, Dan, Levi, Gad, and Zebulun out to inspect herds. They had interpreters whom I trusted and scribes that Mahesa trusted. Judah and Dan went to the Department of the Head of the South, Levi and Gad to the Department of the South. Zebulun took the Department of the North. I also told Judah to organize overseers to keep track of Pharaoh's cattle.

Once again I turned my attention to the Fayyum. Shenbu had tried out six designs for water gates and none of them worked. I wondered if anything would. Until this problem was solved, I would stay at the Fayyum, and Asenath and the boys moved into the house in Itej-Tawy.

The sixth year the nomarchs again approached Pharaoh in desperation. But as always, he sent them to me.

The assemblage appeared much the same as last year, except no one looked at me. They kept their eyes on the floor. Lord Sety stepped forward and started to speak, then he sighed and shrugged his shoulders. "It is no use to hide why we are here, Lord Paanekh. The famine continues, and there is no food in our nomes that does not belong to Pharaoh. We have nothing left. Even the livestock has been sold. We are stripped of everything but our land and ourselves. Now we have come to beg my lord to buy our land for grain so that we and our people do not die. What use is it to Pharaoh to watch us die and the land lie desolate? We have come to sell ourselves for food to eat and seed to plant. We will become servants to Pharaoh. My lord, buy us and our land so that we do not die."

As I studied the crowd, only Lord Mose met my gaze. The suppressed gleam in his eye told me that he had seen, long ago, my double aim in buying up grain, and he had said nothing. He appreciated the danger the nomarchs presented to Egypt, and he had done what he could to smooth my way toward breaking their power, even though that meant the destitution of his own house.

Everyone else had their eyes on the floor. I deliberately stood and bowed deeply to him. He jerked in surprise, then silently bowed back.

"Let it be as you wish," I declared. "I will buy your lands and your fields. I will purchase you and your people. You shall become servants to Pharaoh and shall serve him all of your lives and your families after you. I will give you food and seed for planting. From this day onward, one fifth of the increase from the land and the cattle shall be for Pharaoh. Four fifths shall remain with you, for seed, food, and sustenance."

"That which you have commanded is that which shall be done, Sovereign Lord," they replied.

Afterward I entered the personal audience chamber where Amenemhet III waited. I approached the throne and then knelt and kissed the ground.

Pharaoh sat forward abruptly. "What is it, Lord Paanekh?"

"My lord, almost 13 years ago, you took me from a prison and set me over your household, your palace, and all the lands in Upper and Lower Egypt. I was grateful to my lord for his kindness, and I determined that I would serve my lord with the best that I had in me.

"At that time, my lord gave me an order and told me a wish."

"I remember," he said. "I had taken the biggest gamble of my life, and I was still uncertain whether I had won or lost."

"My lord ordered me to save Egypt, and I have done so. There is grain for the famine, and the people live. There is grain for the countries around, and the land is safe."

"You have done well."

"But my lord also expressed a wish," I reminded him. "I promised my lord to fulfill that wish if I could." I held up a tablet to him. "My lord, the treasure houses are full to overflowing. There is no more of the White, or gold, or copper or bronze in Canaan or in Egypt. My lord possess it all. My lord owns all the cattle in the land and now, my lord, you own all the land in both Upper and Lower Egypt. The lands and wealth of the temples and priests are already part of your household. Today the people of each nome, from nomarch to commoner, have sold themselves as your servants. The nomarchs are yours, my lord."

Amenemhet stared at the tablet in his hands, then at me. "You bought them? They sold themselves?"

"Yes, my lord. They refused to store food, and now there is nothing left but themselves to sell for food. You shall supply them with seed, and they shall return one fifth of the increase from the fields and cattle to you each year."

"Lord Paanekh, I do not know what to say," he stammered. "When Lord Potiphar said that every master you served became rich and received their heart's desire, I was amused and that was all. But you have indeed made me rich beyond counting, and you have indeed given me my heart's desire." He fell silent and I waited.

"Get up, Lord Paanekh," he commanded.

I rose to my feet.

"You have done what I and my fathers were unable to do. You are a greater man than I."

"No, my lord," I said. "My God is greater than any other."

In the silence, the air around us seemed to lighten and stir a little. Pharaoh glanced up, but the doors were all closed. Then Amenemhet gasped and looked around quickly. "Someone is here!" he said. We stilled as El Shaddai's presence filled the room, swelling greater and greater until the glory of my God broke upon us both, enthralling us with the revelation of His power. In that instant we confessed the truth. It is not humanity who commands, and no person is sovereign or lord. El Shaddai alone commands, and humanity obeys, for El Shaddai is the one true Sovereign and Lord. Pharaoh stumbled from his throne, and as one we both fell to the floor and worshiped.

EPILOGUE

So there was glory in the end, the glory of El Shaddai, over-shadowing us that day in the midst of Pharaoh's palace with paintings of other gods on the walls, and belief in other gods all around. But what does that matter to El Shaddai? He is greater by far than any other, for He created all that is.

My story is almost done. Be patient with an old man a little longer while I tell of the end of things. My projects in the Fayyum succeeded at last. Shenbu found the answers to every question, and the first year after the seventh of famine, when the Nile rose for Inundation, it again went far above planting level. But we opened the waterway, and the Nile poured into the great Basin. It diverted enough of the flood that the water receded in time to plant. Egypt had a harvest the eighth year, and the famine ended.

Renseneb and Hetepi raised Little Khay and Geb to manhood. In the end, I bowed to El Shaddai's superior wisdom concerning Lord Khay. He could never have managed the trading network with the ability and finesse of Asenath and Renseneb, and I would have had to do it, robbing me of the time I needed to work in the Fayyum and so thwart the high Nile floods that continued for several years.

Little Khay grew to be a fine man, with all of his father's talent for finding things out, coupled with the judgment and steadiness of Renseneb and Hetepi. He and Geb formed the core of my security force, and they served me well during the troublous times that followed the ending of Amenemhet's dynasty. More than once, I owed my life to Khay's sons and their sons after them.

Mahesa became a brilliant chief of staff, and I depended on him heavily. He married (without telling anyone, I might add. When I chastised him soundly for that, he retorted that as long as I refused to wear a wig, I could not reprimand him on etiquette.) and he trained his sons and grandsons to follow in his steps. His family holds much of the real power in the land. Few realize it, though, for Mahesa's children do not seek empty titles. I honor Mahesa's descendants, for one and all, they know how to serve, and they serve well. And one and all, they serve El Shaddai with a loyalty as deep as their father's came to be.

Abi lived for 17 years in Egypt. He blessed my sons before he died, and I was with him when he left this life. I do not wish to speak of that time, for it hurts me still to think of the sorrow that entered my life when he left his. Pharaoh honored him with a royal embalming, and I buried him in Canaan, in the cave of Machpelah with Leah, Isaac, Abraham, and Sarah.

After he died my brothers came to me again, fearful that now my beloved Abi was dead, I would turn on them in anger for what they had done to me. I told them once more that even though they intended evil for me, El Shaddai planned good, and that I did not hold anger toward them. But I do not think I ever really convinced them, except possibly Dan. He and Benjamin are the closest to me, and I turn to them more and more often. Judah has never called me by name since he arrived in Egypt. I am "my lord" to him, but he has given me an unswerving loyalty that I treasure. I suspect the rest are, deep in their hearts, afraid of me still. It hurts me to think of it, and I shall say no more.

And so I come to the end of my story. Asenath, my beautiful wife, is long dead, but she left me with sons and grandsons and great-grandsons. And now, what remains? Only for me to die, and I feel it in me. Although I am now of Egypt, my heart turns toward the land of my birth. Canaan. Even the sound draws me to it.

Pharaoh—this present Pharaoh— knows that I shall die soon. He will have me embalmed, and I will be buried in the tomb made ready for me in the back of the garden of my palace here in Hatwaret. Pharaoh offered me a tomb with his, but I refused it, as I have refused others. I do not want to be that far from the land El Shaddai promised to my fathers. One day, the time will come to go home. El Shaddai promised it, and what He commands is what will be done, for He is the one true Sovereign and Lord.

To all of you who read this story, I charge you with this one wish as I die. Take my bones with you to Canaan. Do not leave me here in the land where I served first as a slave, then as Tate. My service is done, and I am ready to rest. Take me back to the land El Shaddai chose for my fathers. There let me be buried, for I have given myself wholly to El Shaddai. And that is the secret of all my glory.